FIC DARE TE One
Dare, Tessa.
One dance wit
D0199107
AUG 27 2010

S[illegible] ne
roo[illegible] is
cou[illegible]

B[illegible] e
pou[illegible] his
boc[illegible] nd
tast[illegible]

Devil, damn, blast. He needed to leave this place, immediately.

"Why have we stopped?" she said. "The waltz isn't over." Her voice sounded as though it came from a great distance, filtered through cotton wool.

"It's over for me." Spencer swung his gaze around the room. An open set of doors to his left beckoned promisingly. He attempted to release her, but she clutched at his shoulders and held him fast. "For God's sake," he said, "let me—"

"Let you what?" Her eyes darting to the side, she whispered, "Let you go? Let you abandon me here on the dance floor, to my complete and total humiliation? Of all the unchivalrous, ungentlemanly, unforgivable . . ." When she ran out of descriptors, she threw him an accusatory glare that implied a thousand more. "I won't stand for it."

"Very well, then. Don't."

He slid his hands to her waist, grasped tight with both hands, and bodily lifted Lady Amelia d'Orsay—two, four . . . six inches off the floor. Until they looked one another eye-to-eye, and her slippers dangled in midair.

He spared a brief moment to savor the way indignant shock widened those pale blue eyes.

And then he carried her out into the night.

Also by Tessa Dare

Goddess of the Hunt
Surrender of a Siren
A Lady of Persuasion

Books published by The Random House Publishing Group are available at quantity discounts on bulk purchases for premium, educational, fund-raising, and special sales use. For details, please call 1-800-733-3000.

ONE DANCE *with a* DUKE

A Novel

Tessa Dare

BALLANTINE BOOKS • NEW YORK

Sale of this book without a front cover may be unauthorized. If this book is coverless, it may have been reported to the publisher as "unsold or destroyed" and neither the author nor the publisher may have received payment for it.

One Dance with a Duke is a work of fiction. Names, characters, places, and incidents are the products of the author's imagination or are used fictitiously. Any resemblance to actual events, locales, or persons, living or dead, is entirely coincidental.

A Ballantine Books Mass Market Original

Copyright © 2010 by Eve Ortega

Excerpt from *Twice Tempted by a Rogue* by Tessa Dare copyright © 2010 by Eve Ortega

All rights reserved.

Published in the United States by Ballantine Books, an imprint of The Random House Publishing Group, a division of Random House, Inc., New York.

BALLANTINE and colophon are registered trademarks of Random House, Inc.

ISBN 978-0-345-51885-9

Cover illustration: Alan Ayers

Printed in the United States of America

www.ballantinebooks.com

9 8 7 6 5 4 3 2 1

For my wonderful family

With many thanks to my agent, Helen Breitwieser, my editor, Kate Collins, and everyone on the team at Ballantine. I'm profoundly grateful to Courtney Milan, Amy Baldwin, Jennifer Haymore, Lindsey Faber, Elyssa Papa, Laura Drake, and Janga Brannon for their help with the manuscript, and to Kim Castillo for her excellent assistance with everything else. Mr. Dare . . . as always, I love you!

Chapter One

London, June 1817

Blackberry glaze.

Biting the inside of her cheek, Amelia d'Orsay suppressed a small cry of jubilation. Even at a rout like this one, a well-bred lady's abrupt shout of joy was likely to draw notice, and Amelia did not care to explain herself to the crush of young ladies surrounding her. Especially when the reason for her delight was not a triumph at the card table or a proposal of marriage, but rather the completion of a dinner menu.

She could imagine it now. "Oh, Lady Amelia," one of these young misses would say, "only you could think of food at a time like this."

Well, it wasn't as though Amelia had *planned* to stand in a ballroom, dreaming of menus for their family summer holiday. But she'd been puzzling for weeks over a new sauce for braised pheasant, to replace the same old applejack reduction. Something sweet, yet tart; surprising, yet familiar; inventive, yet frugal. At last, the answer had come to her. Blackberry glaze. Strained, of course. Ooh, perhaps mulled with cloves.

Resolving to enter it in her menu book later, she swept the imaginary dish aside and compressed her grin to a half-smile. Summer at Briarbank would now officially be perfect.

Mrs. Bunscombe brushed past in a flounce of scarlet silk. "It's half-eleven," the hostess sang. "Nearly midnight."

Nearly midnight. Now there was a thought to quell her exuberance.

A cherub-faced debutante swaddled in tulle grasped Amelia by the wrist. "Any moment now. How can you remain so calm? If he chooses me tonight, I just know I'll swoon."

Amelia sighed. And so it began. As it did at every ball, when half-eleven ticked past.

"You needn't worry about making conversation," a young lady dressed in green satin said. "He scarcely utters so much as a word."

"Are we even certain he speaks English? Wasn't he raised in Abyssinia or . . ."

"No, no. Lower Canada. Of course he speaks English. My brother plays cards with him." The second girl lowered her voice. "But there is something rather *primitive* about him, don't you think? I think it's the way he moves."

"I think it's the gossip you're heeding," Amelia said sensibly.

"He waltzes like a dream," a third girl put in. "When I danced with him, my feet scarcely skimmed the floor. And he's ever so handsome up close."

Amelia gave her a patient smile. "Indeed?"

At the opening of the season, the reclusive and obscenely wealthy Duke of Morland had finally entered society. A few weeks later, he had all London dancing to his tune. The duke arrived at every ball at the stroke of midnight. He selected a single partner from among the available ladies. At the conclusion of one set, he would escort the lady in to supper, and then . . . disappear.

Before two weeks were out, the papers had dubbed him "the Duke of Midnight," and every hostess in London was jostling to invite His Grace to a ball. Unmarried ladies would not dream of promising the supper set to any other partner, for fear of missing their chance at a duke. To amplify the dramatic effect, hostesses positioned timepieces in full view and instructed orchestras to begin the set at the very hour of twelve. And it went without saying, the set concluded with a slow, romantic waltz.

The nightly spectacle held the entire *ton* in delicious, knuckle-gnawing thrall. At every ball, the atmosphere thickened with perfume and speculation as the hour of twelve approached. It was like watching medieval knights attempting to wrest Excalibur from the stone. Surely one of these evenings, the gossips declared, some blushing ingénue would get a proper grip on the recalcitrant bachelor . . . and a legend would be born.

Legend indeed. There was no end of stories about him. Where a man of his rank and fortune was involved, there were always stories.

"I hear he was raised barefoot and heathen in the Canadian wilderness," said the first girl.

"I hear he was barely civilized when his uncle took him in," said the second. "And his wild behavior gave the old duke an apoplexy."

The lady in green murmured, "My brother told me there was an *incident*, at Eton. Some sort of scrape or brawl . . . I don't know precisely. But a boy nearly died, and Morland was expelled for it. If they sent down a duke's heir, you know it must have been dreadful."

"You'll not believe what I've heard," Amelia said, widening her eyes. The ladies perked, leaning in close. "I hear," she whispered, "that by the light of the full moon, His Grace transforms into a ravening hedgehog."

When her companions finished laughing, she said aloud, "Really, I can't believe he's so interesting as to merit this much attention."

"You wouldn't say that if *you'd* danced with him."

Amelia shook her head. She had watched this scene unfold time and again over the past few weeks, admittedly with amusement. But she never expected—or desired—to be at the center of it. It wasn't sour grapes, truly it wasn't. What other ladies saw as intriguing and romantic, she took for self-indulgent melodrama. Really, an unmarried, wealthy, handsome duke who felt the need to command *more* female attention? He must be the most vain, insufferable sort of man.

And the ladies of his choosing—all flouncy, insipid girls in their first or second seasons. All petite, all pretty. None of them anything like Amelia.

Oh, perhaps there was a hint of bitterness to it, after all.

Really, when a lady dangled on the outer cusp of marital eligibility, as she did, society ought to allow her a quiet, unannounced slide into spinsterhood. It rather galled her, to feel several years' worth of rejection revisited upon her night after night, as the infamous duke entered at the stroke of midnight, and at twelve-oh-one his eyes slid straight past her to some primping chit with more beauty than brains.

Not that he had reason to notice her. Her dowry barely scraped the floorboards of the "respectable" range, and even in her first season, she'd never been a great beauty. Her eyes were a trifle too pale, and she blushed much too easily. And at the age of six-and-twenty, she'd come to accept that she would always be a little too plump.

The girls suddenly scattered, like the flighty things they were.

A deep whisper came from behind her shoulder. "You look ravishing, Amelia."

Sighing, she wheeled to face the speaker. "Jack. What is it you're after?"

Pressing a hand to his lapel, he pulled an offended expression. "Must I be after something? Can't a fellow pay his dearest sister a compliment without falling under suspicion?"

"Not when the fellow in question is you. And it's no compliment to be called your dearest sister. I'm your only sister. If you're after my purse, you must come up with something better than that." She spoke in a light, teasing tone, hoping against all previous evidence that he would protest: *No, Amelia. This time, I'm not after your purse. I've ceased gambling and drinking, and I've thrown over those ne'er-do-well "friends" of mine. I'm returning to University. I'll take orders in the Church, just as I promised our dying mother. And you truly do look lovely tonight.*

Eyes flicking toward the crowd, he lowered his voice. "A few bob. That's all I need."

Her chest deflated. Not even midnight, and already his eyes held that wild, liquor-flared spark that indicated he was on the verge of doing something spectacularly ill-conceived.

Steering him by the elbow, she left the young ladies to titter amongst themselves and guided her brother through the nearest set of doors. They stepped into the crescent of yellow light shining through the transom window. The night air closed around them, cloying and humid.

"I don't have anything," she lied.

"A few shillings for the hack, Amelia." He grabbed for the reticule dangling from her wrist. "We're off to the theater, a gang of us."

Off to the theater, her eye. Off to the gaming hells,

more likely. She clutched the beaded drawstring pouch to her bosom. "And how will I get home, then?"

"Why, Morland will take you." He winked. "Right after your dance. I've two pounds sterling on you tonight."

Wonderful. Another two pounds she'd have to siphon from her pin money. "At tremendously long odds, I'm sure."

"Don't speak like that." A touch grazed her arm. Jack's expression was suddenly, unexpectedly sincere. "He'd be damned lucky to have you, Amelia. There's no lady your equal in that room."

Tears pricked at the corners of her eyes. Since their brother Hugh's death at Waterloo, Jack had changed, and not for the better. But in rare flashes, that dear, sensitive brother she loved would surface. She wanted so desperately to gather him close and hold tight to him for weeks, months . . . however long it took, to coax the old Jack out from this brittle shell.

"Come now. Be a sweet sister, and lend me a crown or two. I'll send a runner to Laurent's, and he'll send that garish new landau for you. You'll be driven home in the finest style his copper heiress can afford."

"Her name is Winifred. She's the Countess of Beauvale now, and you ought to speak of her with respect. It's her fortune that purchased Michael's commission and supports young William at school. It's thanks to her and Laurent that I even have a home."

"And I'm the worthless ingrate who brings the family nothing but disgrace. I know, I know." His flinty gaze clashed with a forced smile. "It's worth a few coins to be rid of me, isn't it?"

"Can't you understand? I don't want to be rid of you at all. I love you, you fool." She smoothed that incorrigible wisp of hair that always curled at his left temple. "Won't you let me help you, Jack?"

"Of course. If you'll start with a shilling or two."

With clumsy fingers, she loosened the strings of her reticule. "I will give you everything I have, on one condition."

"What's that?"

"You must promise me you'll join us this summer, at Briarbank."

The d'Orsays always summered at Briarbank—a rambling stone cottage overlooking the River Wye, down the slope from the ruins of Beauvale Castle. Amelia had been planning this summer's holiday for months, down to the last damask tablecloth and saucer of currant jelly. Briarbank was the answer to everything, she knew it. It had to be.

Hugh's death had devastated the entire family, but Jack most of all. Of all her brothers, the two of them had been the fastest friends. Hugh had been just one year older, but several years wiser, and his serious bent had always balanced Jack's wilder personality. Without that check on his impulsive nature, Amelia feared Jack's grief and recklessness were conspiring to disaster.

What he needed was love, and time to heal. Time spent far from Town, and close to home and family—what remained of both. Here in London, Jack was surrounded by temptation, constantly pressured to keep pace with his spendthrift peers. At Briarbank, he would surely return to his good-humored self. Young William would come on his break from school. Michael would still be at sea, of course, but Laurent and Winifred would join them, at least for a week or two.

And Amelia would be the perfect hostess. Just as Mama had always been. She would fill every room with great vases of snapdragons, arrange theatricals and parlor games, serve braised pheasant with blackberry glaze.

She would make everyone happy, by sheer force of will. Or bribery, if she must.

"I've a crown and three shillings here," she said, extracting the coins from the pouch, "and six pounds more saved at home." Saved, scrimped, scraped together, one penny at a time. "It's yours, all of it—but you must promise me August at Briarbank."

Jack tsked. "He didn't tell you?"

"Who? Who didn't tell me what?"

"Laurent. We're not opening the cottage this summer. It was just settled this week. We're letting it out."

"Letting it out?" Amelia felt as though all the blood had been let from her veins. Suddenly dizzy, she clutched her brother's arm. "Briarbank, let out? To strangers?"

"Well, not to strangers. We've put the word around at the clubs and expect inquiries from several good families. It's a plum holiday cottage, you know."

"Yes," she bit out. "Yes, I do know. It's so ideal, the d'Orsay family has summered there for centuries. *Centuries*, Jack. Why would we dream of leasing it out?"

"Haven't we outgrown the pall-mall and tea biscuits routine? It's dull as tombs out there. Halfway to Ireland, for God's sake."

"Dull? What on earth can you mean? You used to live for summers there, angling on the river and—" Comprehension struck, numbing her to the toes. "Oh, no." She dug her fingers into his arm. "How much did you lose? How much do you owe?"

His eyes told her he'd resigned all pretense. "Four hundred pounds."

"Four hundred! To whom?"

"To Morland."

"The Duke of Midni—" Amelia bit off the absurd nickname. She refused to puff the man's notoriety further. "But he's not even arrived yet. How did you manage to lose four hundred pounds to him, when he's not even here?"

"Not tonight. Days ago now. That's why I must leave. He'll be here any moment, and I can't face him until I've made good on the debt."

Amelia could only stare at him.

"Don't look at me like that, I can't bear it. I was holding my own until Faraday put his token in play. That's what brought Morland to the table, drove the betting sky-high. He's out to gather all ten, you know."

"All ten of what? All ten *tokens*?"

"Yes, of course. The tokens are everything." Jack made an expansive gesture. "Come now, you can't be so out of circulation as *that*. It's only the most elite gentlemen's club in London."

When she only blinked at him, he prompted, "Harcliffe. Osiris. One stud horse, ten brass tokens. You've heard of the club, I know you have."

"I'm sorry. I've no idea what you're talking about. You seem to be telling me you've wagered our ancestral home against a brass token. And lost."

"I was in for hundreds already; I couldn't back down. And my cards . . . Amelia, I swear to you, they were unbeatable cards."

"Except that they weren't."

He gave a fatalistic shrug. "What's done is done. If I had some other means of raising the funds, I would. I'm sorry you're disappointed, but there's always next year."

"Yes, but—" But next year was a whole year away. God only knew what trouble would find Jack in the meantime. "There must be another way. Ask Laurent for the money."

"You know he can't give it."

Of course he was right. Their eldest brother had married prudently, almost sacrificially. The family had been desperate for funds at the time, and Winifred had come with bags of money from her mining-magnate father.

The trouble was, the bags of money came cinched tightly with strings, and only Laurent's father-in-law could loosen them. The old man would never authorize the use of four hundred pounds to pay off a gaming debt.

"I have to leave before Morland arrives," he said. "You understand."

Jack unlooped the reticule from her limp wrist, and she did not fight him as he shook the coins into his palm. Yes, she understood. Even if nothing remained of their fortune, the d'Orsays would cling to their pride.

"Have you at least learned your lesson now?" she said quietly.

He vaulted the low terrace rail. Rattling the coins in his palm, he backed away into the garden. "You know me, Amelia. I never was any good with lessons. I just copied my slate from Hugh's."

As she watched her brother disappear into the shadows, Amelia hugged her arms across her chest.

What cruel turn of events was this? Briarbank, rented for the summer! All the happiness stored up in those cobbled floors and rustic hearths and bundles of lavender hanging from the rafters—wasted on strangers. All her elaborate menus and planned excursions, for naught. Without that cottage, the d'Orsay family had no true center. Her brother had nowhere to recover from his grief.

And somehow more lowering than all this: She had no place of her own.

Accepting spinsterhood had not been easy for Amelia. But she could resign herself to the loneliness and disappointment, she told herself, so long as she had summers at that drafty stone cottage. Those few months made the rest of the year tolerable. Whilst her friends collected lace and linens for their trousseaux, Amelia contented herself by embroidering seat covers for Briarbank.

As they entertained callers, she entertained thoughts of begonias in the window box. When she—an intelligent, thoughtful, well-bred lady—was thrown over nightly for her younger, prettier, lack-witted counterparts, she could fool herself into happiness by thinking of blackberry glaze.

Lord, the irony. She wasn't much different from Jack. She'd impulsively wagered all her dreams on a pile of mortar and shale. And now she'd lost.

Alone on the terrace, she started to tremble. Destiny clanged against her hopes, beating them down one hollow ring at a time.

Somewhere inside, a clock was tolling midnight.

"His Grace, the Duke of Morland."

The majordomo's announcement coincided with the final, booming stroke of twelve.

From the head of the staircase, Spencer watched the throng of guests divide on cue, falling to either side like two halves of an overripe peach. And there, in the center, clustered the unmarried young ladies in attendance—stone-still and shriveling under his gaze.

As a general point, Spencer disliked crowds. He particularly disliked overdressed, self-important crowds. And this scene grew more absurd by the night: the cream of London society, staring up at him with unguarded fascination.

We don't know what to make of you, those stares said.

Fair enough. It was a useful—often lucrative—thing, to be unreadable. He'd spent years cultivating the skill.

We don't trust you. This he gleaned from the whispers, and the manner in which gentlemen guarded the walls and ladies' hands instinctively went to the jewels at their throats. No matter. It was also a useful thing, at times, to be feared.

No, it was the last bit that had him quietly laughing. The silent plea that only rang louder every time he entered a ballroom.

Here, take one of our daughters.

God's knees. Must he?

As he descended the travertine staircase, Spencer girded himself for yet another unpleasant half hour. Given his preference, he would retreat back to the country and never attend another ball in his life. But while he was temporarily residing in Town, he could not refuse *all* invitations. If he wished to see his ward Claudia well married in a few years, he must pave the way for her eventual debut. And occasionally there were high-stakes card games to be found in the back rooms of these affairs, well away from the white-powdered matrons playing whist.

So he made his appearance, but strictly on his own terms. One set, no more. As little conversation as possible. And if the *ton* were determined to throw their sacrificial virgins at his feet . . . he would do the choosing.

He wanted a quiet one tonight.

Usually he favored them young and vapid, more interested in preening for the crowd than capturing his notice. Then at the Pryce-Foster ball, he'd had the extreme misfortune to engage the hand of one Miss Francine Waterford. Quite pretty, with a vivacious arch to her brow and plump, rosy lips. The thing was, those lips lost all their allure when she kept them in constant motion. She'd prattled on through the entire set. Worse, she'd expected responses. While most women eagerly supplied both sides of any conversation, Miss Waterford would not be satisfied with his repertoire of brusque nods and inarticulate clearings of the throat. He'd been forced to speak at least a dozen words to her, all told.

That was his reward for indulging aesthetic sensibilities. Enough with the pretty ones. For his partner tonight, he would select a meek, silent, wallflower of a girl. She needn't be pretty, nor even passable. She need only be quiet.

As he approached the knot of young ladies, his eye settled on a slender reed of a girl standing on the fringe of the group, looking positively jaundiced in melon-colored satin. When he advanced toward her, she cowered into the shadow of her neighbor. She refused to even meet his gaze. *Perfect.*

Just as he extended his hand in invitation, he was arrested by a series of unexpected sounds. The rattle of glass panes. The slam of a door. Heels clicking against travertine in a brisk, staccato rhythm.

Spencer swiveled instinctively. A youngish woman in blue careened across the floor like a billiard ball, reeling to a halt before him. His hand remained outstretched from his aborted invitation to Miss Melony Satin, and this newly arrived lady took hold of it firmly.

Dipping in a shallow curtsy, she said, "Thank you, Your Grace. I would be honored."

And after a stunned, painful pause, the music began.

The clump of disappointed ladies dispersed in search of new partners, grumbling as they went. And for the first time all season, Spencer found himself partnered with a lady not of his choosing. *She* had selected *him*.

How very surprising.

How very unpleasant.

Nevertheless, there was nothing to be done. The impertinent woman queued up across from him for the country dance. Did he even know this lady?

As the other dancers fell into place around them, he took the opportunity to study her. He found little to admire. Any measure of genteel poise she might claim had fallen casualty to that inelegant sprint across the ballroom. Stray wisps of hair floated about her face; her breath was labored with exertion. This state of agitation did her complexion no favors, but it did enhance the swell of her ample bosom. She was amply endowed everywhere, actually. Generous curves pulled against the blue silk of her gown.

"Forgive me," he said, as they circled one another. "Have we been introduced?"

"Years ago, once. I would not expect you to remember. I am Lady Amelia d'Orsay."

The pattern of the dance parted them, and Spencer had some moments to absorb this name: Lady Amelia d'Orsay. Her late father had been the seventh Earl of Beauvale. Her elder brother, Laurent, was currently the eighth Earl of Beauvale.

And her younger brother Jack was a scapegrace wastrel who owed Spencer four hundred pounds.

She must have sensed the moment of this epiphany, for when they next clasped hands she said, "We needn't speak of it now. It can wait for the waltz."

He quietly groaned. This was going to be a very long set. If only he'd moved more quickly in securing the jaundiced one's hand. Now that Lady Amelia's brash maneuver had been successful, God only knew what stunt the ladies—or more likely, their mothers—would attempt next. Maybe he should start engaging his partners' hands in advance of the event. But that would necessitate social calls, and Spencer did not make social calls. Perhaps he could direct his secretary to send notes? The entire situation was wearying.

The country dance ended. The waltz began. And he was forced to take her in his arms, this woman who had just made his life a great deal more complicated.

To her credit, she wasted no time with pleasantries. "Your Grace, let me be to the point. My brother owes you a great sum of money."

"He owes me four hundred pounds."

"Do you not view that as a great sum of money?"

"I view it as a debt which I am owed. The precise amount is inconsequential."

"It is not inconsequential to me. I cannot imagine that you are unaware of it, but the d'Orsay name is synonymous with noble poverty. For us, four hundred pounds is a vast sum of money. We simply cannot spare it."

"And what do you propose? Do you mean to offer me favors in lieu of payment?" He repaid her shocked expression with a cool remark: "I'm not interested."

It was a small lie. He was a man. And she was a buxom woman, poured into a form-fitting dress. Parts of him were finding parts of her vaguely interesting. His eyes, for example, kept straying to her décolletage, so snugly framed by blue silk and ivory lace. From his advantage of height, he could spy the dark freckle dotting the inner curve of her left breast, and time and again, he found his gaze straying to the small imperfection.

"What a revolting suggestion," she said. "Do you routinely solicit such offers from the distraught female relations of your debtors?"

He gave a noncommittal shrug. He didn't, but she was free to believe he did. Spencer was not in the habit of ingratiating himself, with anyone.

"As if I would barter my favors for four hundred pounds."

"I thought you called it a vast sum of money." *Well above the going rate for such services*, he refrained from adding.

"There are some things upon which one cannot put a price."

He considered making an academic argument to the contrary but decided against it. Clearly the woman lacked the sense to follow logic. As was further evidenced by her next comment.

"I ask you to forgive Jack's debt."

"I refuse."

"You cannot refuse!"

"I just did."

"Four hundred pounds is nothing to you. Come now, you weren't even after Jack's money. He was only caught in the middle as you drove the betting high. You wanted Mr. Faraday's token, and you have it. Let my brother's wager be set aside."

"No."

She huffed an impatient breath, and her whole body seemed to exhale exasperation. Frustration exuded from her every pore, and with it wafted her own unique feminine scent. She smelled nice, actually. No cloying perfume—he supposed she couldn't afford rich scent. Just the common aromas of plain soap and clean skin, and the merest suggestion that she tucked sprigs of lavender between her stored undergarments.

Blue eyes locked with his. "Why not?"

Spencer tempered his own exasperated sigh. He could explain to her that forgiving the debt would do both her brother and her family a great disservice. They would owe a debt of gratitude more lasting and burdensome than any debt of gold, impossible to repay. Worst, Jack would have no incentive to avoid repeating the mistake. In a matter of weeks, the youth would land in even deeper debt, perhaps to the tune of thousands. Spencer had no doubt that four hundred pounds was a large sum to the d'Orsay family, but it would not be a crippling one. And if it purchased Lady Amelia's brother a greater portion of sense, it would be four hundred pounds well spent.

All this he might have explained. But he was the Duke of Morland. As much as he'd forfeited for the sake of that title, it ought to come with a few advantages. He shouldn't have to explain himself at all.

"Because I won't," he said simply.

She set her teeth. "I see. And there is nothing I can say to persuade you otherwise?"

"No."

Lady Amelia shuddered. He felt the tremor beneath his palm, where his hand pressed against the small of her back. Fearing she might burst out weeping—and wouldn't *that* be the final polish on this sterling example of awkwardness—Spencer pulled her tightly to him and whisked her into a series of turns.

Despite his efforts, she only trembled more violently. Small sounds, something between a hiccough and a squeak, emanated from her throat. Against his better judgment, he pulled back to study her face.

The woman was laughing.

His heart began to beat a little faster. *Steady, man.*

"It is true, what the ladies say. You do waltz like a dream." Her eyes swept his face, catching on his brow, his jaw, and finally fixing on his mouth with unabashed interest. "And you are undeniably handsome, up close."

"Do you hope to move me by means of flattery? It won't work."

"No, no." She smiled, and her right cheek dimpled. The left did not. "I see now that you are a positively immutable gentleman, a veritable rock of determination, and my every attempt to move you would be in vain."

"Why the laughter, then?"

Why the question? he berated himself, annoyed. Why not gratefully allow the conversation to die? And why did he find himself wondering whether Lady Amelia's left cheek ever dimpled? Whether she smiled more genuinely, more freely in situations that did not involve debasing herself over large debts, or whether the lone dimple was merely another of her intrinsic imperfections, like the unmatched freckle on her breast?

"Because," she answered, "anxiety and gloom are tiresome. You've made it clear you will not forgive the debt. I can pass the remainder of the set moping about it, or I can enjoy myself."

"*Enjoy* yourself."

"The notion shocks you, I see. I know there are some"—here she raked him with a sharp glance—"who judge it a mark of their superiority to always appear dissatisfied with the available company. Before they even enter a gathering, they have made up their minds to be displeased with it. Is it so very unthinkable that I might choose the reverse? Opt for happiness, even in the face of grave personal disappointment and complete financial ruin?"

"It smacks of insincerity."

"Insincerity?" She laughed again. "Forgive me, but are you not the Duke of Morland? The playwright of this little midnight melodrama that has played to packed houses for weeks? The entire scene is predicated on the assumption that we eligible ladies are positively desperate to catch your attention. That a dance in the Duke of Midnight's arms is every girl's fondest fantasy. And now you call me insincere, when I claim to be enjoying my turn?"

She lifted her chin and looked out over the ballroom. "I have no illusions about myself. I'm an impoverished gentlewoman, two seasons on the shelf, no great beauty even in my bloom of youth. I'm not often at the center of attention, Your Grace. When this waltz concludes, I don't know when—if ever—I shall know the feeling again. So I'm determined to enjoy it while it lasts." She smiled fiercely, defiantly. "And you can't stop me."

Spencer concluded this must now be the longest set in the history of dancing. Turning his head, he dutifully swept her the length of the floor, striving to ignore how every pair of eyes in the ballroom tracked their progress. Quite a crowd tonight.

When he risked a glance down at her, Lady Amelia's face remained tilted to his.

"Can I persuade you to stop staring at me?"

Her smile never faltered. "Oh, no."

Oh no, indeed.

"You see," she whispered in a husky tone, that from any other woman he would have interpreted as sensual overture, "it's not often a spinster like me has the opportunity to enjoy such a prime specimen of virility and vigor, and at such close proximity. Those piercing hazel eyes, and all that dark, curling hair . . . What a struggle it is, not to touch it."

He shushed her. "You're creating a scene."

"Oh, you created the scene," she murmured coyly. "I'm merely stealing it."

Would this waltz never end?

"Did you wish to change the subject?" she asked. "Perhaps we should speak of the theater."

"I don't go to the theater."

"Books, then. How about books?"

"Some other time," he ground out. And instantly wondered what had possessed him to say *that*. The odd thing of it was, despite her many, many unpleasant attributes, Lady Amelia was clearly possessed of some intelligence and wit. He could not help but think that at another time, in another place, he might have enjoyed discussing books with her. But he couldn't possibly do so here, in a crowded ballroom, with his concentration unraveling on each successive twirl.

His control of the scene was slipping.

And that made him frown.

"Ooh, that's a dangerous glare," she said. "And your face is turning a most impressive shade of red. It's enough to make me believe all those dreadful rumors about you. Why, you're actually raising the hairs on my neck."

"Stop this."

"I am all honesty," she protested. "See for yourself." She stretched up and tilted her head to the side, elongating the smooth, pale column of her neck. No freckles there. Only an enticing curve of creamy, soft-looking, sweet-smelling female skin.

Now Spencer's heart slammed against his ribs. He didn't know which he yearned to do more. Wring that neck, or lick it. Biting it might be a fair compromise. An action that mingled pleasure with punishment.

Because she deserved to be punished, the impertinent minx. Accepting the futility of her first argument, she'd chosen to wage a different battle. A rebellion of joy. She might not wrest a penny from him, but she would wring every possible drop of enjoyment at his expense.

This was the very attitude responsible for her brother's debt. Jack would not quit the card table, even when he had no hope of recouping his losses. He stayed in, risked hundreds he did not have, because he wanted to win one last hand. It was precisely the temperament one might expect from a family such as the d'Orsays—a lineage rich with centuries of pride and valor, perpetually strapped for gold.

Lady Amelia wanted to best him at something. She wanted to see him brought low. And through no particular skill or perception of her own, she was perilously close to succeeding.

Spencer came to an abrupt halt. Implausibly, the room kept spinning around him. Damn it, this couldn't be happening. Not here, not now.

But the signs were unmistakable. His pulse pounded in his ears. A wave of heat swamped his body. The air was suddenly thick as treacle and tasted just as vile.

Devil, damn, blast. He needed to leave this place, immediately.

"Why have we stopped?" she said. "The waltz isn't

over." Her voice sounded as though it came from a great distance, filtered through cotton wool.

"It's over for me." Spencer swung his gaze around the room. An open set of doors to his left beckoned promisingly. He attempted to release her, but she clutched at his shoulders and held him fast. "For God's sake," he said, "let me—"

"Let you what?" Her eyes darting to the side, she whispered, "Let you go? Let you abandon me here on the dance floor, to my complete and total humiliation? Of all the unchivalrous, ungentlemanly, unforgivable . . ." When she ran out of descriptors, she threw him an accusatory glare that implied a thousand more. "I won't stand for it."

"Very well, then. Don't."

He slid his hands to her waist, grasped tight with both hands, and bodily lifted Lady Amelia d'Orsay—two, four . . . six inches off the floor. Until they looked one another eye-to-eye, and her slippers dangled in midair.

He spared a brief moment to savor the way indignant shock widened those pale blue eyes.

And then he carried her out into the night.

Chapter Two

Before Amelia could even catch her breath, the duke had swept her straight through the doors. They emerged onto the exact same circlet of terrace where she'd argued with Jack, not a half hour ago. The Bunscombe gardens were getting good use this evening.

Dropping her to the ground with dispatch, Morland warded off her complaint with an open palm. "You asked for it." Then he sagged against a marble pillar, tugging at his cravat. "Bloody hell, it's hot in there."

Amelia quietly reeled on her feet, simultaneously infuriated and exhilarated by the way he'd so easily lifted her and carried her from the room. She wasn't precisely a wisp of a girl. But as sturdily framed as she was, he was definitely more so. As he'd lifted her, she'd felt his dense shoulder muscles rippling beneath her palms.

Oh, yes. He was powerfully built indeed.

Well, and what now? She'd known she was treading untested ground with her bold teasing. But then, she'd been in the mood to take risks. She'd already lost Briarbank, lost Jack, probably lost any remaining marital prospects after her wild charge across the ballroom to claim His Grace's hand. She had no reputation or fortune left to protect; why not have a little fun? He was an attractive, enigmatic, powerful man. It had been intoxicating, pushing the boundaries of propriety as she'd never dared before, not knowing what manner of response she might provoke.

Whatever response she'd expected, it hadn't been *this*. Bodily abducted from the ballroom? Ha. Let those debutantes giggle at her now.

"And to think," she said wonderingly, "I defended you against all those rumors of barbarism."

"Did you?" He made a gruff noise in his throat. "I hope you've learned your lesson. Don't test me again. In the end, I always come out ahead—at cards, at negotiation, at everything."

She laughed. "Oh, do you?"

"Yes." He ran a hand through his hair. "Because I possess the singular bit of sense no one in your family seems to share."

"And what's that, pray tell?"

"I know when to walk away."

She stared at him. Light spilled out from the ballroom, illuminating his sculpted, aristocratic profile. With his curling forelock and the marble behind him, he could have been part of a Greco-Roman frieze. Immortally handsome.

And deathly pale.

"Are you feeling well?" she asked.

"Four hundred pounds."

"What?"

He closed his eyes. "Four hundred pounds, if you leave me this instant. You'll have the bank draft in the morning."

Stunned, she blinked down at the paving stones. Four hundred pounds. Four hundred pounds, and all she need do was turn around and leave? Jack's debt, paid. Her summer at Briarbank, restored.

"Turn those hapless d'Orsay fortunes around, Lady Amelia. Learn when to walk away."

Good Lord. He was serious. She spared herself a brief moment of self-deprecating irony, that while he wouldn't think of paying four hundred pounds for her favors, he was eager to hand over the sum if she would simply go away. Vile man.

Oh, but his face had turned a very peculiar shade. In the ballroom, his cheeks had blazed red with anger, but now his complexion was the color of ash. She could hear the air dragging in and out of his lungs. And was it a trick of the moonlight, or was his hand trembling, just a little, where it rested atop the balustrade?

If he *were* unwell, to simply desert him . . . it would be to abandon every good principle her dear parents had taught her. She would be selling her conscience and good breeding for four hundred pounds.

And there were some things on which one could not put a price.

She took a step toward him. "Truly, you look very ill. Why don't you allow me to get you some—"

"No. I'm perfectly well." He pushed off the marble pillar and paced the terrace perimeter, taking deep draughts of night air. "My sole affliction is a plaguing female in blue silk."

"There's no need to be rude. I'm trying to be helpful."

"I don't need your help." He swiped impatiently at his damp temple with his cuff. "I'm not ill."

"Then why are you so pale?" Amelia shook her head. "Why is it a man would rather swallow nails than accept a lady's assistance? And for pity's sake, can't a duke afford handkerchiefs?"

She unlaced the reticule cinched around her wrist. Now emptied of coin, it was so light she'd nearly forgotten the thing altogether. She loosened the string and withdrew the sole item remaining within: a meticulously embroidered linen square.

She took a moment to admire the stitching she'd finished just a few days ago. Her initials, in dark purple script. Twining around and through the open spaces of the letters, she'd embroidered vines and, in a lighter green, a few curled ferns. A stroke of pure whimsy had spurred her to add a tiny black-and-gold honeybee, buzzing around the apex of the A.

It was, perhaps, her best work yet. And now this treasured, labored-over bit of linen would go to wipe His Grace's noble brow? Just how much would she be forced to surrender on this terrace? Her brother, her home, her last small accomplishment. What was left? She half expected Napoleon to pop out from the hedges and demand her allegiance.

"Morland." The curt baritone sounded from the shadows.

Amelia jumped.

The voice spoke again: low, rough. To her relief, most definitely English. "Morland, is that you?"

The duke straightened. "Who goes there?"

A rustling of greenery indicated the stranger's approach. Impetuously, Amelia went to the duke's side and pressed her handkerchief into his hand. He looked from her to the square of linen, and then back to her again.

She shrugged. Perhaps it was silly, but . . . it was simply that he was one of England's great men, and she did come from one of England's historically great families, and she just couldn't allow him to face an unknown challenge looking as if he'd succumbed to malaria. Not when she clutched a perfectly clean handkerchief in her hand.

"Thank you," he said, hastily wiping his brow and jamming the linen square into his coat pocket as not one, but *two* men emerged from behind the hedge and vaulted the low rail at the edge of the terrace. The duke edged between her and the strange men. It was a chivalrous, reassuring gesture. She did not regret the handkerchief now.

The strangers stood outside the half-circle of available light, so that Amelia could not make out their features. She saw only two silhouettes: one fashionable, one fearsome.

"Morland. It's Bellamy." This came from the fashionable one. "And I know you've met Ashworth," he said, indicating the giant at his side.

The duke stiffened. "Certainly. We're old school chums, aren't we, Rhys?"

No answer from the hulking shadow.

"We've been waiting for you to make your escape," Bellamy said, "but we can't delay any longer. You must come with us at once."

"Come with you? Why?"

"We'll tell you in the carriage."

"Tell me now, and I shall decide if I join you in any carriage."

"Club business," Bellamy said.

He eased into the light, and Amelia peered at him. Ah, now she understood why his name was familiar. His face was familiar to her, too. And there was no mistaking the shock of artfully disheveled hair. He was that infamous hell-raiser, the ringleader of that fast group of young bucks Jack would give his eyeteeth to join. The group he'd lost four hundred pounds trying to keep pace with. Was Bellamy involved in that token nonsense, too?

"Club business?" Morland said. "Do you mean the Stud Club?"

Amelia barely checked an unladylike snort of laughter. Stud Club, indeed. Men and their ridiculous societies.

"Yes, we're calling an urgent meeting," Bellamy said. "And since you're now seven-tenths of the membership, you're required to attend."

"Is it Osiris?" the duke asked, his voice suddenly grave. "If something's happened to that horse, I—"

The tower called Ashworth broke his silence. "It's not the horse. Harcliffe's dead."

The bottom dropped out of Amelia's stomach.

"For Christ's sake, Ashworth," said Bellamy. "There's a lady present."

"Harcliffe?" she echoed. "Dead? As in Leopold Chatwick, the Marquess of Harcliffe?" As in, the boy who'd been raised a half-day's ride from Beauvale Castle and gone to school with her older brothers? The golden-haired, fine-featured, good-humored, and universally admired young man who'd been so kind as to dance with her at her come-out ball? Not just once, as the obligation of friendship warranted, but two full sets? "Surely you don't mean Leo?"

Bellamy stepped forward, tapping his gold-knobbed walking stick on the paving stones as he went. "I'm sorry."

Amelia's hand went to her mouth. "Oh, poor Lily."

"You know his sister?"

She nodded. "A little."

The duke seemed to recall his social duty, as the only person present acquainted with all parties. "Lady Amelia d'Orsay, this is Mr. Julian Bellamy." His voice darkened a shade as he introduced the larger man. "And that's Rhys St. Maur, Lord Ashworth."

"Under any other circumstance, I'm sure I would be delighted." Amelia inclined her head. "May I ask, how is Lily coping with her grief?"

"She has not yet been informed of Leo's death," Bellamy said. "That's why we've come for you, Morland. As the remaining members of the Stud Club, we have an obligation to her."

"We do?"

"Yes, we do."

"What sort of obligation? Imposed by whom?"

"It's in the code. The Stud Club Code of Good Breeding. As your interest obviously lies purely in the horse and not in the club's spirit of fraternity, I don't suppose you've taken the care to acquaint yourself with it."

"I've never even heard of such a thing," said Morland. He looked to Ashworth. "Have you?"

The larger man remained cloaked in shadow, but Amelia could tell that he shook his head in the negative.

"There *is* a code," Bellamy said impatiently. "And you are both subject to it. Else you must forfeit your interest in the Club entirely. Now come along, both of you. We must inform Lily of her brother's death."

"Wait," Amelia said. "I'll go with you."

"No," the three men said in unison. They looked around at one another, as if surprised to find themselves in agreement.

"Yes," she argued back. "Yes, I will. Lily's parents are no longer living. Leo was her only family, correct?"

"Correct," Bellamy said. "Unfortunately."

"Well, you gentlemen may have your clubs and tokens and codes of honor, but we ladies have our sisterhood. And I will not allow the three of you to go trampling Lily's feelings like so many elephants. Tonight, she will learn that her only brother has died and she is alone in the world. She will need understanding, comfort, a shoulder to cry upon. And I refuse to let her suffer through it alone, while you three dolts stand around, arguing the finer points of your asinine club and its asinine code."

There was a prolonged silence, during which Amelia began to regret a few of her words. Such as "dolt," applied to two peers of the realm. And the uninspired repetition of "asinine." But she would not apologize for the sentiment, and she would not be left behind. She knew what it was to lose a brother. She knew what it was to walk down that particular alley of Hell all alone. What she would not have given for Mama's presence on the day they came about Hugh.

At last, the duke spoke. "We will take my carriage. It's readied, and I have the finest team."

"My bays are warm," said Bellamy.

Morland firmed his jaw. "I have the finest team. Anywhere."

A deferential silence followed. It hadn't even been a command, but with those few words the duke had asserted absolute control of the situation. If he had been feeling ill, he now appeared fully recovered.

Fitter than ever, to Amelia's eyes.

"As you wish," Bellamy said. "Can we cut across the gardens? Until we've spoken with Lily, I'm loath to draw public notice."

Again, all three men looked to Amelia.

She paused. Obviously, it would not escape the guests' attention that she and the Duke of Morland had disappeared into the night. But all would be explained, once Leo's death became public knowledge tomorrow. And it wasn't as though they were alone.

She nodded. "Very well."

Bellamy and Ashworth cleared the railing easily. Their boots landed in the flowerbed with a soft squish before they rounded the hedge and disappeared the same way they'd come. Morland went next, stepping over the rail one long leg at a time.

He directed Amelia to sit on the balustrade, then to swing her legs across. She did so, in rather ungainly fashion. A fold of her gown became tangled in the closure of her slipper, and that made for some seconds' delay. At last freed, she prepared to slide down from the rail. It was only a few feet to the ground.

The duke stopped her.

"Allow me," he said, placing his hands about her waist. "It's muddy here."

At her nod of assent, Amelia found herself in those powerful arms for the second time that evening. Lifted effortlessly from the balustrade, swung over the flowerbed, and deposited on the raked gravel path. Gently, this time. Surely she was reading far too much into it, but she couldn't help but imagine he was making amends. Offering an unspoken apology for his brutish behavior in the ballroom.

"Oh," she said, swaying a bit as he released her. "Thank you."

"Thank you," he replied, laying a hand to the coat pocket where he'd placed her handkerchief. "For earlier."

"We needn't speak of it. Are you well?"

"Yes."

Together they followed the path the other men had taken, walking alongside one another. He did not offer his arm. He did, however, point out a toad in the path an instant before she would have stepped on it.

As they rounded the front corner of the house and approached the paved driveway where the carriages and drivers sat waiting, he spoke once again. "What does it stand for, the C?"

"I beg your pardon?"

"Your initial." He patted his pocket again.

"Oh." Understanding dawned. "Claire. It stands for Claire. Amelia Claire."

He nodded and walked on.

Amelia purposely fell behind.

Ninny, ninny. They passed a piece of bronze statuary, and Amelia longed to bash her head against it. What an absolute muffin she was. He'd asked her a question once. She had to answer it *three times*? "Claire," she mimicked quietly, adopting the voice of a parrot. "It stands for Claire. Amelia Claire."

She recognized, and rued, the giddy flutter in her belly: infatuation. It could not have happened at a worse time. Nothing good could come of it. And of all the gentlemen in London, this one? She hadn't been exaggerating in the ballroom, when she'd told him he danced divinely and was undeniably handsome. Nor when she'd confessed an unchaste longing to touch his dark, curling hair. And he really did lift the hairs on her neck. True, all of it true.

He's horrid, she silently told herself. *Loutish, arrogant, insufferable! He refused to release Jack from debt. He insulted you. He bodily hauled you from a ballroom and then offered you money to just please go away! And for heaven's sake, you are on your way to tell Lily Chatwick her twin brother is dead. You are a depraved, deranged woman, Amelia Claire-Claire-Claire d'Orsay!*

It was just . . . something about those few unrehearsed moments, when a strange rustling in the hedge made them forget debts and insults and act on instinct alone. And she'd rushed to his side with her treasured handkerchief, and he'd put his body between her and the unknown. She could not escape the feeling that they'd formed an unspoken alliance and were now acting as a team.

He touched a hand to his coat pocket again. He kept doing that. And every time he did, her knees went weak.

Oh, Lord.

They reached the carriage. It was an impressive conveyance. Jet-black, glossy, emblazoned with the Morland ducal crest, and drawn by a team of four perfectly matched black horses.

The duke helped her in, closing one of his hands about her fingers and placing the other against the small of her back. Bellamy and Ashworth had already situated themselves on the rear-facing seat, leaving Amelia and Morland to share the front-facing one.

Nothing about this situation should thrill her. It was terrible, the way his authoritative command to the driver shot sparks to her toes. It was unpardonable, how she sat toward the middle of the seat and allowed her body to fall against his as the carriage lurched into motion.

"How did Harcliffe die?" the duke asked.

Thank you, Amelia said silently, scooting away from him until she hugged the outer edge of the seat. *Thank you for reminding me of the gravity of our situation and the utter inappropriateness of my thoughts.*

"Footpads," said Bellamy. "He was beaten to death in the street, in Whitechapel. It appears to have been a random attack."

"Good God."

It was too dark for Amelia to make out the expressions of anyone in the coach. She reckoned, therefore, it was too dark for them to see hers. And so she permitted herself a rush of hot, silent tears.

This wasn't right. Waterloo was over; the war had ended. Young, handsome men at the peak of vitality were supposed to stop dying. Only a few weeks ago, she'd spied Leo at the theater. He'd taken a box with some of his friends. The lot of them were loud and disruptive in the way only Leo's friends could be, because Leo was always forgiven everything. Everyone loved him so.

Amelia shuddered. Beaten to death, by footpads. If such a thing could happen to Leo . . . it could so easily have been Jack.

"It could have been me," said Bellamy. "God, it *should* have been me. I was supposed to go with him tonight, but I begged off." His rough voice cracked. "What a damned bloody waste. If I'd been there, I might have prevented it."

"Or you might have been killed, too."

"Better me than him. He had a title, responsibilities, a sister to protect." He swore violently. "What will become of Lily now? This is all my fault. The boxing match was my idea in the first place. And I begged off. I begged off, to spend the evening with that harlot Carnelia." He leaned forward, burying his face in his hands.

Amelia supposed he must refer to the very scandalous, very *married* Lady Carnelia Hightower. Though her mind reeled, she remained silent. The last thing she wanted was to remind all three men there was a lady in the carriage and cause them to temper their remarks. For Lily's sake, she wanted to gather all the information she could. For once, the quality of being invisible to men worked in her favor.

The duke cleared his throat. "You called it a random attack. If that is the case . . . well then, random is random. It might have been anyone."

"It wouldn't have been me." This came from Ashworth, the taciturn giant across from her. "I cannot die."

"Why would you say such a thing?" Amelia asked, abandoning her intention to remain silent. It was such a shocking statement to make, and something in the low rasp of his voice told her he did not speak from arrogance.

"Because I've tried, several times. And as you see, I've failed on each occasion."

She had no response to that.

"Ask your friend Morland," he continued. "I'm bloody hard to knock down."

Beside her, the duke tensed. Clearly the two men had some history of enmity.

"Enough." Mr. Bellamy raised his head, scrubbing at his eyes with his palm. "We've no time for this. Leo is gone. It's Lily we need to discuss. As Leo died without issue, the Harcliffe title, estate, properties—including the town house—will all pass to some distant cousin. She probably has a legacy due her, but given her condition, she cannot live independently in Town."

No, she couldn't, Amelia silently agreed. Poor Lily. She must find some way to help her. "What do you propose, Mr. Bellamy?"

The man looked from Ashworth to Morland. "My lord, Your Grace—one of you must marry her."

"Marry her?" Spencer blinked. "Did you just say one of us must marry her?"

"Yes."

Sighing deeply, he raised a hand to his temple. No offense intended to the deceased, nor to Lily Chatwick and her mysterious "condition." It was just that this situation would clearly require a great deal of discussion, and he'd far exceeded his allotment of civil speech for the evening.

What he wanted to do was to go home, toss back two fingers of brandy, and prostrate himself on the library floor—well, on the carpet; the floor was unforgiving oak, and he wasn't an ascetic monk, after all—until this damned whirling clamor in his head cleared. Come morning, he'd take Juno out for a rambling canter, probably halfway to Dover and back. She was uneasy in Town, unused to the crowds and noise. A long ride over open country would put them both to rights. Afterward, he'd give the mare a proper grooming himself. She was touchy with these London stablehands, and they were never able to do a thorough job. After all that . . . perhaps dinner before he went out in search of cards.

That was what he wanted to do. But, as so often happened, what he wanted and what was required of him were disparate things.

"The Stud Club code states," said Bellamy, "that in the event of a member's untimely demise, the brotherhood is honor bound to care for his dependents. With her brother gone, Lily will need a protector. She must marry."

"Then why don't you do it?" Ashworth asked. "You are obviously well acquainted with her. Weren't you and Harcliffe friends?"

"The closest of friends, yes. Which is precisely why I cannot do it. Lady Lily Chatwick is the sister of a marquess. Her ancestry includes several royals. I believe Leo once told me she's thirteenth in line for the Crown. I am . . ." Bellamy pressed a fist against the seat cushion. "I am no one of consequence."

Well, on that point he and Spencer were in complete agreement. He despised the vain upstart. From what he heard at the tables, Bellamy had arrived out of nowhere some three years ago. Despite the man's vague origins, even the veriest snobs invited him to every rout and card party, for his amusement value alone. He was an uncanny mimic.

Spencer had once watched from a doorway as Bellamy regaled an audience of dozens with his bawdy imitations of Byron and Lady Caroline Lamb. He thought the man a pathetic clown, but the young bucks of the *ton* worshipped him. They mimicked the mimic: imitated his style of dress, his manner of walking, his cutting witticisms. Some went so far as to have their valets apply some noxious mixture of soot and egg whites to their scalp, to imitate his riffled black hair.

Spencer had no interest in the man's hair or fashion, and nothing but contempt for his cheap brand of humor. But he did have a keen interest in one thing of Bellamy's: the brass token that made him a member of the Stud Club.

"It will have to be Morland," said Ashworth. "I'm not marrying her."

"You would be damned lucky to marry her," Bellamy said. "She's a lovely, intelligent lady."

"I'm certain she is. But the last thing I'd do to a woman I admired is marry her."

Spencer couldn't resist. "Oh, you've a shred of decency now? Where did that come from, I wonder? Perhaps you found it lying around a battlefield."

"Perhaps I did," the man said evenly. "I know I didn't meet with you there."

Spencer glowered. Just like the bastard, to deal him a low blow. As a youth, there'd been nothing he wanted more than to follow his father's example and purchase a commission in the Army. But when his father died, Spencer became the late duke's heir. Suddenly he had a title, duties, responsibilities. He would have been risking hundreds of lives in battle, not merely his own. Farewell, visions of glory.

"Why can't you marry her, Ashworth?" Bellamy asked. "You're a lord, aren't you?"

"I've lately inherited a barony. It consists of a worthless expanse of moorland in Devonshire and a house that burnt to the ground fourteen years ago. I had to sell out my commission just to pay the creditors."

"Forgive me," Lady Amelia said, "I'm so sorry to interrupt."

Forgive her? Spencer would have thanked her, profusely. A change in conversation was all too welcome.

"But I knew your name was familiar," she went on, speaking to Ashworth, "and then you mentioned the commission . . . Are you by chance Lieutenant Colonel St. Maur?"

"I am. And yes, I knew your brother."

"I thought so. He mentioned you in his letters, always spoke of your bravery. Were you . . ." Her voice trailed off. "Were you with him, at Waterloo?"

"No, not at the end. He served in a different battalion. But I can tell you he was a fine man, and an excellent officer. Admired by those who served under him, well regarded by his superiors. A credit to his family and country."

"Thank you."

Lady Amelia seemed satisfied, but to Spencer's ears, this speech was flat, unconvincing. Rehearsed. As though Ashworth had spoken those exact words many, many times. He probably had. Perhaps to him, tonight's errand—notifying a young lady of her brother's untimely death—was nothing but routine. It would explain this new gravity in his demeanor. Spencer didn't remember him being so solemn, before.

Not that they'd spent much time conversing at Eton. Difficult to chat while throwing punches.

"Where is his body?" Lady Amelia suddenly asked. "Leo's, I mean."

"At my home," Bellamy answered. "My men are keeping watch until he can be brought to the undertaker's."

"Lily will want to see him."

"No, my lady. She won't."

"She will, I assure you. No matter what his injuries. I . . ." Her voice broke. "I would have given much, for the opportunity to see Hugh. His death would have been easier to accept, I think."

In that moment, Spencer became extremely—there was no better word for it—*aware* of Lady Amelia d'Orsay. His team of blacks hied left, pulling the carriage around a sharp corner, and she fell against him. Soft, warm. Her lavender scent was richer than it had been earlier. As she righted herself, a drop of moisture landed on the strip of exposed skin between his glove and his sleeve.

She was weeping.

Weeping, in absolute silence, presumably too proud to ask for a handkerchief after she'd pressed hers on

Spencer in the garden. His hand strayed to his side pocket, where her precise, cheerful stitches secretly decorated the black satin lining. It was her own fault she was without it—he hadn't wanted the thing in the first place.

But now, perversely, he didn't want to give it back.

"That settles it then," said Bellamy. "Morland will marry her."

Spencer said, "I refuse."

"You can't refuse."

"I just did."

Bellamy leaned forward. "It's in the Stud Club code. Neither Ashworth nor I are suitable prospects, as you've heard. If you hadn't so methodically reduced the number of our members over recent weeks, there might be other candidates. But you did. And as you are now seven-tenths of the club, the burden of responsibility falls on you."

"I don't understand," Lady Amelia said. "How can one man be seven-tenths of a club?"

"It's the tokens, my lady," said Bellamy. "You see, Leo purchased an exceptional stallion some years ago. Osiris was once the finest racehorse in England. He's too old to race anymore, but still valuable as a stud horse. Many gentlemen were asking the favor of breeding rights, and Leo devised the Stud Club scheme as a lark. If you knew Leo, you know how he loved a good joke."

"Oh, yes," she said. "When he and my brother were boys, they once stole the clapper from the church bell just so they could sleep in on Sunday morning."

Bellamy smiled. "Yes, that sounds like Leo. Which brother of yours was this? Lord Beauvale? Or Jack?" When she did not immediately answer, the man added, "Or—God, I'm sorry. Not the one who died in Belgium?"

"No, not Hugh. None of those, actually. This was my brother Michael. He's an officer in the Navy now."

"Good Lord. Just how many of you are there?" Spencer regretted the question instantly. What had possessed him to ask it? Why the devil should he care?

The longer Lady Amelia went without answering, the further the accusatory hush spread through the carriage: *Badly done, Morland. Badly done.* Truly, he *was* capable of civil conversation. Just not at any time before, during, or for several hours following a ball.

At last, she answered. "There were six of us, once. Now only five. I am the only daughter." She paused, perhaps waiting to hear what rude-mannered question would be hurled at her next. When none came, she prompted, "Please continue, Mr. Bellamy."

"Right. Leo had ten tokens fashioned from brass and distributed them to close friends. Possession of a token entitled a man to send mares to Osiris to be mated. But as a matter of club code, the tokens could never be bartered, purchased, or given away. They could only be won in a game of chance."

"At cards," she said.

"Cards, dice, wagers of any sort. That handful of misshapen brass tokens became the most coveted currency in London. Everyone wanted a share of Osiris, of course. But more than that, they wanted to be a part of the club. The fraternity, the camaraderie . . . there's a certain cachet now, among gentlemen of our set, to calling oneself a member of the Stud Club. Not many clubs can be so exclusive as to permit only ten members, and winning a token meant that luck or wits, or both, were with you." Bellamy shot Spencer a cutting look. "Then Morland here came along and ruined the fun. He's collected seven of the ten tokens now. The remaining three belong to me, Ashworth here, and Leo, of course."

The seat cushion resettled as Lady Amelia pivoted in Spencer's direction. "But why would he do that?"

Bellamy said, "Care to answer the lady, Your Grace?"

Spencer stared hard out the carriage window. "Isn't it obvious? I want the horse."

"But Mr. Bellamy has said, one token is sufficient for securing breeding privileges. Why insist on obtaining them all? Why such greed?"

Spencer heard the accusation in her voice. She blamed his "greed" for her brother's debt. "Where Osiris is concerned, I am not interested in breeding privileges. I am interested in possession. I don't like to share."

Bellamy shook his head. "There you have it, Lady Amelia. His Grace is uninterested in brotherhood, friendship, the preservation of a fixture in London society. He only cares for the horseflesh involved. I tell you, Morland—you may not like to share, but you'll have to. You're not getting my token unless you pry it from my cold, dead hands. The Stud Club was Leo's creation, and I'll not allow you to destroy his legacy."

"But you do want me to marry his sister."

"*No*. Er, yes." Bellamy growled with frustration. "I mean, I do not want it. I wish to God there were someone—*anyone*—else. But there isn't."

Lady Amelia made a strange, inarticulate noise. Did it convey dismay? Frustration? Amusement? At least she wasn't weeping any longer.

Clearly, Bellamy could not translate her outburst any better than Spencer could. Cocking his head, he eyed the two of them carefully. "That is, unless you are already engaged. Did we interrupt something on the terrace back there?"

"Oh, no," she said quickly, laughing as she did. "Whatever you interrupted, it was not *that*."

"Then, Your Grace, honor compels you to make an offer to Lily."

"Excuse me," said Lady Amelia, "but precisely what is honorable about deciding a woman's future without so much as soliciting her opinion? If Lily wanted to marry, she might have done so years ago. We are not living in the Dark Ages, sirs. A lady's consent is generally considered a prerequisite before any wedding plans are made."

"Yes, but even in these modern times, sometimes circumstances—such as a death or impending poverty—make a lady's decision for her."

"I cannot speak for Lily, Mr. Bellamy. But I can tell you, I have faced such circumstances. And they have never made the decisions for me."

So, Spencer thought to himself, Lady Amelia had received offers of marriage. And refused them. He had been wondering whether her spinsterhood was a condition arrived at by choice, or merely from a lack of alternatives.

Damn it, why was he wondering about her? Why did he feel this need to know everything about an impertinent, managing, none-too-pretty female? But he did. Oh, he did not want to engage in anything so gauche or peril-fraught as inquiry. He merely wanted a reference—the comprehensive codex of all things Amelia Claire d'Orsay. A chart of her ancestry back to the Norman invaders. The catalogue listing every book she'd ever read. A topographical map indicating the precise location of every freckle on her skin.

Ashworth spoke. "We've arrived."

The carriage rolled to a quiet halt before Harcliffe Manor. As they waited for the footman to open the door, Bellamy leaned forward and spoke directly to Spencer.

"Lily may be deaf, but she is not stupid. She reads lips, and she speaks with diction every bit as aristocratic as yours. Look at her when you speak; that's all that is required. Do not raise your voice or speak in simplistic

Chapter Three

"A duel?" Amelia cried. "Whatever for? So we will have two deaths tonight, instead of one?"

Ignoring her, the duke said icily, "Just try it, Bellamy. I will take pleasure in prying that token from your cold, dead hands."

Really, these men were impossible.

When the carriage door swung open, Amelia rose from her seat and bustled between Bellamy and Morland, who sat trading murderous glares. As she exited the coach, the men followed her.

Rushing up to claim the front stoop, she stood blocking the door and addressed them firmly, in the tone her mother had used to address her quarreling brothers. If these grown men were going to behave like boys squabbling over marbles, someone with sense had to take charge. For Lily's sake.

"Hold a moment, if you please. Before we go in, I will have my say."

The three men stared up at her, and Amelia's resolve began to waver. They may have been behaving like children, but they were, all three of them, quite large, powerful, and intimidating men. A duke, a warrior, a scoundrel. She was unused to commanding the attention of such men. La, she was unused to commanding the attention of *any* men, aside from her own brothers. Her navel was still turning cartwheels whenever she so much as *thought* of glancing in the duke's direction. And thanks to the smoky, amber glow of the carriage lamp, she was getting her first clear look at Lord Ashworth and Mr. Bellamy.

What she saw did not put her at ease.

Ashworth was enormous, in every respect—tall, broad, imposing. A dramatic scar sliced from his temple to his cheekbone. The blow that caused it must have narrowly missed his eye. But for all Ashworth had the look of a marauding pirate, she felt safer with him than with Bellamy. Despite his rakishly mussed hair, Mr. Bellamy's clothing and manner were polished—so polished, they gave the impression of slickness. There was such a thing as a man too handsome to be trusted.

She drew a deep, steadying breath. "Here is what will occur. We will alert the house staff to awaken Lily and ask her to dress. By the time she comes down, I promise you, she will be prepared for the worst."

Any woman, when awakened in the dead of night, prepared herself for the worst. How many times had Amelia stumbled downstairs, tripping over feet numb with dread, certain that disaster had befallen another of her loved ones? Only to discover it was Jack, staggering in from an evening spent carousing with his "friends."

"When she comes down," she continued, "I will speak with her alone. You gentlemen wait in Lord Harcliffe's study, and I will inform Lily of her brother's death."

"Lady Amelia—"

She silenced Bellamy by raising an open palm. "It is not a task I relish, sir. But I will not leave it to the three of you. Forgive me for speaking frankly, but after the past quarter-hour's conversation, I am unconvinced that any of you possess the sense or sensitivity to impart the news in any respectful fashion."

"My lady, I must insist—"

"No, you must listen!" Her voice squeaked, and she pressed a hand to her belly. "You must understand, I have lived through the very experience that Lily is about to endure. And the three of you together, you're a fearsome group. I'm not even certain how I'm able to stand before you without melting into the mist . . . except that this has been a most unconventional evening, and I'm no longer certain of much at all."

Dear Lord, now she was babbling, and they were looking at her with that strange combination of pity and panic with which men regard a woman on the verge of hysterics.

Pull yourself together, Amelia.

"Please," she said. "What I'm trying to say is, allow me to break the news delicately. If Lily gets one look at you, she's going to instantly know—"

With a gentle creak, the door swung open behind her.

Amelia pivoted, meeting face-to-face not with a servant, as she'd anticipated, but with Lily Chatwick herself. For the first time in . . . oh, it must have been two years. Since Hugh's funeral, perhaps. They'd been friends as girls—not the closest of friends, as Lily was a few years older. But after the fever that left Lily without hearing, they'd seen one another less and less. She did not come out in society often.

"Amelia?" Lily swept a lock of dark hair from her face. With her other hand, she clutched the neck of her dressing gown closed. "Why, Amelia d'Orsay, whatever are you doing here at this—" Her sleepy, dark-fringed eyes went to the men.

Amelia squeezed her hands into fists. Lily couldn't have heard her remarks, she reminded herself. Perhaps it wasn't too late to break the news gently.

"Oh, dear God." Lily's hand went to her throat. "Leo's dead."

"I knew it," Lily said some time later, staring blankly at her folded hands. They sat in the parlor. A cup of brandy-laced tea rested on the table, untouched and long gone cold. "Somehow I just knew it, even before you arrived. I'd retired early. I was so very tired last night. But then I woke with a start not an hour later and haven't been able to sleep since. I just knew he was gone."

Amelia moved her chair closer to her friend's. "I'm so sorry." Such worthless, feeble words. But really, in such a situation, there was nothing helpful to be said.

"I wouldn't have been able to believe it, had I not felt it in my own heart. As it is, I've been growing accustomed to the idea for several hours now. We've always known when the other was in danger. Because we are twins, I suspect. Our bond has always been close. During my illness, he took the mail coach all the way home from Oxford, even though no one had written him. I don't know how I'll—" Lily bent her head to her folded hands. "It's just so hard to imagine existing without him, when I never have."

Her slight shoulders shook as she cried, and Amelia smoothed the black plait of hair running down the grieving woman's back. The casual observer would never have guessed that she and Leo were twins. Their appearances could not have been more different. Leo had golden-brown hair, bronzed skin—an aura of health and energy radiated from him. By contrast, Lily was fair and dark-haired, of serene and contemplative disposition. The moon to her brother's sun. Amelia had heard it suggested, in gossipy settings, that the twin birth was a fortunate thing for their mother's reputation—for no one would believe Leo and Lily to be children of the same father, had they not emerged from the womb within minutes of one another.

Amelia squeezed her friend's shoulder lightly until Lily lifted her gaze. "It's hard to imagine Leo gone, even for me. More than anyone in my acquaintance, he always seemed so . . . so alive. He will be greatly missed." She gentled her touch, stroking reassuringly. "But you needn't be anxious. For as many people as there were who loved Leo, there will be equally many eager to assist you, in any way." She threw a sideways glance toward the doors that connected this parlor with the library. "Just in the other room, you have three of England's most powerful men, each of them prepared to swim the Channel, if you asked it."

The corner of Lily's mouth curved. "Mr. Bellamy is responsible for the presence of the other two, I am sure. Sometimes I think that man will smother me under his good intentions."

She must have caught Amelia's fleeting look of skepticism.

"Oh, do not mistake him," Lily said. "Julian is a gifted performer. His favorite, and most successful, role is that of the incorrigible roué. But he has been a steadfast friend to Leo and no doubt views it his duty to assume brotherly guardianship of me now."

"Are you certain his interest is entirely brotherly?" Amelia recalled Mr. Bellamy's behavior in the coach, and his impassioned defense to any remark that might be construed as even mildly disparaging to Lily.

"Oh, yes," Lily said. "On that point, I am quite certain."

"I feel I should tell you, on our way here the three of them were arguing over . . . over who among them should be the fortunate one to marry you."

"*Marry* me? I never thought to marry at all."

"I told them that you would need time to absorb this

news, time to grieve. I tried to persuade them against presenting you with such decisions tonight, but I do not know if I was successful."

More accurately, she did not know if Mr. Bellamy's threats had been successful in removing Morland's reluctance. She hoped not. And not because she would be jealous. No, envy had nothing to do with this. Whatever her own physical attraction to the duke, Amelia was wise enough not to confuse it with esteem for his character. This evening alone, she'd witnessed more than enough evidence of that gentleman's callous attitudes toward debt, death, society, friendship, and marriage to know she would not wish such a husband on any woman she called friend.

"Oh dear," Lily said weakly. Her head sank to the table again. "Don't tell me. This has to do with that absurd club Leo started, with the horse."

"Yes."

"What a ridiculous name he gave it. The Stud Club. I told him, he should have asked me for ideas. I could think of a dozen better things to call it. What's wrong with the Stallion Society?"

Amelia bit back a laugh, then dipped her head to catch Lily's attention. "If you like, I'll send them away. I've stood up to them all once already tonight, and I'm not afraid to do it again."

Pride strengthened her voice as she said this. And why should it not? At some point this evening, between surrendering her last few coins to Jack and claiming the Duke of Morland's hand, Amelia had stepped outside herself, somehow. Or stepped outside that quiet, unassuming, plain, and proper shell she'd been inhabiting all her life. Scolding a trio of intimidating men was only part of it. She'd confronted a duke, even flirted with him during a sensual waltz. With no success, but still—it went beyond anything she'd dared before. Add to all this, she'd departed the ball under mysterious circumstances, and right now the gossips were probably debating precisely when that well-bred d'Orsay girl had become such a brazen adventuress.

Why, at the stroke of midnight, of course. That was the moment Amelia had ceased to be a pumpkin. And no matter what tomorrow brought, she was proud of herself for that.

"I'll go chase them off now," she said, pushing back from the table.

"No," Lily said. "I'll speak with them. I know they are grieving, too, and they mean well. Men do have that incurable need to try their hand at fixing things. Even things that can never be mended."

"I told them you'd want to see Leo."

"Thank you. Yes, I would." Her voice was polite and remote. Amelia knew she had entered that numb void of unreality that followed a great shock. For all Lily insisted she'd sensed the truth hours ago and had grown accustomed to the idea in the interim, Amelia knew Leo's death would not become real to her for some time yet. And when it did, the pain would be near unbearable.

She would not press Lily to confront that grief now. Let her float in that dark nothingness as long as she could.

"Shall I come upstairs with you and help you dress?"

"No, thank you. I'll do. My maid is awake."

"Then I'll wait with the gentlemen until you're ready. May I direct your cook to have a cold supper sent in? The beasts may prove more docile after a feeding. And if you can manage it, you should take some food, too."

"Yes, of course. Direct the servants however you think best." Bracing both hands flat on the table, Lily pushed back her chair and slowly stood. "I'm grateful you're here, Amelia. You are so very good."

* * *

An hour later, the array of cold meats and cheeses laid out on a serving cart remained largely untouched. The duke sat in a winged armchair in the farthest reaches of the library, impatiently leafing through the pages of a book. If he had looked up once in the past hour, Amelia had not noticed it. And, to her frustration, she found herself watching him a great deal.

The only one of the gentlemen to eat anything had been Lord Ashworth, and he now lay reclined on the divan, eyes closed and massive boots propped on the studded leather ottoman. His attitude of repose did not strike her as disrespectful, however. She might have described it as prudent. A military trait, she assumed. Ashworth was clearly a man who did not allow death to interfere with the unceasing work of survival. He would not waste an opportunity to eat, drink, or rest when it presented itself.

By contrast, Mr. Bellamy had not ceased moving since Amelia entered the room. He'd prowled the floor so many times, she feared he would wear a groove in the parquet. When the doorbell rang, he dashed to answer it himself. The caller was an investigator, Amelia gathered through scraps of overheard conversation, charged with tracking down the footpads who'd murdered Leo.

"Some news?" the duke asked, when Bellamy reentered.

"No. Nothing we didn't know already. He was beset in an alley, somewhere in Whitechapel. The motive appears to have been robbery. Some urchins nearby heard scuffling and shouts, but they were too frightened to investigate. It was a prostitute who found his body and called for a hack, but she's since disappeared."

"How did they know to bring him to you?"

"When she came upon him, he was still alive, barely. He apparently gave her my address. A fortunate thing, too, or who knows what might have happened to his body. Sold to medical students, most likely. I'm surprised the whore didn't think of that. She was probably hoping for a reward, saving a nobleman's life."

"Or maybe she simply had a conscience and a good heart," Amelia said.

Bellamy made a sound of skepticism. "Well, no matter how pure her intentions, they weren't enough to save him. He died en route."

"Were you there at home, when they brought him?"

"No." He swore under his breath. "No, they had to send for me. Damn it, if only I'd been with him. This wouldn't have happened."

With a sudden, savage burst of strength, he crashed his fist down on a bookshelf. Amelia jumped in her seat. Lord Ashworth's eyes popped open.

"Don't you see?" Bellamy said. "This is my fault. I can't make it right, but I will do what I can—bring Leo's murderers to justice and see Lily well settled."

"You are unlikely to accomplish either goal tonight," the duke said.

Bellamy started in the duke's direction. "You will offer for her, Morland. If I have to hold a knife to your bal—"

Amelia shot to her feet. "Please," she said, blocking Bellamy's path. "Please, if you care for Lily—"

"I do," he cut in impatiently. "As I would my own sister, if I had one."

"Then I beg you, allow her some time to grieve. Her brother has died. Whether he went violently or peacefully, expected or not—what matters is, he is gone from her life, and this is a tragedy. If you care for her, offer her comfort and understanding, not promises of vengeance or proposals of marriage."

"Very well." Bellamy released his breath. "I will speak

no further of murder and retribution. But he"—he pointed toward the duke—"had better do his duty by Lily. If he wants to hold on to his share in Osiris, he has no choice."

Morland put aside his book. "No choice? I am a duke. I always have a choice. And I do not respond favorably to threats."

"Oh, I'm not threatening you," Bellamy said. "I'm merely reminding you of the Stud Club code. Any member who fails to adhere to the Code of Good Breeding must surrender his interest in the horse."

A thought occurred to Amelia. "But Leo's dead. Doesn't this horse pass to his heir, as the rest of his possessions do?"

Bellamy gave the duke a cold smile before turning to Amelia. "No, my lady. Leo designed the club very cleverly. Had his solicitor draw it all up. Osiris is held in trust, and any breeding rights are contingent on two conditions: possession of a token and adherence to the code. If His Grace fails to fulfill his obligations, he forfeits any rights to the horse."

"That's absurd," Morland said.

Amelia thought the entire enterprise was absurd. She was heartily sick of hearing about this Stud Club and the vagaries of its code.

The duke continued, "This code of yours . . . in the coach, you said members must provide for the dependents of the deceased. I don't recall any mention of marriage."

"I don't see how else you *could* provide for her. She will lose this house, and everything in it. Even with whatever income she may have, she cannot live independently. As much would be true for any well-bred gentlewoman, but when one takes into consideration her condition . . ." He shook his head. "There are no alternatives."

"But of course there are!" Amelia cried, increasingly desperate to save Lily from this ill-conceived plan, which was proving to be nothing but a product of Mr. Bellamy's guilty conscience and the Duke of Morland's greed for horseflesh. "It will take time for the will to be executed. Lily is not in danger of being forced out onto the street tomorrow. And gentlewomen of means *do* live independently. I don't see why Lily's deafness should preclude it, if such is her desire. She could always engage the services of a companion. Some widow or unmarried lady of good breeding but little fortune, to provide her with companionship and assist her in managing the household. Such arrangements are made all the time."

"A paid companion," the duke said thoughtfully. His hazel eyes trained on Amelia. "That would solve matters nicely. If a suitable candidate presented herself."

Cocking his head a fraction, he raised one eyebrow and continued to regard her with that intense, scrutinizing gaze. A meaningful gaze.

She went hot and prickly all over.

Oh, no. No, you don't.

How dare he suggest, even tacitly, that Amelia would make a suitable paid companion? Such employment was for destitute widows and hopeless spinsters. Women with no prospects whatsoever, and no family or fortune of their own. That wasn't her!

At least, not yet.

There he sat, so smugly handsome. She could practically hear the arrogant words echoing in his skull: *I am a duke. I always have a choice. And you may as well abandon all dreams for your future and become a paid companion, because a man like me would never choose a woman like you.*

Yes, well. She'd absorbed that point already, hadn't she? Dozens of midnight snubs had taught her that lesson. But earlier that evening, when she'd taken *his* hand, forced him to listen, given him her opinions—not to mention her handkerchief—Amelia had felt she'd clawed her way to equal footing with the man.

Evidently not. Swiftly, surely, with a ruthless economy of words and those devastating eyes, he had put Amelia back in her place. What was it about this man that made her react so strongly? Despite his fine looks and obvious intelligence—or perhaps because of them—he, more than any man of her acquaintance, had the power to make her feel so vulnerable, lacking, and most decidedly *unwanted*.

Breaking eye contact with the Duke of Morland was not something Amelia wished to do. It was something she *needed* to do, as an act of sheer self-preservation.

For the love of God, why couldn't she?

From the doorway, Lily cleared her throat. "Thank you all for waiting. I am ready now."

Gratefully, Amelia turned away from the duke to face her friend. Lily's long black hair had been replaited, and she'd changed into a dark blue day dress that was elegant in its simplicity. Or perhaps it was elegant simply because Lily wore it. Nearing thirty now, she still had the willowy figure of her youth, and the same dark, doe-like eyes Amelia had always envied. Even in grief, she was stunning. And had she not been so opposed to the idea of her friend marrying any of the gentlemen in this room, Amelia would have taken umbrage on behalf of Lily, and indeed the entire female sex, that any man would have so much as a moment's hesitation when offered the chance to apply for her hand.

With her entrance, both Lord Ashworth and the duke rose to their feet, as etiquette dictated. But then, to Amelia's surprise—to *everyone's* surprise—the Duke of Morland did more than stand.

He came forward.

"Lady Lily," he began. "May I express my deepest sympathies for your loss."

His "deepest sympathies?" Amelia suspected this man's deepest sympathies would not fill a thimble.

"Let me assure you," Morland continued, "that as a friend of Harcliffe's, a fellow peer, and an associate in his club, my honor as a gentleman compels me to offer you any assistance you may require."

"Thank you, Your Grace," Lily replied. She flicked a distressed glance in Amelia's direction, as it became clear the duke was not yet finished speaking.

"In addition, it is my intention to make you an offer," he said.

The room held its breath.

"I should like to make you a substantial offer for your brother's share in the stallion Osiris."

His words skated on the thin, tense surface of quiet. Until they crashed under a resounding chorus from every corner of the room: "*What?*"

"I mean to purchase his token," the duke said.

Ashworth's boots thunked to the floor. "You can't purchase his token. They can only be won in a game of chance."

Morland said coolly, "Was his not a random killing? Bad luck, in its purest form."

That did it. Amelia's impression of the Duke of Morland was now cemented. Not only cemented—cast in bronze. He was the most arrogant, self-absorbed, unfeeling man she'd ever had the misfortune to waltz with, bar none.

"You are supposed to offer her marriage," Bellamy growled.

"I am duty-bound to offer her assistance. And so I have done." He addressed Lily once again. "Madam, tomorrow I will direct my secretary to call. He will be at your disposal in any regard, whether it be making burial arrangements or securing new housing. He will also bring a bank draft constituting my offer for Leo's share in the Stud Club, which you may review and accept or decline as you wish."

Bellamy said, "You bastard. This is a matter of honor, and all you can think of is the damned horse."

"All any of you can think of is the damned horse!" Amelia went to Lily's side. "Lily's future is her own to decide. Stop puffing up your chests and playing at this childish imitation of chivalry. All this going on about honor and duty . . . you own shares in an *animal*, for God's sake. You are not the Knights of the Round Table. By your own admission, Leo devised this club as a joke. Don't you have real duties to tend to, actual human relationships worth your efforts and attention? Or is this all you have in your lives, a bit of play-acting nonsense centered on a horse?"

All three fell quiet, diverting their gaze to various features of the room's décor—tassels, fringes, lacquered trays that had probably never suffered such intense male scrutiny. Perhaps these men truly didn't have anything in their lives worth caring about, aside from this horse and this club. It would certainly explain their pathetic silence.

It was really . . . quite sad.

"It's all right, Amelia," said Lily. She drew a deep breath and addressed the men. "Your Grace, my lord"—she turned to Bellamy—"Julian. I know you are all acting from honorable motives, and I do appreciate your concern. Leo would be heartened to see such evidence of your friendship."

At the sound of Leo's name from her lips, and the slight waver in her tone, the men softened in both posture and expression.

"His death leaves me bereft and grieving, but not penniless. I have means, and I have friends of my own." She squeezed Amelia's hand. "Even if I did wish to marry, I must complete a year of mourning first."

"Those rules don't apply," Bellamy said. "Not in an extreme situation such as—"

Lily shook her head. "There is nothing extreme about my situation, aside from the tremendous shock. Leo is . . . *was* so very young."

"Too young. All the wrong men die young." Swearing, Ashworth kicked the ottoman. "Worthless devils like me? Now, we're damn near indestructible."

"No," Lily said. "No one is immortal—that is the lesson to be learnt from this. If you wish to honor Leo's memory, let his death be your ward against complacency. Amelia is right. Surely each of you has responsibilities more pressing than your membership in Leo's club. Lord Ashworth, don't you have some family, an estate?"

The man swore, rubbing a palm over his close-shorn hair. "A burnt-out stripe of heath in Devonshire. I haven't laid eyes on the place in fourteen years."

"Perhaps it's time you did," Lily said pointedly. When Bellamy looked as though he would protest, she added, "And I'm certain His Grace has duties enough of his own to occupy him, without taking charge of me."

The duke turned toward Lily. "I have a ward. My cousin, though I suppose she was raised as more of a sister to me."

Amelia didn't know why this abrupt admission should move her. And it didn't, not really. It simply caught her by surprise. Surely, other ladies would have known Morland had guardianship of his cousin. She must be the only woman in London society who hadn't spent recent months mooning over the "M" section of *Debrett's Peerage*.

But there was something almost . . . *human* in his face, as he mentioned her. A slight pleating at the corner of his eyes. A hint of uncertainty in the furrow of his brow.

Amelia tore her gaze away. She'd spent entirely too much time looking at the duke this evening, and she couldn't bear to see him humanized any further. Far safer to hold to her demonized version: arrogant, cold, horse-mad. Easy to detest.

Bellamy covered the floor in three quick strides to confront Lily at a distance of inches. His voice was husky and intense. "You know I have no sister. No brother. No estate in Devonshire or anywhere else."

"I know." Lily took his hand in hers. "But we have thought of you as family, Leo and I."

Closing his eyes, Bellamy swallowed hard. "Then you must not deny me the right to look after you."

"I would never try."

Standing at Lily's side, Amelia began to feel as though she were intruding on a very private conversation. Yet it did not seem possible to move away without drawing further attention to herself. She settled for averting her eyes and remaining absolutely still. Beneath her hand, Lily's shoulder began to tremble.

"I promise you this," Bellamy said in a low voice, resonant with emotion. "I will find the men who killed Leo. I will hunt them down. No matter how far they run, no matter where they hide. And I will see them hanged."

Lily began to weep.

"Dear Lily." Bellamy clutched her fingers and brought them to his lips. "Tell me what to do. Give me some way to make it better."

"Just take me to him," she said. "And let me say goodbye."

Chapter Four

As morning dawned, Spencer had still not found the solace of his library carpet, but he had downed a fair amount of brandy, and the whirling din in his head had cleared. He had passed much of the night in silence, which helped. Though he and Ashworth had retreated to Bellamy's garden while Lily wept over her brother's battered corpse, by tacit agreement there'd been no conversation. He'd spent the carriage rides to and fro in quiet contemplation, as had they all.

He peered out the coach window into the gray-amber dawn. The London streets swarmed with fruit and fish vendors, live-out servants and laborers on their way to their posts. The early-morning bustle slowed the coach's progress considerably.

But then, he was in no great rush. The two other men and Leo's grieving sister had already been deposited at Harcliffe Manor. He and Lady Amelia were the sole passengers remaining, and the coachman was welcome to take his time. For once, Spencer was not eager to be alone.

"This has been a most extraordinary night," he said softly, almost to himself.

"Indeed," she replied.

Fatigue, coupled with the incredible nature of the

night's events, had left him in a strange state. He had taken Lily's exhortations to heart. Harcliffe's death was indeed an effective *memento mori,* as the medieval saying went. "Remember that you will die." Were something to happen to him, Spencer would not want Claudia caught in Lily's predicament. Fortunately, there were concrete actions he could take to avoid such an outcome, and he intended to see to them directly.

This very morning, as a matter of fact.

"It was a very grave shock," he said. "But Lily seems to have taken it well."

"Perhaps it seems so, to you. But I know better. Leo's death is only now becoming real to her. When the shock wears off, she will be stricken with grief. I will call again this afternoon. Perhaps offer to stay with her for a few days." She shot him a look, her blue eyes catching a sharp gleam from the window glass. "Only until other arrangements can be made."

He tried to understand the anger in her tone, and failed. It was becoming a maddening habit, this trying to understand her.

"Your Grace, if I may speak freely—"

"I haven't yet managed to prevent you."

"Your 'offer' to Lily last night was unconscionable. I have never encountered a person so vain, arrogant, presumptuous, self-absorbed, and utterly heartless."

Her charges surprised Spencer, but they did not wound him overmuch. When spoken in such a distraught, irrational tone, words were easy to dodge—like so many china shepherdesses hurled in a fit of pique.

She continued, "From all evidence, you care more for horses than for people."

"You have concluded wrongly."

"Oh, have I concluded wrongly?" she said, mocking his deep tone. "How so?"

"It is true that I find the average horse more pleasant

to be around than the average person. Most true horsemen would agree. But it does not follow that I value all horses above all people. And I am not pursuing ownership of Osiris simply because he is *a* horse, but because he is *the* horse I am determined to have, at any cost."

"Precisely," she muttered. "At any cost, including that of friendship, dignity, honor."

Spencer shook his head. It would be futile to explain his reasons for wanting that horse. She couldn't comprehend them, even if he tried.

The carriage rattled on, and their elbows rattled against each other. They sat sharing the front-facing seat. Spencer supposed he might have crossed to the opposite seat, once the others had alighted. That would have been the proper thing to do. But he hadn't felt like moving. Lady Amelia was leaning against him, just slightly—no doubt fatigued and chilled. And once again, he found himself enjoying the soft weight of her body against his.

As that pleasure gathered and spread, so did his unbiddable curiosity. He could not rid his mind of it, this desire to keep speaking with her, to listen to whatever she might say. To discover, to know, to *understand*.

He said, "You disdain the importance I place on horses."

"I do. With all due respect to the horses."

"What is it then, that's most important to you?"

"My family," she replied instantly. "And my home."

"A house in Bryanston Square?" Spencer could not mask his surprise. From the direction she'd given, he knew it must be one of those newer, boxy town houses. Not the sort of history-rich, time-faded abode in which he would picture Lady Amelia d'Orsay.

"No, not that house. That is Laurent's house, built to his wife's tastes. I refer to our ancestral home in Gloucestershire. Beauvale Castle is in ruins, but we have a cottage where we summer. It's called Briarbank, for its position directly overlooking the River Wye."

"A pleasing prospect."

"It is. I don't believe I've ever seen a house more happily situated. Mama and I, we used to walk out every morning to gather lavender and fresh—" She sniffed. "All my fondest memories are of Briarbank."

"Will you be leaving Town soon, to summer there?"

She tensed. "Not this year. This year, my brothers intend to let the cottage out. You see, Your Grace, my brother Jack has a debt to pay."

"I see," he said, after a pause. "So this is the true root of your anger, my refusal to forgive your brother's debt. Not my offer to Lily."

"Well, the root of my anger has since forked into several branches of irritation, and your treatment of Lily is one of them. But yes." Jutting out her chin, she turned her face to the window.

Spencer couldn't bring himself to fault her persistence. Throughout his life, if there was a common trait amongst the few people he'd unreservedly admired, it was loyalty. But in this case, the sentiment was severely misapplied. That brother of hers was on a swift course to ruin her entire family. "I fail to see how—"

"Your Grace." She cut him off with an impatient gesture. "By my counting, we've spent close to seven hours in one another's company. And you've spoken more words to me in the last few minutes than in previous six-and-some hours combined. Are you always this chatty in the mornings?"

Chatty? Spencer had been called many unflattering things in his life, but no one had ever accused him of being *chatty*. Remarkable.

"No," he said thoughtfully. "I'm not. Are you always this inhospitable?"

She gave a breathy sigh. "No. But as you say, it has

been an extraordinary night. Even before you arrived at the Bunscombes' ball."

Her remark put him back on that darkened terrace and had him mentally searching his pockets for her handkerchief. He shouldn't like to lose it. She'd obviously invested great care in its design and creation. But unlike the young ladies who netted purses and lacquered tea trays as a means of displaying their dubious "accomplishments," Lady Amelia had embroidered that square of linen for no one's appreciation but her own.

This intrigued him.

As did the fact that, for all her harsh words declared him an enemy, her body seemed to have formed a fast friendship with his. She was still leaning against him.

"You are not intimidated by me," he observed.

"No," she said musingly. "Honestly, I am not. Oh, I would have been at this time yesterday. But as Lily said, this night has taught me that no one is immortal. It's a dire realization in many respects, but oddly enough I find it somewhat freeing. Brash impertinence holds a sudden charm. I shall have to look out, or I may be in danger of becoming a real termagant." She laughed softly to herself. "Yesterday at this time, I would have seen you as the unapproachable, imposing Duke of Morland. And you would not have seen me at all."

No doubt it would have been the politic thing to object. To say, *Oh, certainly I would have noticed you. I would pick you out from a crowd of ladies.* But that would have been a lie. In all likelihood, she was right. If they'd crossed paths in the street this time yestermorn, he would not have spared her a second glance. And that would have been an unfortunate thing, for she was a woman who greatly improved on second glance. At this moment, he was discovering that the warm, even light of dawn did her features better service than the harsh shadows cast by candlelight and coal. She looked almost lovely, in the morning.

She touched a finger to the window glass. "Today, I know we are merely humans. Two flawed, imperfect, mortal beings, whose bones will one day crumble to dust. Just a woman and a man."

At her words, space inside the carriage seemed to collapse around him. Not in a suffocating, oppressive manner, but in a way that evoked the pleasanter aspects of human closeness: physical pleasure and emotional intimacy. It had been some time—an imprudently long time, on reflection—since he'd enjoyed the former. He'd spent most of his adult life avoiding the latter. Surely the extraordinary nature of the night's events was to blame, but Spencer found himself suddenly, intensely hungry for both.

No sooner had he thought it, than she nestled closer still. Was she seeking comfort? Or offering it?

Just a woman and a man.

Slowly, deliberately, he lifted one gloved hand from his lap and placed it on her leg, a few inches above her knee.

Her thigh went rigid beneath his palm. He did not move, did not acknowledge her startled response. He simply sat there, cupping the plump curve of her thigh and enjoying the way it filled his hand.

Though for practical reasons he favored pretty little nothings in a ballroom, when it came to bed sport, Spencer's tastes ran to substance, in multiple senses of the term. He liked a woman with something to her, both physically and intellectually. Lady Amelia met both qualifications.

True, she was no great beauty, but she had an undeniable appeal. Her mouth, in particular, he found alluring. Her lips were full and voluptuous, like the rest of her, and a lovely shade of coral pink. Then there was that lone, obstinate freckle still clinging to the inner curve of her left breast. The tiny mark only called attention to the otherwise creamy perfection of the bosom it adorned.

And after the night they'd just passed wandering through Death's shadow, it was only natural for a man to crave . . . well, to crave.

In sum, he wanted her. Quite fiercely.

He eased his hand up her thigh—one inch, perhaps two. Past the concealed ridge of her garter. Her breathing went from uneven to erratic as he began brushing his thumb back and forth in a slow, even rhythm. He applied enough pressure that his touch dragged the fabric rather than sliding over it, allowing them both to enjoy the sensation of silk and linen gliding over her bare skin. Whatever petticoat she had on was delightfully spare, worn soft and supple by many launderings. Beneath the fabric, her flesh was just the right pliancy. The taut, smooth texture of a ball of risen dough—perfect for grasping, kneading, shaping with his hands.

Erotic images flooded his mind; lust pounded in his blood. He wanted to haul her straight into his lap and wrap those creamy, abundant curves around his body. He would bury his head in that magnificent bosom and clutch her bottom with both hands as he took her, right here in the carriage, letting the swaying motion of the coach bring them closer and closer to release . . .

Yes, she could offer him all manner of comforts—if she were the sort of woman to oblige a man that way. Simply because she remained unmarried, it did not necessarily follow that she was untouched. In fact, some alteration in the latter condition might explain the former.

There was only one way to find out.

Spreading his fingers, he gave her thigh a light, appreciative squeeze.

With a startled cry, she wrested her skirt from his grasp and scuttled sideways like a crab. There, wedged into the opposite corner of the cab, she stared hard out the window and steadfastly ignored him.

Well, that settled that.

And now Spencer looked out his own glass and prayed for a sudden snarl of unnavigable traffic. For they were nearing Bryanston Square, and thanks to his vivid imagination, he was in no condition to be seen in public.

By the time the coach drew to a halt before an ostentatious rococo edifice, his lust had ebbed. Somewhat. Enough to restore his silhouette to respectability. Spencer alighted first and then posed at the bottom, hand outstretched to assist Lady Amelia in making her descent.

She ignored his hand. And would have walked straight past him altogether, had he not grasped her elbow.

She slowly pivoted to face him. "Your Grace, I thank you for delivering me home. I shall keep you no longer." When he did not release her, she added through gritted teeth, "You may go."

"Nonsense," he replied, steering her up the stairs to the front door, which was already held open by a footman. The servant's rose-pink livery did much to subdue any lingering carnal impulses. "I'll see you in. I must speak with your brother."

"Jack won't be here. He has his own rooms in Piccadilly."

"Not him. I meant Lord Beauvale."

They entered the house two abreast. Only one of the two doors had been opened, forcing them to squeeze together momentarily as they stepped over the threshold. God, her body felt good against his.

"I can't imagine why you would wish to speak with Laurent."

"Can't you?"

"He won't make good on Jack's debt, if that's what you mean."

The woman was obviously not thinking straight, but Spencer decided not to hold it against her. It had been a long and trying night, after all. "By all public appearances, I've abducted you from a ball and kept you out all night. Your brother will no doubt appreciate some explanation and assurances."

Pulling one of his cards from his breast pocket, he flicked it on the butler's salver. "We will await the earl in his study." There, Spencer hoped, he might be safe from these revolting gilt plaster cockleshells hugging the ceiling like barnacles.

Once ushered inside Beauvale's wood-paneled, shell-free study, they stood awkwardly in the center of the room. As a gentleman, he could not sit until she did—and the idea of sitting had apparently not occurred to her. Her hair had half-fallen from its coiffure, giving her a lopsided appearance. The blue silk that had so closely hugged her curves the evening previous now showed obvious signs of fatigue.

Her eyes widened at the way he was boldly appraising her form.

Spencer gave her an unapologetic shrug. "That gown has done its service, and then some. Earned its pension, I should say."

Red bloomed from her throat to her hairline. Her jaw worked a few times. "Are you quite finished insulting me?"

"I did not insult you. That gown insults you."

"You—" She made a gesture of exasperation. "You, sir, have no understanding of women. None at all."

"Does any man?"

"Yes!"

Spencer cocked his head. "Name one."

At that moment, the Earl of Beauvale entered. His hair was damp and freshly parted, and his cuffs remained unfastened. Obviously, he'd dressed in a hurry.

He bowed in Spencer's direction. Lady Amelia crossed to her brother immediately and threw herself into his arms.

"Amelia. For God's sake, where have you been?" Beauvale pulled back from the embrace and studied his sister. "What's happened to you?"

"Leo is dead," she said, burying her face in her brother's coat.

"Harcliffe?" The earl directed his question at Spencer.

He nodded. "Attacked by footpads, last evening. We have spent the night attending his sister. She was—and remains—in a state of shock."

"Yes, poor Lily," the earl muttered, rubbing his sister's arms. "Poor Leo. I can't believe it."

"I can't either," she said. "He was so young, so vivacious and well-liked. He was . . ." Her eyes met Spencer's. "He was the answer to your question, Your Grace. A man of true understanding. In all the years I knew him, Leo never once spoke an unkind word to me."

"Yes, well. We can't all be Leo, can we?"

This bitter, ill-conceived remark was repaid with cold silence. As it deserved to be. Even Spencer realized it had been an unfeeling thing to say, motivated by envy.

Envy for a dead man, at that. How nonsensical.

Nothing about this night had made sense, from the moment she'd caromed across that ballroom and grasped his hand in hers. He'd danced with her, argued with her, carted her from the dance floor like some sort of primeval cave dweller, and then together they'd spent the night attending an impromptu vigil. On a morning that should have found him taciturn and withdrawn, she'd made him *chatty*. Now he found himself taking spiteful swipes at the poor dead fool who earned a word of her praise. It all added up to one inescapable conclusion.

He was rather taken with Amelia Claire d'Orsay.

Irrational, perhaps; unexpected, certainly. But there it was.

The earl spoke over his sister's shoulder. "Thank you for seeing her home, Your Grace."

It was a clear dismissal, just like her less eloquent version at the doorstep: *You may go*. But Spencer remained undeterred. He was the Duke of Morland; he would not be dismissed. And once he'd set his mind on something—or someone—he couldn't rest without making it his.

He said, "I should advise you, Beauvale, that upon hearing of this tragedy, we left the Bunscombe residence together in surreptitious fashion. To others in attendance, it may have appeared to be an illicit assignation."

"I see." The earl frowned. "But nothing happened."

Spencer looked to Lady Amelia.

"Amelia?" Beauvale prompted. "Nothing happened, did it?"

"Oh, no. *No*. Most definitely not." Her deep blush did not lend the impression of veracity.

"I see." Beauvale glared in Spencer's direction. "People will be talking?"

"Yes, they will. It cannot be helped. In fact, the gossip is likely to increase with the announcement of a betrothal. We may as well make the engagement brief."

Silence.

Brother and sister stared at him in open-mouthed shock. Spencer rocked idly on his heels, waiting.

Lady Amelia left her brother's side and went to the nearest chair. At last, the thought had occurred to her to sit.

"Forgive me, Your Grace," she began, "but this has already been a rather unbelievable night. And it is giving way to a positively apocryphal morning. I thought I just heard you refer to an engagement."

"Yes. Ours."

More stunned silence.

Spencer cleared his throat. "It is not my aim to be cryptic. Allow me to make my intentions perfectly clear. Beauvale, I am offering to marry your sister."

The earl lifted a brow. "Do you mean you are *requesting* the honor of her hand?"

"Is that not what I just said?"

"No," Lady Amelia said, with an odd little laugh. "No, it is most definitely not." Regarding Spencer closely, she added, "Laurent, will you leave us?"

"Yes," her brother said, drawing out the word. "Reluctantly. I shall wait in the parlor."

"Thank you," she said coolly. "We won't be long."

Chapter Five

Amelia stared at the duke. His health was robust, his expression composed, his bearing everything ducal, if not downright regal. He looked quite fit indeed. Still, the question tumbled out.

"Are you insane?"

"No," he answered swiftly. "No, I am in possession of my mental faculties, and in excellent physical health. If you wish further assurances prior to the wedding, I can refer you to my personal physician."

Good Lord, was he serious?

His mild expression told her he was.

"That will not be necessary. Allow me to rephrase my question. What on earth are you thinking, suggesting we should marry?"

"Isn't it obvious?" He sat casually on the edge of Laurent's desk. "Your reputation is endangered."

"Only because you are endangering it! Nothing happened between us. Why would you lead my brother to believe otherwise?"

"You are the one who led him to believe otherwise, with your stammering and blushing. I am merely taking the honorable course, by not contradicting you."

"The *honorable* course? Well, this is a fresh development. Were you taking the honorable course when you groped me in the carriage?"

"That was . . . an experiment."

"An experiment," she echoed in disbelief. "Pray tell me, what did you learn?"

"Two things. First, it assured me of your virtue."

"My virtue? You were—" Oh, there was no use in mincing words now. "You were able to divine my virginity, by fondling my leg."

"Yes."

She covered her eyes with one hand, then traced her left eyebrow with a fingertip. "Forgive me, Your Grace. Are you suggesting a woman is some sort of . . . piece of fruit to you? One squeeze, and you know if she's ripe?"

"No." He laughed softly. A low, brief chuckle. It took her by surprise, for she had not thought him a man capable of humor. "It was not *what* I squeezed that convinced me, but rather your reaction to being squeezed."

Amelia's face burned as she recalled her squawk of surprise, and the alacrity with which she had sought the farthest corner of the cab. Even that distance had not been far enough. The heat of his touch had lingered on her thigh, then melted and spread over her entire body. Her mind had been in upheaval, her pulse a mad riot.

She was not sure she had recovered, even now.

She took a deep breath. "You say this experiment of yours brought you to two conclusions, Your Grace. Dare I ask, what was the second?"

He gave her a bold, scorching look. "That I would not find it a chore to bed you."

Oh, Lord.

What, pray tell, was the appropriate response to *that*? Her own body could not come to an accord on the matter. A blush burned on her cheeks, her stomach twisted itself into a knot, and her blood skittered merrily through her veins.

Don't react as though you were flattered, she told herself sternly. *Do not take perverse excitement in the fact that the Duke of Morland has evidently given a good deal of thought to the idea of bedding you, perhaps even imagined the act in detail. Do not—do not—dream of imagining it yourself!*

Too late, too late.

Amelia pushed the carnal image away and struggled to tamp down any sensation that might be construed as a thrill. The duke had not called her desirable. He had deemed her beddable, and in highly insulting fashion at that. No doubt he would say the same of any chambermaid.

"I cannot credit this," she finally said.

"You believe me insincere?"

"I believe you inconsistent. Here you are offering to marry me this morning. Yet not seven hours ago, you were ready to duel Mr. Bellamy rather than offer for Lily. And she, I might add, has a greater claim on your honor." *And more beauty. And more grace. And more money.*

"I did not wish to marry Lily."

The back of Amelia's neck prickled, against all her attempts to remind it that the duke's statement was not a compliment to her.

"Lady Amelia," he continued, "in all our conversations, you have paid me the compliment of unflinching honesty. May I be completely frank with you now?"

She waved her hand in invitation.

"As Lily advised, I have taken Leo's death as a reminder of my own mortality, and as a call to action. I have a ward, several years my junior. It will be two years before her introduction, and longer still before she is ready to wed. If some misfortune were to befall me in the interim, my title and estate would pass to distant relations, and her fate would be in the hands of strangers.

I cannot risk it. Therefore, I have decided to marry and produce an heir."

"Just this morning, you have decided this."

"Yes."

"Why me, and not Lily? Why not one of the other ladies you've auditioned, over the course of dozens of balls?"

He looked taken aback. "Auditioned? Is that what people believe, that I have been conducting a search for my bride? Trial by waltzing?"

"Yes, of course."

He laughed again. Twice in one morning now. Astonishing. And this time, his laugh had a rich, velvet quality that stroked her with heat from crown to toe.

"No. That has not been my purpose, I assure you. But I will answer your question honestly. I wish to produce an heir, as quickly as possible. I have no inclination to court, flatter, or otherwise woo some silly young chit scarcely half my age. Neither do I have the patience to engage the hand of a grieving woman who will be in mourning for the next year. Dowries are of no importance to me. I simply need a sensible woman from suitable bloodlines, of robust constitution and even temperament, with whom to create a few children."

She stared at him in horror. "You want a broodmare!"

He said evenly, "When you draw that comparison, you demean us both. I have many fine mares in my stables, and yet there is not a one of them I would allow to mother my children or manage my household, much less introduce my cousin to society. No, I do not want a broodmare. I want a wife. A duchess."

At that moment, the magnitude of his offer struck Amelia with sudden force. It was fortunate she was still sitting down. This man would make her the Duchess of Morland. If she accepted him—barbaric, unfeeling creature that he was—she would become one of the highest-ranking, wealthiest ladies in all England. She would host grand parties, move in the most elite circles of society. And at last—oh, her heart turned over at the thought . . .

"I would be mistress of my own house," she whispered.

"In point of fact, you would be mistress of six. But I almost never travel to the Scottish one."

Amelia gripped the arm of the chair, hard. As if she might slide right off it and fall into wedlock if she didn't hold on with all her strength. Good heavens, six estates. Surely one of them could use a vicar. She could convince Jack to resume his studies and take orders, see him settled in a wholesome country vicarage, far away from his ruffian friends . . .

No, no, no. There were a thousand reasons why she must refuse the duke. There had to be. She just couldn't think of them right now.

"But . . ." she stammered, "but we scarcely know one another."

"In the past several hours, I have observed you at a social event, witnessed your composure during a difficult ordeal, and engaged you in conversation that hovered some distance above the usual banalities. I am familiar with your ancestry, and I know that you come from a family rife with sons, which bodes well for my purposes of getting an heir. For my part, I am satisfied. But if you wish, you may ask me questions." He cocked an eyebrow in anticipation.

She swallowed. "What is your age?"

"Thirty-one."

"Have you other close family, besides this cousin?"

"No."

"Does she have a name?"

"Of course. She is Lady Claudia, fifteen years of age."

"Is she here with you, in Town?"

"No. She has spent the past few months in York, visiting her mother's relations."

Amelia paused, uncertain where to go from here. What sort of questions did one ask a gentleman of his stature? It would seem absurd to inquire after a duke's favorite color, or preferred glovemaker. Finally she blurted out, "Do you object to cats?"

He grimaced. "Only in principle."

"I should like to keep cats." She perked in triumph. Here it was, her escape route from this bizarre proposal.

He tapped a finger on the desktop. "If you can keep them out of my way, I suppose that desire can be accommodated."

Drat. No escape there.

She tried again. "What is the last book you read?"

"*A Vindication of the Rights of Woman*, by Mary Wollstonecraft."

"You are joking."

"Yes, I am." The corner of his mouth curled in a sly, sensual manner. "Actually, I read that book some years ago."

"Truly? And what did you think?"

"I think . . ." He pushed off from the desk and stood, regarding her with cool challenge in his eyes. "I think you are stalling, Lady Amelia."

Her pulse did stall, for a moment. Then it jolted back to life, pounding feverishly in her throat. Why didn't God apportion fine looks in equal accordance with deserving personalities? A horrid man ought to be horrid-looking. He should never be gifted with dark, curling, touchable hair; nor the noble, sculpted cheekbones of a Roman god. He most especially should not possess entrancing, deep-set hazel eyes and a wide, sensual mouth that was near devastating in repose, but even further improved by the presence of a knowing little smile.

Time for desperate measures.

"If I marry you, will you forgive Jack's debt?"

Say no, she willed silently. *Please say no, or I cannot be responsible for my actions. If you say yes, I may be driven to embrace you. Or worse, give my consent.*

"No," he said.

Waves of relief and disappointment crashed within her, leaving Amelia feeling rather adrift. But her course was now clear. "In that case, Your Grace, I'm afraid I cannot—"

"I will, of course, settle a substantial sum on you, as part of the marriage contracts. Twenty thousand, I should think, and some property. In addition, you would receive a generous allowance for your discretionary spending. Several hundred pounds."

"Several hundred pounds? A year?"

"Don't be absurd. Quarterly."

Amelia's mind blanked. In recent years, she'd become expert at counting up small sums of money, down to the last ha'penny. Two shillings, ten pence at the draper's, and so forth. But sums so large as these . . . they simply weren't in her arithmetic.

"Your allowance will be yours to spend as you wish, but I would advise against wasting tuppence on your brother. Even if you pay his debt, you won't be summering at your cottage. You'll come to my estate in Cambridgeshire."

"Braxton Hall."

He nodded.

She knew it well by reputation. Though the current duke never entertained, his aunt and uncle had, and the older society matrons sometimes waxed nostalgic about the epic grandeur that was Braxton Hall. It was said to be the largest, most lavish house in East Anglia, surrounded by beautiful parklands and gardens.

She allowed herself one quiet, plaintive sigh for those gardens.

"Have no doubt that I will provide for your every material comfort. In return, I ask only that you continue to receive my attentions until such time as a son is born. And of course, I will demand your fidelity."

She recalled his terse words last night, when he spoke of that blasted stallion: *I am not interested in breeding privileges. I am interested in possession. I do not like to share.* Such words, such a tone, such an attitude of absolute entitlement—they were repugnant in reference to a horse. They were perfectly debasing, when applied to a woman. Debasing and demeaning and . . . God help her, arousing.

"I see," she said, struggling for equanimity. "And may I expect your fidelity in kind?"

"Curse that Wollstonecraft woman. Very well. Until you have birthed a son, you may be assured of my faithfulness. At that time, we can revisit our arrangement. If you wish, we need not even live on the same estate."

It only became worse. So she was not even to be possessed, but merely to be *rented*.

When confronted with her stunned silence, he added, "Is that not egalitarian?"

"Egalitarian, yes. Also cold, convenient, and heartless."

"Well, you can hardly be expecting romantic declarations. They would be transparently false, and an insult to us both."

Amelia rose to her feet and said calmly, "I do find myself sufficiently insulted for one morning."

"My patience is also at an end." He met her in the center of the room. "I have made you an offer of marriage. I am certain it is the most generous and beneficial offer you will ever receive—likely the last such offer you will ever receive. I have answered all your impertinent questions and made you some extremely generous promises. Now, madam, may I have your answer?"

Oh, yes. She would give him an answer.

But she would take some satisfaction from him first.

"One last question, Your Grace. You have said earlier, you would not find it a chore to bed me. How am I to be assured of the same? Perhaps I would find it a chore to bed *you*."

He took a step backward, as though he needed the extra distance to properly glare at her. Or perhaps because he suspected her of carrying an infectious disease of the brain.

She smiled, enjoying the triumph of setting him on edge. "Don't look so alarmed, Your Grace. I do not intend to squeeze your thigh."

At this moment, she made the error of dropping her gaze to those thighs. Those very thick, very muscular thighs that looked as squeezable as granite.

"Don't you?"

She wrenched her eyes back up to his face. "No. You see, when it comes to such matters, women appreciate a touch more finesse."

He gave a derisive, but—she imagined—also *defensive* laugh.

"I may be a virgin, Your Grace, but I am not ignorant."

"Don't tell me. More subversive reading material?"

She ignored his feeble attempt at taunting. "Before I give an answer to your proposal, I would like to perform an experiment of my own."

A wild panic flared in his eyes. Or perhaps that amber spark was desire?

Don't be ridiculous, she chided herself. It was panic, surely panic. And she relished it.

"What sort of experiment did you have in mind?"

"A kiss."

"Is that all?" He stepped forward, angling his head as though he would press a chaste kiss to her cheek.

She held up a hand between them. "On the lips, if you please. And do it properly."

"Properly." Disbelief echoed in his tone.

His gaze searched her face, and Amelia inwardly cringed as she pictured herself through his eyes. Plump cheeks, gone bright pink with a blush. Puffy eyes, certainly not improved by the purple circles under them this morning. Disheveled blond hair, hanging loose against one side of her neck. What had she been thinking, to bait him thus? Why not simply refuse his proposal and be done with it?

Because she wanted this, she admitted. She wanted this kiss. She wanted to feel *wanted*. In all honesty, some depraved part of her wanted to go back to his carriage and do everything differently. To find out what would have happened if she hadn't startled and moved away, but allowed him to keep caressing and kneading her thigh. Perhaps trail his fingers up and up, to the warm, damp place between her legs . . .

The very thought made her weak.

His gaze settled on her lips.

She held her breath. Braced herself. Grew an inch out of sheer anticipation.

And then he took two steps away.

Oh, Lord. He'd rejected her. In a darkened carriage, she was good enough for a squeeze, but one honest look at her in full daylight, and he'd decided she simply wasn't worth the trouble.

He cleared his throat. "If I'm to do this properly . . ."

With his left hand, he began loosening his right glove. First, he undid the small closure at the wrist. Then he began at the little finger and worked inward, working the close-fitted black kid loose with firm, confident tugs. After separating his thumb from its leather sheath, he raised his hand to his mouth. A shiver ran through her as he caught the middle finger of the glove between his teeth . . . and pulled.

Oh, his hand was lovely. Amelia couldn't tear her gaze from his fingers as they worked. They were long and dexterous, graceful yet strong. Soon he had the second glove loosened, and when he stared her straight in the eye, took that nub of leather between his teeth, and slowly pulled his right hand free . . . she couldn't help it.

She sighed. Audibly.

At once, she understood why men threw away so much money on opera dancers. She wondered why similar establishments did not exist for ladies. Perhaps they did, and she was simply innocent of them. There was a powerful, illicit thrill to watching a man bare himself—even these relatively innocent parts of himself—for her benefit.

Tossing his gloves atop Laurent's desk, the duke closed the distance between them. He raised his hands—not to her face, but to her hair. Those long, deft fingers plucked the hairpins from her debilitated upsweep. He stood close to her as he worked, almost as though he held her in an embrace. The pose gave Amelia an intimate view of the strong line of his jaw, and the exposed curve of his throat beneath it, where the rough beginnings of whiskers dotted his skin. He smelled of brandy and leather and starch; and beneath all these commonplace scents simmered the unique musk of his skin. She inhaled deeply.

As he freed the last pin, her hair tumbled around her shoulders. His fingers raked deliciously over her scalp as he arranged the locks to his satisfaction.

"There," he said. Strong, warm hands cupped her face and tilted it to his. "Now we can do this properly."

A surge of excitement flooded every inch of her body. And it didn't come from the heat of his breath on her lips, or the firm pressure of his hands bracketing her face. Its origin was that tiny word: "we." *Now* we *can do this properly.*

It wasn't that *he* would kiss *her*. *They* were going to kiss.

His lips brushed hers, slowly, sensually. And in an abrupt, volcanic explosion, Amelia d'Orsay's world gained a whole new continent.

She'd suffered a number of Mr. Poste's kisses, back when he'd courted her. Could it truly have been almost ten years ago? Those horrid kisses still lurked in her memory: wet, grabby embraces that had made her feel helpless and ashamed.

But this was different. So different. The Duke of Morland had spent the past several hours assaulting her feelings with one rude, arrogant remark after the other. The man had no notion of polite discourse.

But this kiss . . . now, this kiss was a *conversation*. Again and again, he pressed his lips to hers, then retreated, inviting her to reciprocate. And reciprocate she did, with unabashed pleasure.

"Yes," he murmured, as she gingerly placed her hands on his shoulders. "Yes, that's the way."

Encouraged, she moved her hands higher, clutching his neck. His hands slid backward to fist in her hair, and she followed his example, at last twining her fingers in those dark, touchable curls. Oh why hadn't she removed her own gloves? She would have given much at that moment to feel his hair sliding between the sensitive webs of her fingers. But she took heart in the little growl he gave when her gloved fingertips stroked his nape. Satin did have its advantages.

He paused to draw breath.

Oh, don't stop. Don't stop.

She caressed his neck again, and he renewed the kiss with even greater vigor. Her body went soft to the bones. His lips were insistent, demanding. But what he demanded was not her surrender, but her escalating response.

She hadn't known kissing could be like this: not a conquest, but a trade. A steady bartering of caresses, licks, gentle nips. She'd never known the corner of her mouth to be so exquisitely sensitive, until he touched the spot with his tongue.

Oh, this was dangerous. Delicious, but dangerous.

He was not just teaching her, he was empowering her. And he was forcing her to reveal far more of herself than she ought. How could he fail to sense her desire for him, when she purred with it? When she drew his lower lip into her mouth to mirror the way he gently sucked her upper one? And oh—oh, Lord—once their tongues had done *this*, how could she convincingly use this same mouth to refuse him?

And then she finally stopped thinking and gave herself over to sensation. Blissful, all-consuming sensation. Her body sang, shivered, ached. She needed more. She needed to feel his hands on her body, somewhere below the neck. Everywhere below the neck.

Lacing her fingers behind his collar, she pitched forward. Her breasts met the welcome resistance of his hard chest. And he rewarded her by sliding his hands from her shoulders, to the small of her back, over the swell of her hips and all the way down to her bottom, which he cupped firmly in both hands. He pulled, bringing her hips flush against his. Pleasure, sharp and intense, burst through her.

He moaned. "*Amelia.*"

Here was a gesture she couldn't reciprocate. For she didn't recall his Christian name, and to call him "Morland" seemed just wrong. She certainly couldn't call him "Your Grace"—not with his hands on her backside.

Then his tongue was in her mouth again, and she couldn't have called him anything at all.

After some time—it might have been minutes, or hours or eons, for all Amelia knew; this kiss had rendered her quite insensible to such frivolous things as the passage of time—he gently pulled away. Shamelessly she chased him, pulling his face down and pressing one last kiss to the corner of his lips.

He laughed—a breathless, husky, arousing laugh.

"So," he said, "not a chore, I think."

"No."

He regarded her closely. One eyebrow quirked. "That wasn't your answer, was it?"

"No," she said hastily. "Or . . . I don't know. My answer to what?"

"I'm confused."

"So am I."

She slid her hands from his neck and clutched them together in front of her. Oh, what a miscalculation this had been. She'd asked for the kiss. She'd hoped it might be enjoyable. She hadn't expected it to alter her understanding of the world. How was she supposed to tell him, *No, no, a thousand times no. Take your insulting proposal and begone*, when every corpuscle in her body was screaming, *Yes, yes! Please, Your Grace, may I have some more?*

"Perhaps we should begin again." He covered her knotted fingers with his. "Lady Amelia, will you do me the honor, et cetera."

"Did you just say 'et cetera' in a proposal of marriage?"

"No, I believe I said 'et cetera' in reprising my proposal of marriage. Have you arrived at an answer yet? I think you're stalling again."

"I'm not stalling."

He drummed his fingers on the tops of hers, making it quite clear to them both that she was, indeed, stalling.

"We don't get along at all," she said desperately.

"That's not true. We've been getting along quite well for several minutes now."

Yes, they had. They had.

Knowing herself to be a very poor liar, Amelia opted for honesty. "I'm infatuated with you, I cannot deny it. Physically speaking, you're a very attractive man. But I don't like you, the vast majority of the time. So far as I can gather, you behave abominably in public and are only marginally better in private. I only find you remotely tolerable when you're kissing me."

He gave her a chastening look. "Even from that stinting description, we'd have a better foundation for marriage than many couples."

"Yes, but it's still nowhere near the marriage I'd dreamed of having."

"Well." The duke released her hands and stepped back. "It would seem you have a choice. Will it be the dreams? Or me?"

"No woman should have to make such a choice."

But she knew that women did, all the time. Every moment of every day, somewhere a woman surrendered her blissful fantasies to the cruel reality of the world. Years ago, she'd managed to delay the inevitable, but now Amelia knew in her bones—her day, her moment had come. It was her turn to lay down those fantasies of romantic love and grab what she could: security, the opportunity to help her brothers, and something undeniably tempting—the chance to explore physical passion. As for love . . . well, there would be children. And Amelia would love those children as no mother had ever loved. No mother except her own, of course.

She knew what she ought to do; what she *would* do. Still, she could not say the words.

"Don't make the choice, then," he said. "Come here."

It was not a request, but a command. And she complied, gratefully. His confidence drew her forward, as though he pulled her to him with a string. She stopped, just inches from him, staring up into his handsome face.

"Kiss me."

Another command. Another so easily obeyed, because it was exactly what she wanted to do. He bent his head, and she pressed a warm, unhurried kiss to his lips. She would know a lifetime of these kisses. She would know what it was, to see this formidable man unclothed and vulnerable, to feel the weight of his naked body stretched out over hers.

The kiss ended.

"Now," he said, "say yes."

She would be a duchess. She would be mistress of six houses. She would be married from St. George's in Hanover Square, in front of all London, wearing a gown of the divinely embroidered and obscenely expensive ivory brocade she'd seen last week in Bond Street. She would serve white cake at the wedding breakfast, with three different fillings and rolled gum icing cut in the shape of blossoms—orchids, not roses. Because everyone had roses. She would have real orchids in her bouquet, and she would visit the hothouse this very week to order them.

Some of her dreams could still come true.

"Say yes, Amelia."

"Yes," she said. And because it came more easily than she'd expected, she said it again. "Yes."

"Good girl."

He gave her a smile—slight, yet devastating—and to that subtle quirk of his lips Amelia impulsively hitched all her hopes and dreams. For better or for worse.

"I'll go speak with your brother." He gathered his gloves from the desk.

"Please do give my name to your secretary," she said, giving in to a flutter of bridal excitement. "We can begin compiling the guest list, making the arrangements."

"That won't be necessary," he said. "We'll be married here, in this room. Tomorrow."

Chapter Six

Not thirty hours later, Amelia sat in the Rose Parlor—actually, one of two rose parlors Beauvale House boasted, thanks to Winifred's fondness for pink. With a fretful sigh, she squeezed Lily Chatwick's hand and asked for what must have been the fifth time, "Are you certain you don't mind?"

"I don't mind," Lily answered.

Amelia chewed her lip. "It just feels all wrong, to have you here."

It all felt wrong, full stop. A wedding, before Lord Harcliffe was even in the ground? It was so tasteless, so arbitrary . . . and so sadly lacking in rolled icing and orchids. But evidently the Duke of Morland considered her whispered "yes" to be Amelia's last word on the matter. Plans for these hasty nuptials had proceeded apace, whether she liked it or not. Yesterday afternoon had seen a flock of messengers descend on the Beauvale doorstep, delivering legal papers, the special license obtained from the archbishop, trunks emblazoned with the Morland crest in which to pack up her belongings. But before all these, a *modiste* had presented herself, flanked by two seamstresses and armed to the teeth with straight pins. Apparently the duke had been serious, when he spoke of pensioning off her blue moiré silk.

For the better part of the hour, the three women had flitted about her, measuring and clucking their tongues portentously, as if they were the three Fates of Grecian myth, sent to snip and stitch the precise shape of Amelia's destiny.

Then early this morning, a footman had marched the long path to Amelia's small bedchamber at the rear of the house, bearing a tower of boxes. The largest package held clouds of white petticoats and a mist-thin chemise; the smallest contained a coil of perfectly matched Baroque pearls. And one of the boxes in the middle had opened to reveal a tasteful, stylish gown of dove-gray satin. The color was understated and respectful—but quietly lovely. Amelia ran her fingers lightly over the skirt, twisting it in the sunlight to coax a lilac shimmer from the fabric.

"It's a beautiful dress," Lily said.

Amelia balled her hand in a fist, ashamed to have drawn attention to her own vanity. She ought to have refused to wear it and put on her plain black bombazine instead. But she had such a weakness for fine-milled fabric.

"You deserve it," Lily said, as if she understood Amelia's thoughts. "And you must not feel guilty on your wedding day. I'm grateful to be here, truly. What else should I be doing? Sitting weeping at home? I found ample time for that yesterday; tomorrow will bring a fresh supply of empty hours to fill. Today, I am glad for the distraction. And to be completely honest, I'm a bit relieved."

"Relieved that you won't have to marry him?" Amelia laughed dryly. "Yes, I understand. Better me than you."

"I didn't mean it that way. I'm certain His Grace will make you a fine husband."

"Are you? I wish I could say the same."

Lily's gaze caught hers. "Amelia, you would not believe what he sent to the house yesterday."

"Not seamstresses, I hope."

"No, no. A bank draft."

Amelia buried her face in her hands to disguise her unladylike response. "Not that blasted horse again."

"It's not so bad as you suspect. I was astonished to see the—"

Bang.

The parlor door swung open with such force, the hinges rattled in the doorframe. Alarmed, Amelia shot to her feet. Lily followed suit, with considerably more grace.

The Duke of Morland filled the doorway. Tall. Dark. Handsome. Irate.

Not even the brown-black curls at his temple had the temerity to rebel this morning; they appeared to have been ruthlessly subdued with comb and pomade. His impeccable black topcoat and Hessians were matched by an equally dark expression. The duke looked angry, commanding, arrogant—and so intensely attractive it actually pained her to look him in the face. Truly, Amelia felt as though she'd swallowed all three of his nimble little seamstresses, and they were currently stitching the lining of her stomach into pleats.

From behind the duke's imposing figure, Laurent made a chagrined expression. "Beg pardon. I tried to prevent him."

"Good heavens, what is it?" In a defensive move, Amelia crossed her arms over her chest. Then she impulsively uncrossed them and clasped her trembling hands behind her back. He was just a man, she reminded herself. Just a mortal, imperfect man. She couldn't let him cow her—not now, not ever.

"Lady Amelia," he accused, "you are . . ." He raked

her with a glance, and beneath the pearly silk, a thousand pins pricked her skin. "You are late."

"Late," she echoed, disbelieving.

"Eight minutes late." Striding into the room, he drew a timepiece from his waistcoat pocket. "The wedding was to begin at half-ten. It is now ten thirty"—he raised an eyebrow and paused dramatically—"nine. Nine minutes late."

Struggling to remain calm, Amelia advanced to meet him in the center of the room. "Your Grace," she muttered, "you have allowed me a betrothal of precisely twenty-seven hours. Twenty-seven hours, in which to reorder my life from that of an unmarried woman to that of a duchess. Now you would begrudge me nine minutes' delay?"

He glowered at her. "Yes."

Laurent crossed to her side and laid a hand on her shoulder, drawing her away. "Amelia," he said quietly, "it's not too late. You needn't do this, you know."

At the warm solicitude in his voice, her resolve nearly crumbled. For something like twenty-six hours now, Laurent had been urging her to reconsider this whole enterprise. If she said no, even at the last moment, Amelia knew her brother would support her decision. He'd done the same ten years ago, when she'd been unable to stomach marriage to that horrid Mr. Poste. *Never mind the money*, he'd insisted, *your happiness is worth more than gold.*

When she'd been granted that reprieve, Amelia had felt nothing but relief. At the age of sixteen, she never could have conceived that Papa's debt would balloon so catastrophically, nor that a country widower's suit would be the last she'd entertain.

Amelia lowered her voice to a whisper. "This is an opportunity, Laurent. An opportunity for *us*. Once I am a duchess, I can help our brothers in ways even you cannot. The alliance will greatly improve Michael's chances of marrying well. Perhaps I can secure a living for Jack, get him out of London and away from his unsavory friends."

Her brother shook his head. "I fear Jack may be a lost cause."

"Don't ever say that. If Mama were here, could you say that to her face?"

"If Mama were here, could you marry this man? She wouldn't have wanted this for you. She wanted her children to marry for love."

"And yet you defied her," she said gently.

After Papa died, the debts had mounted higher and higher still. Laurent had made the very sacrifice at which Amelia had once balked: he'd married, sensibly and disaffectionately, to secure the d'Orsay family's future. She loved him for it and often despised herself for leaving him no other choice. "I can't cry off this time, Laurent. It isn't only about the family. I want my own household, my own children. This may be my last chance. I'm not sixteen any longer."

No, she was older and wiser—and undeniably lonelier. And disagreeable as his demeanor might be, the Duke of Morland compared favorably to Mr. Poste. Morland wasn't thirty years older than she. He had straight teeth. He didn't reek of tallow and sweat. He knew how to kiss. Properly.

And he was a duke. A duke with six estates, who would settle twenty thousand pounds on her, and some property besides. In her shortsighted, selfish girlhood, she'd let slip one chance to help her family. If this man saw fit to offer her security and children, Amelia supposed she could promise him punctuality in trade.

"Are you absolutely certain?" Laurent cast a wary glance at the duke. "I've no compunction about tossing him out on his ear, if you like."

"No, no. You are very good, but I am decided." She truly believed the sentiment she'd expressed to the duke the other night, during their waltz. Contentment was largely a matter of individual choice. "I am decided, and I will be happy."

Spencer was displeased. Greatly displeased. Twelve minutes now. He could have been married already, perhaps even ordering the carriage for their departure. Instead he was standing here awkwardly in the center of the room, watching his intended bride confer with her brother in heated whispers.

Damn it, he hated weddings. He didn't remember ever attending any others, but he was certainly making this one his last.

To think, not an hour ago, he'd been congratulating himself on his brilliance. He needed a wife, and here was his chance to obtain one without the nuisance of a courtship. When a man of his wealth and station proposed marriage to a lady of hers . . . They both knew she couldn't possibly have refused.

But she had no problem keeping him waiting. Spencer didn't like being made to wait. The waiting was making him uneasy, and he didn't like feeling uneasy.

This was why he'd insisted on a small, private ceremony in her home. If there was no crowd, no music, no fanfare, he reasoned, he would remain perfectly calm and in control. Except that now a ten-minute delay had him fretting like a schoolboy. And that fact had him resenting her further, because he was intelligent enough to realize that this churning tempest inside him must mean *something*. Something about him, something about her . . . something about *them*, perhaps? He didn't know. He just wanted to marry the woman, take her home, and puzzle it out in bed.

"Your Grace?"

His head whipped up. Lady Amelia stood before him. And whatever exorbitant sum he'd paid that dressmaker, it hadn't been nearly enough.

Standing with her hands clasped behind her back, she played her figure to its best advantage. Her waist was trim and defined, her hips cuppable, her bosom delectable. Silk covered those lushly proportioned curves, clinging in all the right places. Its silvery, iridescent shade reminded him of dew on heather, or the belly of a trout; and it contrasted pleasantly with the warm, milky texture of her skin. She was all softness and sleekness, and his gaze slipped over her easily even as his thoughts snagged. He wrestled to make sense of her, define her, understand what it was she signified to him and why. He couldn't say she looked elegant or stunning or beautiful.

Refreshing. Her appearance was refreshing, like cool, clear water on a sun-baked summer's day. And he gratefully drank her in.

She gave him a deferential nod. "I apologize for my tardiness, Your Grace. I am ready. Has your groomsman arrived?"

He stared at her.

"You . . . you do have a groomsman to stand up with you? Someone to sign the register as a witness?"

He shook his head. The thought hadn't even crossed his mind. "Won't Beauvale do?"

"Laurent?" Her brow wrinkled. "I suppose he could, but I hate to ask. I'm rather doing this against his wishes. And unfortunately, he's the only one of my brothers here. Michael's at sea of course, and Jack—well, Jack is necessarily avoiding you." She swept a glance around the room, finally settling it on the butler. "I suppose we could have Wycke. But surely you don't want a servant?"

If it meant they could be married within the next

quarter hour, Spencer would gladly have opened the door and dragged in the first ruffian off the street. "He'll do." He made a curt motion to the butler. "Bring the curate. We may as well do it in here."

At the clergyman's entrance, Spencer summoned the man to his side with nothing but a pointed look and the arch of one brow.

The curate inclined his balding head. "Yes, Your Grace?"

"There's a very generous donation in the parish's future if you make this fast. Ten minutes, at the most."

Frowning, the man fumbled open his liturgy. "There's an established rite, Your Grace. Marriage must be entered into with solemnity and consideration. I don't know that I can rush—"

"Ten minutes. One thousand guineas."

The liturgy snapped closed. "Then again, what do a few extra minutes signify to an eternal God?" He beckoned Amelia with a fluttering, papery hand. "Make haste, child. You're about to be married."

Spencer scarcely heard the fevered rush of words that constituted his wedding. In principle, he agreed with the curate. Marriage should be a solemn, sacred enterprise, and the length of time Spencer took to make a decision had no correlation with how seriously he considered it. This wasn't something he approached lightly, else he would have married years ago. Somewhere in between mumbled "I will's" and parroted vows, he managed a brief, silent petition for a few male children and whatever other blessings God saw fit to grant them. It wasn't much, but it would have to do.

At the curate's direction, they exchanged simple gold bands. All his aunt's pieces were at Braxton Hall; she'd have her selection of jeweled rings there. Her fingers were chilled, and irrational anger spiked through him. Why was she cold? Hadn't the *modiste* sent gloves?

"I pronounce you man and wife."

There, it was done.

He turned to his bride, looking her in the eye for the first time since the ceremony had begun. And he promptly kicked himself, because this would have been far more pleasant if he'd been looking at her the whole time. Her eyes were really quite lovely—large, intelligent, expressive. A patient, sensible shade of blue.

He very much wanted to kiss her now.

And as if she'd heard the thought—God, he hoped he hadn't said it aloud—she gave a tiny shake of her head and whispered, *"Not yet."*

With a plunk, the curate laid open the parish register on a side table and thumbed to the appropriate page. Once their names and the date had been recorded, Spencer took up the quill and signed his name on the line. His was a long name; it took a while. After he'd finished, he dipped the quill again before passing it to Amelia.

She paused, peering down at the register.

As the moment stretched, Spencer's heart gave an odd kick. *Oh, come along.*

Before she could lay pen to parchment, a commotion in the hallway disrupted the scene. Julian Bellamy stormed into the parlor, followed by Ashworth. Spencer groaned as the two made straight for him.

"What the devil do you mean by this?" Bellamy demanded.

"I mean to be married."

"I know that much, you despicable blackguard." Sneering, Bellamy shoved a rectangle of paper in Spencer's face. "This. What do you mean by this?"

It was the bank draft he'd sent over yesterday morning, as promised. "It's just as I said. I'm offering Lady Lily compensation in exchange for her brother's token."

"In the amount of twenty thousand pounds?"

Beside him, Amelia gasped.

"Twenty thousand pounds," Ashworth said. "There's no racehorse in the world worth that, much less one retired to stud."

"I didn't base my offer on the market value of the horse. I offered what the token is worth to me." Spencer turned to Bellamy. "And it's Lady Lily's to accept or decline. Not yours."

The slender, dark-haired woman stepped forward. "I'm very grateful, Your Grace, but you know I cannot accept."

"If you find my offer insufficient, we can discuss more generous—"

"It's not that," Lily said. "Your offer is beyond generous. It's charity, and I cannot accept it in good conscience."

Bellamy cut in. "She cannot accept it because Leo's token is gone."

"Gone?" Amelia said. "Gone where?"

"Precisely what I'd like to know." Bellamy shot Spencer a murderous look. "Care to tell us, Morland?"

"How should I know where it's gone? Wasn't it with Harcliffe's belongings?"

Ashworth shook his head. "We've gone through everything, twice. It wasn't on his body, either. Must have been stripped by his attackers."

"Simple robbery, then," Spencer said. "Or perhaps he'd already lost it in a wager."

"Never," Bellamy said. "Leo would never have risked that token, and you know it. You know you had no other way of getting it from him."

"What the hell are you suggesting?" A cold, leaden weight settled in Spencer's gut. "Surely you don't mean to suggest I had some hand in Harcliffe's death?"

Bellamy only raised his eyebrows.

"Surely you don't mean to suggest it," Spencer

repeated coolly, "because if you did slander my character in such an outrageous, unfounded manner, I would have to demand satisfaction."

"So you can get my token, too? Pry it from my cold, dead hands?"

Amelia wedged herself between them. "Why are the two of you so determined to kill one another? Mr. Bellamy, with all due respect and sympathy—your charges make no sense. If His Grace already had possession of this token, why on earth would he offer Lily twenty thousand pounds for it?"

Fortunately someone in the room had some sense. And more fortunate still, she was the one he was marrying.

"Guilt. Blood money, to ease his conscience." Bellamy gave him a cold stare. "I've remembered something, Morland. You were there in the card room the other night, when Leo and I made plans to attend the boxing match."

Was he? Spencer supposed he could have been, but he certainly hadn't been paying attention to Harcliffe and Bellamy. His sole focus had been winning Faraday's token. "What if I were? So were a dozen other gentlemen."

"None of them had a reason to kill Leo. You've destroyed fortunes in pursuit of Osiris already. Why should I believe you'd stop at violence? You knew exactly where Leo was going to be that night. You knew I was meant to be with him. Were you hoping to get us both in one blow?"

"You're mad."

"You're sickening," Bellamy said. "My gut twists, to think I almost allowed you to marry Lily. And it makes perfect sense, why you wouldn't. Imagine, sitting across the table from her every day for the rest of your life, knowing you were responsible for her brother's death. Keeping company with your own damning guilt."

"Stop this," Lily said. "Julian, you don't know what you're saying. This is nonsensical. We have no reason to believe that missing token had anything to do with Leo's death. And simply because His Grace declined to—"

Bellamy ignored her. "Couldn't stand the thought of it, could you? No, you'd sooner pay Lily off." He jerked his chin toward Amelia. "And shackle yourself to the first available female just to settle the matter."

It had been fourteen years since Spencer had lashed out at a man in a moment of blinding white fury—but he hadn't forgotten how to land a punch. His knuckles made a satisfying thwack as they connected with Bellamy's jaw, sending the man sprawling. The bank draft fluttered to the carpet as Bellamy struggled to his feet.

Spencer hauled back his fist for another punch, but before he could swing, Beauvale leapt forward to grab his arm.

"You see?" accused Bellamy, rubbing his jaw. "He's dangerous. He wants to kill me, too."

"I do now," Spencer ground out. He shrugged out of Beauvale's grip.

"And need we guess who's next? Everyone knows what you did to Ashworth at Eton."

"Oh, do they?" Spencer turned to the soldier. "And what, precisely, did *I* do to Ashworth at Eton?" Damn it, he'd been sent down for that fight. He'd tacitly accepted all the blame. The blackguard had better not sell him out at his own wedding.

Ashworth shrugged. "Obviously something less than killing me."

"Julian, please." Lily went to Bellamy's side. She touched a finger to the corner of his mouth, where blood oozed from his cracked lip. "I know you are hurting and angry. I know you want someone to blame, some means of avenging Leo's death. But surely you're mistaken."

"Am I?"

The room went quiet. Uncomfortably quiet, as all eyes trained on Spencer. He felt the keen scrutiny of every person in the room: Bellamy, Lily, Ashworth, Beauvale, the curate . . . Amelia.

She spoke first. "You are mistaken, Mr. Bellamy. I was there when he learned of Leo's death. It took His Grace completely by surprise, I assure you."

Bellamy dabbed his bleeding lip with the back of his hand. "Forgive me, but your assurances aren't worth much."

The knave. Spencer wanted to grind him into this revolting pink carpet and cast both pieces of refuse out onto the street. But he wouldn't waste the effort. There were more effective ways of wounding a man. Julian Bellamy came from nothing. In the eyes of the *ton*, he *was* nothing. And there was no one so well positioned to remind him of it as the fourth Duke of Morland.

"You will refrain," he said with crisp, aristocratic diction, "from addressing my bride in that familiar manner. You will refrain from speaking to her at all, unless you afford her the respect and deference her superior rank demands. Know your betters."

A flash of jealous hatred crossed Bellamy's face, and Spencer knew his cut had slashed deep. Obviously the man harbored a poisonous mix of envy and loathing for the social elite. Someone ought to inform him such an attitude was a grave weakness, ripe for exploitation. But that someone wouldn't be Spencer.

"As to the value of Lady Amelia's assurances," he continued in a low voice meant for Bellamy's hearing alone, "I assure you, they are worth far more to me than your miserable life. Disparage her again, and you will find yourself at the point of a blade."

"Spoken like a murderer," Bellamy growled.

With a careful appearance of nonchalance, Spencer bent to retrieve the bank draft from the carpet. "If Harcliffe's token is missing, I also have an interest in locating his killers. In one hour's time, meet me at the mews where Osiris is stabled. We'll discuss the matter further. But for now . . ." He carefully pocketed the bank draft, then finally had the satisfaction of speaking the words he'd been longing to say since Bellamy entered the room. "Get out."

"No, wait." Amelia clasped her hands together. "Don't leave. We still need a groomsman."

Unbelievable. Spencer blinked at her. "Are you seriously suggesting this . . . this *cur* should witness our wedding?"

Bellamy put in, "After all you've heard and seen, are you still seriously planning to marry this villain?"

"Do I have a choice?" Amelia tilted her face to Spencer's and studied him quietly.

"It's not yet official," he made himself say. "You haven't signed. I will release you, if you've given some credence to Mr. Bellamy's accusations."

After a moment's lip-biting hesitation, she reached forward and touched one hand to his. The light touch dissolved the tension in his wrist, and his fingers uncurled. He hadn't even realized he'd been holding them in a fist.

Wordlessly, she bent over the register and wrote her name in careful, deliberate strokes. After blowing lightly over her signature and returning the plume to its inkwell, she straightened and said simply, "There."

It took a great deal to humble Spencer, but his bride—his *wife*—had just managed to do it.

Lily came forward next. She took the quill and signed in one of the two spaces marked "Witness" before extending the pen to Bellamy. "I think you should sign it, Julian. You know what an amiable sort Leo was. When he conceived of the Stud Club . . ." She paused. "Forgive me, I still can't say that without wanting to laugh. Anyhow, he began it with the purpose of making new friends. This was why he decreed membership should be dependent on chance—he wanted to draw together people from different classes, form unlikely alliances. Don't let his death tear that apart." She pushed the quill at him. "Please. Do it for Leo. Or if not him, then—"

Cursing, Bellamy ruffled his hair. "Don't ask it, Lily."

"Then do it for me."

With a strangled groan, he snatched the pen from her grip and bent as if he would sign. At the last moment, however, he cast the quill away. "I can't do it. Even if I believed . . ." He swore. "I just can't."

"For Christ's sake, I'll do it," said Ashworth. The battle-scarred warrior elbowed his way past Spencer. "There's your unlikely alliance, my lady."

Unlikely indeed. "You don't think me a murderer, then?" Spencer asked. Strange, that Ashworth should become his defender. In his entire life, Spencer had only come remotely close to killing one man, and it was him.

"No." As he bent to scrawl his name across the register page, Ashworth spared him a cryptic glance. "You don't have it in you."

The tone of his remark hardly made it a ringing endorsement of Spencer's character. Then again, Spencer didn't really care. "Meet me at the mews," he told the men. "One hour."

Chapter Seven

"This is a travesty." As he approached the mews, Spencer swore quietly into the late-morning fog.

Osiris, the greatest racehorse of a generation—champion at Newmarket, Doncaster, Epsom Downs—was stabled here, amongst common carriage horses?

The barn was dark and dank as a cave inside. A blizzard of dust motes whirled in the lone shaft of light penetrating the gloom. The horses' stalls were cramped, as they always were in Town. Spencer's nose wrinkled at a trough of stale, fetid water—in Cambridgeshire, his grooms drew fresh water twice daily from the stream.

At his order, the groom opened the door of the stallion's stall and released him into the small yard. The horse shook himself, nostrils flared and head swinging from side to side. The groom jerked roughly on the halter, and Spencer's jaw clenched with anger. Had the man been in his employ, that one move would have cost him his post.

"How is he exercised?"

"We turn 'im out twice a day. Sometimes a walk about the yard on a lead. Don't like to be saddled no more, this one. Touchy with the grooming, too."

"So you're letting him tell you what to do, instead of the other way around?"

Tsking softly, Spencer circled the horse. His dark bay coat was in dire need of a brisk raking with a currycomb. Gray hairs mingled with the ebony, giving a hoarfrost look to his forelock, a sign of the stallion's advancing age. He'd worn a bald patch on his right flank, likely from chafing against the stable wall. Despite the deplorable state of his grooming, however, Osiris remained an impressive example of horseflesh. His high, taut haunches and long, arched neck displayed his Arabian ancestry.

Spencer circled to the front again, standing slightly to the horse's side, allowing the animal plenty of space to see him, and several snorting breaths to investigate his scent. The look he saw in the stallion's large, dark-fringed eye pleased him, as did the haughty head toss that yanked the groom off-balance. There was spirit there, and fierce arrogance. That look said, *I'm better than this.*

"Most certainly," Spencer agreed. The horse was spoiled as the devil and would need a great deal of retraining with an expert handler, but at least his spirit hadn't been broken.

He removed his gloves and tucked them beneath one arm, murmuring gently as he approached. After extending his hand palm-down for the stallion to nose and inspect, he laid it against the horse's withers.

"Far better than this," he said, giving the horse a brisk rub. The horse turned and nosed his palm, displaying the narrow blaze of white that ran the length of his nose, with the look of a lightning bolt.

Spencer was tempted to saddle the beast and ride him straight out of the mews. But as it was, he already stood accused of murder. It would seem unwise to add horse theft, another hanging offense, to Julian Bellamy's list of suspicions.

"Holy Christ."

Spencer's gaze jerked to the entrance.

Ashworth strode into the barn, chasing the fog of his breath with a low whistle of admiration. "That is one magnificent animal."

Spencer's opinion of the man took a small leap in favorability. No matter their history as youths, there was something to be said for a man who recognized quality horseflesh when he saw it. Or, for that matter, a man who recognized a baseless accusation when he heard one.

"That he is," Spencer said, pride enriching his voice. "His grandsire was Eclipse; his dam's line goes back to the Godolphin Arabian, with several champions in between. No finer pedigree to be found in English horseflesh." He took the stallion's halter himself, dismissing the groom with a glance.

Ashworth tilted his head to examine the horse further. "Had a gelding once from the Darley line. Red chestnut, white markings. Fast as a demon, with a temperament to match. I must have pushed that horse over every moor in Devonshire. Perfect mount for an angry, overgrown youth."

Spencer wouldn't have said it aloud, but he too had spent more hours of his youth in the saddle than in the schoolroom. "What's happened to him now?"

"Dead."

"In battle?"

"No."

Ashworth paced idly toward the rear of the yard, and Spencer sensed that he didn't want to speak of the matter. Strange, that the man would so easily discuss the deaths of his fellow soldiers, only to fall silent when the deceased was a red chestnut gelding.

Or not so strange, perhaps.

"So why are we here?" Ashworth said.

"I'm wondering that myself." Julian Bellamy swaggered

into the yard, turned out in a suit of rumpled cobalt velvet that looked like he'd slept in it. Or *not* slept in it. His hair always appeared slept-upon; that much was no surprise. Why a man would go to such meticulous effort to cultivate a slapdash appearance, Spencer couldn't imagine. But then, neither could he fathom why anyone would stable a priceless racehorse in this place.

"We're here to discuss the investigation of Harcliffe's murder," Spencer said. "But first, these boarding conditions are unacceptable."

"What's wrong with them?"

He ticked off the list on his fingers. "Fetid water. Rotting hay. Inexpert grooms. Poor ventilation. Cramped stalls. And I haven't even started in on the lack of proper exerci—"

"Enough already." Bellamy flashed an open palm. "To my eye, looks no different from the stabling of most Mayfair gents' cattle."

"This isn't a carriage horse, nor a gelding for the occasional prance down Rotten Row. Osiris is a former racehorse, from the most noble of bloodlines." Spencer gave him a cutting look. "I wouldn't expect a man like you to understand."

Julian Bellamy's cheeks blazed a very satisfying shade of red. And the red contrasted most pleasingly with the purpling bruise on his left jaw. The man was simply too easy to provoke, once one discovered that raw, tender gash of bitter jealousy.

"I see," Bellamy said hotly. "Only the purebred nobleman can truly understand the purebred horse, is that it?"

Spencer shrugged. His own breeding had nothing to do with it, but he definitely knew what was best for this horse. "Proper handling of a horse like this is no simple matter. He was trained to race, from birth. Not only to race, but to be the best. Once a champion, he was spoiled with attention and permissive handling. Add to that, he's an ungelded male, with a strong natural mating drive. It all adds up to a horse with a mile-wide streak of arrogance, bloody bored out of his mind. Without proper exercise and opportunities to mate, all that aggressive energy festers. He becomes moody, intractable, withdrawn, destructive."

Ashworth raised an eyebrow at Bellamy. "Is it just me, or is this conversation becoming uncomfortably personal?"

Spencer fumed. "I'm not referring to myself, you ass."

Suddenly Ashworth was all wide-eyed mock innocence. "Oh, of course you aren't, Your Grace." He slyly added, "But it would explain a few things if you were."

"It would indeed," Bellamy said. "Like this." He indicated his bruised jaw.

"I was thinking more of His Grace's hasty nuptials," Ashworth said. "Though by that logic, his temper ought to improve markedly tomorrow morning."

"Enough." Spencer's jaw tensed with the effort of self-restraint. "Make all the fun you like. You won't think it so humorous when Osiris meets with an early death."

Now that earned the two men's attention.

Bellamy gave a low whistle through his teeth. "You are a violent one, aren't you?"

"For God's sake, it wasn't a threat," Spencer said impatiently. "All issues of breeding and training aside, this horse requires superior accommodations by sheer virtue of his value. Personally, I wouldn't stable a draft horse here, let alone a priceless racehorse. The risk is too great."

"He's kept in the most secure stall," Bellamy said. "The grooms watch in shifts, and the gate is chained and locked at all times."

"The locks are part of the problem. Look at the condition of this barn." Spencer swept a gesture toward the cobwebbed rafters. "Dust everywhere, loft crammed with dry hay. It's a firetrap. One spark would turn this whole structure into an inferno, and all your chains and locks would simply seal the horse's fate."

"On that point he's right," Ashworth said, all hint of humor gone from his voice. "Stable fires are a nasty business." He looked to Spencer. "If the two of you want to move him, I'll take no issue with it."

"Would you be interested in selling out your share?" Spencer asked. "I'd be generous."

Ashworth fell silent, as though he were seriously considering the offer. Excellent. If he'd been forced to sell out his commission to pay his estate's creditors, the man had to be short on funds.

"He can't sell out his share," Bellamy protested. "The tokens can only be won or lost in a game of chance."

"Something of that nature could be arranged," Spencer said. "Fancy a game of cards, Ashworth?"

Ashworth began to respond, but Bellamy interrupted with a forceful, "No!"

The stallion's head jerked, and Spencer adjusted his grip on the halter, muttering a litany of soft, soothing imprecations that Bellamy was all too welcome to overhear.

"I won't allow it," Bellamy said. "Leo devised this club. He laid down the rules of membership and the code of conduct. Now the man's dead. The least you can do to honor his memory is to respect the spirit of fraternity this club represents."

"Some spirit of fraternity," Spencer said. "Interrupting a man's wedding with unfounded accusations of murder? Listen, the both of you. I'll forfeit all interest in the remaining tokens, on one condition. That Osiris be stabled at my estate in Cambridgeshire."

Bellamy shook his head vigorously.

"Just hear me out," Spencer said. "The rules remain the same. Any member of the Club may send mares to be mated—"

"All the way to Cambridgeshire?" Bellamy snorted.

"My stables are the finest in the country, and I include the Royal Mews in that assessment. Large stalls, enclosed pasture. My stable master and grooms are the most capable to be had, anywhere. I also keep an expert veterinarian on my staff. At Braxton Hall, this stallion will be among his equals in lineage and ability. Fed properly. Exercised properly. Bred properly." He reached up to smooth Osiris's jet-black mane. "This horse belongs with me."

"You mean the horse belongs *to* you." Barely bothering to turn his head, Bellamy spat in the straw. "You believe you're entitled to this beast, just as you believe you're entitled to everything. What makes you so much better than the two of us? Your title? The remarkable accomplishment of being born to a noblewoman instead of your father's favorite chambermaid?"

Oh, now Spencer was thoroughly angered. Whatever clashes they'd had in Spencer's adolescence, his father had been a decent, honorable man. "Just because you know nothing of your own father," he warned, "do not pretend to know something of mine."

Hatred burned in Bellamy's eyes. "It's naught but luck. Simple, dumb, blue-blooded luck is all that separates a man like you from a man like me. Leo understood it. He never thought himself the better of anyone. That's why he created this Club, made its membership contingent on the kind of good fortune that comes *after* one's birth, not before it." His glare alternated between Spencer and Ashworth. "I'll be damned if I'll allow the two of you to destroy that. I'll fight you to my last breath if you try to take this horse from London."

"You'll lose." Spencer narrowed his eyes. "Mark my words, those tokens will be mine, in time. This horse will be mine, in time. And if you think all that separates the two of us is simple, dumb luck . . ." He shook his head in contempt. "One wonders why you spend such time and effort courting the favor of people you claim to despise."

Before Bellamy could recover, Spencer changed the subject. "What do we know about Leo's death?"

"Seems like I should be asking you that question."

Spencer shrugged off the implicit accusation. "Has the prostitute been found yet? The driver of the hack?"

Bellamy shook his head warily. "Spent all night combing the louse-ridden pig's arse that is Whitechapel. I'll be headed straight back when we're through here. Don't suppose Your Grace cares to come along?"

"Not particularly." Spencer beckoned the groom with a nod, then passed him the stallion's lead. Reaching into his breast pocket, he withdrew an envelope sealed with the Morland crest and extended it to Bellamy.

The man stared at it with resentment. "What's that?"

"The reason you're here." He pushed the envelope into Bellamy's hand. "Guard it well. Inside, you'll find the bank draft for twenty thousand pounds."

Bellamy stared at the letter, his sneer fading.

"Use it to hire every runner and investigator in London. Search every seedy tavern and grimy hole; question every prostitute and footpad. Perhaps you'll discover some long-lost relations in the process, but you'll find nothing connecting me to Harcliffe's death."

"We'll see about that." Bellamy grasped a corner of the envelope and tugged.

Spencer kept his grip on the other edge. "When the killers are found, the remainder goes to Lily. The token comes to me."

He let go, and Bellamy accepted the envelope with a begrudging nod.

Ashworth spoke up. "I don't have that kind of coin, but when it's muscle you need, send for me. If it's a court trial you're wanting, though"—his neck cracked menacingly—"I can't promise there'll be much left but scraps to stand before the magistrate."

"Duly warned," Bellamy said warily. "I thought you barely knew Leo. You'd kill for him?"

The soldier shrugged. "I've killed for less."

Right. Impatient to end this, Spencer said, "If you refuse to allow me to move Osiris, I insist on sending one of my own grooms to oversee his care. I'm for Cambridgeshire tomorrow. Keep me apprised of any and all developments. For that kind of money, I expect a daily express."

"Fleeing Town rather speedily, aren't you?" Bellamy asked.

"I am not fleeing anything. I've business at my estate."

"Honeymoon business, I'd wager," Ashworth said. "A series of pressing engagements with the ducal mattress?"

As the two others exchanged looks, Spencer blew out an impatient breath. Maybe they were right. Maybe he really did just need a good tumble. All the more reason to end this meeting and return home to Amelia, who had both the good sense to disregard these ridiculous accusations, and the lush body to make him forget them completely.

"I still say it's suspicious," Bellamy said. "All of it. That hasty wedding, your leaving Town so soon."

The already-fragile thread of Spencer's patience snapped. "And if I remained in Town, you would accuse me of tampering in the investigation and impeding justice. Nothing I say will convince you of my innocence, because all you can see is your own culpability. You were supposed to be with your friend that night; instead you were out whoring. Now the guilt's eating you alive, and until Leo's killers are found, you're going to make my life miserable. So much is clear." He jerked on his gloves. "I don't care what the devil you think of me. Just find the killers. I want to see them brought to justice every bit as much as you do."

And I want that token more than you could possibly understand.

"Find them," he repeated, staring Bellamy down. "Find the token. And then we'll meet to discuss the future of this club."

A low rumble of laughter dispersed the angry tension in the air.

"Sorry," Ashworth said, still chuckling, "It's just amusing, don't you think? The three of us, comprising the membership of any club."

Julian scowled. "It's absurd, is what it is."

"Yes, well." Spencer brushed the dust from his sleeves and motioned to the groom for his mount. "You did say Leo loved a good joke. This one seems to be on us."

Chapter Eight

Amelia was beginning to wonder if her husband ever intended to bed her.

When staring blankly at the lavender walls of the duchess's suite passed tedium and strayed toward madness, she flopped back on the counterpane with a frustrated sigh and stared up at the bed's purple canopy. It seemed to be embroidered with birds. Joyless, awkward birds with wings sprawled at odd angles. Perhaps they were meant to be cranes? To her, they resembled dead partridges ready for plucking. Hardly an inspiring vision for a new bride to contemplate whilst performing her wifely duties. She hoped the duke preferred darkness, when he came to consummate this marriage.

If he came to consummate this marriage.

They'd left Beauvale House shortly following that mockery of a ceremony. A tense, silent carriage ride conveyed them to Morland's residence. At the door, he'd handed her off to the housekeeper with the terse statement: "Tripp will show you to your chambers. See that you rest."

She had not seen him since.

She had rested. She'd taken tea. She'd thought to spend the afternoon unpacking her trunks and becoming acquainted with the house, but her new lady's maid informed her that wouldn't be necessary. His Grace had decreed they'd be leaving for Braxton Hall tomorrow.

Tomorrow?

Confronted with that disquieting information, Amelia had sought refuge in a hot bath. She had dressed with great care for dinner, and then she had dined alone. When she finally summoned the courage to inquire after His Grace's whereabouts, she was informed that the duke had gone out riding.

Pah. Her wedding day, and already she'd been abandoned for a horse.

Now, several hours after that solitary dinner, Amelia lay on the counterpane in her sheerest muslin shift, fingering the eyelet neckline and wondering if she'd made a terrible mistake. Her thoughts returned again and again to that morning, and to Mr. Bellamy's accusations. At the time, she had rejected the idea instinctively. The Duke of Morland might be a disagreeable, arrogant, cold sort of man, but she couldn't believe him capable of murder.

But then she thought of that bank draft. Twenty thousand pounds. He was willing to pay twenty thousand pounds for a one-tenth share in a racehorse—the exact same amount he'd settled on Amelia, who came all of one piece. Independent of any aspersions cast on the duke's character, those amounts spoke eloquently of his priorities.

And then there was that breathtaking, violent punch to Bellamy's jaw.

No doubt another lady would have found that moment thrilling, when her bridegroom sent fist crashing into face to defend her honor. But Amelia had had five brothers, each of whom had thrown punches ostensibly in her defense, and she knew better. Men hit one another because they felt like hitting one another, and the "fair lady's honor" bit was usually no more than a convenient excuse.

If the duke had slammed Mr. Bellamy to the floor for insulting Amelia . . . what might he be capable of doing, if the stakes were something he truly cared about?

No, no, no. She'd been with him that night at the ball. Granted, he'd arrived after Leo was already dead, but . . . his behavior hadn't been that of a murderer. Had it? Amelia had to be honest; she had no idea how a man would act after committing a murder. Might he promptly show his face in public, to allay suspicion? Become pale and ill when challenged, perhaps even abscond to a secluded terrace? Toss obscene amounts of money at the victim's surviving family, marry the only witness to his suspicious behavior, and make hasty arrangements to leave town?

She flung her wrist over her eyes. Oh, Lord. What had he done?

What had *she* done?

She snapped up in bed. Perhaps it was not too late. The marriage was not yet consummated. If she could just escape this house and get back to Laurent's, she could request an annulment. She rose from bed, threw a wrapper over her shoulders and opened the window. For an early summer night, it was quite cool. But if she could dress on her own, evade the servants, slip down to the street somehow, find a hack . . .

No, there was too much danger inherent in a furtive escape, and Amelia wasn't stupid. Whatever Morland had done, she doubted he posed a threat to her life. She could not say the same for the miscreants who roamed the darkened London streets.

Maybe she could simply send a note to Laurent, and he would come for her in the landau. Yes, that was it. She would bribe a footman to deliver it without His Grace's knowledge. Or if everything else failed, she could feign illness and demand a doctor's attention. It wasn't even that late yet. It was only just now—she peered at the mantel clock—

Twelve.

A latch scraped open, and she jumped in her skin.

The duke entered through the connecting door, and Amelia clapped a hand over her mouth to suppress a bubble of inane laughter. What a ninny she'd been, to expect his arrival even a minute earlier.

After all, this was the Duke of Midnight.

Even she had to admit he lived up to the romantic appellation tonight. Standing in the doorway, dressed only in a shirt and loose trousers, he regarded her with unwavering, unnerving intent. He was obviously fresh from a bath, for his hair was still wet. Dark, untamed curls caught a warm gloss from the firelight. Amelia's gaze bounced from one newly revealed piece of him to the next—his sinewy forearms, the wedge of chest exposed by the open collar of his shirt, his bare feet. He was so sinfully attractive, he could have been the Devil himself.

"Are you well?" he asked, his brow creasing. He probably hadn't expected to open the door and find his bride standing at the open window, pressing a hand to her mouth.

Amelia considered feigning illness. Clutching her belly, falling to the floor, writhing in agony until a doctor or her brother arrived to rescue her. With a rueful sigh, she decided against it. From her childhood, she'd been a very poor liar.

"I am well," she said slowly. "Only disturbed by my thoughts. And by the birds."

"The birds?" He tilted his head and looked toward the window.

"On the canopy," she clarified.

He crossed to the bed and flung himself on it, rolling

over onto his back. The mattress protested with a loud creak.

"Yes, I see," he muttered, lacing his hands behind his head and staring upward. "Disturbing indeed. Are they vultures?"

"I think they're meant to be cranes."

"Cranes?" He cocked his head for a different angle.

Amelia averted her eyes. It seemed indecent, somehow, to keep staring at him as he lay on the bed, all rangy limbs and masculine sprawl. At least, the sight took her mind to indecent places.

"Whatever they are," he said, "they'll be gone the next time we're in this house. We can't have such an affront in your bedchamber."

"I don't know that I'd call it an affront. An affront to cranes, perhaps."

"No, it's an affront to anyone with eyes. But especially to you."

"Why especially to me?"

"You're accomplished with a needle, are you not?"

"I suppose." Puzzled, Amelia folded her hands over her belly. She was indeed proud of her skill at embroidery, but how would he know that?

Ah, yes. The handkerchief. She wondered briefly what had become of it. Then she wondered briefly what had become of her wits. He could have her silly handkerchief, and welcome to it. She had to get out of this room, out of this marriage.

"For tonight," he said, rolling onto his side and propping himself on one elbow, "I'll simply put out the light."

"*No,*" she blurted out.

"No?" He drew up to a sitting position. "Then let's move by the fire. It's gone drafty in here."

Amelia watched in silence as the duke rose from the bed and shut the window. He then gathered the pillows and blankets from the bed and arranged them in a heap by the hearth. Taking up the poker, he added more coal and stirred the fire until she could feel the flames' warmth from the center of the room.

Was this the same arrogant, ill-mannered man she'd married this morning? Dukes didn't close their own windows or arrange their own pillows or build their own fires. And yet he performed these simple tasks with an unaffected, manly strength that was both reassuring and arousing. Here was that flash of humanness again. He certainly hadn't the look of a cold-blooded killer.

As the light and warmth of the fire grew, her shadowy suspicions receded, until she began to feel a bit silly for entertaining them. Had she truly been standing at the window a few minutes ago, contemplating scaling the drainpipe in her dressing gown to escape her villainous bridegroom?

Really, Amelia. This isn't a gothic novel, you know.

In her heart, she just couldn't believe this man capable of murder. But then, she knew herself to be a trusting soul—often to a fault. Nevertheless, if she wanted some assurance of his innocence, there was nothing to prevent her from asking for it.

"There," he said, clapping the coal dust from his hands and wiping them on his trousers. "No more disturbing birds. What of the disturbing thoughts? Is there something I can do to exorcise them?" He sat down before the fire and motioned for her to join him.

"Perhaps." She gingerly arranged herself atop a pillow and pulled a blanket over her lap. "Where have you been? The butler told me you'd gone riding."

"I did, for a while. I was attending to various matters in preparation for our departure. We leave tomorrow for Cambridgeshire."

"So my maid informs me." Beneath the blanket, Amelia crossed her legs. "Why so soon?" she asked, trying not to sound too disheartened. Had he even considered whether she would wish to leave London tomorrow? She wouldn't have a chance to bid her brothers farewell. And where was the fun in being a duchess, if her old friends couldn't pay calls and ply her with "Your Grace"s until they all collapsed into girlish giggling?

"My ward, Claudia, will soon return from York. I'm eager to see her again, and eager for her to make your acquaintance. Besides, I have no further business in London at the moment."

"Because you have married now?"

He shook his head. "I told you, I didn't come to London for a wife. I came for the horse."

She quietly groaned. Not that horse *again*.

"I meant to win Osiris fairly, but the contest is now stalemated. One of the tokens is in unknown hands, and neither Bellamy nor Ashworth will risk his share. There's no point to my remaining in London. I despise city living."

"I see," she muttered, trying to come to terms with her status in his life as a sort of consolation prize, barely worth making plans around. "If you did not come to London for a wife, tell me again why it is you've married me?"

He was silent for several moments. "I'd rather show you."

Her heart stuttered. What with the pillows, the toasty fire, and all this unpleasant murder business . . . she'd nearly forgotten the entire reason behind his visit to her bedchamber.

Evidently he had not.

Her blood heated as he swept her with a possessive gaze. She felt a blush rising on her neck and throat. Beneath the translucent fabric of her shift, her nipples rose to tight, self-conscious peaks. She was certain he saw them. She imagined he gave a little smile.

He reached out to grasp the hem of her shift where it peeked out from beneath her blanket. She stared at his fingers as he teased the bit of fabric, sliding the muslin back and forth over his thumb. He wasn't even touching her, but her nerves didn't seem to understand that. Her breath caught audibly, and his smile widened. She had the sense that he was toying with her, just as he toyed with that edge of her shift. Demonstrating that even his smallest actions had such power over her. The wolfish glint in his eyes said, in no uncertain terms, that before the night was out he meant to conquer her absolutely.

She gulped. And said, "Did you murder Leo Chatwick?"

Poof.

He fell back against the pillows, as if she'd kicked him in the chest.

Amelia took advantage of that increased distance to draw a deep breath. Thank heaven. Now she had him on the defensive.

"What did you just ask me?"

"Did you murder Leo Chatwick?"

The hollows of his cheeks blanched. "You would ask me this now? You seemed convinced of my innocence this morning."

"Yes. But then you left me alone all day, with only my thoughts and those ghastly cranes for company. And as I recall the scene now, I realize . . . you never truly answered the question."

"I didn't think there *was* any question. No one who knows me could give any credit to Bellamy's accusations."

"But that's my point. I don't know you, not very well."

"Well enough to consent to marry me."

She tugged on a blanket, drawing it up to her breasts

and wrapping it snugly around her body. "I consented to a betrothal. Normally those last longer than one day."

He arched a brow at her.

She repaid the sardonic gesture with an arched brow of her own. Perhaps it was unseemly of her to pursue this line of questioning. But it was true that he'd never expressly denied Mr. Bellamy's charges. Not that morning, not now. He seemed to think it beneath his effort, and Amelia didn't like being made to feel beneath his effort. A man ought to be willing to earn his wife's trust. "Where were you, before you arrived at the Bunscombes' ball that night?"

"I was here."

"Alone?"

"Yes." His brow furrowed. "The servants would support that, if asked."

"If they are loyal servants who value their employment, I'm certain they would support whatever their master said."

His jaw tightened with anger. "See here. I have just this morning given that guttersnipe Bellamy twenty thousand pounds to fund an investigation into Harcliffe's death. Why would I do such a thing if I were responsible?"

"I don't know," Amelia said. "I do know that twenty thousand pounds is a sum you toss around rather lightly. It seems to be the going rate for everything you purchase—wives, shares in horses . . . why not exoneration too?"

He stared hard at her for a long moment, those hazel eyes burning into hers. Then he rose to his feet and quit the bedchamber, slamming the door behind him.

She winced. That was it, then. Would she find herself tossed out on the pavement? Or would he be so charitable as to send for Laurent's coach?

The door crashed open again. The duke entered, carrying a small lockbox under his arm and a ring of keys in the other hand. He crouched beside her, setting the box on the floor and selecting a key from the ring. Once he had the velvet-lined cache open, he positioned the contents for her perusal.

"There," he said. "Count them."

Amelia stared down at the scattered brass discs that represented membership in the Stud Club. Each token was stamped with a horse's head on one side and, logically, a horse's tail on the other. So irreverent; so boyish; so very Leo. How could anyone think these misshapen coins worth killing for? "I don't need to count them. I know there are seven."

"You believe me, then."

"I believe you far too intelligent to place Leo's token with the others, if you did have it."

With a huff, he flung his arms wide in a posture of martyrdom. "Search the house, if you like."

"That would likely take a week. And this is but one house; you have six, and doubtless some bank vaults besides."

"You can't honestly suspect me of murder. Here I thought you were a woman of some sense."

"Then treat me like one! You've given me no opportunity to know you, no chance to judge your character for myself. All I have are my own observations, and what I see is a man with a great deal of wealth and influence, and very little respect for others' feelings, who has arranged his life around the procurement of a racehorse, heedless of the lives he ruins in the process. From a purely rational standpoint, I have more reason to suspect you than trust you."

Muttering an oath, he ran a hand through his hair. "Amelia . . ."

"Yes, Spencer?"

He blinked, obviously surprised at her use of his Christian name.

"It was in the vows," she explained. "Would you prefer I call you Morland?"

"I would prefer you call me Your Grace, if you mean to seek an annulment. Is that what you want?"

"I want some answers, that's all. I'd like to feel I know something of your character, before I allow you . . ." She blushed. ". . . certain liberties."

"I invited you to ask me questions when I proposed." His gaze was flinty, affronted. "You asked me about cats."

Amelia knotted her fingers in her lap. It was true, she'd accepted him easily enough, without questioning much of anything outside his bank accounts. She hadn't considered that her lack of curiosity might be construed as an insult. To be truthful, she hadn't believed him possessed of emotions at all.

He sat back on his heels. "Tell me what it is you'd like to know. Specifically."

"Specifically, I want to know my husband is not a murderer. But to that general purpose, I'd like to understand why this horse is worth so much to you. Why you would happily ruin my brother's hopes in pursuit of it, but you'd draw the line at killing Leo. I want to know why you became ill at the ball—and you were ill, don't try to deny it. Why did you insist we marry so quickly, so quietly? Why are you hustling me off to the country, away from all my family and friends? Was your youth truly as wild and uncivilized as they say? And on that subject, what's this mysterious history with Lord Ashworth?"

He blinked. "That's a very long list of questions."

"Yes. Precisely my point."

"Very well," he said, his voice dark and intense. "Then here are mine. I'd like to know whether that freckle on your left breast is a solitary mark, or part of a vast constellation. I'd like to know if your nipples are the same coral-pink as your lips, or a darker, tawny shade. I want to know if you've touched yourself, learned how to give yourself pleasure. And"—he leaned forward, and her heart leapt into her throat—"I have a deep, desperate need to hear the little noises you make when you come. Specifically."

Oh my. Amelia quietly reeled. The idea of a man—*this* man—entertaining such lascivious thoughts about her . . .

Her? *Her.*

He raised a brow. "Well?"

Amelia prayed her voice would not tremble as violently as her thighs. "You first."

He swore and turned away, clearly exasperated. "We reached an agreement. I'm giving you security; you're giving me an heir. Your body was part of the bargain. An inquisition into my life's history was not. I'm not in the habit of explaining myself, to anyone."

"Not even to a wife?"

"Especially not to a wife." He poked at the fire. "God damn it, Amelia. When I offered to marry you, it was because I expected things between us to be easy."

His words made her wilt inside. Yes, of course. He wanted her because she was easy. Convenient. Desperate. A woman he needn't take trouble to court or woo. A wife he wouldn't find it a chore to bed. A vessel for his seed. But did he honestly believe she should surrender her body to him, when he couldn't be bothered to secure her faith in his basic human decency? If he had the right to question her about her private activities under the coverlet on lonely nights, surely she had the right to be assured he was not a murderer.

She said, "Yes, well. No doubt you'll think me a foolish, deluded spinster for it, but I've decided I'm worth a modicum of effort."

"Effort? Do you suppose it an easy task, to arrange our wedding and departure from Town in the space of a single day?"

"For a man of your means and influence? Yes." When he did not respond, she hugged herself and added, "We seem to be at an impasse."

"An impasse," he repeated. "Allow me to be absolutely certain I understand you. You refuse to consummate the marriage until you're convinced of my innocence? Bellamy's investigation should unearth that proof soon enough. It had better, considering the funds I've provided him."

"Well, then. Is it so inconceivable to request a few days' delay?" She closed her eyes and exhaled slowly. It took no small amount of courage, to set him a hurdle like this. But if she did not assert herself now, she knew she would never have a chance. "Leo's death, our betrothal, now the wedding—it's all happened so fast. Too fast for my comfort. I see it angers you, that I cannot take you at your word. It disappoints me, too. A wife *should* be able to trust her husband implicitly. If you gave me some time, allowed me to understand you better . . ." She bit her lip. "Maybe tonight, we could simply talk."

"Talk," he echoed.

"Yes. You know, chat."

"*Chat.*" From the disdain in his voice, one would think she'd suggested they quilt, or polish silver. For heaven's sake, what was so revolutionary about the concept?

Perhaps it was just a matter of choosing the right topic. Even Michael, the quietest of the d'Orsay men, could go on about celestial navigation until the stars faded at dawn. "To begin with, why don't we talk about horses? Why is owning Osiris so important to you?"

"I don't want to talk." He relocked the box of tokens and shoved it aside. "I don't want to chat. About horses, or murder, or anything else. I want to bed my wife and then get some sleep."

Leaning forward, he prowled across the cushions that separated them until he had her body caged between his broad, muscled arms. With a swift tug, he robbed her of the blanket she clutched. His long fingers roughly encircled her thigh, branding her flesh through the thin chemise. "As your husband, I am entitled to certain rights."

"Yes." Her pulse pounded in her throat, and she swallowed hard around it. "And it would certainly tell me something of your character, if you mean to take them by force."

"The same way I 'forced' you to embrace me in Beauvale's study?"

His grip on her leg went slack, but he didn't release her. Rather, he began dragging teasing arcs with his thumb, caressing her inner thigh. Her skin burned beneath his touch.

When he spoke, his voice was firm but husky. Deeply arousing. "Do you truly want to know me, Amelia?"

She nodded.

"Then know this." Lifting his hand from her thigh, he trailed his fingertips over her collarbone, dipping to trace the neckline of her shift. "I've been waiting to kiss you all damned day."

The words alone left her breathless. And then his mouth took hers in a dizzying kiss.

She kissed him back. Imprudently. Wantonly. Foolishly. Passionately.

This was exactly the paradox that had landed her in this situation. She never would have consented to marry him, if not for this kiss. Whenever he spoke, he used that wide, sensuous mouth to dismiss and insult her. But when his lips met hers, he became a different man. Solicitous, considerate. He afforded her respect, never overpowering her with his strength. He encouraged her cooperation with gentle sweeps of his tongue.

And he made it far too easy to imagine there was something besides mere lust behind this kiss.

Don't think it, she told herself. In his own words, this was a business transaction. Her security for his heir.

But as he deepened the kiss, she sighed. Her hand went up to clasp his neck.

She teased her bare fingertips through his damp, luxuriant curls, and he rewarded her with a guttural moan that echoed and swelled in her most feminine places. Her aching breasts. The damp cleft between her legs. Her heart.

He could claim them all, far too easily. She knew herself too well to believe otherwise. Already her blood pounded with lust for him, with the bone-jarring force of an army marching out to war. With the slightest encouragement, her affection would no doubt traipse blithely behind, like the village idiot. As the only woman in a family of five brothers, unreasoned devotion to undeserving men came all too naturally to her.

The enormity of the day's events struck home with sudden force. She'd married a virtual stranger. Given him license to possess her body, but taken no precautions to safeguard her soul. With a twenty-seven-hour betrothal, she simply hadn't had time to prepare. To draw the boundaries that would protect her in this cold, impersonal bargain they'd struck. *Within these borders lies the essential Amelia: You may come this far, and no further.*

"Amelia." He breathed her name against her ear. "I must have you."

She began to tremble, and a whimper caught in the back of her throat.

The sound gave him a start. He pulled away and stared hard at the slope of her shoulder, where her flesh quivered under his touch. "You are truly frightened."

"Yes," she said honestly. "You frighten me."

"Damn it, I didn't kill anyone. You've no reason to fear me."

"Oh, I do. I have every reason." And none of those reasons had a whit to do with Leo's death. Her fears were originated right here, in the heat between them and the veiled emotion in his eyes. Could she dare put them into words?

I'm afraid of imagining you feel more for me than you do. Afraid of wanting too much, needing you more than you'll ever have a use for me. I'm terrified that there's more to you than I suspected, but you'll never let me see it all. That I'll give you everything I have, and you won't even offer a few answers in return. And I need some time—just a little time—to learn how to offer you my body without risking my foolish, fragile heart.

"Leo's token," she whispered. "When it's found, I'll know you're blameless."

His eyes hardened as he withdrew his hand. "Very well. While Leo's killers walk free, I'll not come to you. But once that token is recovered and I am proved innocent, there will be no further delay. And when I do take you, I will have all of you. Touch all of you. Taste all of you. You'll deny me nothing."

She stared up at him, paralyzed with longing and fear.

"Say yes, Amelia."

"Yes," she managed. What a devil's bargain she'd just sealed.

He rose to his feet and made to leave the bedchamber. Amelia fell back against the pillows and pressed her thighs together, attempting to ease the sweet, maddening ache in her womb.

At the door, he stopped. "And Amelia? Even though I've pledged not to come to you, there's nothing to keep you from coming to me." With one last burning glance, he reached for the door handle. "The door's unlocked, if there's anything you need."

Chapter Nine

Juno's hooves danced under him as Spencer eased into the saddle. He exchanged a nod with his outrider. The groom had been walking her for most of the morning, but now the mare had reached the end of her patience. As had he. A good, hard ride was what they both needed. They'd outpace the carriages for this last leg of the day's travel and he'd see about procuring rooms at the inn.

At Juno's impatient whicker, he nudged the mare into a canter. As the horse found her pace, a fresh breeze whipped through his hair—a refreshing burst of coolness on this warm afternoon. He ought to have been taking in the pleasant countryside, Spencer supposed, but instead all he saw was Amelia, as she'd appeared last night. The soft gold of her unbound hair, burnished by firelight. The enticing pink curves of her flesh, covered by the sheerest white muslin.

Her clear blue eyes, filled with fear.

Devil take it. That fear had come as a stab to the heart. Her courage and sensible nature were what attracted him to her in the first place. From her teasing during that that cursed waltz, to the kiss she'd demanded before accepting his proposal—she infuriated, intrigued, and aroused him, all because she refused to be intimidated. Just as she'd said that morning after Leo's death, in the carriage: When they were alone, they were just a woman and a man.

Not anymore, evidently.

Now, thanks to the esteemed membership of the Stud Club, they were a woman and an alleged murderer. This morning ought to have found him a well-satisfied bridegroom, and instead he was frustrated in every way. All because Julian Bellamy had an irrational hatred of aristocrats, Rhys St. Maur had been a hot-tempered youth, and Leo Chatwick had had the poor sense to go walking in Whitechapel alone at night. Now Amelia feared him.

And then—of all the addled feminine notions—to remedy the problem, she'd suggested they sit up all night and *chat*. She wished to submit him to her own version of the Spanish Inquisition, examine his sins, his failings, his family history and moral principles.

Good God. He couldn't imagine a worse strategy for earning her trust. How, precisely, would that interview go?

Very well, Amelia. I'll answer your questions. Yes, I spent a wild youth in Lower Canada, disappearing into the wilderness for weeks at a time with people you'd consider heathen savages, causing my excellent father no end of grief. Yes, during my first year in England, I nearly pummeled Rhys St. Maur to death at Eton. Yes, I ruined your brother's fortunes in pursuit of a horse, for reasons you will find inexplicable and unforgivable. There, now. Can't you see I'm not a villain?

Oh, that would go over splendidly.

And if she thought he would *ever* discuss his true reasons for abducting her from that ballroom . . . well, she would wait in vain. If there was one indisputable advantage to being a duke, it was never having to explain himself to anyone.

That didn't mean they couldn't know one another. Ever since their waltz, he'd been seized by an intense desire to know everything about Amelia Claire d'Orsay. Hell, he'd married her in part to assuage it. He just didn't see why words must be involved. He wanted to learn his new wife from the inside out, starting with the sweet cleft of her womanhood and working his way to her delicate fingers, which he'd discovered last night to be capped with neat round calluses from needlework.

If they were to become acquainted, Spencer could think of no more logical beginning than to know one another in the biblical sense, as God and Nature intended.

Fortunately, Spencer had considerable experience winning over wary creatures, undoing the damage wrought by other men. It had been nearly two decades since he'd broken his first mustang to halter in Canada, and at his stud farm he'd gentled countless horses since—most notably Juno, the mare carrying him now. The trick of it was knowing when to walk away. He'd give a fearful horse a few minutes' tenderness—stroke her behind the ears, murmur encouragement, give her a reassuring pat on the withers. Nothing too bold. Just enough attention to keep her wanting more. The moment the horse began to relax and enjoy his touch, Spencer would walk away. The next time he entered the enclosure, the once-frightened horse would approach him, eager and unafraid. The technique never failed.

Of course, he'd never plied it on a woman before. He'd never needed to. He knew some men took perverse excitement in conquering a reluctant lover, but he wasn't one of them. He liked his bed partners to be just that—partners. Willing, engaged, aware of themselves. He'd wanted Amelia because she not only possessed the virtue and lineage he required in a wife, she met his ideals for a lover. When he kissed her, she responded with an instinctive, inventive passion that made his bones weak.

Until those damned accusations planted doubt in her mind, and she'd trembled. Not with pleasure, but with fear. Oh, he could have persuaded her into consummation if he'd wished. But she would have despised him for it this morning, and he wouldn't have liked himself much, either.

He would coax her out again. It might take a few days—time he really didn't want to bide—but he was a man of self-discipline. With cards, horses, negotiation . . . He knew how to be patient when the situation required it, and how to elicit the desired response. Before a week was out, his wife would come willingly, eagerly to his bed.

The key was all in knowing when to walk away.

Amelia surveyed the rooms Spencer had procured. If indeed these accommodations truly counted as "rooms." The inn's best suite consisted of a small bedchamber and an even smaller antechamber. The antechamber was furnished with a table and two chairs, plus a sleeping cot, likely intended for servants. Yet both her and Spencer's trunks had been carried up to the suite, so she assumed he meant to join her.

What he meant to do then, she was afraid to imagine.

One of the inn's serving girls had brought up a dinner tray. After a day of rough coach travel, the mere smell of stewed beef had Amelia's stomach roiling. She managed to choke down a bit of bread and tea. Her next thought was to undress quickly and slip into bed before the duke even returned. Surely he wouldn't disturb her if she was already asleep. Just to be safe, she'd barricade the connecting door with her trunks.

Before she could act on the plan, however, the door opened with a rude creak. In came the duke. He had to fold nearly double to avoid hitting his head on the doorjamb, and with the addition of his imposing presence, the "rooms" shrank further.

A curt nod was his only greeting. And, as he'd caught her with a mouthful of tea, her reply was an audible gulp.

Lord, he was so handsome. She didn't understand it, but somehow she forgot, when they were apart, what a fine-looking man he was. And every time she reencountered him, the simple fact of his masculine beauty startled her again with fresh, sudden force.

This man is my *husband*.

This man is *my* husband.

Surely one of these days the novelty would fade. Or at least she would learn to adjust more quickly, so each time they crossed paths in the corridor, she wouldn't pull up short and simply stand there, open-mouthed and struck stupid.

Rather as she was doing now.

He removed his coat, unfastened his cuffs, turned up his sleeves, and lathered his hands at the small washstand. As he rinsed them, he asked, "You've eaten?"

"As much as I care to. And you?"

He nodded. "Downstairs."

After carefully folding his coat and laying it across a trunk, he worked loose his cravat. Next he sat in one of the chairs and began on his boots. He really was remarkably self-sufficient, for a man of his rank. Amelia supposed he must not have been raised with a valet.

"You needn't sit with me, if you'd rather be downstairs," she said nervously. Didn't men prefer to be down in the tavern, drinking and carousing?

He gave her a disbelieving look. "You think I'd leave you alone in a public inn? Not a chance. This is one of the better establishments, but still . . ." He shook his head. "At any rate, crowded alehouses really aren't my idea of a pleasant evening."

"Why have we stopped at an inn at all? Cambridgeshire isn't so very far. Couldn't we have pushed through to your estate?"

"Breaking the journey sets a kinder pace for the horses."

Well, to be sure, she thought to herself bitterly. *Heaven forfend we place human convenience ahead of the horses' comfort.*

He began unbuttoning his waistcoat. Just how far did he intend to disrobe, right in front of her?

She rose from her chair. "Well, I'm rather fatigued. I think I'll retire early."

To her dismay, he also stood. "Excellent idea."

Surely he didn't mean to go to sleep *with* her. Hadn't he promised to leave her be? "On second thought, I'm not sleepy just yet. I believe I'll work on my embroidery."

She went to the smallest of her trunks and unbuckled the straps, knowing her needlework basket to be at the top. She imagined she felt him ogling her bottom as she bent at the waist to retrieve it, and she straightened so quickly, all the blood rushed from her head.

She stumbled, and he grasped her by the elbow to steady her. His firm, arousing touch was of no benefit as she struggled to collect her wits. Curse this wretched infatuation that turned her into a perfect simpleton whenever she came within breathing distance of his warm, male scent. It made her want to fall straight into his arms, never mind if he was a murderer or the very Devil himself.

She was used to being around strong, protective men—her brothers—and used to being embraced and comforted by them. Now she was miles away from all of them: homesick and weary, and direly in need of a hug. It occurred to her that the duke was her only potential source of strong, engulfing masculine embraces in the vicinity, and that thought made her sad indeed. For while she was tolerably certain he'd bed her tonight if she gave him the slightest encouragement, she knew she'd never be able to ask him for a hug.

She cringed to imagine his response, if she did. He probably didn't even know how to give one.

He released her as she sank back into her chair. Drawing closer to the light, she busied herself unpacking linen, thread, and scissors. "What is your usual habit in the evenings, Your Grace? Do you keep country hours?"

"I keep my own hours, wherever I am. I typically retire around midnight."

The word "midnight" sent a shiver through her. "And until then?"

"Until then?" His eyes caught hers, a glint of wry humor in their dark, entrancing depths. "You mean, in the absence of other nighttime activities?" He paused, giving her mind ample time to fill with other, very nocturnal activities. "When I'm not plotting my next vile act of treachery?"

He leaned forward. Heat prickled along her skin.

Finally, he said in a deep, suggestive voice, "I read."

She stared at him, suddenly unable to speak.

"Books," he added, as if for clarification.

"Oh," she replied, as if she were stupid enough to need that clarification.

He opened a small valise, revealing it to be full to brimming with volumes of all sizes, in a variety of bindings. The sight caused a swift, surprising pang in her chest.

"My," she remarked. "You must be a great reader."

"Whenever I'm in London, I take the opportunity to add to my personal library." He removed a few books, turning them over in his hands to read the bindings. "I didn't attend university, you see. Extensive reading has been my only education."

"Didn't you want to go to university?"

"Not especially. Even if I had, my uncle thought it best not to send me."

"Because of what happened at Eton? When you were sent down for the brawl with Lord Ashworth?" She was guessing, but it seemed the logical explanation for both the rumors she'd heard and the strange tension she'd observed between the men.

He gave her a long, pointed look. Well, there was one of her questions answered.

"Because," he said coolly, selecting a book and packing the others away, "my uncle's health was already failing, and I was his heir. Estate management was a more pressing topic of study than Latin or mathematics. I continued my studies independently."

"Ah. Yes, it's like that for many of us."

His brow wrinkled in confusion.

"Oh, I didn't mean *us*, as in you and me." Peering at her needle, she threaded the eye with a strand of blue floss. "I meant, it's like that for many of *us*." She patted a hand to her breast. "Women. We don't attend university, either, but many of us still seek to improve our minds through books."

Clearly the duke had no idea how to receive that comparison. Frowning a little, he sat down with his book. Amelia smiled at her stitches, rather pleased with herself.

"What are you reading?" she asked, feeling emboldened and just a bit coquettish.

He held up the book for her inspection.

"Not *Waverley*? I thought you called yourself a great reader. You must be the last person in England to read that book."

"I'm not. I've read it already, more than once." He riffled the pages. "I don't have the concentration for philosophy or German this evening."

Amelia fell momentarily silent to focus on the evenness of her stitches. At length she said, "*Waverley*. I'll admit, I'm surprised to hear it's a favorite of yours."

"I can't imagine why. As you noted, it's a very popular book."

"Well, yes." She gave him a coy glance. "But it's a romance."

"It is not." He held the green-covered book at arm's length and stared at it, as though she'd said, *But it's a pineapple*. "It's a historical novel about the Scottish uprising. There are battles."

"There's a love triangle."

He made an offended huff. "Listen, am I permitted to read the thing in peace, or not?"

Suppressing a laugh, she forced herself to be quiet and sew. Soon she lost herself in her work—in the precise, familiar rhythm of stitches, the careful selection of colored threads. The room went quiet, save for the low crackle of the fire and the occasional sound of a page being turned. As she worked, her sleepiness increased. When she sensed her stitches becoming less and less even, she knotted off one final strand of blue and cut it free before turning the whole square face-up and surveying her work.

"How did you accomplish that?" Spencer asked, reaching over her arm to indicate the rightmost section of the cloth.

Startled by his sudden nearness, Amelia jumped in her chair. When had he moved his chair beside hers? How long had he been looking over her shoulder?

"Right there," he said, pointing to the little brook she'd stitched tumbling through a glen. "It truly looks like water. How did you accomplish it?"

"Oh, that." A hint of pride seeped into her voice. She *was* rather happy with that bit. "It's very thin strips of ribbon in different shades of blue, worsted with silver thread. I twist the needle as I sew, and in that way each stitch catches the light in a different way. As sunlight might dance on a rippling stream."

He said nothing. Likely he hadn't been *that* interested, to warrant a needlework lesson. Well, he had asked.

The longer he stared silently over her shoulder, however, the more self-conscious she grew. "I was going to make it into a little settee cushion. Or perhaps use it as the center of a chair cover." She turned it this way and that in her hands, tilting her head to examine the piece from different angles. Perhaps she ought to frame it in strips of velvet, and use it for a larger pillow, or—

"A cushion?" he said abruptly, pronouncing the word as though it were caustic on his tongue. "What an abhorrent idea."

Amelia blinked. *Abhorrent?* "Wh-Why?" she stammered, taken aback. "I'll keep it in my own room, if you don't care for it. You needn't see it."

"Absolutely not. That"—he pointed at her needlework—"is never adorning a chair or settee in my house."

"But—"

"Give it here."

Before she could protest, he snatched the embroidered square from her hands, opened his valise again, and thrust the fabric inside before slamming it shut with a decisive motion. The nerve of the man! Rather than argue, Amelia hastily packed away the remainder of her needles and thread, worried His Grace might suddenly decide to cast the entire sewing kit into the fireplace. She could always retrieve the embroidery later. She hoped.

"Enough reading and needlework. We'll play cards," he said, drawing out a deck of cards and sitting down. "Piquet." He split the deck and began to shuffle the cards effortlessly. He moved so rapidly, fingers and cards were nothing but a colorful blur. The effect was entrancing, and subtly erotic.

He noticed her staring. One dark eyebrow rose in question.

"You're quite adept at that."

He shrugged. "I'm good with my hands."

He was indeed good with his hands. But Amelia knew that already. She remembered with near-painful clarity the exquisite pang of yearning she'd experienced when he'd pulled them free of his gloves that day in Laurent's study. She remembered the way those strong fingers had unpinned her hair, then tilted her face to receive his kiss. And some moments later, clasped her bottom, bringing her body flush against his . . .

Thwack. He rapped the deck against the table to square the edges, jolting her from her reverie.

"Perhaps just one hand," she said.

"You do know piquet?" he asked, beginning to deal.

"Yes, of course. Though I cannot claim to be an expert."

"I hope not. If you were, you should have taught your brother better strategy."

Amelia's anger spiked at the mention of Jack and his gaming debt, chasing away any lingering fatigue. "I thought it was brag you played."

"It was, the night he lost the four hundred." He gathered his cards.

She likewise retrieved the pile of cards in front of her and began sorting them in her hand. "So it was not just the once, then? You played together several times?"

"I would not say several. On a few separate occasions." He selected four cards from his hand and discarded them.

She exchanged three of hers. He immediately declared his point to be forty-one, signaling he held one of the strongest hands possible in piquet.

"Drat," she muttered.

"I see you don't like to lose any more than your brother does."

"No one likes to lose."

When it came to games and sport, Amelia did have a competitive streak. Losing always put her in a foul temper. Therefore, her temper grew increasingly short as the hand progressed, for Spencer, after building an insurmountable lead in the reckoning of points, went on to take nearly every trick. But it wasn't simply losing the hand of cards that had her frustrated. No, it was everything else she'd lost thanks to this man. If not for the duke's equine obsession and luck with cards, at this moment she could have been packing her belongings for a summer at Briarbank. And Jack would have been coming with her.

Once her defeat was confirmed—confirmed, and then underscored—Amelia quietly gathered the cards and began to shuffle them anew.

"I thought you only wanted to play one hand," he said dryly.

She spared him no word—just a brief, sharp look. As if her pride would allow her to walk away after that drubbing she'd just been handed.

"You should have discarded the knave of hearts," he told her as she dealt. "Don't aim to collect sets, aim to win the tricks."

Discard the knave, indeed.

But though she hated taking his advice, she did so. Once again, she had two knaves in her hand; this time she discarded both and reaped a king in return. Spencer still won the game, to her chagrin, but by a much narrower margin.

"Better," he said, as he gathered the cards for his deal. "But next time, lead with your ace."

And so it went, over several hands. She gained on him slowly, coming closer and closer to victory—but each time still falling short. After each hand, he offered her a point of strategy, which she begrudgingly incorporated into her own play. At last, on one of his turns as dealer Amelia reaped a very lucky hand of cards, including two aces and a septième. Falling silent to marshal all her powers of concentration, she discarded strategically, played her cards in the most advantageous sequence, caught a stroke of luck when he had no red king . . . and won.

"I won," she said, staring with disbelief at the played-out cards on the table.

"You did. This once."

She smiled. "Watch me do it again." She reached out to gather the cards for her deal, but he put out a hand and trapped hers against the table.

"Care to make it interesting?"

His hand was heavy atop hers, and warm. Amelia's heart began to beat a little faster. "Do you mean a wager?"

He nodded.

"Four hundred pounds," she said impulsively. If she could win back Jack's debt, her brother would not have to avoid Spencer any longer. Perhaps he could even come to Braxton Hall for an extended, wholesome country holiday, away from London and his wastrel friends.

"Very well. If you win, I will pay you four hundred pounds." He released her hand. "And if I win, you will come sit on my lap and lower your bodice."

Oh dear. Her hands curled into tight fists—one still on the table, the other in her lap. "I . . . I beg your pardon?"

"You heard me. If I win this hand, you must come sit on my lap, lower your bodice, and expose your breasts to me."

"And then what will you do?"

One of his dark brows lifted in a clear signal of carnal intent. "Whatever I wish."

Amelia's mind whirled. Dare she take his wager? The odds were against her. He was clearly the superior player, despite her gains of the last hour and this one paltry victory. But she wanted so badly to clear Jack's debts on her own.

Even more than that, she wanted to best Spencer at his own game and watch that superior look slide straight off his smooth-shaven face.

But another part of her—a heated, yearning, deeply feminine part of her—perversely wanted to lose. To sit on his lap and strip this dress from her body and feel those strong, sculpted hands cup her bared breasts. And that ought to have been the strongest argument for getting up and leaving the table that instant.

"You will remain clothed?" she asked. She was an utter fool.

"But of course."

"There must be a time limit."

He nodded his agreement. "A quarter hour."

"Five minutes."

"Ten." He removed a timepiece from his waistcoat pocket and laid it on the table.

Her fists uncurled, and she ran one damp palm over her skirts before reaching for the cards. "Agreed."

With trembling fingers, Amelia began to gather the cards. The duke's small discard pile lay off to one side, with the result that she reached for it last and added it to the bottom of the pile. As she turned the deck on its side to divide it for shuffling, the card she saw gave her a violent start.

The ace of spades.

Quickly masking her surprise, she split the deck and shuffled with energy. The duke had discarded the ace of spades. It made no sense. No one discarded an ace in piquet. There was only one way to account for such a thing.

He'd sabotaged himself and allowed her to win. She'd thought herself gaining on him in skill, improving to his level. But in reality, he'd been in control of their match since the very beginning, manipulating the results. And now . . .

She looked up, and his intent, desirous gaze trapped hers.

Now she'd played right into his hands.

With an odd sensation in her chest, equal parts dread and anticipation, Amelia dealt the cards. She played them as best she knew how. And she lost. Badly.

She never had a chance.

"A stroke of luck," he said. In a matter of seconds, he had the cards stowed and the table shoved aside. Then he patted his knee meaningfully. It was uncomfortably close to the gesture one might use to call a dog.

She needn't obey it. He could make no claim on her honor, when he'd secured the wager through trickery.

Oh, but she wanted . . .

She *wanted*.

"Ten minutes," he said. "No more. I'm a man of my word, remember? Come here, then." He extended a hand to her, in almost a gallant gesture.

And Amelia accepted. She'd wanted to learn how to enjoy physical passion without risking her heart. Wasn't this the perfect opportunity? It was only ten minutes.

She rose from her chair and crossed the short distance to his seat before turning sideways and perching awkwardly on his knees.

"Not like that," he said impatiently. Grasping her by the hips, he lifted her and half-stood, repositioning them both as he sat back down.

Amelia discovered, with some horror, that she was

now straddling his lap. The thick folds of her skirts bunched up between them.

"Much better," he said, still cupping her hips in his big, strong hands. He raised his eyebrows in expectation. "You remember the penalty. Lower your bodice."

"On my own? But my buttons . . ."

"I daresay you can manage."

Drat him, he was right. A lady didn't grow up in genteel d'Orsay poverty without learning the trick of undoing her own buttons. She slowly raised her arms and folded them at the elbows, reaching behind her head for the topmost button of her gown, positioned at the base of her neck.

Clutching her hips tighter, he released a soft groan.

It took just a brief glance downward to learn the reason for it. With her arms raised like this, the bodice was straining at the seams. At the same time, the position thrust her breasts upward, with the combined result that twin scoops of flesh threatened to overflow her neckline.

His eyes fixed on the exposed tops of her breasts, and Amelia felt unspeakably tawdry. Her fingers trembled as she released the first button. Then another and another still. By the time she'd reached the fourth, her bosom was rapidly lifting and falling with her nervous breaths, and the duke's breathing had taken on an audible rasp. She paused, unable to reach the fifth button.

"More," he whispered roughly. Desire was plain in his voice. "Go on."

Carefully, she lowered her arms and bent them behind her back, flexing her shoulder blades together and stretching her fingers toward the valley between them. His breath caught again. If the previous posture had put her breasts on display, this position all but served them up. His face hovered inches from her brimming cleavage as she undid the fifth button, then the sixth. Although her neckline gaped, her tightly laced stays kept her breasts pert and round.

Seven now. Then eight.

How many buttons were there? Ten? Twelve? Twenty wouldn't be enough. She loved the way he was looking at her, and the power she wielded over him as she eased each button loose. She didn't feel tawdry anymore. She felt erotic and sensual and wanton . . . and completely not herself, for those were certainly not words that applied to Amelia d'Orsay.

But she wasn't Amelia d'Orsay any longer, was she? She was Amelia Dumarque, the Duchess of Morland.

She was this man's wife.

As her fingers neared the midpoint of her back, the bodice began to fall away from her body. His pupils widened with anticipation.

With a little roll of her shoulder, she dislodged one sleeve from its tenuous position on her arm. The fabric slid downward, taking half of her bodice with it. She pulled that arm free, and then easily bared the other. A chemise and stays still covered her torso, but she'd never felt so exquisitely naked. Uncertain what else to do with them, she allowed her hands to dangle at her sides.

With possessive leisure, his eyes roamed every curve of her body. Perspiration beaded in the valley between her breasts. The room was thick with leftover afternoon heat, and even if it weren't—his bold appraisal was heating her from the inside out. No man had ever looked at her this way. Oh, she'd been ogled by Mr. Poste, and by a fair number of other men since. When framed by the right neckline, her bosom never failed to draw men's notice. Unfortunately, none of her other attributes held their attention beyond that brief, greedy glance.

The duke's gaze was different, though. Not leering,

but appreciative. Speculative. There was more than idle admiration going on behind those eyes. There was thoughtful planning and intelligent strategy. His eyes drew sweeping arcs over the thin gauze of her shift, as though he were mapping out each possible approach.

What a novel sensation, to be the object of strategy. What would it be like, to be pursued by this man with just a fraction of the determination and resources he devoted to pursuing that wretched stallion? Heat swirled through her at the idea, and she felt herself melting between her legs.

"God." He tightened his grip on her waist and hauled her forward, bunching her skirts higher between them and bringing her pelvis in sudden, startling contact with his.

A little gasp escaped her. Obviously men did not melt between the legs. No, they grew hugely, demandingly hard. In response, her own body softened further.

"Your stays," he choked out. "Unlace them."

Breathless, she shook her head. "Only the bodice. That was the wager."

Groaning, he released her hips. She closed her eyes, suddenly afraid. Not afraid she'd angered him, but afraid this interlude would end.

A touch, whisper-soft, grazed her hand where it dangled at her side. Soon the sensation echoed on the other hand—not only matched, but multiplied. He swept light caresses over the backs of her hands, her sensitive palms, and up the delicate skin of her wrists. Amelia wanted to moan. His touch was so sweet, so unbearably sweet.

Slowly, gently, with excruciating care, his fingers climbed her arms, lingering in the tender hollows of her elbows and skimming over the rounded flesh of her upper arms. He caressed the exposed planes of her upper back, and she shivered with pleasure as his fingertips traveled up her spine and traced the sweeping curve of her collarbone. He dipped a single finger into the tender valley of her cleavage, then just as quickly drew it out.

She wished she'd obeyed him and unlaced her stays, so labored was her breathing now. She was faint with longing. Her eyelids trembled, even though she kept them tightly closed.

She felt him shifting, closing the gap between them. His breath warmed the curve of her neck. And then his lips pressed against her pulse.

Her eyes flew open. If he was kissing her neck, he couldn't meet her gaze . . . and in that case, she wanted to see everything. As he lightly nibbled the underside of her jaw, she studied the peeling wallpaper with ridiculous concentration. *This is real,* she told herself. *The Duke of Morland is tasting my neck as though it were the most luscious, succulent fruit this side of Eden's gates, and this is all real. There is the wallpaper to prove it.*

Grasping her by the shoulders, he gave her a necklace of kisses—kisses that grew increasingly hungry and fierce. By the time he reached the other side of her neck, he grazed her flesh with his teeth.

And then he really did bite her. Gently, but still she cried out in surprise.

"Hush," he soothed, licking at her ear. "I've been wanting to do that ever since that damnable waltz." Before she could even conceive of a reply, he added, "This, too."

His hands slid around to claim her breasts. Greedily, possessively. He kneaded and shaped them, his fingers molding around the soft cups of her stays. Then, resting his forehead to her shoulder and releasing a lustful sigh, he burrowed his long fingers under the edge of her chemise, curved them under the swells of her breasts, and lifted. Her breasts sprang free with a nearly audible pop.

"God, yes." He reclined, holding them up for his examination. Her nipples contracted to tight peaks. Amelia felt like closing her eyes again, but she just couldn't.

His finger covered the small freckle on the inner curve of her left breast. "Just the one," he said softly. He trailed the same finger down, drawing a wide circle around the circumference of her areola. "And tawny, like spice."

This is real. The Duke of Morland is eyeing my naked bosom with raw, unmitigated lust, and there are his dark, unwavering eyes to prove it.

If she required any further evidence of his desire, it pulsed hotly against her feminine core. Bright pleasure sparked through her. Then his thumb brushed her hardened nipple, and she thought she would explode.

Pushing her breasts together, he leaned forward and buried his face in them, nuzzling either side in turn and swiping teasing licks over her breastbone. Then he pulled back and drew her left nipple into his mouth.

She couldn't hold it in a moment longer. She moaned. But fortunately, so did he, so it wasn't quite so embarrassing.

Keening low through her teeth, she brought one hand to the back of his head, teasing her fingers through his soft, curling hair as he sucked and licked. He transferred his attentions to her other breast, and the sensations began anew—so sharp and acute at first, then sweet and dark and deep. Without even thinking what she did, she rocked her hips against his, grinding against the hard ridge of his arousal.

"Yes," he said, breaking away from her breast and kissing his way back up her neck. His hands slid to her hips, and he rocked her against him again. And again. Stoking her pleasure to a near-unbearable plateau.

"Yes." He panted against her neck. "This is how I wanted you, that morning in the carriage. Just. Like. This."

Truly? That morning they'd quarreled in the carriage, he'd imagined them doing *this*? He dragged her over his hard length again, sending a fresh surge of pleasure through her.

Her lips parted, and his name rushed out with her breath. A helpless plea for mercy, but he seemed to take it as encouragement.

"Amelia." He clutched her hips tighter, nuzzled her ear. "God, we'll be good together. I've known it from the first."

No, no. Such dangerous words. She tried to block them out, but her shields faltered, and she let herself imagine, for just a moment, there was more than lust behind them. In her ears, his words echoed and altered, warping around all her girlhood fantasies and romantic dreams. *We'll be good together. I've known it from the first. I've known you from the first. Oh God, Amelia. I've loved you from the first.* The foolish, useless craving for affection throbbed in her blood, made her hot between the legs. And her heart . . .

She didn't think her heart could bear it if he spoke again, so she kissed him, out of sheer self-preservation. Stupid, stupid mistake. The emotions unleashed in that rough press of mouth against mouth . . . oh, they were a thousand times worse. His taste was too familiar now. He explored her mouth so thoroughly. It was all so unbearably intimate, it made her ache deep inside. She broke the kiss, intending to break away entirely.

But then he had his hands on her breasts again, and his mouth captured her nipple . . . Pleasure swamped her last hold on resistance. She was lost. Her hips moved of their own accord, rocking against his in a steady rhythm.

Hot sensation gathered between her thighs, spreading sweetly through her limbs. And still she craved more. She'd never imagined she could achieve pleasure this easily—still mostly clothed, her body not yet attuned to his rough, masculine touch. But, oh, she was close. So close. That shimmering pinnacle of bliss hovered just beyond her reach, but she was striving toward it. Climbing higher . . . higher . . .

Thud.

She fell straight back to earth.

He lifted her by the waist, abruptly breaking the contact between their loins. "Enough," he rasped.

Enough? Amelia consulted her body. No. No, that was most definitely *not* enough.

Pushing her farther away, he straightened in the chair. "Ten minutes." Red-faced, he nodded at his watch. "They're over. The wager is satisfied."

Was he mad? Perhaps ten minutes were up, but Amelia wasn't nearly satisfied. And neither was he, from the looks of the straining bulge in his trousers.

Nevertheless, he rose from the chair and half-carried her into the bedchamber, abruptly releasing her. His hasty retreat left several paces' distance—and the connecting door—between them. "Go to bed, Amelia."

Reeling, she grasped the bedpost for support. Her whole body felt like blancmange, soft and quivering. And she ached . . . oh, how she ached for completion. Surely he knew how aroused she'd become, from the way she'd wantonly ridden him. Goodness, from the *sounds* she'd made. He conquered any resistance with his seductive touch and that hot, wicked mouth. Caught in that haze of lust, she would have surrendered her virtue easily.

"We agreed on ten minutes," he said, turning away to make discreet adjustments to his trouser fall. "And I gave you my word."

Was she to believe he was being honorable? From the moment he'd drawn out that pack of cards, he'd drawn her straight into his clutches. Literally. And now he was walking away, leaving her a frustrated, trembling mass of thwarted desire and unfulfilled need.

"You don't need help with your laces?" he asked.

She numbly shook her head.

"Good night, then." He started to pull shut the connecting door, then paused to give her an enigmatic look. "I'm just here, if there's anything you need."

Chapter Ten

Alone in the antechamber, Spencer unscrewed the top of his flask with trembling fingers. He tossed back a quick, scorching swallow. Then another.

His movements jerky and agitated, he stripped himself of his waistcoat. He flung open a trunk, pulling out a set of clean linens and snapping them open to cover the narrow cot. As if he'd be able to sleep.

He strode to the table to light a fresh candle. When his fingers refused to work the flint properly, he cast the damn thing away. Swearing quietly into the darkened room, he tugged at the buttons of his breeches placket, untucked his shirt, and stopped postponing the inevitable. Bracing one hand on the table, he freed his aching erection with the other. He was still hard as a pike, and primed for release.

Oh, God.

Her breasts. Her hips. Her mouth on his. Her softness and heat. Her little mewls of pleasure. The sound of his name from her lips. The taste of her skin. Her breasts again, because they bore repeating. And those nipples . . . God, she had the most pert, luscious nipples he had ever—*ever*—laid eyes or thumbs or lips upon. And the look on her face, when he'd carried her to the bedroom. Bewildered, mussed. Half-naked and fully aroused. She was there, right now, in the bed. He could join her. He could have her under him. Surrounding him. Gripping him tight. Panting and writhing and—

Sweet. Holy. Merciful . . .

Behind his eyelids, the world went searing bright. Gritting his teeth against an involuntary cry, he came in a frenzy of brisk, tight-fisted strokes, spurting jet after jet into a loose fold of his shirt. His breath grated in and out of his chest as he clutched the table's edge for support.

After a minute, he straightened, pulled the soiled shirt over his head and cast it aside, then flopped onto the cot to savor the numb, joint-loosening sensation of release.

Release, yes. Relief, no. For she was still fewer than six paces away, and he could be hard for her again in a matter of three minutes. Perhaps two. *Don't ponder it overmuch*, a throb in his groin warned.

The evening really had not gone as planned. Well, it had gone as planned, up to a point. The cards, the wager, her breasts in his hands . . . all these he'd counted upon. He'd only meant to give her a bit of skillful stroking. Not too much. Just enough to loosen the tension in her body and offer a taste of the pleasure they could share. Just enough to prove he could be trusted, and keep her wanting more.

Well. This was clearly a different endeavor from horse-breaking.

In his best imaginings, he wouldn't have guessed that Amelia would respond to him so passionately. He couldn't have dreamed how strongly he'd respond to *her*. As a younger man, Spencer would have counted it with great pride, the fact that he'd taken an inexperienced lover from clothed and uncertain to half-naked and teetering on the verge of climax—all in under ten minutes. But the triumph rang a bit hollow tonight, as he realized his victory came with a forfeit.

He was left wanting more, too.

Not just more pleasure, more heat, more skin . . . although he did want all those things, and desperately . . . but more *Amelia*. He wanted to sit at the table and watch her worry that plump lower lip with her teeth as she embroidered. He wanted her to tease him for his reading choices. Most of all, he wanted to catch her staring at him, when she thought he wasn't looking.

And he wanted the look in her eyes to be fondness, not fear.

He stared hard at the connecting door, as though he could swing the warped panel on its rusted hinges by sheer force of will.

Come to me, Amelia. You crossed a ballroom to confront me while hundreds looked on. Open that door tonight.

But when dawn came, he awoke alone.

God had a very cruel sense of humor.

Here Amelia was, the newly minted Duchess of Morland, arriving at Braxton Hall in all its early summer splendor. Through the square carriage window, she spied endless acres of rich farmland dotted with neat barns and cottages, then a pleasing expanse of rolling green parklands, and now, as they neared the Hall, a wall of towering, manicured hedges that must contain equally well-maintained gardens. Of this prestigious, lovely, verdant estate she was now mistress.

And she was a shambles.

Amelia had never traveled well. The rolling motion of a carriage always nauseated her, and she felt the effects even more strongly in warm weather. Their first day of travel hadn't been too distressing, but the farther they went from London, the worse the roads became. Late spring rains had left this particular dirt lane rutted and uneven, so that she had not only rolling to contend with, but violent jouncing as well. She ached all over, her muscles stiff from long hours of bracing herself on the seat, and her head throbbing with a persistent, dull pain. Her gown—a sensible chocolate-brown traveling habit two years past its fitting—was wrinkled and coated with a fine layer of dust.

She was the sorriest-looking duchess to ever live, she was sure of it.

As they turned the corner onto a smoother drive, Amelia glimpsed the Hall's brick-and-limestone façade in the distance. She hastily patted her face and smoothed stray wisps of hair, anxious to make herself presentable before facing Spencer again.

Dear Lord, how *would* she face him? A blush scalded her cheeks at the mere idea. What had happened last night, at the inn . . . Those ten minutes in his lap had been a sensual thrill the likes of which she had never thought to experience. And by undeniable, abundant evidence, his desire for her had not been feigned. She hadn't felt sorry-looking in his arms last night, but attractive and wanton. Until he'd abruptly called a halt to the evening, leaving her confused and frustrated instead. Had he truly meant to respect their agreed-upon boundaries, or to punish her for setting them?

The carriage door opened, and harsh sunlight flooded the velvet-lined interior. Her headache renewed with double force. She hadn't expected the sun to be so strong in late afternoon. But as she accepted the footman's hand and alighted from the coach, Amelia realized it was not the direct rays of the sun that blinded her, but rather their reflection off the gleaming white marble entrance to Braxton Hall.

Blinking, she raised her hand to shield herself from the stabbing attack of grandeur. Briarbank was covered in ivy and moss, and it never made her wince. In a defensive move, she turned her head to the left. No marble there. Just an endless façade of crimson brick, glittering limestone, and glazed windows that faded into the distance, most likely somewhere near Cambridge. She swiveled her head to the right. An equally impressive, equally long façade fronted the Hall's east wing, seeming to stretch half the distance to the sea.

And it was hers. All hers to manage, to make both a showplace and a home. Amelia battled the urge to hop up and down with delight.

She confined herself to a discreet twirl instead, turning just in time to watch Spencer dismount from his horse in one smooth, elegant motion. Of course, he looked magnificent. A touch of dust dimmed the shine on his Hessians, but it only enhanced his masculine appeal, as did the healthful glow of physical exertion and the bronze cast to his complexion after two days spent in the sun. As he handed the reins to a waiting groom and exchanged a few words with the man, she noticed a relaxed, easier way to his manner. He was even smiling.

Then he turned and caught her eye. The smile disappeared.

"Good Lord." His boots clicked against stone as he covered the distance between them, and just as Amelia was learning to expect, he took what could have been a mildly awkward situation and made it twelve times worse. "You look dreadful."

She squirmed under his gaze. "I'm sorry. The carriage . . ."

"Yes, obviously. Come inside and rest." Laying a hand to the small of her back, he guided her up the marble steps toward the open door. The muscles flanking her spine were bunched and stiff. His thumb found the worst of the knots and traced firm circles over it. She sealed her lips over a grateful moan.

"Why didn't you say something?" he chided her.

"You might have ridden part of the journey, if you'd liked."

"I don't ride."

He halted, looking down at her. "You don't ride," he repeated in a tone of disbelief. "At all?"

"No," she said, chastened.

"Surely you're joking. I know your family epitomizes noble poverty, but don't the d'Orsays have some cattle to their name?"

"Of course we do. I just never cared to learn."

He merely shook his head and resumed guiding her up the stairs and into the house. The butler and housekeeper came forward to greet them.

"Welcome home, Your Grace." The silver-haired butler bowed to the duke. He then turned to Amelia and made the same gesture of respect to her. "Your Grace."

"I gather you received my express," Spencer said.

"Yesterday morning, Your Grace." The housekeeper curtsied. "Our congratulations on your marriage. Her Grace's chambers are aired and readied."

"Very good. Her Grace is unwell. See that she rests." In a brisk tone, he introduced the servants as Clarke and Mrs. Bodkin.

"What a lovely entrance hall," she said, by way of indirect compliment. She hoped to make the housekeeper a quick ally. Peering at one of the dozen gilt-framed paintings on the far wall, she wondered aloud, "Is that a Tintoretto?"

"Yes," Spencer answered.

"I thought so." Her family had owned one quite like it, once. It had fetched enough at auction to pay their expenses for a year.

"Spencer!"

Amelia's gaze jerked to the top of the staircase, where a young woman stood clinging to the banister.

"Spencer, you're home!"

And this must be Claudia. Hadn't Spencer said his ward was visiting relations in York? But it could be no one else. The family resemblance was subtle, but clear. The cousins shared the same dark, curling hair and fine cheekbones—features that must recall their fathers' side of the family. Claudia's innocent features contrasted with a developed figure. She teetered on that fulcrum between youth and womanhood.

"What are you doing home?" Spencer called to her. "You're meant to be in York another week yet."

"Oh, I begged them to send me home early. And when the decrepit old bat refused, I simply misbehaved until she was glad to be rid of me. We sent a letter, but it must have crossed you on your journey." The young lady tripped down the cascading river of marble that formed the front hall stairs, pale pink muslin fluttering behind her. As she hurried toward the duke, everything about her—from her fists balled in excitement to her bright, flushed expression—bespoke joy and affection. The girl clearly adored him.

"Incorrigible chit." The words might have been a reproach, but Amelia didn't miss the warmth softening his eyes. In his own reserved, masculine way, he clearly adored her, too.

The realization hit Amelia very queerly. It was encouraging, she supposed, to learn that her new husband was capable of genuine, tender affection. But it was also disheartening, to contrast that depth of emotion with his treatment of her.

When Claudia reached the bottom of the stairs, she rushed toward her guardian at a startling velocity. At the last second, however, she pulled up short and looked askance at Amelia. "Is this my new companion?"

Amelia's already-upset stomach clenched further. This didn't bode well.

"No," Spencer said slowly. "No, she is not your new companion."

"Of course not." Claudia smiled. "Just from looking at her, I knew she must be the new companion's lady's maid, but I wanted to be certain she wasn't the companion first. It would have been rude of me to assume otherwise, wouldn't it?"

Amelia swiveled to face Spencer, so slowly she heard her own vertebrae creak. Then she lifted her eyebrows. It was all the reaction she could manage.

Oblivious, Claudia went on, "Is my new companion traveling separately?"

Spencer clenched his jaw. "There is no new companion."

"But . . ." Her brow wrinkled. "But you promised that when you came back from Town, you'd br—"

"*Claudia.*" At the sharp command in his voice, the girl startled and looked up at him with the bewildered eyes of a puppy that had just been kicked. Heavens, this just became worse and worse.

Spencer lifted Amelia's hand, tucking it into the crook of his elbow. She stared stupidly at her own fingers, resting leaden and numb atop his arm.

"*Lady* Claudia," he said firmly, obviously hoping to inspire some return to decorum, "may I introduce Amelia Claire d'Orsay Dumarque, the Duchess of Morland. She is not your new companion. She is my new bride."

"Your . . ." Claudia stood blinking at Amelia. Then she turned and blinked up at Spencer. "Your . . ."

"My wife. The duchess. Your new cousin." He gave her a pointed look. "The lady to whom you must curtsy and apologize. Now."

The girl dipped in a curtsy, tripping over a few words of apology. Then she looked up at Spencer with the resentful eyes of a puppy that had been kicked not once, but many times.

"I'm . . ." Amelia cleared her throat. "I'm so happy to meet you, Claudia. The duke has told me many wonderful things about you."

"How curious," she said. "None of his letters mentioned you at all."

"Claudia," Spencer warned.

Amelia squeezed his arm, then withdrew her hand. "I do hope we can be friends," she said brightly, moving forward to lay the same hand on Claudia's wrist. It was probably futile, but she had to make the attempt.

A prolonged, awkward silence ensued. Just when Amelia thought the tension could not possibly become worse, it did.

Claudia began to cry.

"You *married*?" Ignoring Amelia entirely, the girl turned brimming eyes on Spencer. "Without even telling me? How could you—"

"Hush," he muttered, drawing his ward aside. "Don't make a scene."

Amelia almost laughed. Too late for that bit of advice. Truly, she couldn't blame the girl. In any normal betrothal, they would have become acquainted well before the wedding. Claudia would have had weeks or months to adjust to the idea of a new duchess at Braxton Hall, rather than having Amelia thrust upon her unawares one afternoon. No, she couldn't fault the girl for her resentment. She faulted Spencer for it. It was just one more example of the duke making an impulsive, arrogant decision with no regard for the feelings of those affected.

"Well," she said, "the two of you must have a great deal to discuss." She turned her back on Spencer. "Mrs. Bodkin, would you be so kind as to show me to my chambers now? We can discuss dinner arrangements on the way."

The housekeeper brightened. "Oh, yes, Your Grace.

Cook will be so pleased to receive your direction. Have you special recipes or menus?"

"I do." A genuine smile warmed Amelia's face. Here was some consolation. "An entire book of them."

The handful of hours between Amelia's arrival at Braxton Hall and dinner were a whirlwind. Ill or no, she had little time to rest. This was her first evening in residence as the Duchess of Morland. She might have entered the house looking like a poorhouse case, but by the time she descended those marble stairs for dinner, she was resolved that she would look and act the part of a duchess.

No one would mistake her for a paid companion, or worse, a lady's maid.

Dinner plans were no simple task. She was forced to rely on Mrs. Bodkin's estimate of the kitchen stores and devise an elegant yet simple menu that could be prepared from available foodstuffs within the allotted time. Fortunately, the housekeeper seemed overjoyed to assist in any way. After sending the older woman off to the kitchens with a list of dishes, a few custom recipes, and many verbal instructions for the cook, Amelia permitted herself ten minutes' rest on a chaise longue covered in sumptuous brocade. Her entire suite of rooms—she'd counted six of them so far—was decorated in positively regal shades of royal blue, cream, and gold. From where she lay, she studied the intricate Greek key pattern trimming the plastered ceiling. If she let her head fall to one side, she saw four exquisitely turned wooden legs supporting a polished stone tabletop, which held a blue-and-white Chinese vase, which in turn accommodated a large arrangement of fresh-cut flowers.

Orchids. At last, she had her orchids.

The entire tableau was one of beauty, elegance, and harmony. Merely gazing upon it filled her with quiet joy.

After years of living with Winifred's ostentatious displays of pink shells and overfed cherubs, Amelia reveled in the abundant evidence of her precursor's restraint and good taste.

For ten minutes. And then she went back to work.

Once the maid had drawn her bath, Amelia sent her off to press the new pearl-gray silk from her wedding. The gown was unquestionably the best she had, and this occasion demanded her best.

Amelia could manage a bath on her own—she'd done so for years—but time was short, and she couldn't be late for dinner. This was what she'd been waiting for all her life, to be mistress of her own house. She would show Spencer and Claudia both. Soon they would adore *her*. They would wonder how they'd ever survived without her. One well-planned, satisfying meal, and the duke would realize his immense fortune in marrying a plain, unassuming spinster. He might even rise from his seat, walk the length of the table, and humbly kneel at her side, gazing up at her with sheer worship in his eyes. *Amelia,* he would say, in that husky, thrilling voice of his, *I don't know how I've lived without you. You've made our house a home. I'll do anything, say anything. Just promise me you'll never, ever leave.*

Or so it was amusing to dream.

Working quickly before the water could go cold, Amelia wrestled out of her traveling habit. Stripped down to chemise and stays, she then stood in the center of the room, uncertain what to do with the dress. She didn't want to just throw the whole dusty mess atop a clean bed. Another lady might have dumped the garments in a heap on the floor, but Amelia's sense of tidiness and her respect for good fabric just wouldn't allow it. Surely this room had a closet with a hook or two . . .

Turning slowly in place, she spied a sliding wood panel to one side of the bed. It blended so perfectly into the wainscoting, she hadn't noticed the closet on first inspection.

Enjoying the way the carpet's thick pile cushioned her bare toes, she hurried to the door. It was heavier than she'd expected, but by leaning her full weight into the effort, she managed to slide it open.

On the other side was Spencer.

Upon seeing her, he froze—right in the middle of removing his shirt.

"Oh!" Mortified, Amelia dropped the entire bundle of fabric. Which only increased her embarrassment, since she now stood before him in just her shift and stays. "I'm so sorry," she stammered. Her eyes riveted to the rippling muscles of his abdomen and the line of dark hair bisecting them. "I . . . I thought this was a closet."

Lowering his shirt, he flicked a bemused glance at the room behind him. "No. Not a closet."

"Of course not." Her face burned. Obviously it was the duke's bedchamber—an exact mirror of her own, but done up in rich, masculine colors and fabrics—and this sliding door connected the two suites. "I just wasn't expecting . . . I mean, this arrangement is very—"

"Convenient?"

"Unusual. That's what I meant to say."

She shifted her weight uneasily. His gaze dipped to her bosom.

She added, "I mean, I've never seen this sort of papering before, done up in such complimentary colors. It's so clever, the way the gold in my room is mirrored with a dark blue in yours, but both carpets have the same pattern of . . ."

"Mm-hm." He nodded thoughtfully at her cleavage. He wasn't hearing a word she said.

"The same pattern of unicorns. Alternating with rounds of cheese."

Another vacant nod. "Indeed."

Amelia's face heated. Here she was, dreaming of elaborate menus and blathering on about room décor—and he didn't care. He'd married her for one reason only, and if she'd momentarily forgotten it, the intensity with which he was currently staring at her breasts would have been a certain reminder. He wanted to bed her, and get an heir. That was all. Despite his assurances to the contrary when he'd proposed, she was here in his home as a glorified broodmare.

No, scratch the "glorified." He likely treated his broodmares with greater affection.

She stepped back, nearly tripping over the heap of clothing at her feet. No way to pick it up without giving him an even bolder view of her cleavage. Discreetly kicking the garments aside, she put one shoulder to the door panel and prepared to slide it closed. "I'll see you at dinner, then."

His hand shot out to grasp the edge of the door. Amelia pushed anyway, but the slab of oak wouldn't budge.

"About Claudia," he said. "She's very . . . young." He sighed. "I wish that had gone differently, downstairs."

Was this what constituted an apology, in Spencer's world? It didn't quite merit absolution in Amelia's. She nodded. "So do I."

His gaze seemed to have settled on her hips now, his lips curving in masculine approval. Yes, yes. They were wide and strong. Excellent for breeding, as she'd been informed by many a well-meaning matron in her day.

Amelia cleared her throat. The message in the inarticulate sound was clear: *Hullo? I'm up here.*

He dragged his eyes back up to her face. But he took his time about it, and as his gaze stroked over her, a pleasant warmth buzzed through her veins. Lord, what a hopeless situation. She enjoyed being lusted after; there was no pretending otherwise.

But she couldn't stop herself from craving affection in the bargain—even though he'd never offered it, and she'd accepted him knowing that full well. He was a man. Not just a man, but a powerful, attractive duke. He could separate his physical needs from his emotions—but for Amelia, the two were hopelessly entangled. That meant he had all the power.

Not to mention the physical force. As they stood there—her whole strength marshaled to close the door and his one hand holding it open—it occurred to her how easily he could overpower her, if he wished. For God's sake, he'd lifted her six inches into the air in that ballroom, and she wasn't especially light.

Her eyes went to the door handle.

"There's only one latch," he said, guessing her thoughts. "It's on my side."

She swallowed hard. "I see."

"Don't worry." With an arrogant grin, he released his grip on the door and stepped back. "I'll never lock it."

Amelia shifted her weight, and the door slid shut with a satisfying bang. She thought she heard him laugh.

Chapter Eleven

Dinner was a miserable business.

Against all reason, Spencer had hoped for a swift improvement in Claudia's demeanor. Obviously, the fact of his marriage had taken his ward by surprise. But with a few hours to grow used to the idea, perhaps she would embrace Amelia as a welcome addition to the household.

No. No embracing going on tonight.

Spencer sat at the head of the table. Amelia and Claudia faced one another across an arctic expanse of white linen and bevel-cut crystal, but their eyes never met. One would think the fish course had been served live and wriggling, considering the violence with which Claudia stabbed it.

"How was your time in York?" Spencer asked her. "Can I expect good reports from your tutors?"

"I don't know." She jabbed at a fillet of turbot. "I was rather a disappointment to my German master."

"What of your music?"

"The music master was rather a disappointment to me." Sniffing, she laid down her fork. "The shops were lovely, though."

"I sent you to York so that you might improve your mind, not distribute your pin money to the local merchants. Why should I bother arranging for tutors if you learn nothing from them?"

Resentful eyes snapped up to his. "Perhaps you shouldn't."

"Aren't you hungry, dear?" Amelia interjected in a smooth, conciliatory tone. She nodded at Claudia's abandoned fish. "You didn't touch your soup, either."

The girl still refused to look at her.

"Please excuse me." Chair legs scraped the floor as Claudia rose to her feet. "I've little appetite this evening."

With that, she fled the room. Spencer braced his hands on the arms of his chair and started to rise. He froze halfway. Should he even bother going after her, or would that only make matters worse?

"No, don't," Amelia said, reading his thoughts. "She needs time."

He lowered himself back into his chair.

With a sigh, Amelia signaled the servants to remove the fish. "Spencer, what do you intend to do about her?"

He was too fatigued to be anything but honest. "I don't know." He hadn't known what to do with Claudia for some time now.

"How old was she, when she lost her parents?"

He started to answer, then hesitated as liveried sleeves reached between them. The servant positioned a roast of lamb in the center of the table. Spencer impatiently motioned for the knife and carving fork. Perhaps dukes didn't typically carve their own roasts, but he found it easier to talk when his hands were occupied.

And surprisingly enough, he wanted to talk about this.

"She was an infant when her mother died. That was shortly before my uncle summoned me from Canada. He had no wish to remarry and produce an heir of his own, so he and my father agreed I would come here and prepare to assume the duties of the title. Claudia was nine years old when the late duke passed away. Since my own father had died in the meantime, that's when I inherited the dukedom and assumed her guardianship."

And he'd begun failing her almost immediately thereafter. At least, that's the way it had felt. He *had* tried. He'd kept her close for the year or two after her father's death. Let her travel with him, taught her to ride, read aloud to her in the evenings from Shakespeare, Homer, Milton—never letting her guess that the classics were new to him, too. She was a clever child, and endlessly greedy for affection. He'd given her as much attention as he could, considering the demands of his own new title, but he'd always known she deserved more. And the older she grew, the less he knew what to do with her. She needed education, refinement, guidance, exposure to society—none of which he could adequately provide.

"Of course," he said, flicking aside a sprig of rosemary as he sawed the meat, "I've hired governesses through the years. The past few winters, I've been sending her to her great-aunt's in York. She was supposed to have the benefit of some masters there."

Amelia sipped her wine. "No wonder she resents me. Poor girl."

"Why should she resent you?"

Her eyes widened at him over the wineglass, but Spencer truly didn't understand. He'd hoped Claudia would be happy to have a feminine influence in the house, since she'd never known her own mother.

"Spencer, you are the sole adult she's lived with all her life. To her, you are like cousin, brother, guardian, and God Himself, all rolled into one. It was plain from one minute's observation how much she adores you, and here you've only been sending her away. She came home early just to see you, only to learn you've married with no warning whatsoever. For the first time in her life, she has a rival for your attention. Of course she resents me."

He had the vague understanding that he'd put Amelia in a very awkward situation. The portion of meat he slid onto her plate seemed poor compensation.

"Have you considered," she said, testing the lamb with one tine of her fork, "that Claudia might have hoped to marry you herself?"

He dropped the carving knife with a clatter. "Lord, no. We're cousins. I'm her guardian. She's fifteen years old, for God's sake. Barely more than a child." He suppressed a shudder. Marry Claudia? The idea made him ill.

"I know, but . . ." She shrugged, cutting into the meat. "Such matches do happen. And she isn't unthinkably young. When I became engaged for the first time, I was barely older than she is now." She took a bite.

"You were engaged? To whom?"

It took her an eternity to chew that damned bit of lamb.

Finally, she swallowed. "To no one you'd know. A wealthy squire, in Gloucestershire."

"What happened?"

"He was so old, and . . . well, I just couldn't go through with it." She poked at her lamb again, looking tense and fragile. Spencer already felt such welling hatred for this Gloucestershire squire, he had no idea how to question her further without . . . breaking something. And that wouldn't do much to assure her of his nonviolent nature.

Suddenly she said, "Aren't you going to eat?"

He shook his head. "I don't care for lamb."

"That's absurd. Who doesn't care for lamb?"

"I don't."

Amelia sighed. "She needs your attention. Claudia, I mean. We should make a fuss over her."

"A *fuss*?" Though he was grateful for the sudden change in topic, Spencer wasn't sure he liked the sound of this. He had a longstanding prejudice against fuss, in all its forms. "What do you mean?"

"Spend time with her, to start. Talk to her. Listen to what she has to say. Every girl her age needs a confidante. I'll try to reach out to her, but that will take time. She needs wider society. If she's to make her debut in Town, she ought to begin moving in less formal circles now. I don't suppose we could take her to Bath or Brighton?"

"We've only just arrived here. My desk has accumulated so many papers in my absence, it resembles a snowdrift. Add to that, it's stud season and I've mares to—"

"All right, all right. It was only a thought. No travel. A party, then." She clapped her hands. "I can do a lovely party, and Claudia can help me with—"

"No. No parties."

"Well, it needn't be a grand affair. No dancing. We'll just invite a few good families, with young ladies her age—make it a musicale, perhaps. You did say she plays. That will give her an opportunity to perform in front of—"

"No," he said, bringing his fist to the table with a forceful crack. He needed to shut down this discussion, immediately. Braxton Hall—his home and refuge—swarmed with giddy girls and their obsequious relations? His brain spun at the thought. It would be as if Dante had created him an elite tenth circle of hell. "Listen. Claudia is my ward. She is my responsibility, and I will deal with her as I see fit. She's not ready to begin moving in society."

"But I thought if she—"

"Your thoughts aren't required. Not on this."

"I see." Her eyes fell. She looked utterly conquered.

Devil, damn, and blast. Spencer picked up his wine-glass and drained it.

"Well, I've little appetite tonight. Fatigued from the journey, I suppose." With quiet precision, she positioned her silver on her plate, then folded her napkin and set it aside. When she rose from her chair, he stood too.

"Will you show me to my suite?" she asked quietly. "Or must I ask a maid for directions? I haven't learned the trick of these corridors yet."

He offered his arm, and together they proceeded in silence. Through the hall, up the stairs, down the passageway toward her rooms. When they'd nearly reached her suite, she pulled up short.

He halted beside her. "What is it?"

"Now that we're alone . . ." She scanned the empty corridor, then abruptly released his arm and wheeled on him. Her eyes sparked with anger. "You will not do that to me again. I've waited my entire life to be mistress of my own house. As if it wasn't bad enough to be mistaken for a servant on my arrival, now you would humiliate me in front of the real ones? On my first day in residence? If you're going to berate and belittle me, at least pay me the courtesy of waiting to do it in private."

He didn't know how to respond. Not verbally, at any rate. His body, however, was responding to her with primal eloquence. His pulse accelerated; blood surged to his groin. At last, here was Amelia again—the bold, spirited woman who provoked him in every possible way.

"And you may not 'require' my thoughts on the matter," she went on, "but you're going to have them. I've known since we met how arrogant and self-absorbed you can be, but this is the first time I've known you to be stupid. That girl adores you. With the slightest effort on your part, you could make her so happy. Instead, you're driving her away, devastating her through your own inaction. By the time you deem the relationship worth your effort, it may be too late.

"What's more, I could help you. I was once a girl, and I understand how Claudia feels. Now I'm a lady, and I understand how to make a home, welcome guests, care for people who need it. I know you married me solely to get a few children, but if you bothered to look, perhaps you'd see something beyond my breeding potential." She put a hand to her temple. "You have no idea what more I could offer you."

"*Offer* me? You sound like a woman presenting herself for employment. I thought you took offense at the notion of being a paid companion."

"I do," she said, bristling. "You're the one who said your very reason for marrying was to protect Claudia's future. It's obvious you care deeply for her. When's the last time you told her so?"

For God's sake, he didn't know. Never?

He said, "If it's so obvious, why should I have to say it? I provide for her material needs and her education. I establish boundaries to protect her."

"Oh, yes. You're so generous. You give her everything but your affection."

"Well, if that's the remedy for everything, tell me again why your brother's a worthless rogue?"

She glared at him, chest heaving. Moments passed. "Are we going to play cards tonight or not?"

Nothing she could have said would have stunned him more. Or aroused him further. He looked to the door of her suite. "Are you inviting me in?"

"To the sitting room. No further."

He reached past her and opened the door. "By all means."

She entered and settled herself on a divan. He located a pack of cards in a drawer, then pulled up a table and a chair for himself.

"Will it be piquet again?" he asked, striving for a bored tone as he split and shuffled the cards.

"As you wish."

He'd been pleasantly surprised last night at how quickly her piquet improved. She'd adapted with each successive hand, integrating new points of strategy into her play. With more practice, she might prove a challenging opponent for him. Typically Spencer had to handicap himself by discarding his best cards, just to keep things remotely interesting.

But if she thought she could best him tonight, she was deluding herself. The only way that could happen is if he purposely lost.

Perhaps he ought to let her win. At least the first hand.

As he prepared to deal, she stopped him. "One round will do tonight, I think. Shall we set the wager now?"

"Very well," he said, surprised anew. "What is your forfeit? Four hundred pounds again?"

"Four hundred pounds, *and* you will allow me to plan and host a musicale for Claudia."

"Agreed," he said. "And if I win, you will come sit on my lap and undress me to the waist."

She sucked in a breath. Her wide-eyed gaze seemed to settle on one of his waistcoat buttons. "And . . . and then what will you expect me to do?"

"Whatever you wish."

"Ten minutes, as before?"

He nodded in agreement.

"Very well."

Guilt dragged his heartbeat as Spencer dealt the cards. He'd been planning to let her win the first round. Winning had cheered her last night, boosted her confidence. And victory had looked well on her, painting her cheeks a lovely shade of rose pink.

But he couldn't let her win this wager. Opening his

home to a bevy of young chits who *thought* they could sing and play? Being forced to listen to them try? No, he had no desire to host a musicale, but he did want to feel Amelia's hands on his bare skin. Very much wanted it, with an intensity that concerned him.

Amelia gathered her cards. Her pale eyebrows drew together as she studied them. Of course, carnal satisfaction wasn't what she had in mind. She wanted to save her brother and lift Claudia's spirits, and perhaps her own as well. Bloody hell, she just wanted to be helpful, and he was going to deny her that.

He picked up the cards he'd dealt himself. They included three aces and a royal quart. His victory was all but assured.

Before he could think better of it, Spencer flung the ace of hearts away. There. He would still play to win, but now she at least had a sporting chance.

As the round progressed, her play was distracted and rash. She made foolish mistakes. Even if Spencer had been trying to lose, he would have had a deuced difficult time of it. In the end, he won handily.

She clasped her hands in her lap and gave him a reproachful look, as if to say, *Well, you blackguard, I hope you're satisfied.*

But he wasn't. Suddenly the whole game left a bad taste in his mouth. He'd manipulated her last night at the inn, to be sure. But if she hadn't become a most eager participant in his arms, he never would have let matters go so far. If he'd wanted a fearful, timid lover, he would have taken her on their wedding night.

"Amelia," he said slowly, knowing he would soon regret it, "it's late, and we're both tired. We can forget the wager."

"Oh, no." She rose from her seat and skirted the table. "Let it never be said that a member of the d'Orsay family does not honor her debts." She held out her hand. "I believe you'll have to stand, if I'm to remove your coat."

He stood. He was a man, not a saint.

Beginning at his navel, she ran her hands up his chest, cleaving the sides of his coat from the waistcoat beneath. That brisk, sensible touch, even muffled as it was by several layers of fabric, nearly undid him. Her hands worked over his shoulders, loosening his sleeves. He made his arms straight and pushed them slightly back, and the coat slid off easily. She shook the garment out and carefully laid it aside, so it wouldn't be wrinkled. He stood waiting impatiently. She could have trampled the thing, and he wouldn't have cared.

She attacked his cravat next, pulling the starched linen loose from his neck with sharp tugs. Nimble flicks of her fingertips freed his waistcoat buttons, and soon the carefully folded silk joined his coat.

Spencer's breath was ragged. He was painfully hard. There was nothing coy or seductive about the way she was undressing him, but it was undeniably feminine, and powerfully arousing. Hers wasn't the touch of a lover; it was the possessive, efficient touch of a wife.

His wife.

As she freed his shirt from his trousers with a swift yank, she bobbled a bit on her feet. His hands took her waist. Then they slid over her hips and down, cupping the twin curves of her firm, rounded bottom. He hadn't bid them to do so, they just did of their own accord.

With a chiding arch of her brow, she took his hands in hers and removed them forcibly. "Not part of the wager." Laying her hands flat against his chest, she pressed lightly and added, "Be seated."

He obeyed, gladly.

Hiking the filmy gauze of her skirts, she straddled his lap, just as she had last night. The same as last night, except that much less fabric separated them. He could already feel the heat of her skin burning through that meager excuse for a petticoat.

His erection throbbed against his trouser fall. Surely she could not fail to notice his aroused state, and virgin or no, she seemed too clever a woman not to understand what it meant. Instead of bringing her pelvis flush with his, however, she sat back toward his knees, denying his aching groin any direct contact. Her hands went to his waist and she gathered the fine lawn of his shirt in trembling fingers, drawing it slowly up.

As she exposed his bare torso, her tongue darted out to moisten her lips. "Lift your arms." Her words were a husky whisper.

He obeyed in silence, and she stretched up on her haunches, pulling the shirt over his head. She didn't fold it this time, but tossed it carelessly aside.

His flesh blazed as she surveyed his bare chest. Her breathing was shallow, her throat and bosom prettily flushed. However she'd felt about paying this forfeit a few minutes ago, she was a more than willing participant now. Her obvious desire only multiplied his own.

Still she sat there, hesitating.

"Whatever you wish," he scraped out. "Do whatever you wish."

Her hands went to cover his. She traced each finger individually and smiled, evidently amused by the way he was clutching the chair's upholstered armrests. Good. Let her know what she did to him. *Yes, Amelia. I'm clinging to restraint by an ever-fraying thread. And if I don't bed you soon, I may lose my grip on sanity forever.*

Her touch feathered over his wrists and up his forearms, tracing the prominent cords of muscle and sinew. She progressed to his upper arms, pressing her palms flat against the solid swells of his biceps. Just to tease her, he flexed. A little gasp was his reward. Women usually enjoyed exploring the contours of his arms and chest—unlike most gentlemen of his station, he was strong and toned from working the horses.

She paused, hands balanced on his shoulders. A fresh wave of blood rushed to his groin. As if that part of him needed any further reinforcement.

Her fingertips swept to the back of his neck. A hot thrill shot to the base of his spine and simmered there. She was repaying him for last night, mimicking his attentions caress for caress—just as he'd hoped she would. It was torture to sit passively and take it, but his inaction was exactly what the situation required. He had to be patient, so patient . . . even if it killed him.

Her gaze dropped to his chest.

Yes. Yes. Touch me there. God, kiss me there.

He fought the urge to grasp her fingers and direct them, the desire to tangle a hand in her upswept hair and drag her open-mouthed kiss everywhere he craved it. His lips, his neck, his chest, his—

She leaned in close to whisper in his ear. "You said last night, you'd been wanting to . . . to lick me. To bite me."

"Yes." Those carnal words, from her innocent lips . . . the image of her neat, delicate teeth closing over his earlobe, her tongue stroking over his skin . . . Oh, God. His hips bowed upward, seeking friction to soothe his rampant arousal. His erection brushed ever-so-slightly against her belly—but it wasn't nearly enough. The light, teasing contact only increased his desperation.

"Well." Warm, rhythmic breaths caressed his neck. "I've been wanting something, too."

Sweet heaven. Was it too much to hope that what she'd been wanting required full nudity and a firm mattress? Because he was absolutely ready to oblige. When she hesitated, he couldn't keep silent any longer. "What?" he asked into her hair. "What is it you want?"

"You'll laugh."

"I won't. I swear it."

"I have your word?"

"Yes, of course." Every muscle in his body tensed with the effort to keep still. His mind churned with depraved fantasies. What carnal act spun from a virgin's imagination could possibly make her so abashed? Whatever it was, it was bound to be good. Very, very good.

"This," she whispered finally. "Just this."

Her hands slid over his shoulders and linked behind his neck. She bent her head, and her soft breasts flattened against his chest. Excitement rushed over his skin. Every inch of him anticipated the imminent, exquisite sensation of her kiss.

But she didn't kiss him. Instead, she rested her cheek against his collarbone, tucking her face into the curve of his neck. And then she released a deep, full-body sigh and went still.

Spencer was confused. Had she changed her mind? Perhaps embarrassment had conquered her desire. Damn.

"Won't you hold me?" she murmured, nuzzling further into his neck. "Please? I'm homesick and tired, and it's been a wretched day."

Oh.

Oh, sweet holy infant. What a lust-addled fool he was. She hadn't shied away from some lascivious fantasy. This *was* what she wanted. A chaste, comforting embrace. A hug.

"It's not so very difficult," she said. "Just put your arms about me. Husbands do it all the time."

Damned if he knew how to refuse.

His arms went around her waist, gathering her close. She was so soft, and so warm, and she all but melted against his bare chest. As some consolation to his frustrated lust, the embrace brought them closer, until her thigh wedged snug against the hard ridge of his arousal. She didn't startle or squirm away. For his part, Spencer resisted the urge to grind his hips. And so there they sat, hugging. Him in the chair, her on his lap, and the world's most insistent erection between them. If he'd wanted sweet torture—by the devil, he had it. In trumps.

The longer he held her, however, the more he became aware of sensations that didn't originate in his lap. The soft contours of her breasts soothed his pounding heart. Her eyelashes fluttered sweetly against his neck. And she smelled so good. Her enticing perfume blended her usual lavender scent with hints of vanilla and some kind of spice . . . was it clove? Perhaps she'd visited the kitchens today.

He stroked her back, once. Purring, she nestled closer in his lap. An unfamiliar tenderness swelled in his heart. Encouraged, he repeated the touch, skimming his fingers up the delicate ridge of her spine. Up, then down. Slipping the pads of his fingers over each vertebra, as if counting pearls on a string. The slow, steady tempo calmed them both. Their lungs seemed to arrive at some instinctive agreement, and their chests ceased struggling against one another. Instead, they breathed in a rhythm, trading the air back and forth between them. Warm. Fragrant. Intimate.

More deeply arousing than anything he'd ever known.

"Your parents," she murmured. "Did they love each other?"

"I . . . I'm not certain."

What a question. He couldn't recall his mother much, but he remembered his father had wept when she died. They'd wept together, the confused young boy and the hardened soldier. And then they'd never spoken of it again. When he'd learned of his father's death years later, Spencer hadn't shed a tear. He'd lashed out with fists instead, because he'd found it too devastating to contemplate weeping alone.

She said, "Mine did. They were devoted to one another. I always thought myself fortunate to have grown up with their example." She shivered in his arms. "Now I'm not sure. Perhaps it only prepared me for disappointment."

He brought her closer, until the heat of her skin seared his chest. That breath they kept trading back and forth—it came more quickly now, and hot. Places inside him were softening, thawing. He recalled her words to him in the corridor: *You have no idea what more I could offer you.* Oh, he did. He most definitely did. He'd watch his innards removed through his navel before admitting it, but on some fundamental level, he knew why he hadn't been able to let her go that night. Why he'd bodily removed her from that ballroom; why he'd proposed to her scant hours after that. Because this woman displayed such loyalty to a no-account wastrel of a brother, and he just one of five. Surely somewhere in that boundless reserve, she could find a spare bit of devotion for him. He didn't deserve it, but he wanted it just the same.

"Amelia, look at me."

Keeping her hands clasped behind his neck, she lifted her head. She went perfectly, absolutely still in his arms. She seemed to have ceased to breathe.

He kissed her. Without warning, without permission. Without even deciding to do it, but simply because he couldn't have done anything else. He needed that breath she was holding. It belonged to him, and he wanted it back.

Her lips were warm and soft, her tongue cool and

slick against his. Bracketing her face in his hands, he angled her head to deepen the kiss. She squirmed in his lap, but he held her tight, taking more. And then more. Stroking deep with his tongue, clashing teeth against teeth. He had to have this taste, this softness, this heat, and devil take it, he knew he was going to ruin everything by scaring her away, but he couldn't stop.

He slid one hand to her breast and squeezed hard, because part of him wanted to punish her. Inside him, things were cracking and shifting with the deep, bone-shivering howl of ice splintering off from a glacier. Old pockets of emptiness were filling in; new chasms of need split asunder. It hurt. He was being rearranged in deep, forgotten places, and this woman was to blame. He kneaded harder, pinching the tight knot of her nipple, because he wanted her aching, too. It was unforgivable, and so damned unfair. Somehow she'd managed to get inside him before he'd gotten inside of her.

She made a startled cry against his mouth, jerking him into consciousness. He froze, breaking the kiss.

"Ten minutes," she said, panting. "You have to let me go."

"I can't."

Struggling against him, she choked on a sob. "Spencer, please."

"If I release you, will you come to me tonight?"

He felt her head shake before he heard her answer. "No."

"Don't tell me you're still afraid."

"I'm more frightened than ever."

He swallowed a roar of frustration. Damn it, hadn't he shown her inhuman amounts of restraint? Aside from that little slip just now? How could she sit in his arms like this if she thought him capable of murder?

Swearing softly, he slid his hands from her body. She

couldn't even meet his gaze. Her eyelashes trembled against her cheeks.

"Go." He closed his eyes and tried to master his breathing. Gripping the armrests so hard his knuckles went numb, he growled out, "*Go*. Damn it, get off my lap this instant, or I will not be responsible for my actions."

She obeyed in haste, pressing her palms against his thighs for leverage as she rose. His chest sagged with relief as she left him. He leaned forward, bracing his elbows on his knees and letting his head drop into his hands. His own labored breathing was a roar in his ears.

"Good night, Spencer," she said quietly.

He heard a door latch click, but he didn't look up. There were three doors leading from this room, and if he knew which one she'd exited through, there was an excellent chance he'd be breaking it down a second later.

After several moments spent wrestling his own lust into submission, Spencer raised his head. Scrubbing one palm over his face, he blinked at the card table, where their round of piquet remained played out before him. No matter how he stared at the cards, they didn't make sense. Once he'd handicapped himself by discarding the ace, Amelia had a true chance to win. She'd neglected to reckon her points correctly and played the cards far below her skill level. On impulse, he reached for her discard pile and flipped it over.

A one-eyed knave winked up at him, and beneath it, two kings.

She couldn't possibly have been so stupid as to discard those cards. There was only one way to explain it. She hadn't even tried to win. All that talk about hosting a party, reaching out to Claudia—what she'd wanted, more than any of it, was simply to be held. By him. And of course, he'd sent her fleeing in fear.

Emotion caught in his throat, prickly and raw. His patience was exhausted, and he felt shabby as hell. One thing was certain—the next time he took Amelia in his arms . . .

He would not let her go.

Chapter Twelve

The summer she was twelve years old, Amelia made the grave mistake of screeching at a speckled toad within her brothers' hearing. Therefore, naturally, her brothers had spent the next month foisting toads upon her. They'd hidden them in her cupboards, her sewing kit, even under her pillow . . . Pharaoh was plagued by fewer toads than Amelia shooed from her room that summer. She detested the bulge-eyed animals, but could she do the expedient thing—pick up the toad lurking in her empty chamber pot and merely toss it out the window? No. She had to catch the loathsome lump in her hands, carry it outside in the dead of night, and turn it loose in the garden no worse for wear. Because that was what Amelia did. She was a nurturer. She couldn't help but take care of creatures, even the vile, unwanted ones.

Especially the vile, unwanted ones.

It was perverse and irrational and likely the sign of some severe mental defect—but the further Spencer displayed his gross incompetence as a sensitive human being, the more he engaged her sympathy. The worse he bungled every opportunity to put her at ease, the greater her own desire to soothe. And the longer he kept her at arm's length—emotionally speaking, at least—the more she yearned to hold him tight.

When she awoke the next morning alone, staring up at the stamped plaster ceiling, Amelia had to be honest with herself. She'd been delaying consummation in hopes of girding her heart first. But after last night, she knew it to be a hopeless cause. That embrace had stirred her too deeply. True, Spencer had abandoned their chaste hug to press for further liberties, and his lustful aggression should have dispelled her cravings for tenderness. But when he aroused her desire with those demanding kisses and skillful hands, the longing wouldn't stay put between her legs. It filled her, consumed her. The longer she denied him her body, the more she risked her heart.

Well, then. That was that. She would go to him today.

Bolting upright in bed, she threw off her coverlet. She wrapped a light blanket around her shoulders and moved to the edge of the mattress, sending her bare toes down to scout the carpet for her slippers.

Inwardly, she resolved to banish all craving for romance. And even if that resolve faltered—what was the worst that could happen, really? She would waste a few months' unrequited affection on him; he would remain indifferent to her. The world had seen graver injustices. Before long, a baby would fill the void. And the sooner she shared Spencer's bed, the sooner that baby would come along.

Softly, she padded across the carpet. Now that she'd made the decision, she didn't want to wait. Nighttime encounters were too personal, too intimate. Surely the act would feel anything but romantic in the bright light of morning. She wouldn't even bother to brush her hair.

Putting her muscle into it, she slid open the connecting door to Spencer's room.

He wasn't there.

A woman was. Two women, actually—a pair of chambermaids, briskly making the bed. Each froze instantly, pillow in hand, to gawp at Amelia. Behind them, a curtain fluttered in the open window, silently mocking her surprise.

"Good morning, Your Grace," the maids said, curtsying briefly before returning to their work.

Amelia firmed her spine and cleared her throat. "My husband . . ."

"Oh, he's not here, ma'am. Mr. Fletcher said business took His Grace away early this morning," said the younger girl. "Before dawn, even."

Crisp linen snapped. The elder maid gave her partner a stern look, but the young girl chattered on. "The duke's not expected back until very late, is what I heard."

"Yes, I know that," Amelia said firmly, even though she'd had no idea. She made a mental note to speak with Mrs. Bodkin about the staff gossiping, and to question why this Mr. Fletcher was having predawn words with a fresh-faced chambermaid. "What I meant to say was, my husband's bed linens should have no starch. Remove those, and start again."

She made as graceful an exit as she could, considering the circumstances. At least she managed not to shut her wrapper in the door. It hadn't been a lie, that bit about the starch. When she'd removed Spencer's shirt last night, she'd noticed reddened skin at his throat and wrists—no doubt he was sensitive to whatever starch was being used on his collar and cuffs. She'd speak with his valet later about using an alternate preparation.

If she was going to be mistress of this house, she was going to do it right.

Since she'd worn her gray silk the evening previous, she was forced to select a frock from her own faded, worn wardrobe today. Even the best of her summer dresses—a striped muslin done up just last year, with sage grosgrain ribbon trim—looked drab here at Braxton Hall. Most un-duchessly.

It didn't help matters when Amelia entered the breakfast room to encounter Claudia dressed in a remarkably similar high-waisted striped muslin frock, except hers boasted lace-trimmed flounces. Two of them. She truly was a lovely girl, with the prospects of becoming a great beauty. But she needed someone to gently guide her behavior, and clearly Spencer wasn't up to the task.

"Good morning." Smiling, Amelia laid a plate of kippers and eggs on the table and prepared to seat herself.

Claudia stared at the plate, her features contorting in disgust. Before Amelia's bottom even touched the chair, the girl shot to her feet and made for the door, two lace flounces bobbing pertly in her wake.

"Claudia, wait."

She halted, one hand on the doorjamb.

Amelia squared her shoulders. "It may not be my place to say it. But whether you dine with family or strangers, it's unacceptable to leave the table without excusing yourself."

"I am ill," she said mulishly. "And it's not your place to say it."

Amelia sighed. The girl was so . . . so *fifteen*. And desperately in need of a hug. "You look very well, to my eyes. Won't you sit down? We need to have a talk. An honest one, woman to woman."

Claudia let go the doorjamb and slowly turned. "Whatever about?"

"I know you resent me."

"I . . ." The girl flushed. "Why, I'm sure I don't—"

"You resent me. Of course you do. I'm a stranger who has invaded your home without warning and taken your late mother's role. Perhaps the role you wished to one day assume?"

"I don't know what you mean." Claudia blushed as she studied the carpet.

"I can't fault you for being angry," Amelia said calmly.

"I'd feel the same, were I in your place. And to be perfectly honest, I cannot claim to be any better. If it helps at all, I rather resent you, too."

She looked up. "You? Resent *me*? Whatever have I done to you?"

"Nothing. Nothing at all. But you're young and pretty, and you look better in stripes than I ever have or will." She smiled gamely. "When I look at you, I can't help but see myself at fifteen, when the world was all marvelous, romantic possibility."

"You know nothing of me. Don't speak as if you do."

"Fair enough. At the moment, I grant that we are little more than strangers. I would like, eventually, to be your friend. But I know that's too much to expect just yet, given the circumstances. I won't interfere in your daily routine. I will let you be." She reached for a tray of jam tarts from the sideboard and extended it. "But you can't keep running away from every meal. I insist that you eat."

"You *insist* that I eat?" The young lady eyed the pastries. Instead of taking one, however, Claudia grasped the entire tray and removed it from Amelia's hands altogether. "Very well," she said, stuffing a tart into her mouth. "I'll eat." Then she and the tray of pastries flounced from the room.

Well, Amelia would count that as progress. At least the girl would not waste away. Settling down to her own breakfast, she opened her mental recipe book and headed a blank page, "Claudia." Under that, she noted: "Jam tarts. No kippers."

As she ate, she wondered where Spencer had gone for the day. It shouldn't be surprising that he had business. After spending some months in Town, surely he must have many estate matters requiring his attention. But wherever he'd gone, she wondered if he was angry with her, after last night. Or disappointed by her. Or yearning for her.

She shook herself. The man was busy. He likely wasn't sparing her a second thought.

Amelia kept busy, too. She interviewed each member of the staff and acquainted herself with every inch of Braxton Hall—the interior, at least. The gardens would have to wait for another day. As she moved through the rooms with the housekeeper at her side, she made careful note of any fixtures that needed replacing or improvement, any arrangement of furniture that struck her as less than pleasing or efficient. After fifteen years without a mistress, the house was still well maintained but beginning to lag where style was concerned. She limited herself to the public and common rooms, not wanting to encroach on Claudia or Spencer's privacy.

The task took her all day, and well into evening—at which point she was glad that Spencer had not yet returned and Claudia remained cloistered with her tarts, for Amelia had no time to plan dinner. Instead, she and Mrs. Bodkin shared a cold supper as they discussed modernizing the kitchen. Afterward, they began an inventory of all the household silver. Hours later, the entire dining table was covered in gleaming rows of forks, spoons, knives, ladles, tongs . . .

All of which began to rattle in unison, just as the clock's largest hand neared twelve.

Amelia grasped the table edge in alarm. Beneath the low clatter of silver, the thunder of hoofbeats swelled.

"That will be His Grace," the housekeeper explained, the corners of her mouth creasing as she suppressed a yawn.

Spencer. Amelia's heart kicked into a furious rhythm. Until this second, she hadn't acknowledged how much she'd been anticipating his return. But she had. She'd been waiting for him all day, every second. Why else would she have spent the day working her fingers to nubs rather than allow herself a stray moment for thought? Why else would she be sitting up counting silver at midnight? And poor Mrs. Bodkin, forced to keep watch with her.

"You're dismissed," she told the housekeeper. "We'll just lock this room overnight and finish in the morning. Thank you so much for your help."

Amelia rushed from the room, smoothing her upswept hair and shaking the wrinkles from her skirts. How much time did she have before Spencer would enter the house? Surely he would just hand his horse off to a groom and come inside. Pausing in the corridor to check her reflection in the glass covering the clock face—not much to see, but at least the dim light confirmed her features had not suffered any dramatic rearrangement—she went to the entrance hall and waited.

And waited. Several minutes passed, and no sign of him. Could he have come in through another door? Perhaps by the kitchens . . . he would be hungry, after a long ride.

She walked toward the rear of the house, crossing into a narrow gallery that connected the main residence with the service wing. It was tiled in marble and lined with windows on both sides, which made it rather cold at night. Amelia hugged herself and quickened her pace. She supposed she might have simply gone up to her suite and awaited Spencer there. But that would mean choosing between her bedchamber and his, and she wanted to meet him on neutral territory. She was going to keep this calm and cool. As emotionless as possible.

Step one: A smoothly delivered, dispassionate declaration. *Your Grace, I thank you for your patience. I'm now ready to consummate the marriage.*

Step two: Lie back and think of Briarbank.

Through the blackened gallery windows, a flash of torchlight drew her eye. She halted and turned toward it, walking up to the window and cupping her hands around her eyes to peer into the darkness. Down a gravel-packed lane lined with intermittent lamps sat a low, ranging building with a sloped roof. Golden light emanating from the building's interior outlined a wide, square door and men moving within. The coach house, she discerned, and stables. Perhaps Spencer had taken the horse in himself.

Eyes still straining out into the night, Amelia took slow paces sideways. She discovered that toward the far end of the gallery, one of the tall windows was not truly a window at all, but a door. She still had a set of house keys tied at her waist, and she tried each of them in turn until one slender finger of metal turned the tumblers of the lock. The door swung open with a creak, and she walked outside.

She didn't follow the drive, but walked straight across the green, not caring to draw attention to herself. The grass was damp with nighttime dew, and it wanted clipping. The blades brushed her exposed ankles as she walked, ticklish and cool. Moths fluttered out of her path.

The stables drew her like a lodestone. She wanted to see this place that merited so much of Spencer's effort and attention. It was certainly the largest horse barn she'd ever seen. In construction and outward appearance, it looked finer than most houses she'd ever seen.

A few grooms milled in the entryway, talking to one another. They didn't notice her as she skirted the main entrance and plunged into the shadows at the side of the building. Barns always had more than one entrance. Before long, she came upon a human-sized door. She ducked inside and found herself in a dimly lit, meticulously kept tack room. The smells of leather and clean horse mingled in air heavy with the dust of hay. Amelia pressed her hands to her face and sneezed into them.

In the ensuing silence, she froze—waiting for someone to have heard her and come looking. No one did. However, she did hear a voice echoing from the rafters—a low, calming murmur much like the sound of rushing water, coming from somewhere nearby.

She moved through the tack room and into a wide aisle lined with stalls, taking care to make her steps light. A recumbent horse whickered softly as she stepped toward the low, mesmerizing voice and a flickering light at the far end of the aisle. She paused at the edge of the last stall, well out of the golden aura cast by a single hanging carriage lamp. Cautiously, she craned her neck around the post.

This was a larger, open area, designed for grooming. And in the center was Spencer, rubbing down a regal dark filly. Amelia observed the pair in silence, digging her fingers into the wooden post to keep her balance.

The horse was freed of saddle and bridle, restrained only by a simple halter tied to a ring. Spencer was dressed in an open-necked shirt, knee boots, and breeches of tight-fitting buckskin. Both man and beast were damp in places. Perspiration shone a glossy black on the horse's flanks, just as it matted the dark locks of hair at Spencer's nape. The inseams of his breeches were dark with sweat, too. The sight did strange things to her, in analogous places.

The horse's breathing was audible, and Spencer rubbed the filly's withers and back with a towel, wiping the lather from her coat in a smooth, confident rhythm. And as he worked, he spoke. Crooned, really. Amelia could scarcely make out his words, but they were soft and tender. Affectionate.

"Softly, then," he said, coming to stand before the horse and carefully wiping the animal's nose and ears with a corner of the towel. "Hold just a moment, my sweet." The horse snorted, and Spencer gave an easy, good-natured laugh that resonated in Amelia's bones.

He kept up the steady stream of words as he hung the towel on a hook and bent to check each of the horse's hooves. Each time he asked the horse to raise a hoof, he did so with more patience than Amelia had ever seen him ask a person for anything, with words like, "This one, if you please," and "Thank you, my pet."

Her heart ached. She was seeing an entirely new side of him—a gentle, caring, thoughtful side she would never have guessed he possessed. Having grown up with five brothers, she did understand that paradox about men. They found it easier to display emotions where animals were concerned. Laurent had been her rock at both Mother and Papa's burials, but when his boyhood sheepdog slipped into permanent rest at the age of fourteen, Amelia had watched her brother weep like a child.

And seeing Spencer tend the horse with such patience and care, even when he believed himself to be alone—it confirmed what Amelia had known in her heart, from their wedding on: This man could never be capable of murder.

"Nearly done, my dear."

He took a brush to the horse's coat, gently brushing the dirt from her fetlocks and murmuring more tender words. As Amelia watched, a sick feeling gathered in her stomach. She'd known from the first that people came second to horses in the duke's priorities. After all, that was the entire reason they'd met. He'd all but ruined Jack—and by extension, her own happiness—in pursuit of a stallion. But somehow viewing this scene recast that reality in a new, harsh light. There was no further denying that this man possessed the capacity for real tenderness and solicitude. He just couldn't—or wouldn't—reveal those things to her.

Oh, God. Ladies were supposed to become embittered wives when their husbands strayed to other women's beds. Amelia was going to spend the rest of her life feeling envious of *horses*. The complete absurdity of it made her tremble.

She needed to leave, immediately. He would finish grooming his mount soon, and the last thing she wanted was to be caught out here and forced to explain not only her presence, but the tears burning her eyes. She began her slow retreat, feeling her way backward across the tiled brick floor rather than making too much rustle with a turn. But shadows clung to the ground, obscuring her steps, and her slippers were still wet with dew. She slipped.

Drat, drat, drat.

Throwing her arms wide, she made a wild grab for the door of a nearby stall. Her fingers closed over the edge, and somehow she stopped her fall before she sprawled completely to the ground. She froze, her pulse pounding in her throat and her spine contorting in ways she'd surely rue tomorrow. At any second, she expected Spencer to round the corner and make her humiliation complete.

He didn't. After several moments' uneventful silence, Amelia struggled to unknot her limbs and regain her feet. For once, luck was on her side. Her wild scrambling had gone unnoticed.

By Spencer, at least. The same couldn't be said for the horse whose door she'd borrowed for a crutch. An offended snort came from the darkened stall, and Amelia heard the horse coming to its feet.

She addressed the animal frantically, making as many mollifying clucks and shushes as her predicament would allow. She didn't want Spencer to hear the horse, but she didn't want him to hear her, either. Perhaps she should have simply turned and fled, but her instinct was to quiet the beast first, rather than rouse the whole barn.

Through the shadows, she could just make out the

horse swinging its head from side to side, ears flat and nostrils flared. The beast's breathing grew heavier. Noisier. Now the horse's agitation was not only inconvenient, but threatening. This was why she'd never learned to ride. Horses always frightened her. All that intimidating strength, and they never heeded her wishes whatsoever. Just like now.

"Oh, please," Amelia pleaded through her teeth. "Please hush, please."

Boom.

The horse kicked at the bottom of the door, sending a bone-jarring vibration up the rails and through Amelia's arms. With a startled cry, she released her grip and leapt back, only to collide with an unseen obstacle. She whirled in defense. Strong hands grasped her shoulders and she fought instinctively against them, struggling and lashing out with her fists until reason and the carriage lamp illuminated the obvious. These were Spencer's hands holding her.

The ensuing wave of relief dissolved what remained of her strength.

"Oh, God." She sucked in a lungful of air, trying to locate the courage to meet his eyes. "Spencer, I'm so sorry."

"You should be. What the devil are you doing in here?" He looked her up and down, as he often did, but this time his gaze sought her angles instead of her curves.

"I'm unharmed," she told him, hoping that's what he meant to assess. Behind her, the horse gave another booming kick at its stall, and she jumped in her skin.

With a rough curse, Spencer released Amelia's arms. Fairly shoving her out of the way, he went to the door and reached his hand toward the horse. The animal nosed his fingers roughly, as if in reprimand, and stamped the floor. Undeterred, Spencer murmured a steady stream of placating words. Eventually the mare—for Spencer's soft endearments left no question the horse was female—tossed her head and offered her left side for his touch. He obliged the request, rubbing the horse behind the ear.

And Amelia stood there awkwardly, arms crossed over her chest, wondering why it should surprise her in the slightest that when confronted with a frightened mare and frightened wife, Spencer would choose to calm the horse.

He turned to her and said with cool, even disdain, "Who let you in here?"

"No one."

"Damn it, tell me—" At his harsh tone, the horse started. Spencer paused a moment to calm her again, then made a visible effort to temper his voice before speaking again. "Tell me who let you in here," he said calmly. "Whoever he is, he's just lost his post."

"I'm telling you, no one let me in. I came on my own. I entered through the tack room." The anger in his eyes as he stared at her, juxtaposed with the tender way he still caressed the mare's ear . . . it was just too much. Too insulting, too disheartening.

"God, Amelia." He shook his head. "What the hell were you thinking?"

"I don't know. I heard you ride up to the house. I thought you'd be in directly, but then you weren't. I was tired of waiting and tired in general, and I've been wanting to speak with you so I thought . . ." She clapped a hand over a sudden burst of laughter. If only he knew what she'd come out here to say.

He frowned at her, and she giggled again. Suddenly, the situation was unbearably funny. Her absurd envy for a horse. His unfailing knack for saying the wrong thing on every occasion. The whole dratted marriage.

"I was thinking of you, you insufferable man." She

laughed into her palm, then wiped her eyes with the back of her hand. "All day long, I've been thinking of you."

Spencer stared at her, his jaw working as he debated what to say. If he told her he'd been thinking of her all day, too, would it sound trite and insincere? Would it even do the truth justice? To say he'd been merely "thinking" of her seemed inadequate. What was the word for it, when over the course of an endless, wearying, ultimately fruitless day, one's every act, thought, intent, and breath were directed toward a single purpose—a single person? He supposed he could tell her he'd been "thinking" of her so fiercely all day long that when he'd seen her standing there in the shadows, gripping the door of Juno's stall, for a moment he'd wondered if his extreme fatigue and longing had conspired to create a hallucination. And that when she'd startled and he'd caught her, and there'd been no further doubt that the soft, trembling flesh beneath his fingers was absolutely real—he hadn't been sure how to keep touching her without completely losing control.

But whatever he wished to say, before he could get a word of it out, she turned on her heel and fled.

Just bloody perfect.

After wiping his hands and tossing a word or two to the groom at the entry, he hurried after her. She was halfway up the green by the time he caught up. Head down, arms tucked securely around her middle, she made purposeful strides through the grass. The hem of her frock was damp and translucent, tangling about her ankles. The sight made him thirsty.

"Listen to me," he said, matching her stride for stride. "You're welcome to visit the stables any time you wish, but don't ever sneak in alone like that. The mare you startled—she can be dangerous when provoked. Not only does she kick, she bites. She's taken a few fingers in her day."

"Ah. So that's the key to earning your affection, is it? Perhaps I should try snapping at you, and then I'd merit better treatment."

It was his turn to laugh. "You've been snapping at me since the night we met."

"Well, then. That hasn't worked."

"What do you mean? I've married you, haven't I?"

Her stride hitched. Then she resumed her pace. Then she stopped again.

"You've married me, yes. And when you proposed, you told me you wanted a duchess, not a broodmare. Silly me, to assume the former ranked above the latter in your taxonomy."

He bit off his response, because it would only have angered her further. It would doubtless be a very grave error to tell her he found her pronunciation of "taxonomy" indescribably arousing.

Huffing at his silence, she turned and forged on. And now Spencer was beginning to find the entire conversation gratifying.

She was jealous. Envy was the farthest thing from fear. It implied she wanted more from him, not less. She'd come out to the stables looking for him. By her own admission, she'd been thinking of him all day.

"For two people married a total of four days," he observed, catching up to her again, "we seem to argue a great deal."

"Are you expecting me to apologize?"

"No. I rather enjoy it." And he did. He loved the give-and-take of it, their even match of wits, the responses she provoked from him. She drew him out of his own head and forced him to interact, in a way few people could do. And then there was the lovely pink of her cheeks and the way a defiant posture emphasized her bosom. He enjoyed those things, too. "But I think we're just using it as a substitute."

"A substitute? For what?"

"For what we're not doing." He lifted one eyebrow and slid his gaze down her body.

"Is that all you ever think about? Getting me in a bed?"

"Lately? Yes. Just about."

She shot him a glare that didn't quite disguise her satisfied blush. He allowed himself to fall behind a few steps, that he might enjoy the brisk sway of her hips as she walked. Perhaps this day hadn't been so fruitless after all.

He followed her to the back of the service wing, where she approached the nearest entrance, a small door at the rear. She pulled a key from her chatelaine and fit it in the lock. How did she know the house so well, so quickly? Damn, Spencer had lived at Braxton Hall for almost fifteen years, and he'd never even used this door.

"Where are we going?" he asked as they navigated a dim, narrow corridor.

She turned and stared at him. "The kitchen, of course."

"Oh. Of course." Shaking his head, Spencer followed her into the kitchen and watched as Amelia went to a cupboard and pulled out two covered dishes. She set them on the butcher-block counter in the center of the room, then snagged a plate and flatware from a shelf.

"Are you hungry?" he asked, watching her arrange a single place setting, then pour a large glass of wine.

"No, you are."

She whipped the cover from a platter of cold meats. Spencer counted ham, roasted beef, chicken legs, tongue . . .

"No lamb," she said. "And there's bread."

He stared at the growing buffet before him. "What was it you wished to speak with me about?"

"Beg pardon?" Using the side of her wrist, she brushed back a stray lock of hair.

"Out in the stables. You said you'd waited up to speak with me."

"It will keep until morning. Here's pickle."

"No," he said, bracing his hands on the wood surface. "No, I don't think it will keep. It was important enough to keep you up late, drive you out of the house in search of me. What was it?"

Ignoring his question, she plunked a small crock down on the table. "Butter."

"For God's sake, I'm not interested in butter!"

"Very well." She took the crock away.

He thrust a hand through his hair. "Damn it, Amelia. What's going on?"

"Why won't you eat?"

"Why do you care?"

"Why don't you treat me like you treat your horses?"

He could only stare at her.

Looking a bit embarrassed, she crossed her arms and regarded the ceiling.

"Why don't I treat you . . ." He shook his head to clear it. "Here's a thought. Perhaps because you're not a horse?"

"No, I'm not. In your view, it would seem I am some lesser creature by far. At least the horses are turned out now and then."

She grabbed the butter crock again and thunked it down on the table, reaching for a knife. With her other hand, she split open a roll. "No one eats in this house," she muttered. She dipped her knife in butter and coated the bread with short, tense strokes. "I may not be a woman of any exceptional accomplishment. Nor do I possess a great deal of beauty or grace. But I'm good at this." She leveled the knife at him. "Planning menus, managing a household, entertaining guests. Taking care of people. And you would deny me the chance to do any of it."

"I haven't denied you anything." Good Lord. If anyone was being denied in this marriage, it was him.

"You've denied me everything! I've been removed to the country, away from all my family and friends. My meals are spurned, as are my overtures of friendship. I'm not permitted to host guests. You wouldn't even allow me to make a silly little seat cushion." She threw the knife down, and it landed with a loud clatter. "What does it signify to you, anyway?"

"Amelia . . ."

"And that's another thing. The horses are 'my dear,' 'my sweet,' 'my pet.' I'm just *Amelia*." She pronounced the name in an exaggerated drawl, mimicking his deep voice.

Spencer's chin jerked. She'd overheard him in the stables? How long had she been standing there? The thought of her eavesdropping on him inflamed his irritation.

"*Just* Amelia," he repeated. "Very well, I confess to the egregious offense of addressing you by your Christian name. But with God as my witness, I have never referred to you, in speech or in thought, as 'just' anything."

She set her jaw.

"Do you wish me to address you in endearments, then? Do you truly want to be known as 'my dear,' 'my darling,' 'my pet'? I cannot yet truthfully call you my wife."

"No," she said. "You are right. Insincerely uttered endearments are much worse than none at all. Please forget I ever voiced the complaint." She took an angry sip of wine. And then another. "I'm tired of arguing."

"So am I." Rounding the table, he came to stand directly in front of her. Heat built between their bodies. He took the wineglass from her hand, brushing her hand with his fingertips. Just that simple touch electrified him. God, he was more than taken with her. He was damn near consumed.

Never breaking eye contact, he drained the remaining wine. As she watched him, her tongue darted out to moisten her lips. Spencer casually set aside the wineglass, and tension all but audibly crackled between them. He thought it might have been the last dregs of his patience, evaporating into the air.

"Well?" he said darkly.

She didn't miss the alteration in his tone. Anxiety overtook her expression. She blinked furiously, looking everywhere but at him. Reaching for the butter crock, she said, "I should clean up here."

He grabbed her wrist. "Leave it."

She gasped, and the breathy sound stoked his desire. He wanted to make her gasp again. And again. Moan, whimper, call out his name.

Eyes widening with apprehension, she tugged against his grip. "Then I'll just go to bed."

Lifting her into his arms was the work of an instant. Oh, and the gasp she gave that time—it made his blood sizzle.

"Not without me, you won't."

Chapter Thirteen

"You can't do this," Amelia protested, even as Spencer carried her swiftly up the stairs, proving he could, quite easily, do this.

At the top of the staircase, he turned in the direction of her suite.

"You gave me your word," she said breathlessly. "If you break it now, I'll never be able to trust you."

"Damn it," he growled, shouldering open the door to her parlor, "stop pretending you don't want this, too. You're so wet for me beneath those skirts, I can taste it from here."

Oh, my. If she hadn't already been damp between her thighs, that little speech would have done it.

"I don't want it like this," she said, a little less firmly than she'd like. Yes, she'd intended to share his bed, but not in the heat of passion.

As he swept her through the door, she cowered into his chest, not wishing to hit her head on the doorjamb. A frantic pulse beat at the apex of her sex, matching the rhythm of his pounding heart. She pressed her cheek to his strong chest, feeling threatened, protected, desired, conquered. Thrilled, in a dozen different ways.

He carried her through the parlor and antechamber,

straight into her bedchamber. Oh, God. He really meant to take her, tonight.

He stopped short of the bed, dropping her to her feet.

Dizzy, she reeled on her toes. "I . . . I think you should leave."

He made a sound of exasperation. "Amelia, turn around."

She turned. And immediately berated herself for it. Why did she obey his arrogant commands so instinctively? He said "sit," she sat. He said "stand," she stood. He told her to remove her bodice, she stripped herself to the waist faster than a master chef skins an eel. It was a fortunate thing he hadn't yet ordered her to go to the bed, lift her skirts, and be still.

A fortunate thing, indeed. Or a considerate one, on his part. Perhaps even a patient, generous, honorable thing?

Now she was more confused than ever.

"Look to your right," he said. "What do you see there, just to the side of the mantel?"

She raised her hands in bewilderment. "A chair?"

"Between the mantel and the chair."

"Oh." There was a small silver frame hanging there that she didn't recall seeing before. She took a candle from her dressing table and stepped closer, peering at it hard. "It's . . ." *Oh, goodness.* It was her needlework—the little country scene she'd finished the other night—stretched tight and framed under spotless glass. The silver frame complemented the silver threads she'd woven into the brook, and the whole effect was . . . even if she did say it herself, it was really quite charming.

"You had it framed?" she asked, still staring at the embroidered vignette. "I thought you said you'd never allow it in this house."

"I said it would never adorn a settee in this house." His voice deepened as he came to stand behind her.

"But . . . but you took it from me."

"Of course I did. Because you threatened to make it into a pillow." He placed both hands on her shoulders. Their weight felt like a reproach. "A pillow, for Christ's sake. Why should it have to justify its existence by serving some mundane function? It's lovely. It's art. In this house, we don't sit on art. We hang it on the wall and admire it."

She didn't know what to say. *Thank you* came to her lips, but she wasn't sure he meant his words as a compliment. In fact, she felt strangely unsettled by them.

He turned her to face him. "You are so eager to define yourself in reference to others. Jack's sister, Claudia's sponsor, this house's mistress. You rail at me for not treating you as I would treat one of my horses, my possessions. For not measuring your worth by the food you serve or the musicales you could host." He gestured impatiently toward the framed embroidery. "From the moment we met, you've resisted me, provoked me, demanded my respect. Then we arrive at Braxton Hall, and here . . . It's as if you wish to be a settee cushion, and you're vexed with me for refusing to sit on you."

She shrugged off his grip on her shoulder. "You have no right—"

"Oh, I have every right." He closed the distance between them, taking the candlestick from her hand and placing it atop the mantel. "I'm your lord and your husband, and I have all manner of rights I've chosen not to exercise. Yet."

That last word gave her chills.

His hungry, dangerous gaze trapped hers. "There's a lot going on behind those pretty blue eyes, but somewhere between those delectable ears and that remarkable brain is a seriously faulty connection, if when I call you 'Amelia' you hear it prefaced with 'just.' Believe me, I could have married 'just anyone' years ago."

Did she still have knees? If so, she couldn't feel them.

Believe him, he said? Believe that she had pretty eyes and delectable ears and a remarkable brain. Delectable. Her. Believe that a wealthy, attractive duke had held off marriage for years, but something about her—an impoverished, impertinent spinster—had changed his mind overnight.

Now his words were more than unsettling her. They were threatening everything she believed about herself, and everything she knew about him.

Which was hardly anything, come to think of it.

"What predictable arrogance," she said, jabbing her finger in his chest. It was a juvenile gesture, but for some reason she needed to touch him. "What utter hypocrisy. You would stand here and . . . and analyze my character, pretend to understand all the innermost workings of my mind? This, from the man who lavishes affection on horses, but doesn't know how to hold a wife."

Only a fleeting spark in his eyes betrayed his surprise.

"You have no right to judge me." She made a fist and thumped the flat side against his chest. Was that his heart, pounding against it? "Don't you belittle me for valuing family and friendship and hospitality, simply because you can't be bothered to care. And how dare you chastise me for seeking ways to be useful, when you've brought me here just to give you an heir. You married me for the most mundane function of all."

"Oh, believe me. When we share a bed, it will be anything but mundane." His hand shot out and captured her chin. "Do you know how I spent my day, Amelia?"

She shook her head. Just a little, because he held her jaw fast.

"With whores."

"With . . . ?" Her voice died in her throat. *Oh, Lord.*

"Yes, whores. I rose before dawn and rode hard, all the way to London, exhausting three horses on the way.

I then spent the entire afternoon turning Whitechapel's most undistinguished establishments inside out, searching for the prostitute who found Leo's body. I spoke to whores of every shape and size. Dark ones, fair ones, plump ones, thin ones, ugly ones, pretty ones . . . a rare few who were genuine beauties. And for a shilling, any one of them would have cheerfully dropped to her knees or hiked her skirts for me. But I didn't want any of them. The whole damned day, I thought only of you."

His eyes bored into hers. "I thought of you as I rode home, without changing horses in Cambridge as I should have done. I pushed that horse harder than I had any right to do, and yes, she deserved a bit of soothing and apology for it. I never abuse my cattle, but I came damn near to it today. And I didn't do it because I just wanted a 'mundane' tup, Amelia. I sure as hell didn't do it because I wanted to come home to roast beef and a nice buttered roll. I did it all just to find that blasted token. So I could show you I'm not a murderer. Earn your trust, convince you there's nothing to fear."

With a bitter chuckle, he released her chin. "And the damnedest thing of it is—at this moment, you *should* be afraid. Terrified."

He advanced on her, backing her up until she collided with the wall. The beaded edge of the paneling pressed against her spine. His desirous gaze roamed over her body, turning her firm in places and soft in others.

"You should be trembling in your slippers, because I am tired and frustrated and about two heartbeats away from throwing you to the bed, ripping that dress from your body, and making you mine, whether you wish it or not."

"You wouldn't do that."

He braced his arms against the wall, caging her between them. His heat and scent surrounded her.

"You're right. I wouldn't. I'd take you right here, never mind the bed."

His eyes were dark and wild and hungry, and the intensity in them was enough to make her feel invaded already. Gone was the man who'd kissed her in Laurent's study with such patient skill. There was nothing of seduction in his manner now—only possession, naked and raw.

Though she was shivering to the roots of her hair, she forced herself to hold his gaze and remain absolutely still. Until the heat smoldering between their bodies could melt steel.

At last, her patience was rewarded. He sighed, and the strength tensed in his arms relaxed. It was plain he was exhausted, in both body and mind.

"For God's sake, Amelia . . ."

She took that narrow window of opportunity and bolted through it. Ducking under his arm, she darted sideways and ran for the other side of the room.

With a curse, he lunged at her. Instead of skirting the bed as she had, he vaulted atop it, attempting to cut off her path of retreat. He fell to his knees on the mattress, pitching forward to grab at her as she passed. He caught only a fold of her skirt, and the fabric tore as she wrestled away.

She hurried toward the connecting door, glancing back to see him sprawled on the bed, clutching a swatch of shredded muslin and glaring pure murder.

"Damn it, don't you run from me."

Marshaling all her strength, she slid back the panel. The creak of wood was matched by a creak of the mattress as he hastened to rise and give chase. With a little cry of alarm, she scurried through the door and began to slide it closed. Just as the panel was nearly shut, his hand shot into the narrowing gap. But the door's momentum and Amelia's desperate energy were too much for him this time. The door banged home, mashing his fingers against the jamb.

Roaring in pain, he withdrew his hand, and the weight of her body propelled the panel to its resting place. With trembling fingers, Amelia fitted and secured the door's only latch, locking herself in Spencer's bedchamber.

Breathing hard, she turned her back to the door and melted against it with relief.

Bang.

She jumped. He pounded the door again, and then again.

"Let me in there," he demanded, his voice muffled by the thick wood.

She swallowed hard. "No."

"What's to keep me from walking around and entering the other way?"

"I've locked that door, too," she lied, rattling the keys on her chatelaine.

More muffled curses. Then the loud crash of something breaking against the wall.

She hugged herself tight, trying to stop trembling. Suddenly, the door panel shifted against her back, as if he'd leaned his weight on the other side.

And everything went quiet.

On the outside, at least. Inside Amelia, a whole symphony was playing. Her pulse drummed furiously in her ears. A phantom violist played frantic melodies on the taut strings of her nerves. And in her heart, a chorus of thousands sang. Hallelujah, hosanna, glory be to God on high!

Spencer wanted her. He really, truly, desperately wanted *her*. Her, Amelia. She wasn't "just" a wife to him, a mother for his heirs. He'd said it himself, he could have married "just anyone" years ago. She was reason enough for a duke to debase himself by crawling through the seediest districts of London. Reason enough for the most horse-mad gentleman she'd ever known to risk the health of a valuable, favored mount.

She had pretty eyes. And delectable ears. She touched her fingers to her own earlobes, absurdly wishing she had some way to taste them and judge for herself.

He'd called her an artist. She had a remarkable brain, he'd said. He enjoyed arguing with her. He'd thought of her all day.

Oh, my. Oh my God.

She'd waited her whole life to feel this way. Really, truly wanted. Not just nice to have around, or vaguely lusted after, but *desired* for both her body and her mind. Joy shouted from every corpuscle of her body—and she needed to be alone with it for just a little while longer, or . . .

Or she would fall in love with him so hard, so fast, she would crash straight through the floor.

"Amelia?" His voice was very near, and rough with fatigue. She pressed her ear to the door to make it out. He said, "I hope you didn't like that china shepherdess."

She smiled a wide, secret smile. Quintessential Spencer apology.

"I'm bloody tired," he said, sounding defeated. "I'm going to sleep in your bed now."

The door didn't move. So she knew, neither had he.

Turning her head, Amelia spoke softly—at a volume he could only hear if he was pressing his own ear to the door and listening very hard. "Is your hand all right?"

Moments passed.

"I think so."

"I'll have a look at it in the morning."

"On second thought, it may be broken."

Smiling again, she ceased leaning against the door and stood under her own power. With a little rattle, the panel shifted as he removed his weight from the other side. She slid back the latch and pushed open the door to find him waiting for her.

"Let me see," she said, extending an arm.

He laid his wounded hand in hers, palm up. His breathing was a slow, seductive rasp as she made her examination. His skin was dry and warm and a little roughened with wear, but each finger wiggled easily. She noted no swelling or blood.

"It's fine," she said.

"I know."

They stood there in silence, just touching. Both staring at his hand, as if she were a gypsy fortune-teller, peering into his palm to divine the future.

He said quietly, "I'm not a murderer, Amelia. I know I've flattened a man in front of you and behaved like a brute since the night we met. But with God as my witness, I hadn't raised my hand in violence for fourteen years before our wedding day. I don't know what the devil you've done to me, but you make me lose control. You make me laugh. You make me *chatty*. You make me hard with a word, or even a look—and there's damn near nothing I wouldn't do right now to get inside you. But don't run from me as if I were a villain, and don't ever lock me out. I didn't kill Leo, I swear it."

She lifted her head, and their gazes tangled. He didn't even try to mask the vulnerability in his eyes. At last, this was something he needed from her. She was a nurturer, and he didn't want to be nurtured. She was a caregiver, and he didn't wish to be looked after. But she had a trusting soul, and he needed this—someone to believe in him.

It just wasn't in her to refuse.

"I know. Oh, Spencer, I know you didn't." She lifted his hand, dropping a kiss in the center of his palm before pressing it to her cheek. "In my heart, I never believed you did."

He sucked in a shaky breath. "Then why—"

"I was afraid. Of getting hurt in other ways. To be truthful, I still am."

His thumb stroked her cheek. "I would never hurt you."

"I don't think you can promise me that." She squeezed his bruised fingers. "But it makes things a bit more equal, to know that I can hurt you, too."

His gaze fell to her lips. He said simply, without any trace of irony, "You are killing me."

He moved through the doorway, taking her into his arms in one swift motion. Together they fell to the bed, and his lips found hers. With no preliminary, he pried her jaw wide, probing her mouth with deep, unrelenting sweeps of his tongue. She clung to him, surrendering to the wild passion of the kiss, her only goal to take from him as much as she gave.

He lifted his head and stared into her eyes. "We're going to do this."

Again, that thrilling little word. *We.*

"Yes," she whispered.

"No fears tonight. No regrets tomorrow."

"None."

He sat back on his haunches and pulled her up, until they both stood on their knees in the center of the bed. After fumbling with the row of buttons at her back, he peeled the bodice from her torso, and she helped by wriggling her arms free of the sleeves. He found the laces of her stays and impatiently yanked them loose, casting the entire undergarment aside within seconds and eagerly taking her breasts in his hands, through her thin summer chemise.

She swallowed hard as he admired them, lifting and kneading the soft globes with his fingers. He seemed lost in those curves—his touch unhurried, his breathing slow and thick. Her nipples grew painfully hard, gathering to tight, prominent peaks that chafed against the thin fabric.

He eased her neckline down. The gap wasn't generous enough to afford him access to her nipple. Instead, he bent his head and suckled her straight through her shift. Oh, God. The sensation of his soft tongue licking her through the rough fabric . . . it was so intensely pleasurable, she couldn't help but moan.

She reached for the hem of his shirt, tugging it free of his waistband and sliding her hands beneath, running her palms over the tight muscles of his abdomen and the faint trail of hair leading to his groin. Emboldened by his gruff sound of approval, she slid her hand downward, cupping the rigid length tenting his breeches.

"You'll have to tell me what to do," she said, lightly tracing the shape of him.

He raised his head from her breast. Seeming to abandon his efforts to undress her, he finished pulling his own shirt loose. "There aren't any rules to this. If I do something to you, and you enjoy it"—he yanked his shirt over his head and tossed it aside—"there's an excellent chance I'll enjoy it if you do the same to me."

"Oh. Very well."

As he reached for the closures of his breeches, she bent forward and took his nipple in her mouth.

He hissed out his breath, and she jerked back. "Not good?"

"Good," he assured her, sliding a hand over her neck. "Very good."

Smiling to herself, she bent and tried again. This time she licked first, teasing the small, flat circle to a tiny bud. He groaned as she fitted her lips around it, suckling gently, then nipping with her teeth.

"Holy God," he grit out.

Heat surged between Amelia's thighs. She'd never felt so sensual, powerful. With a few swipes of her tongue she'd incited a man to blasphemy, and she cupped the proof of his rampant desire for her in the palm of her hand. As she transferred her attentions to his other nipple, she tentatively stroked up and down his length.

"Enough." He clapped a hand over hers, pressing her palm firmly to his groin.

She lifted her head. "Not good?"

"Too good." With a pained expression, he pulled her hand away. "I've waited much too long for this, for it to be over before it starts. Lie down."

She complied, smiling to herself. He said "sit," and she sat. He said "stand," and she stood. He told her to "lie down," and she lay down . . . because at her core, she trusted him instinctively. She always had, from that very first night.

Kicking her slippers to the floor, she drew the counterpane back before reclining on the pillows. With focused concentration, he divested her of stockings, petticoat, and drawers, until she lay atop the sheets in only her chemise. The dampened cloth clung to her nipples as feverish breaths lifted her chest. He sat at the edge of the bed, wrestling briefly with his boots and then standing just long enough to slide his breeches and smallclothes down over his hips.

Fully naked now, he straddled her thighs, making no attempt whatsoever to hide his erect member from her view. For about two seconds, a vestige of modesty diverted her gaze elsewhere, but she quickly gave into temptation and stared. His proud, thick shaft jutted out from a nest of black hair, making a dramatic impression against the white lawn of her shift. She had no grounds for comparison, but she found his sheer size and eagerness rather daunting.

"Don't be timid." The hint of amusement in his voice made her blush. "It's going to be inside you. You ought to see it first." He picked up her hand where it lay at her side, whispering, "Touch me."

He wrapped her fingers around his shaft, guiding her hand slowly up and down his full length. Petal-soft skin slid with her palm, slipping over thick veins and rock-hard need. This softness, this strength—it would all be inside her soon. Her feminine places ached pleasurably at the thought.

She stroked him again, and a drop of clear moisture glistened at the tip. Intrigued, she dabbed it with her fingertip.

His hand tightened, immobilizing hers. "No more of that."

He pulled her hand away and retreated to grasp the hem of her chemise. Skimming his hands up the slope of her calves, then her thighs, he pushed the fabric to her waist. After pausing briefly to adjust his weight, he hiked the shift higher still, exposing her soft, rounded belly and the swells of her breasts. Fabric wadded beneath her arms. Should she sit up, so he might remove the garment entirely?

He seemed too impatient to bother. His hands ranged greedily over her body, grasping her breasts, hips, thighs. With one hand, he reached between her legs, parting her sex. She was already damp there, and his fingers slipped easily between her folds. He explored her gently, his breathing growing rough. Growing self-conscious, she found herself wishing he'd at least kiss her while he touched her this way. But then his thumb found that sensitive nub at the crest of her sex, and she just didn't care anymore. Her back arched, thrusting her breasts upward. With a low moan, he bent and took her nipple in his mouth, sucking firmly as he circled that needy spot with his thumb. He slid a finger inside her, and her intimate muscles clenched around it.

"Bloody hell." When he spoke again, his voice shook. "You're so tight."

"Is that bad?" She moaned as he worked his finger in and out, dragging against exquisitely tender flesh.

"It's unfair. This is going to be damn amazing for me, and damn uncomfortable for you, at best." He increased the pace of his circular caresses, and her hips jerked with a fierce jolt of pleasure. "Can you come for me? If you come first, it will go easier."

What a request. Just like him, to be so straightforward. Could she? Amelia wasn't sure. She most definitely wanted to. His touch incited unbearable sensation in her, and he drove her closer to the edge with every tiny caress. But there was trusting him, and then there was *trusting* him. She'd never come for anyone other than herself. It was as though she hovered on the brink of pleasure, but a thin cord of inhibition held her back.

And then his words began to unravel it.

"I want to see you come. I've been dreaming of it, did you know?"

No. No, she hadn't known. She could never have guessed, in a thousand years, that he would be dreaming of that.

"Both asleep and awake, I've been dreaming of it. What your face will look like. How tight your nipples will get. Exactly what shade of pink you'll turn, and in precisely which places."

Rocked by a fresh surge of pleasure, she let her head roll back and threw her wrist over her eyes.

He pulled her arm away, while with the other hand he stroked her in a brisk, firm rhythm. "Oh, no. Don't you hide from me. I'm selfish, and I want to see. Right now I ought to sink between your thighs and bring you there with my tongue, but I won't, because I have to see you when you come for me."

She could barely comprehend the carnal picture his

words painted, but her body responded to it with enthusiasm. She was so aroused, her body made wet, erotic noises as he plunged his finger into her again and again.

He had her so close, so close. She whimpered, desperate for release.

"Tell me," he said. "Tell me what you need."

Were there words for it? She couldn't find them. He'd decimated her vocabulary.

"Softly," she managed. "Softly."

He eased the pressure off his thumb, jiggling it lightly over her swollen bud. "Yes?"

"Yes." She panted and bucked, biting her lip and grasping handfuls of the bed linens.

Yes yes yes . . . Yes.

The last strand of her resistance snapped. She came so fiercely, the climax jolted her hips from the bed. He slid a second finger inside her, doubling the intensity of her peak. The pleasure went on and on, in wave after wave. The last tremors were still rippling through her as he withdrew his hand and positioned himself between her legs.

"I must have you," he muttered, forcing her thighs wide and thrusting into her quivering core. "Now."

She gasped at the fresh spear of pain mingling with the ebbing wave of pleasure.

He swore, rooting deeper. "Can't stop." *Thrust.* "Too good."

With short digs of his hips, he pushed further and further into her. Her tender flesh ached and stretched. Just when she thought she couldn't possibly take any more of him, he grasped her backside in both hands, angled her hips, and sank deeper still. Her neck arched as she struggled for breath. She was so full of him, she felt him everywhere.

At last fully seated, he rested atop her for a moment, panting against the curve of her neck. The joining hurt, but it also felt indescribably right. She was a woman.

She was made for this. She loved the fact that she could take him inside her and hold him there, so tightly, that there was nowhere else on earth he'd rather be.

"You put me through hell for this," he said, punishing her with a sharp nudge against her womb. "And I want you to know, it was worth every moment."

She laughed, and the brief spasm made the pain even worse. But better, at the same time.

Kissing her quiet, he began to thrust again. Gently now. Her body had adjusted to his, and he moved easily, gliding in and out with smooth, powerful strokes. Within seconds, the act ceased hurting so much and began to feel warm, and quite pleasant indeed. She relaxed her thighs, spreading her legs to take him deeper. Reveling in the weight of his body atop hers, the firmness of his muscled shoulders and arms, the sleekness of his back. As his tempo increased, she ran her hands possessively over the hard angles and planes, even daring to cup the taut, flexing muscles of his buttocks.

He made a gruff sound, and she sensed a shift in him. Consideration was banished; raw need took its place. He rose up on his knees, lifting her hips from the bed in his strong, sculpted hands. The tendons in his neck stood out like ropes. Her breasts jounced wildly as he pistoned his hips, taking her hard and fast in ruthless pursuit of his own pleasure.

Now she understood why he'd insisted on watching her peak. Even with his eyes closed, even through the shadows of night . . . the look on his face told her he'd rather die than withdraw from her body right now. This was it. This was the very best part. Feeling so desired, so needed. More essential to him than air.

He made a rough noise, something between a growl and a moan. And then he collapsed atop her, shuddering and helpless in the throes of his release. She wrapped her arms around his shoulders, smoothing the damp hair from his brow. He made a pillow of her breasts and sighed her name against her skin.

Maybe she'd spoken too soon. Perhaps this was the very best part. Holding him, in every way. Feeling as close as two people could possibly be.

It didn't last long enough.

All too soon, he withdrew from her body. "Are you terribly hurt?"

"Not terribly. I'll do."

"Good." He rolled over and slumped onto his back. "I failed miserably at that gentleness bit."

"I noticed." She eased the fabric of her shift back down over her body. "It's all right."

With one arm, he drew her close, tucking her body against his. She rested her head on his chest, enthralled by the forceful, distant thumping of his heart. It eventually slowed, as did his breaths.

"It will get better," he mumbled sleepily. "You'll see. It only hurts the once." His grip on her arm went slack as he drifted into sleep. A gentle snore rumbled through his chest.

She clutched his waist, shivering despite the heat he radiated. Could he have any idea what she'd just surrendered to him? Not just her body, but her trust, her heart, her future. She would love him soon, if she didn't already. From this moment forward he possessed the ability to make her indescribably happy, and the power to devastate her completely. He'd revealed to her flashes of true emotion and vulnerability tonight, but then—tonight he'd been at an extreme of frustrated lust. What would the morning bring? She could only cling to a thin cord of optimism and hope that his . . . desire, or regard, or whatever he felt for her . . . hadn't been exorcised with the force of his climax.

You'll see. It only hurts the once.

She prayed it was the truth.

Chapter Fourteen

Amelia awoke with the first rays of dawn, desperate with need—for the chamber pot.

That urgent matter resolved, she tiptoed to the washstand and quietly washed her face, rinsed her mouth, and brushed out her hair. The knowledge that Spencer lay abed nearby excited her, no matter that he was asleep and oblivious. The mere fact of being in a handsome, virile man's bedchamber—and of being that handsome, virile man's lover—gave her a quiet thrill. As she brushed her hair, she imagined he was awake and watching her intently, growing aroused at the undulation of her unbound breasts beneath her shift, and the silhouette of her thighs through the sheer muslin.

After finishing her toilette, she turned to find him still asleep. However, as she watched, he made a low moan and turned over onto his back. At least the arousal part of her fantasy had been true. The bed linens tangling about his hips outlined an impressive ridge. Just looking at him, recalling the force of his passion last night, her own sex heated and grew damp.

But she didn't want to wake him, not yet. Not while she had his whole suite to herself, and the opportunity to explore.

Explore she did. Oh, she did not snoop. That would

have been low, and demeaning to them both. She didn't open a single drawer or cupboard. But what lay open to her for observation, she absorbed—thoroughly, and with a certain greed.

She looked at all the paintings on the walls and she imagined she could tell which ones had been hanging there for generations and which ones Spencer had brought in himself. It was plain to see why he appreciated her embroidered vignette. He favored landscapes—wild, rugged ones in particular. Seascapes, mountain ranges, forests, and vast plains.

Adjacent to the bedchamber, he had a small room like a study, with a desk he clearly never used. She supposed the library downstairs was his center of business. But there was one side of the room it seemed the maids were forbidden to touch. A generous leather armchair lounged near the hearth, and a low table supported a haphazard pile of sporting newspapers, ledgers, cards, and books. Several books.

My, but the man had a great many books.

There were six chambers in all, and in every room there were books. Even the dressing room had a niche of built-in shelves that were likely intended for hats but had been overtaken by books. And none of the volumes were in any order whatsoever. Not that she could discern, at any rate.

Amelia skipped her fingers over the leather bindings. Several titles were familiar to her, but three times as many were not. Still, she felt among friends. She never would have classified herself a scholar or a bluestocking; she was simply a great reader. A lover of books. And she found ample evidence to suggest that Spencer shared her affection. She found novels, plays, philosophy, several agricultural tomes, the stray scientific treatise, and volume after volume of poetry. Cracks and creases on the spines proved that most of the books had been read, at least once, and the wide variation of subject matter suggested their collector to be in possession of not only a keen mind, but an open one.

If she'd been aroused earlier, she was desperate for him now. She smiled, wondering what he would say if he knew this worn, jumbled collection of books was such a powerful aphrodisiac.

She moved noiselessly to the bedchamber and perched on the mattress edge, careful not to disturb his sleep.

The soft, early morning light was kind to him. He was always handsome, in any lighting, but dawn had a way of illuminating his features evenly without casting those harsh, judgmental shadows on his deep-set eyes and slashing cheekbones. He looked so youthful. The way his eyelashes rested against his cheek—long and thick, as only undeserving men's eyelashes grew—gave the throbbing pulse of desire a sharp, sweet edge. How had she ever thought this would feel less intimate in the morning?

Dark stubble covered his jaw and throat. She extended an open hand, flexing her fingers backward as she lowered her palm toward his face, until the sharp bristles just pricked her sensitive skin.

When he'd turned over, he'd flopped one arm across his belly. The tight ripple of his biceps, the thick cords of sinew on his forearm . . . so many lines drew her gaze downward. With a feather-light touch, she traced a prominent vein on his wrist. He stirred, mumbled something incoherent in his sleep, then lay still again.

A narrow escape, but she couldn't resist tempting fate once more. His body was so intriguing, so different, so male. Shameless, she drew a single fingertip downward, tracing his hard length through the sheets.

"Wha—"

His hand latched over her wrist. He bolted upright with a start, flipping her back and pinning her to the mattress. Confusion and alarm warred in his eyes as he blinked down at her.

"It's me," she gasped, breathless and dizzy from the sudden inversion. "Only me. Amelia."

Oh, please, she prayed. *Please let him still want me.*

Recognition softened his face. "Amelia."

The way he breathed her name, with such an intoxicating blend of reverence and lust, she wondered why she would ever wish him to call her anything else. No endearment could be uttered with greater tenderness, or to more potent effect. His voice reached places deep inside her, plucked a string connecting her heart to her womb.

"Yes," she whispered, sweeping back the hair that had fallen over his eyes. "Your wife."

They stared into one another's eyes, both breathing hard. Her nipples drew tight beneath her shift, and anticipation coursed through her veins. Releasing his grip on her wrist, he rolled his weight between her legs, spreading her thighs wide. In gentle hands, he cradled her face as his hips pressed home against hers. Pleasure streaked through her, even as she winced.

"Hell," he muttered, pulling back. "You're tender. It's too soon."

She was wondering how best to convince him otherwise—words or deeds?—when a low rumbling sound demanded her attention. At first she thought it her stomach, or his. They'd both gone to bed hungry in more ways than one. But it grew progressively louder, until it became clear that the noise originated from without their chamber. From without the house, perhaps.

He noted her distraction. "A carriage in the drive," he explained. "Most likely a delivery I'm expecting."

"Something to do with the horses, I suppose?"

In reply, he merely tweaked her ear and rolled to a sitting position. Well, she guessed she was lucky to have held his attention this long.

"Do you really have to go meet it?" she asked, running a fingertip down his bare back.

"No. I don't really have to. But I think I should."

Before she could protest, he rose from the bed. Nude, he walked across the room and disappeared into his dressing area. Well. Now she was completely at a loss for words.

"Amelia?" he called from the other room.

She nodded stupidly, then realized he couldn't hear her. "Yes, what?"

"Leave. Go into your suite and shut the door."

Dismayed, she sat up in bed.

His head and shoulders poked through the doorframe. "Go. Or I'll come ravage you like a barbarian again, and I'd rather hoped to accomplish the act with a bit more finesse the next time."

He disappeared again, leaving her wearing a broad grin. She didn't find the prospect of being ravaged nearly so unpleasant as he seemed to think—but on the promise of *finesse,* she could be persuaded to take a long, hot bath.

She rose from bed and crossed to the doorway he'd just exited through. Remaining on the bedchamber side, she leaned one shoulder against the doorjamb and said coyly, "I'll go . . . under one condition."

"Oh, and what's that?" His voice deepened, as if muffled by fabric. Perhaps he was pulling on his shirt.

"I want riding lessons."

He was silent for a long moment. The words had surprised even her. She hated horses. Or feared them, more accurately. But after last night, she just couldn't abide the thought of being locked out of this part of his life forever. She wanted to understand him, which seemed to mean she would need to understand horses, too.

Suddenly his head and shoulders poked through the doorway again. He had indeed donned a fresh shirt, but his hair was wilder than ever and he still smelled of . . . of *them*. He was close enough to kiss, but Amelia just barely restrained herself. The expression on his face was far too amusing to disturb.

"Did you say riding lessons?" he said darkly, cocking an eyebrow. His gaze slid down her body.

Amelia blushed as she gathered the other, more carnal interpretation of her words. "On a horse!" she protested, even as her nipples peaked.

He clutched the doorjamb so hard she thought his fingers might leave dents. "Woman, your chances for finesse are dwindling by the second. Go away. Now."

And so she went with a smile. And a sway in her step, because she knew he was watching her leave.

She went into her suite, shut the door, rang for the maid, and ordered her bath. Then she flopped contentedly on the bed, easing under the blankets to wait for the water to be drawn and heated. Her brain hummed with nervous energy. She found herself wishing she could steal back into Spencer's chambers and borrow one of his books to distract her mind. Or maybe just to feel close to him.

Oh, dear. She was already lost.

When the door swung open a half hour later, Amelia expected to be called to her bath. Instead, a parade of chambermaids entered, each laden with brown-paper-wrapped parcels and hatboxes.

"What's all this?" she asked her lady's maid.

"Your new wardrobe, Your Grace. Only now arrived from London."

This was the delivery?

Amelia inspected one of the parcels and immediately recognized the lavender ribbon binding. These packages were from the London dressmaker who had fashioned her wedding gown. Spencer must have ordered an entire wardrobe for her, but of course it could not have been completed in one day. It was a small miracle that it had been completed in a week. She surveyed the growing mountain of boxes. They must contain at least a dozen dresses. And if the new gowns were even one fraction as fashionable and lovely as the pearl-gray silk she'd been married in, she likely now qualified as the best-dressed lady in Cambridgeshire.

Giddiness rose in her as she pulled at the first ribbon bow. She was going to open each package on her own, and she was going to do so slowly. This was better than a lifetime of birthdays.

"Your Grace?" An apologetic maid interrupted her little party. She extended a folded note.

Amelia opened and read it.

Somewhere in these, you will find a riding habit. Join me in the stables at ten.
—S.

Amelia stared at the note for a long time. His handwriting transfixed her, just as it had the first time she'd seen it, on the parish register they'd signed after exchanging vows. He didn't follow any of the rules well-bred English children were taught by schoolmasters and governesses. Nevertheless, his writing was eminently legible—also strong, vigorous, unapologetic. Every pen stroke displayed confidence. She found it oddly arousing, then and now.

But most entrancing of all was a stray mark just before the word "join." As though he'd begun a word, then thought better of it. Amelia studied the diagonal slash, capped with the beginnings of a loop . . . to her eye, it looked like an aborted "p." And even though she knew there were probably ten thousand words in the

English language that began with the letter "p," she could not help but speculate the unthinkable had occurred.

Spencer had nearly written "please."

"Oh, she's ready, Your Grace. A bit nervous, as she's a maiden yet." With an abrupt whinny, the mare danced sideways. The groom corrected her with a word and a flick of the halter. "She's an anxious one."

Spencer shook his head. His own cattle were meticulously trained, and it annoyed him no end when gentlemen sent their unprepared horses to his stables. If any animal had a natural instinct to please, it was the horse. An owner failing to secure his horse's trust and cooperation was, to him, as unfathomable as failing to feed or water the beast.

He reached out and patted her bay withers, murmuring low. "Did you give the teaser a pass at her?" he asked the groom.

"Aye," the groom replied. "She was receptive enough, but reared up when he tried to cover her. We'll need to hobble her, else she'll kick."

Spencer nodded his assent, moving to scratch the mare behind one dark-tipped ear. Teaser stallions were used to test a mare's readiness for mating, so as not to fatigue or endanger a valuable stud horse. The teaser would chase her about the paddock, go through the motions of equine courtship, test the mare's receptivity to being mounted—and then the handlers would pull him back before the deed could be accomplished. It was standard operation for a stud farm, and Spencer had never thought much about it. But this particular morning found him unusually contemplative.

On the one hand, he wondered if the practice could be detrimental to his stallions' health or sanity. His own constitution felt remarkably improved, now that he was no longer playing the part of teaser himself. On the other, he felt it as a silent yet stern rebuke, that Amelia's accusations had been true. He gave more consideration to the comfort of his broodmares than he had his own wife. Remembering the way he'd pounded her against the mattress last night, on their very first time together . . . it made him wince with guilt. It also made him semi-hard within seconds.

He sighed, resolving to turn his thoughts to something else.

The groom led the mare away, and Spencer leaned against the wall, making a show of kicking the straw from his boots and trying not to look as though he were waiting. The world waited on a duke, not the other way around.

"Spencer?"

His boot thunked against the brick-tiled floor. He looked up, and there, framed by the tall, square entryway, was Amelia. Or some new, luminous version of her.

"You . . ." His voice died as he remembered he just wasn't the sort of man to blurt out *By God, you look lovely* in the middle of a horse barn. Or anywhere. He cleared his throat. "You came."

"You sound surprised." Lifting her eyebrows, she gave him a coy smile. "Thank you," she added, dropping a hand to her skirt. "For this."

Spencer rebuffed her thanks with a wave of his hand. Really, he should be thanking *her*. He didn't recall specifying a color for her riding habit, but he couldn't have possibly chosen better. The dark blue velvet skirt was cut and draped to stunning effect. The jacket was pieced together like mother-of-pearl inlay, angled and sewn so that each panel's brushed nap caught the light differently, and the result was that Amelia shone. Sparkled, really, like an expertly cut and polished sapphire, offset by the gold filigree curls of her hair, and—

And bloody hell. When had he started thinking like this? About anything?

The longer he stood there, staring and not speaking, the further her smile widened.

"I'm ready for my first lesson," she said. "Are you?"

"Yes." Though his lips formed the word easily enough, his boots seemed rather bolted to the floor.

As she approached him, Spencer realized he'd been utterly wrong—it wasn't anything about the new dress that made her look so appealing. The allure was all in the way she wore it. The way those curvaceous hips traded her skirts back and forth as she walked. She was cloaked in sensual confidence, and by God, she wore it well.

He cleared his throat. "We're going to take this slowly. Of course I don't intend to put you in a saddle today, not after . . ." He cleared his throat again. His face felt hot. God, could he truly be *blushing*?

"Is this a bad idea?" she said, looking suddenly self-conscious and unsure. "Perhaps we should wait for another day."

"No, no. It's a very good idea. Every lady should know how to handle horses. For her own safety, if nothing else."

And it was a good idea for other reasons, he admitted to himself. He looked forward to spending time with her, outside of a bed. Showing her this important part of his life, so that she might come to understand what the stud farm meant to him, as well as what it didn't. Gratifying as it had been to view her jealousy last night, he didn't wish to awaken to her resentment every morning.

She craned her neck, surveying the vaulted ceiling. "This place looks very different in daylight. Would you give me a tour?"

He released the breath he'd been holding. "Certainly."

He offered his arm, and she took it. They ambled

slowly through the stables and outbuildings as Spencer told her of the history of the structure—built by his grandfather, expanded by his uncle, improved yet again by him—and explained the operations of the stud farm. Her comments and questions were few, but they reflected genuine interest and appreciation. No polite "I see"s or disingenuous "How very interesting"s, but rather "Is this brick locally produced?" (Yes), and "Do you breed your mares every year?" (No), and "Have you foals? Please, may we go see the foals?"

Well, of course. He should have known to start with the foals. Good Lord, the way she cooed and fawned over the ribby, spindle-legged creatures . . . As she crouched in the grass to stroke a white filly through the fence, Spencer considered putting the animal on a ribbon and letting it follow him around Braxton Hall. At least he'd be assured his wife's warm reception whenever he entered a room.

"How old is she?" Amelia clapped with delight as the filly made a gangly dash for the far side of the paddock.

"Going on three months. And showing off already."

"She's beautiful. Can I have her?" She turned and smiled up at him. "For my riding lessons, can I choose her?"

"Absolutely not."

Her brow wrinkled in disapproval.

"As a yearling, she'll fetch a thousand guineas, at least," he protested. "She can't be saddled for a year, and even then she wouldn't be a safe mount for you. She's from racing stock, bred for short bursts of reckless speed. Her dam's last colt won at Newmarket. What you need is a mature, steady gelding."

"Do you at least have a pretty one?"

He chuckled. "Take your pick, and I'll have the grooms braid ribbons in his mane."

"A thousand guineas," she said thoughtfully, propping

one fist on a fencepost. "For one foal . . . Why, this farm must bring in a fortune each year."

"We do well. Well enough that I haven't raised my tenants' rents in six years." Spencer couldn't keep a hint of pride out of his voice. His uncle had disagreed with him over expanding the stud farm. The late duke had thought the large pastures a waste of good farmland—land that could have been earning rents. Spencer had insisted that the stud farm would more than pay for itself, and time had proven him right. "I also employ a small army of local men, and more than a few farmers make their annual income just supplying our oats and hay. But none of it would be profitable if we didn't produce the finest racehorses in the country. They don't admit it aloud at their Jockey Club meetings, but England's wealthiest racing enthusiasts all bring their custom to me."

"But you're not a member of the Jockey Club yourself? You don't race any of the horses?"

"No."

"Why not? You're a stone's throw from Newmarket."

He shrugged. "Never wanted to. I don't like attending the races." When she looked as though she might question him further on the subject, he quickly added, "I'm not interested in the glory."

"And you don't really need the money. So why do it?"

"Because I'm good at it. And I enjoy it."

She rested her chin on her hand, in an attitude of reflection. "Two ways of saying the same thing."

"I suppose they are."

As they watched the foals a minute longer, he warmed inside. Somehow he'd known, from the moment she pressed that meticulously embroidered handkerchief into his hands, that she would comprehend this. The deep satisfaction that came from doing something exceptionally well, with both care and skill, regardless of public acclaim. And he understood, suddenly, why she kept angling to plan meals, host guests, nurture everyone around her. These were the things she did well; the things that brought her true enjoyment.

"And Osiris?" she asked. "You're so determined to have him for your own—or at least reduce the number of the club. That's to protect the superiority of your breeding stock, I assume? If he's too widely available, the demand for your horses could decrease."

He loved how quickly her mind worked. She'd grasped the business rationale instinctively. Spencer often purchased retired racehorses he had no intention of breeding, just so their offspring wouldn't dilute his own stock's value. And he gave them an idyllic pension in open pasture, so it worked out well for the horses, too.

"Yes," he said, "limiting his breeding will be one benefit."

"But it's not the real reason you want him. That benefit can't be worth tens of thousands of pounds."

Suddenly he realized how far this conversation had strayed, and how it was now on course to collide with some long-held secrets. His body stiffened, as though encased in armor. "How does this pertain to riding lessons?"

"It doesn't. But I'm not truly here for the horses. I just want to know you, Spencer. I want to understand."

She laid a hand next to his on the fence rail. Her little finger just barely grazed his, but the warmth in that touch went a long way toward melting his resistance. His conscience tore down the rest.

Long before his uncle died, he'd made a bargain with himself. Yes, he would assume the title and do his duty, but he'd do it on his own terms. To the devil with what people said or thought. He wasn't going to explain himself to anyone. But cards aside, he had a keen sense of fairness. On their wedding night, he'd demanded her body, her loyalty, her trust. In return, she'd asked only some answers. Now that she'd given him everything so freely, it felt wrong to deny her this.

"Very well." He offered his arm, and she took it. "I can better explain inside." Keeping her close, he led her back into the horse barn and down to the farthest end. She tensed against his arm as they neared Juno's stall, and he knew she was remembering his harsh words to her the night previous.

"I regret shouting at you," he said, stopping a few feet from the mare's stall, "but I was concerned for your safety. As I've said, Juno bites. And kicks, as you saw last night. She doesn't like new people. Or most people, for that matter." He sighed heavily. "She's the devil's own nag, is what she is."

Amelia cast a wary glance at the mare, and Juno released a gruff snort, as if in confirmation. "Then why do you keep her?"

"Because no one else would. She's the first horse I ever bought in this country. My father left me a small legacy, and when I came of age, I took the funds to an auction and came home with this creature. I was young and stupid—made my decision based on pedigree without taking temperament into account. She was four years old and had noble bloodlines and some modest racing success. Thought I'd made a fine bargain. What I didn't know was that she'd always trotted the line between spirited and flat-out dangerous, depending on her rider, and she'd spent the previous year boarded at some country estate, in the care of an incompetent stable master. She'd been kept tethered in a dank stall, barely groomed, beaten often."

He stopped and drew a deep breath. Even now, he felt the old fury rising in his chest. When he'd mastered his voice, he went on, "By the time I bought her, her trust in men had been completely destroyed. No one could saddle her. No one could even get near her without risking his fingers. Clearly we'd never be able to breed her. My uncle wanted to put her down, but I wouldn't allow it."

"You wouldn't?" Amelia stroked his arm in a sympathetic manner.

"Oh, it wasn't so noble as it sounds," he told her. "Pride was my true motive. I'd bought the damned mare, and I didn't want to lose the investment. Or admit defeat." Releasing Amelia, he walked forward to offer his hand to Juno. She nosed his fingers with rough affection, then turned her head to offer him her favorite spot under her left ear. She liked to be rubbed there, so he humored her for a bit.

"I took personal responsibility for her and then turned her out to pasture for a full year," he said. "Made no attempts to train her, asked nothing of her. I fed her, watered her, groomed her as much as she'd allow. Even once I'd gained her trust, it took a full year of slow training to ride her. With time, I was able to break her to halter, bridle, eventually saddle . . . Strangely enough, those rides were what finally improved her disposition. As if that's what she'd been waiting for, been needing—the chance to carry a rider and gallop across an open park. So I began riding her regularly, and her mood improved. Now it's our habit. She'll let the stablehands feed and groom her, but to this day, I'm still the only rider she'll allow."

He looked to Amelia, and she gave him a slight, disarming smile. It occurred to him he'd been talking for an uncharacteristically long time, and she'd been standing there patiently for a long time, too—pointedly silent, unwilling to interrupt until he finished.

"She's getting old," he went on. "Too old to be ridden by anyone, much less a man my size. I've always been more weight than she really ought to carry. But if I try tapering off the frequency of our rides, she grows touchy again. Starts refusing to eat, kicks at the stall. I hate to keep riding her, but I'm more concerned about what will happen if I stop altogether." He rubbed the mare's withers briskly, then stepped back and folded his arms. "That's where Osiris comes in."

"Osiris?" she asked, obviously baffled.

"It's difficult to explain."

Again, she gave him that patient, friendly silence.

So he explained, and found it wasn't so difficult after all. "I'd been trying to learn more about Juno's early years, to see if there might be something else to calm her, or some*one* else she once trusted. A groom, a jockey perhaps. It wasn't easy, so many years after the fact. But I found the farm where she'd been bred to racing age, and the old stable master was pensioned but still living nearby. He remembered her, of course. He told me she'd always been difficult—no surprise—but that in her second year she'd formed a strong bond with an orphaned colt. Horses are much like people, you see. They form friendships and often remember one another, even if parted. We once had a pair of geldings who'd been separated for years, but once they . . ."

He stopped, absorbing the fact that her blue eyes had grown wide as shillings. God, he knew this would sound ridiculous spoken aloud.

"So this colt that she bonded with . . . it was Osiris?"

"Yes." He tapped his heel defensively. "I know it sounds absurd, but it was the only possibility I could think of. Juno's never socialized well with the other horses here. But I thought if she'd bonded with Osiris in her early years, before the horrific abuse she endured, perhaps she'd warm to him again and have some companionship to . . . to soothe her."

They stared at one another for a while.

"So . . ." She pursed her lips around the drawn-out

word. "This is why you're pursuing Osiris. You're willing to spend tens of thousands, rearrange your life, risk the fortunes of others—including my own brother—all so your ill-tempered mare can be reunited with her childhood friend?"

"Yes."

The surprise in her expression suggested she'd been expecting him to protest, but really . . . Amelia was a clever woman. She had it pegged. He hadn't anything else to say.

"Yes," he repeated. "Yes, I put your brother in insurmountable debt just to buy my old, crotchety horse a consort. Make of it what you will."

"Oh, I'll tell you what I make of it." She closed the distance between them, step by slow, deliberate step. "Spencer . . . Philip . . . St. Alban . . . Dumarque. You"—she jabbed a finger in the center of his chest—"are a romantic."

The air left his lungs. Damned inconvenient, that—because bloody hell, if ever there was an accusation he *needed* the breath to refute . . .

"Oh, yes," she said. "You are. I've seen your bookshelves, and all those stormy paintings. First *Waverley*, now this . . ."

"It's not romanticism, for God's sake. It's . . . it's simple gratitude."

"Gratitude?"

"This horse saved me, as much as I saved her. I was nineteen, and my father had died. I'd spent my youth bashing about the Canadian wilderness, and suddenly I was here, preparing to inherit a dukedom. I was angry and unfocused and out of my element, and so was this horse, and . . . and we tamed one another, somehow. I owe her a debt for that."

"You're only making it worse, you know." She smiled.

"Keep talking, and I might just deem you a sentimental fool."

He was about to object, but then her hand flattened and crept inside his coat. The bronze fringe of her eyelashes fluttered as she leaned forward. Her breasts pressed against his chest, soft velvet on the surface and softer still beneath. Perhaps he should rethink his disavowals. Really, he had no objection to *this*.

He put a finger under her chin and tilted her face to his. And then, because it suddenly seemed he should have had a reason to do that, he asked her, "You know all my names?"

"Yes, of course. From the parish register."

He froze, recalling the image of her poised over that register, quill in hand, peering down at it for long, agonizing moments. He'd thought she was having misgivings, and she'd merely been memorizing his name. Some emotion ballooned inside him, hot and dizzying and much too vast for his chest to contain it. And for a moment, Spencer wondered if he just might be a sentimental fool after all.

"It was just . . ." Her voice broke as he slid his hand along the smooth, delicate flesh of her neck. "You already knew my middle name."

"Claire," he murmured.

Her pulse leapt against his palm.

Smiling a little, he lowered his lips to hers. "It's Claire. Amelia Claire."

Ah, the sweetness of this kiss. The softness, the warmth. The soul-shaking beauty of it. He took her mouth tenderly, and her arms slid around his chest under his coat, and . . . and oh, God. This was so, so different from any of their kisses since they'd wed. They hadn't kissed standing up since they'd shared that first incendiary embrace in her brother's study, and deuce if he knew why not. When they kissed like this, it emphasized how small she was against him. He had to bend his head to reach her lips, shore her up with his arms so his kiss wouldn't send her stumbling back on her heels. When he held her this way, she felt delicate and breakable in his arms. And he knew Amelia was anything but fragile, but for some loutish, deeply male reason he liked pretending she was. Cradling her tight against him, giving her the heat of his body, inclining his head to cherish her lips with the softest, most tender of kisses . . . as though her mouth were a delicate blossom and those dewy pink petals would scatter if he dared breathe too hard. As though he needed to be very, very careful.

Because then it became an easy thing to imagine she trusted him. Not only trusted him, but needed him. Relied upon him. He liked imagining that, because he was beginning to worry, in some rogue corner of his mind, that the truth was quite the other way around.

Then something changed. She stiffened in his arms, breaking the kiss.

"On second thought"—her gaze focused—"perhaps you are merely a fool. Has it occurred to you, that instead of bankrupting my brother in pursuit of this stallion, not to mention enduring suspicions of murder, you might simply be honest with Lord Ashworth and Mr. Bellamy?"

"I tried," he said. "I offered to stop pursuing the remaining tokens if they would let me stable Osiris here. They refused."

"Did you tell them your true reasons for wanting him?"

He snorted. Oh, yes. Because it was his life's ambition to hear Bellamy and Ashworth deem him a romantic, sentimental fool. "They won't give a damn. Why should they do a thing for me, much less an old, maltreated mare?"

"Because they're your friends."

"Precisely what gave you that impression? The part where Bellamy accused me of murder? Or the part where I ground him into the carpet? I took my swings at Ashworth years ago, no need to revisit those."

"No," she said evenly. "The part where I asked if you'd nothing more important in your lives than a silly club and a handful of tokens, and the three of you discovered a sudden fascination with your boots." Her arms tightened around his waist. "Maybe you're not friends, not yet. But if you expend the time and effort to *make* friends with them, they'll give you what you want."

"Are you mad? They believe I killed Leo."

"Lord Ashworth doesn't. And Mr. Bellamy's investigation will clear your name any day now."

"It may not. Amelia, I turned that neighborhood upside down and shook it with vigor. There's a very real possibility Leo's killers will never be found."

"Then you will prove yourself and earn their trust. Just give them a chance to know you, the same as you've done with me." Her lips curved in a smile. "Much as it might pain you to do it, you'd save yourself a great deal of trouble simply by revealing your most deeply buried secret of all."

"Oh? And what's that?"

She touched his cheek with the back of her hand. "That against all reports to the contrary, you're a decent, kind, shockingly likable man. At least . . ." She paused. "I know I'm coming to like you, a great deal."

What a sweet thing she was. Not innocent or naïve, just . . . truly good-hearted. Only the most generous of souls could conceive of such a thing—three men putting aside class, fortune, hatred, and suspicion and becoming the sort of friends who traded heartfelt secrets over port. Even men who *weren't* divided by class, fortune, hatred, and suspicion didn't trade heartfelt secrets over port. That's what made them men.

But staring into those clear blue eyes, he almost wished he could make it happen, just for her.

And suddenly, a thought came to him. The best idea he'd had since proposing to this woman. By God, every once in a while he scared himself with his own brilliance.

He couldn't help but grin with self-satisfaction as he asked, "Would you do me a very great favor?"

"Ask me, and see."

"I want to have a house party. Just a small one," he added in a rush, before her eager gasp of excitement carried her away. "I'll invite both Ashworth and Bellamy, and the three of us will hash out this business once and for all." Not in the way Amelia was envisioning, but she need never know. That part would take place behind closed doors. But to execute his plan, he needed the other men loosened up first. Relaxed, well fed, content, and complacent. "I need a hostess. Do you mind?"

"I'd be delighted, and you know it. But only two guests, in such a grand house as Braxton Hall?"

"No, not here. I think it's best if we meet on neutral ground." Here was the truly brilliant part. "I'm thinking of renting a summer property. I've heard there's a cottage for lease, in Gloucestershire."

Gripping his shoulders, she pulled back to stare at him.

"The rent's horribly inflated," he went on. "Four hundred pounds, for a summer cottage? For that price, it had better not be drafty."

Her fingers laced behind his neck. "Briarbank is the loveliest cottage you ever saw. And only the slightest bit drafty." She launched herself into his arms. "Oh, Spencer. You'll love it there. It's beautiful country, with the valley and the river. You can take the men angling.

May I invite Lily? She told me she'd be returning to Harcliffe Manor, and it's quite nearby. I'm sure she'd be glad for the company."

"I don't see why not." In fact, the idea struck him as fortuitous. If anyone could make that idiot Bellamy see sense, it might be Lily Chatwick.

"Will Claudia go with us?"

"Yes, of course." There was no way he could leave her behind.

"Oh, good. Then my dinner table will have equal numbers of ladies and gentlemen. And it will be so good for her. For you both. No one can be unhappy at Briarbank, it simply isn't possible." She slid back to the ground. "When can we leave?"

He laughed at her impatience. "Not for a few weeks, at least. I'll need to make arrangements, and so will you, I imagine. And in the meantime"—he stroked her back—"we'll be occupied with your riding lessons. It's three days by carriage to Gloucestershire, and you'll be miserable if you can't ride part of the way."

She nodded in acquiescence, catching her plump lower lip between her teeth. Oh, how he needed to kiss that mouth.

But before he could act on the impulse, she kissed him first, throwing her arms around his neck to pull him closer. Her tongue teased his, stoking wild sensations in his blood. Raw lust powered through him, sweeping away any vestige of restraint. Together they stumbled into an unused stall, and he threw an arm out to soften the impact as her back collided with the wall.

So much for fragility. And tenderness be damned. Her fingernails raked his scalp, and the kiss was barely a kiss anymore, but more a series of hot, gasping clashes of mouth against open mouth. He slid his palms over all her velvet-cloaked curves—breasts, hips, bottom, thighs.

"Amelia. We shouldn't begin this if . . ."

"I want you," she breathed, rolling her hips against his.

Between the husky promise of her words and the grinding friction of her pelvis, Spencer thought he might spill right then and there. He fisted his hands in her skirts, lifting the folds of velvet above her knee and thrusting his fingers into the flurry of petticoats. She said she wanted him, but he wanted proof. He needed to feel it.

She sighed, biting her lip as his fingertips grazed her bare inner thigh.

The devil in him wanted to tease her, draw out the contact inch by torturous inch—but he'd expended his reserve of patience days ago. He cupped her sex in his palm. A low groan escaped him. God, was she ready. Her most feminine places were hot and wet and quivering under his touch, both erotic and innocent.

But much as he wanted to take her now, he hated to take her *here*. A sweaty tup against the wall, in a barn reeking of horses—on the second day of their true marriage? He'd planned to make love to her properly the next time, with patience and care. He'd spent the past several days caught up in a haze of his own unrelenting want, and he was beginning to realize, as the fog cleared, that Amelia might have wants of her own.

"Spencer?" Leaning forward, she licked the underside of his jaw and ground her moist heat against his palm. "Last night, when you threatened to take me against the wall, never mind the bed?"

Oh, Jesus.

"Could you do that now?"

Yes. Yes, if that was what she wanted, he most definitely could. And if she met him halfway with the buttons, they could be under way in seconds.

"Hullo?" A faraway voice echoed through the barn. "Hullo there! Amelia, are you in here?"

"Wh—?" Her eyes sparked like candles. Her hands instantly flew to her riding habit, redraping the skirts and smoothing the bodice. Craning her neck, she called to the rafters, "Yes. We're just here!"

What the devil? Spencer jerked around, hastily running one hand through his hair and adjusting his breeches with the other. He knew that voice, but he couldn't place it.

"Don't tell me this is the duchess's suite." The voice and accompanying footfalls approached. "Marriages of convenience are all well and good, but I rather expected Morland to provide you finer accommodations than these."

Spencer still didn't know who it was, but whoever it was, he felt like hitting the man. But Amelia . . .

Amelia blushed. And laughed.

She dashed into the aisle to greet the newcomer, and Spencer followed her. When the owner of the irreverent comments came into view, he instantly understood. Understood that a very promising afternoon had just gone to hell.

Biting back a groan, he watched his wife embrace her brother.

"Jack," she said warmly. "I'm so glad you've come."

Chapter Fifteen

"I must admit," Amelia said some time later, directing the servant to deposit the tea service on the table, "it's quite a surprise to see you."

"A happy one, I hope," said Jack, shoving his blond hair back from his face. He shared Amelia's fair coloring—all her brothers did—but he had a greater share of their mother's refined features. He'd always been "the handsome brother," long before he'd eagerly donned the black-fleece mantle of "the ne'er-do-well."

"Yes, of course," she replied. "Claudia, would you be so good as to pour?"

Even Spencer's ward had made an appearance, obviously curious about the arrival of this impromptu house guest. The young lady accepted the tea-pouring duty with reluctance, but Amelia offered her no reprieve. Claudia needed the practice serving, and Amelia needed to think.

Why on earth was Jack here?

Of course she'd hoped he'd come out for a visit. She'd spent the last several months dreaming up methods of removing Jack from his debauched London life. That was why she'd sent him a hasty note the day of her marriage, extending him an open invitation to stay at Braxton Hall whenever he wished. But the very same week?

"I would have come even sooner, had I known what lovely scenery Cambridgeshire has to offer." He gave Claudia a dashing smile, and worry twanged in Amelia's gut. That quintessential Jack grin worked entirely too well on impressionable young ladies.

It did little for Claudia, however. The girl's eyes widened a fraction, and then she simply turned her head.

Good for her.

Shrugging, Jack reached for a sandwich and bit into it eagerly. "Traveling all night on the mail coach leaves a man devilish hungry. The cooks in those posting inns have nothing to match your skill, Amelia."

"It's only a bit of cold ham. I've ordered all your favorites for luncheon, though."

"Ah, I knew you would. Even removed to Cambridgeshire, you're the best sister a fellow could hope to have."

As Claudia busied herself with the tea things, Amelia leaned forward and addressed him in a low, confidential tone. "The duke will join us any moment. Dare I hope this visit means you've raised the funds to pay him?"

"Oh, that?" He reached for a second sandwich. "That debt's been dispatched already. Rents from the cottage, you remember."

"Oh." Amelia blinked. "Yes, of course. That was . . . fast."

Why hadn't Spencer mentioned this? She supposed he hadn't yet received the payment. So much for their country house party. She hated thinking of Briarbank occupied by strangers, but it did lift a weight from her shoulders, to know that Jack was clear of debt. Perhaps that was the reason for this new lightness in his demeanor.

"How long will you stay?" she asked.

"A few weeks, if you can put up with me. Thought I'd

ride over to Cambridge one of these days and see about resuming my studies."

Her heart soared into her throat, and she swallowed her tea with difficulty. She couldn't have dreamed of a better morning. First her conversation with Spencer, where he'd finally begun to reveal to her what a good-hearted, remarkable man he was—if inexplicably determined to hide it from the world. And now Jack's fortuitous arrival, his intention to reform.

It was all so perfect. Jack could stay here for several weeks, away from his miscreant friends. Spencer would be such a good influence on him. Perhaps Jack could even live here when he resumed his studies—Cambridge was only a nine-mile ride away. In time, Spencer could find Jack a living somewhere: a nice vicarage, a few hundred pounds a year. It wasn't much perhaps, but it would be a good life—and as much as the fourth son of impoverished nobility could reasonably expect. With a summer like that, she would scarcely miss Briarbank.

Brimming with optimism, Amelia nipped a lump of sugar into her tea. "Who did let it, in the end? Briarbank, I mean."

Instead of answering, Jack rose to his feet. It took her only a moment to discern why.

Spencer stood in the salon entrance, freshly bathed and dressed in immaculate linen and dark, chocolate-brown wool.

Oh, dear. All the sensual excitement of their encounter in the stables . . . it rushed back in the space of a moment. When Jack had arrived, Amelia had carefully banked the fire of her lust—she'd had no choice—but beneath her every motion and every breath, desire had been quietly smoldering all the while. And now Spencer appeared, and he was . . . the poker, or the bellows, or the very long straw one used to light tinder—heavens, take any crude male analogy, and it fit. One glance at his tall, strong, handsome figure, and heat washed over her, instantly. Perspiration beaded in inconvenient places—the cleft of her bosom, the backs of her knees, her inner thighs. Even her mouth watered. Her choices seemed to be two: look away, or liquefy. She opted for the former, hoping to spare the silk upholstery of her chair.

"Your Grace." Jack made an elegant bow. He did have very pretty manners, when he chose to use them.

"Mr. d'Orsay."

"Oh, come now, Morland. Won't you call me Jack?" Jack took his seat. "We are brothers now, you know."

Amelia risked a glance at Spencer then. His face revealed no pleasure at Jack's sudden familiarity. His eyes were hard and unforgiving. Magnetic and entrancing. Demanding and arousing.

Look away, look away. A good hostess doesn't salivate.

"Well, Jack." He strode into the room and joined their group, dropping his muscled frame onto a slender, straight-backed chair that looked, Amelia worried, rather unequal to the challenge. "Let's dispense with the pleasantries, then. What is it you want?"

"What do you mean?" she said. "He's come for a visit."

"Oh, has he?"

Amelia couldn't fathom the reasons for Spencer's suddenly cool demeanor. But Jack didn't seem overly surprised.

"Yes, of course." Her brother chuckled nervously. "A visit. Fine way to welcome me."

Spencer raised his eyebrows in a clear expression of skepticism.

"Perhaps I want to see how you're treating my sister," Jack said, his voice growing defensive. "You took her from us rather quickly, don't you think? And there's talk"—he leaned forward—"about you."

"What sort of talk?" Claudia asked.

Everyone froze, surprised by the young lady's sudden question. By appearances, she'd spent recent minutes arranging lemon slices with tiny silver tongs rather than heeding the conversation.

"The usual talk?" Claudia's dark eyelashes fluttered with interest. "Or something new?"

Amelia bit her lip, both appalled at Claudia's rudeness and eager to hear Jack's answer. Obviously Claudia knew nothing of Leo's death and the mysterious circumstances surrounding it, but Amelia wondered if Julian Bellamy had been spreading his suspicions through Town. She prayed not. Spencer would be proved innocent eventually, but the stain of scandal was difficult to scrub clean. Rumors of the duke's involvement in a murder would damage the prospects of all connected with him. Claudia, most of all.

"Claudia." Spencer addressed the girl without even looking at her. "Leave us."

"But—"

"I said, leave us. Now."

His tone was rapier-sharp, and though Amelia understood his reasons for wanting Claudia gone, she hurt for the girl. No one deserved that sort of dismissal, especially not in front of a guest.

"It's all right, dear," she whispered, laying a gentle touch atop Claudia's wrist. "We'll see you at luncheon."

Tears gathering in her eyes, Claudia rose from her chair. "No, you won't."

As she fled the room, Spencer winced just a little. Amelia filed away a thought for some later date: *Give His Grace some lessons on the care and feeding of children.* He did well enough with foals, but he was a disaster with young humans. She'd best find a way to work on that, before birthing him a child of his own.

Oh, heavens. The mere thought of carrying his babe inside her . . . Her heart gave a sweet, sudden kick.

"Now, then." Spencer braced his elbows on his knees and leaned forward over his linked hands. "Let's settle this. You've come here to see how I'm treating Amelia?"

Jack fidgeted in his chair. "Yes."

"You. The devoted brother who deserted her at a ball without chaperone, transportation, or a coin to her name. Who played high with money he didn't have, to the detriment of her hopes and prospects. Who failed to appear at her wedding. *You* . . . are questioning *my* treatment of her. Do I understand this?"

Jack blinked.

Spencer turned to her abruptly. "Amelia, how are you being treated? Well enough?"

After a stunned moment, she replied, "Very well."

"There you have your answer, Jack. The reason for your visit is satisfied. You'll remain here as my guest tonight, and tomorrow you'll head back the way you came."

"Tomorrow?" Amelia blurted out. "Why, he traveled all night by coach just to get here. I'd hoped he could stay for some weeks. He means to ride over to Cambridge and see about resuming his—"

"Tomorrow." The word was a verdict, not a suggestion. End of discussion. But his gaze trapped hers, and the conversation continued.

Why? she felt herself silently asking. *Why are you retreating to this cold, arrogant behavior, after the lovely morning we just shared? If I truly mean something to you, why can't you extend the slightest consideration to my kin?*

There were answers there, in his eyes. But she couldn't quite make them out.

And then something clattered to the table between them, breaking the silent communication with a sharp, metallic clang.

Amelia's eyes flew to the object instinctively, and she gasped at what she saw. A small, roundish disc of brass, stamped with a horse's head.

Leo's missing token.

"Oh my . . ." She reached for it in surprise.

Jack clapped a hand over the coin. "I have what you want, Morland. And I know what it's worth to you."

"I seriously doubt that," Spencer said.

Enmity sparked between the men, exploding all Amelia's hopes for a happy, idyllic summer.

"However did you get that token?" she wondered aloud. "There are investigators searching all London for that scrap of brass."

"Yes, well. The investigators haven't come asking me." Jack's lips quirked in a strange little smile, and a sliver of fear pierced Amelia's heart. Oh, God. He couldn't have been involved in Leo's murder. Not her own brother. No, no, no. It simply couldn't be.

No.

It simply couldn't be.

She replayed the events of the evening, slowly filling her lungs with relief. Jack had been with her at the ball all evening. True, he'd departed early, at half-eleven. But Mr. Bellamy and Lord Ashworth had appeared not an hour later, and Leo had already been dead for some time. Jack could not possibly have been involved. Thank God. But the question remained . . .

"How did you get your hands on that token?"

"It was the damnedest thing," her brother said, speaking to Spencer. "I'd been passing some time with a—" His gaze flicked toward Amelia. "With an acquaintance, a few days ago. We had cause to exchange a coin or two, and I spied this in her purse. Offered her a guinea for it, and she happily made the exchange."

Amelia's stomach turned. This "acquaintance" had to have been the prostitute who found Leo. She knew Jack had been sinking lower and lower . . . but this exceeded even her worst imaginings.

As usual, Spencer didn't mince words. "So where's the whore now? Could you find her again?"

Jack stammered a bit, rising to his feet. "Look, man. Perhaps we could discuss this alone."

"Why? Amelia's no simpleton. She already knows you've been taking her money and throwing it away on dockside bunters." Spencer stood, too. "It's a bit late to spare her the shame, Jack. If you want to try redeeming yourself, start with information. Where did you find this woman? Where did she take you? What does she look like? What did she tell you about the attack, about Leo?"

"Why should I tell you anything? So you can get to her first and hush her up?"

The room went very quiet.

Jack strolled forward. "Julian Bellamy thinks you killed Leo."

"I don't give a damn what Julian Bellamy thinks."

"Perhaps not. But others do. When he talks, the *ton* listens. And public suspicion like that is hard to live down. Your pretty little ward there"—Jack's chin jerked toward Claudia's exit route—"might suffer for it. As would my sister."

"Well, if you're so concerned for Amelia, you have the evidence to exonerate me right there in your hand. Julian Bellamy thinks I killed Leo to get that token. Obviously, I don't have it."

"No, you don't." Jack flipped the coin into the air and caught it in his hand. "I do."

Amelia's heart plummeted. Of course. He needed money. Though his debt to Spencer was dispatched, he must have landed himself in worse straits now, and he hoped to buy his way clear with that token.

"Oh, Jack," she said, coming forward. "Just tell us what trouble you're in. There's no need to extort assistance from the duke. As you say, we are all family now. We can find some way out of your scrape, surely."

"He's not getting a penny from me," Spencer bit out.

"Don't misunderstand me, Morland," Jack said. "I'm not a blackmailer. Now that would be low, even for me. Besides, the Stud Club tokens"—he tossed the coin and caught it again—"can't be bought or sold. Everyone knows that."

"You want me to play you for it," Spencer said.

Jack nodded.

"By God, you truly are an idiot. A prideful, stubborn idiot." He shrugged. "But if you insist . . . In my library, then."

He walked swiftly from the room, with Jack following after him. Amelia stood there for a moment, stunned. Then she picked up her skirts and gave chase.

"Jack," she said, catching her brother by the sleeve halfway down the corridor. "What is it? Are you in debt again?"

He didn't say a word. He didn't have to.

"Don't do this," she pleaded. "I have access to funds now . . . We'll find some other way. You'll never win against the duke."

"You don't know that." He shook off her grip and kept walking. "It's a game of chance," he said dryly. "That's what makes it so very exciting."

Chance had nothing to do with it. Not against Spencer.

Abandoning all hope of reasoning with her brother, Amelia charged forward and overtook her husband. At least *he* had a logical mind, if not compassion. She pulled up short, stopping him in front of the library entrance.

"Please," she whispered through her teeth. "Please. Don't."

"This doesn't concern you, Amelia."

"Of course it does. We both know Jack has no chance to win against you. And he's clearly in trouble with someone. If he leaves here defeated and upset, he'll only dig himself deeper still."

"That's not my problem."

"No, it's mine. And if you . . ." Her voice trailed off, leaving the remainder of the sentence unspoken and obvious. *If you care for me at all, you won't do this.*

"For God's sake, Amelia." Jack stepped between them. "This is men's business. Stop meddling in my life, for once."

Before Amelia could even begin to respond—Jack wasn't there anymore. He was on the carpet, moaning in pain, and Spencer was shaking out his fist.

"You—" She clapped a hand to her cheek and gaped at Spencer. "You hit him!"

"Yes. But not half as hard as I wanted to." He pushed a hand through his hair. "Damn it, d'Orsay. That was barely a punch. Pick yourself up. It's embarrassing."

A stunned Jack struggled to his feet, rubbing his mouth.

"Now apologize."

"Sorry," he muttered through rapidly swelling lips.

"Not to me, you jackass. To Amelia."

Staring at the spot of blood on fingertip, Jack swore incoherently, then mumbled, "Solly, Ameeya."

Spencer flung open the library door. "Now let's finish this."

It took all of twenty minutes.

Amelia waited in the corridor, arms crossed over her chest, pacing in time to the hall clock's ominous ticks. Dread welled inside her with each passing minute. Surely Spencer could have beaten her brother in the first round, had he wished to. Perhaps he was toying with Jack, the way he'd toyed with her. Drawing him further into the game, building false confidence . . . and of course, Jack would not know when to walk away.

Finally, the door swung open, and Jack emerged. Amelia flew to him, scanning his expression for clues to his state of mind. "Will you be all right?" she asked. No need to ask whether he'd won or lost.

He stared vacantly at the wainscoting, rubbing his neck with one hand. An impressive bruise bloomed across the left side of his jaw. "I don't know. I don't know what will become of me now. I thought . . ." He blew out his breath slowly, then turned and gave her a defeated half-smile. "I wish you better luck than mine, Amelia. I fear you'll need it, married to that man."

He kissed her cheek, then strode off down the long, carpeted passageway.

"Wait," she called after him. "You're not leaving already?"

He did not break stride to answer—which was, she supposed, an answer in itself.

"Jack!"

He halted, but did not turn around.

"Have you enough for your fare home?"

"Yes, just."

"When will I see you again?"

"Soon," he replied, throwing her a cryptic glance over his shoulder. "Or never." He jammed his hand into a pocket and resumed strolling away. Turning right toward the entrance hall, he disappeared from view.

Amelia wheeled around and charged straight into the library. "How could you do that to him? How could you do it to me?"

With deliberate calm, Spencer closed the drawer he'd been holding open, then stood from his desk chair. The crisp linen of his shirt stretched taut across his shoulders as he rose. He'd removed his coat for the game, evidently.

"How could I not?" His eyes went to Leo's brass token, which lay in the center of the ink blotter. He scooped the coin into his palm. "I couldn't risk allowing him to leave here with this. God knows where he'd lose it, or what further damage it might cause, should it fall into the wrong hands."

"Yes, but why take it from him this way? He is in financial straits; you want that token. Why not find a solution beneficial to you both?"

He gestured toward the door. "You heard your brother. He didn't want a price for it. The damn fool wanted to play. Was I supposed to refuse?"

"Yes! You know better, even if he doesn't."

"I don't know where you expect your brother to get some sense, if you keep thinking for him." He folded his arms. "Perhaps now he'll have learnt his lesson."

"He's learned nothing, except not to visit me again."

"I can't say that comes as a disappointment." He walked out from behind his desk.

"Not to you, perhaps. It's a grave disappointment to me." More than a disappointment. More like devastation. She hated to even think about what would happen once Jack returned to Town.

"For God's sake. Jack is a no-good wastrel. He takes your money and in return gives you no end of worry. And yet you defend his horrid behavior. You coddle and reward him for it."

"No, I don't." Her voice shook. "I continue to love him despite it. And I hold out hope he'll reform. You needn't have simply thrown him money. Jack told me he wants to resume his studies at Cambridge. Take orders in the Church." He hadn't truly said that last bit, but it was the logical extension. "You could offer him a living as a vicar, or some other chance to earn back his debts."

"My tenants are my responsibility. You want me to place their spiritual welfare in *Jack's* hands? Inconceivable." He shook his head. "And he didn't come here with any intention of resuming his studies or taking orders, Amelia. He came for money. He changed his tale the moment I challenged him."

"He changed his tale the moment you cast him out! Without so much as a word to me, I might add. I thought after this morning, you might begin to see the virtue in engaging your wife in open conversation. We might have at least discussed the matter before you swindled him out of that token and tossed him out on his ear."

When his only answer was a gruff sigh, she pressed a fist to her chest. "You say your tenants are your responsibility. Well, my brothers are mine."

She'd been ten years old when Young William was born. Mama had been so weakened from the birth, it was all she could do to tend the baby. Hugh and Jack were seven and six at the time, and their care fell to her. *You must be my little mother, Amelia. Look after the boys.* And she'd done her best, ever since.

"Spencer, please. I've already lost Hugh. I can't lose Jack, too."

He came to stand before her. His face was dark with emotion, his posture one of power and strength. His sheer physical nearness roused her body, and she recalled the way he'd tangled his limbs with hers in the stable, kissed her throat, stroked her bare thigh . . . Despite her anger, she was a breath away from launching herself into his arms and begging him to hold her, kiss her, pleasure her, care for her.

Love her, and understand.

And then he said quietly, "Jack is already lost, Amelia."

No. Amelia gaped at him, tears burning in her eyes. Marrying Spencer was supposed to mean her brother's salvation, not his doom. He'd exhaust his fortune for an ill-tempered horse, but he'd write off her brother with a single remark?

"Don't you say that," she whispered. "You don't know him. He and Hugh were just a year apart, and such close friends. It's like a part of Jack died with him, and he keeps trying to fill that emptiness with gaming and drink. You don't know how he was, before."

"And you are blind to the man he is now. I've seen this before, in reckless youths with a taste for high stakes and brains starved for good sense. I tell you, he is lost. He may yet find his way back, but only if he discovers the will and strength within himself. Nothing you can do will make him change. You need to snip his leading strings, for both your sakes. No more consoling, no more cajoling. No more money. If you're not strong enough to cut the ties, I'll do it for you."

"*Cut the ties?* With my own flesh and blood?" She couldn't believe that this was the same Spencer she'd conversed with in the stables this morning. He knew how important her family was to her. How could he even suggest this? "Of all the arrogant, unfeeling . . ."

"Ah, yes." With a humorless laugh, he unfolded his hand. Between them, the brass token glittered in his palm. "*I'm* the villain. Jack can show up at this house, drowning in gaming debt, having recovered this coin from a low prostitute. He can impugn my honor, threaten my cousin's reputation, and insult you to your face—"

"You hit him!"

"—and I'm the villain." He muttered a vicious oath. "I've spent a week laboring under wrongheaded suspicions. I've exhausted every scrap of patience and consideration, worked day and night to see these accusations proved false. You claimed to believe me, even when my efforts failed. Now Jack appears with the very evidence of my innocence in his pocket, and I'm the deuced villain. Worthless ingrate that he is, *he* gets your loyalty. He's the one you defend."

The wounded look in his eyes . . . God, she felt it twist in her heart. But what could she say? "He's my brother."

"I'm your husband!"

The force in his voice sent her stumbling a half-step in retreat. The predatory gleam in his eyes sent her back another two. Her heart drummed furiously in her chest.

"I am your husband. We exchanged vows, in case you've forgotten." He held up the token between his thumb and forefinger as he advanced. "And that same night, you made me a pledge. Once this token was found, I would have all of you. You would deny me nothing."

"What do you mean? You've just threatened to forcibly separate me from my family. Now you expect me to behave as if nothing has changed? Lie back on the bed like a good, obedient wife?"

"No." In a rush of strength, he caught her by the waist and swept her backward, until she collided with the wall. "I'll take you right here, never mind the bed."

He lifted her slightly, wedging his legs between hers and supporting her weight with his thighs as one hand dropped to burrow beneath her skirts. She gasped for air as he shoved the heavy velvet up to her waist, too stunned to resist. His fingers found her sex, and she was still wet for him from earlier, still tender from the night before. The sensation was overwhelming. Without preliminary, he pushed two fingers inside her, and her inner muscles cinched around their girth.

He stilled, breathing just as heavily as she. "You wanted this."

Wanted what? To marry him in the first place? To be taken hard and fast against the wall? To witness the hurt in his eyes and feel that sharp edge of retribution, after the way he'd devastated her just now?

"Yes," she breathed. Yes, she wanted all of this.

He withdrew his fingers, and she felt him tugging at the placket of his trousers. He gritted his teeth as he struggled to free himself, supporting her weight and endless wads of velvet with one arm as he worked the buttons with his other hand. Amelia let her own arms dangle at her sides. She didn't want to help him, but neither did she want to push him away. Despite all her anger and wounded feelings, she still yearned for the pleasure he could give. It was as if her heart had walked out the door with Jack, but her body was still here, mindlessly craving.

Once he ceased struggling with the buttons, he grasped her hand in his and pulled it between them, tunneling through all the layers of cloth. He wrapped her fingers around his swollen, rigid length. His skin was hot to the touch, scalding against her palm.

"Show me you want it." He tightened his fist until she was sure their combined grip must be hurting him. "Guide me in."

He released her hand, leaving her clutching his manhood between them. He cupped her thighs in his hands and lifted, spreading her legs wide.

Using the hard, pulsing handle he'd provided her, she pulled him closer. Not down between her folds, where she knew he wanted to be, but where *she* wanted him. She rubbed his engorged crown against the sensitive place at the top of her cleft. Pleasure rolled through her as she massaged the swollen bud with his hardness and heat.

He groaned, and his fingers bit into her thighs as he tilted her pelvis. His hips bucked, and he thrust against her, dragging his full length through the moist folds of her sex. She tightened her grip, pulling him away. He'd given her control, and she wouldn't relinquish it now. This was what she wanted—to grind against his hard length, to rub his velvety heat against her in just the way she liked. She wouldn't have dreamed lovemaking could be so good when begun in anger instead of tenderness . . . but it was. Oh, it was.

Writhing her hips, she worked herself closer and closer to release. As the sweet tension grew, she released her breath in a low, taunting purr.

"Curse you." His hips jerked again. "Guide me in."

And she did. Not because he'd told her to, but because it was what she wanted now. To feel him inside her, filling her, thrusting with helpless abandon.

She clutched his neck and stared at the ceiling. He gripped her thighs and pressed his face to her throat. There was no more eye contact, and no more conversation. Just a frantic rhythm and building sensation and a climax so sharp, so stunning, her mouth fell open in a silent scream.

He growled against her shoulder, filling her deep as he reached his own peak.

And in the aftermath, as he slumped breathless and shaking against her—a miracle occurred. Amelia put her hands on his shoulders. And then she pushed him away. The physical bliss of her climax had nearly split her in two, but her anger and confusion remained intact. She had no foolish desire to hold him, to cradle him close and stroke his hair. No deep, secret wish to hear him murmur words of praise and love in her ear. She'd taken what she wanted from him, and she was satisfied.

Finally, she'd reached a position of equality with her husband. She'd learned how to give him her body without risking her heart.

What a cold, bitter triumph it was.

* * *

Spent and trembling, Spencer withdrew from his wife's body. His knees locked as he lowered her to the floor.

She said, "I thought I was promised finesse."

Spencer winced. He wasn't especially proud of that performance. It had been brutish, angry, brief . . . and goddamned amazing, which somehow made it worse. "Do I owe you an apology?"

"Don't be absurd." Her eyes were the pale blue of river ice. "We both enjoyed it."

He turned aside to straighten his garments, needing to escape her gaze. He'd just enjoyed the most intensely pleasurable sexual experience of his life, with the eager participation of his creative, willing lover. And he felt lower than the carpet fringe.

Shaking out her skirts, she said, "When can I have my money?"

"What?" Had she honestly just asked him for money? As if she were a common whore, lifting her skirts in a darkened alley for a tup against the wall? There was angry but amazing, and then there was . . . coarse.

"As you've just reminded me, we had an agreement when we married. I give you children; you give me security. Those were *your* words, Spencer. Specifically, you promised me twenty thousand pounds. I'd like to know how soon I can have it. If you refuse to let me see my brother, I'll help him on my own. I'll . . . I'll . . ." Her words tumbled together, growing increasingly fraught with emotion. "I'll do *something*. Perhaps I can send him back to university, or buy him a commission, or just find some place for him away from Town . . ."

Spencer put a hand to his temple. Her loyalty to Jack was admirable—and the very reason they'd met—but her protective efforts were doing her brother more harm than good. There was no way in hell he was going to hand over thousands of pounds and let her squander it by proxy in London's seediest brothels and worse. "The money is held in trust. I can't just give it to you. It doesn't work that way."

"I'm certain you could make it work that way, if you wished. You're quite free with your chequebook when it suits you." She cast a glance at the wall they'd so recently buttressed. "I'm holding up my end of the bargain."

Bile rose in his throat, giving his words an acid tinge. "You're not with child yet. By that logic, I don't owe you anything until a son is born."

"Half," she said numbly. "I want half in advance. Or there'll be no son at all."

"What the devil has come over you? Holding your favors for payment, as if you were a harlot? This conversation is beneath you, Amelia. It's beneath us both."

"You've driven me to it!" A tear streaked down her face. "Don't you have the slightest capacity for empathy? Leo was attacked while wandering the same neighborhoods Jack's frequenting. Jack could so easily have been the one who was killed. I can't just idly sit by and wait for him to come around. By the time he does, it could be too late. Yes, I would barter my body to save him. I would give my life, if that's what it took." Turning away, she buried her face in her hands.

A rough sigh deflated his chest. He closed the distance between them and slid an arm around her shoulders. She flinched, but he held her tight. He might not have possessed a natural talent for this hugging business, but he'd always been a quick study. He stroked a hand down her spine. "Jack doesn't deserve that kind of devotion."

"Who truly does?" She ceased struggling and buried her face in his waistcoat, and he folded both arms around her. "But you can't ask me to stop loving him. It isn't fair."

He held her as she cried, trying to come to grips with his own painful conclusion—that he couldn't ask his wife to stop loving her fool of a brother, any more than he could force her to feel the same for him. He let himself imagine, for a treacherous moment, what it would be like to know that Amelia would do anything for him. Give her last worldly possessions, her body . . . her life if it came to that. If he were ever so fortunate as to be the recipient of such affection, he damned sure wouldn't be spurning it to chase idle pleasure in gaming halls.

All he need do was throw some money at Jack, and he'd be in her good graces again. But the whole cycle would just repeat. Sooner or later—most likely sooner—Jack would resurface, having squandered it all, promising to reform if only they'd give him a little more. And Spencer would be forced to refuse, and Amelia would cry . . .

No amount of reasoning or explanation could change her mind right now. She was too compassionate, too tenderhearted to break the pattern. He had no choice but to be the arrogant, unfeeling villain and do it for her.

"Spencer, please. If you could just talk to—"

"No," he said firmly. "There will be no discussion, Amelia. My decision is made. I cannot, in good sense or good conscience, give your brother any funds. Now that he's realized that, I think you'll find Jack will be the one cutting the ties."

She cried some more. He would have held her longer, but she pulled away. Instead he just stood there awkwardly, watching her weep. It was a miserable way to pass a quarter hour.

"Well?" she said finally, hugging her arms across her chest. "Where do we go from here?"

"We go to Briarbank. As soon as possible." At least he could offer her that much consolation—a holiday at her cherished cottage. "Now that Leo's token is in my possession, it won't help my cause with Bellamy. More than ever, I need to gather him and Ashworth in one place and talk matters through."

She stared at the carpet, and he sensed two factions warring within her: the wish to see her home again, and the desire to rebel.

Spencer might not yet have the key to her heart, but he did know the five words that would improve her disposition and win her cooperation. The same ones that must have worked for Jack, time and time again. He played that trump card now. "Amelia, I need your help."

Her shoulders softened instantly. God, it was so easy, he almost felt guilty about it. She lived to be of service to those around her, to the point that she would deny her own happiness to secure others'. It might be low of him to take advantage, but if it was that or lose her completely . . .

She wiped her eyes with the back of her hand. "Didn't Jack tell you? Briarbank is already let for the summer. You'll have to rethink your house party plan."

"No, I won't."

Her brow crinkled. "You won't?"

"I . . ." He sighed. Brilliant. Now he was lying to her. He abhorred deceit, but if he told her the truth now, she would take it all the wrong way. He'd forfeit whatever remaining grain of esteem she might still have for him. "I'll make them a better offer. Will you still want riding lessons?"

Will you still want to spend time with me?

She shook her head. "If we're to leave as soon as possible, I'll be too busy." She looked toward the door. "I should go begin writing letters now."

But she didn't move. She just stood there, staring at the door, as if waiting for him to say something. It felt like a test, and he'd spent his boyhood living in terror of just such oral exams. He never knew the right thing to say.

"Amelia . . ." He exhaled slowly. "I still need an heir. But as you ask, I'll honor our initial agreement. If, once you have borne me a son, you no longer wish to live with me . . ." He hated the thought of it, but at least he had the better part of a year to change her mind. "I will release the entirety of your trust and provide you with a completely separate home."

Her lower lip trembled. Then thinned. Then folded under her teeth and all but disappeared.

Wrong thing. Wrong thing to say, completely. Devil, damn, blast.

For midday in summer, the air in the room took on an odd chill.

"Yes," she said, avoiding his eyes. "That was our agreement, wasn't it? I should never have expected more."

"I just . . ." Damn it, how had this past hour gone so wrong? This morning, they'd been on the cusp of something wonderful. Closeness. Friendship. Intimacy. Now there was a wall between them. "Amelia, I just want you to be happy."

"Oh, I shall be." Lifting her chin, she smoothed her palms down her stomach and hips. "I am going to Briarbank, and I have a house party to host. Of course, I will choose to be happy." Her cheeks tightened with a forced smile as she headed for the door. "Well. Now that's settled. If you'll excuse me, I have dinner to plan."

So silence it was.

Claudia remained aloof, as ever. Her presence at meals was unpredictable, as was her mood at any given moment. She rebuffed every one of Amelia's attempts at friendship, and eventually Amelia ceased making them. The girl would doubtless come around in time, but in the interim, a duchess had more pressing matters demanding her attention. Such as writing invitations to her guests, and sending servants ahead to Briarbank with supply ledgers and lists of cleaning tasks and heaps of crisp linens.

She was so busy, the appointed date for their departure arrived before she expected it. Rather than take the longer route through London, Spencer had decided they would travel directly west, to Oxford and then Gloucester. But the roads were smaller and poorer, which made for slow and nauseating travel. Both Amelia and Claudia spent their time jouncing about the coach and trading the basin between them.

As they crossed into Oxfordshire on the third morning, Amelia perked up. She'd written to her second cousin, now styled Lady Grantham, and arranged for the party to break their journey at Grantham Lodge. Amelia had never been particularly close to Venetia, nor even particularly fond of her. But she did keep a lovely home in Town and had a rapacious taste for the society of nobility, so Amelia had hopes for warm hospitality.

The sun was still high in the sky when Grantham Lodge came into view. It was a friendly looking manor house, quite modern in its architecture. The shallow reflecting pool before the house provided a mirror image of the white façade and its many glazed windows. A swan or two paddled idly about. Sir Russell must be doing rather well for himself, Amelia mused. But then, the Granthams had always been an ambitious couple.

The carriages rolled to a halt in the drive. When she

and Claudia alighted, Sir Russell and Lady Grantham were waiting to greet them. Venetia wore apricot silk and that same strange, thin smile Amelia remembered. Her cousin had elaborate theories about too-wide smiles causing premature wrinkles. Amelia thought she would rather look wrinkled and happy than smooth-skinned and camphorized.

"Amelia, dear child. It's been far too long."

It had barely been two months by Amelia's counting, but she embraced her cousin and accepted a kiss on the cheek.

"Oh!" the lady gasped and gave a little laugh. "But I must call you Your Grace now, mustn't I?"

"Of course not," Amelia assured her. "We are family." Internally, though, she couldn't help but wonder if Lady Grantham's slip were truly an accident. Was she destined never to be recognized as a duchess? Always taken for some impoverished relation or lady's maid?

She introduced Claudia, whose ill pallor provided a convenient excuse for her usual withdrawn demeanor. Soon Spencer joined the group, having dismounted and passed his reins to a waiting groom.

"Your Grace," Lady Grantham said, dropping a graceful curtsy. "We are honored to welcome you to Grantham Lodge."

No one ever mistook Spencer for anything less than a duke. Well, and why would they? He looked magnificent, as always. Tall, handsome, noble, perfect, and only improved by a day spent in the sun. He acquitted himself as well as could be expected in the introductions, which was to say he nodded curtly and refrained from making any outright rude remarks.

"Do come inside." Sir Russell's waistcoat could barely contain his excitement as he made a beneficent sweep of his arm.

Venetia cozied up to Amelia, taking her arm as they

followed the men toward the door. "It's so good to see you, my dear. When we heard of your marriage, we were so disappointed to have missed the chance to celebrate. And I knew you must have been disappointed as well, long as you've waited. But now you are here, and everyone is so excited to welcome you both."

"Everyone?" Amelia asked, as they breached the entrance hall.

Lady Grantham made an expansive gesture by way of a reply, and Amelia looked around her to see . . .

Everyone.

Or at least, the better part of the population of Oxfordshire.

Applause broke out amongst the assembled guests, mingled with cheers. Good heavens, there were dozens of them. A few Amelia recognized as relations or old acquaintances, but the majority she assumed to be the neighborhood gentry, all drawn by the promise of a newlywed duke and duchess.

She caught Claudia's eye. The girl swallowed hard, looking positively ill.

Spencer blinked disdainfully at the crowd, which was typical Spencer behavior.

"Isn't it wonderful?" Venetia whispered, gripping her arm. "I know you were cheated out of an engagement ball or a proper wedding breakfast, but never despair. Lady Grantham is here to put matters to rights. We've a whole evening planned. Dinner, music, dancing."

"How . . . how very kind of you," Amelia said, allowing her cousin to draw her to the center of the room, but at the same time trying to keep Claudia close. The girl needed protection from this horde.

"Come now, you must meet everyone," Venetia said. "It will take the footmen some time to bring in your trunks, at any rate."

Out of the corner of her eye, Amelia saw Sir Russell

give Spencer a hearty slap on the back, propelling him forward into the crowd. The introductions began. And went on. And went on. Amelia pasted a polite smile on her face and warmly greeted each old and new acquaintance. She kept a watchful eye on Spencer, who clearly did not appreciate Sir Russell's bold familiarity. Amelia couldn't make out their words in the din of conversation, but by appearances, Spencer was about as happy to greet the assembled guests as he would be to devour their hats and bonnets, plumes and all. Amelia sighed. She knew this sort of gathering didn't appeal to him, but couldn't he at least make the pretense of etiquette?

Lady Grantham took her arm again to steer her toward another group of waiting ladies. Craning her neck to keep watching Spencer, Amelia looked on as a tall, elderly man smiled and nodded through Sir Russell's fulsome introduction, then made a sweeping, elegant bow as was once the style at Court. While the man was still doubled over his extended calf, Spencer turned on his heel and quit the room.

Oh, now Amelia was incensed. Had he truly just cut that elderly gentleman, mid-bow? Without very good reason, such a move was the height of rudeness. And here they were guests in her cousins' home . . . His complete disregard for her relations was insupportable.

A murmur of dismay made a small ripple through the assembled guests, only increasing Amelia's mortification.

"Lady Grantham," she said, "will you please forgive me? I've realized there's an important parcel amongst my things that requires very special attention. I meant to mention it to the footman, but it slipped my mind. I'll just go out and see to it, and then I'll return in a moment." Before the lady could object, Amelia pulled away. "Won't you introduce Claudia to your daughter Beatrice? She's fifteen and eager for new friends."

Leaving Claudia in the hands of her cousin, Amelia

hurried out the door the way Spencer had left. Not seeing him immediately, she turned left and followed the drive that led toward the coach house and stables. No doubt he'd spurned human company to look after the horses again.

She hadn't gone but twenty paces before a harsh, choked cough drew her eye to a side garden. Surprised, Amelia walked toward the sound, passing through a shaded arbor.

What she found astonished her.

"Spencer, is that you?"

Oh, Christ. He knew he should have gone farther from the house.

He tugged fiercely at his cravat, pulling the cloth loose from his neck. He cleared his throat. "It's nothing. Just needed some air," he said, striving for a calm, collected tone. "Bloody hot in there."

"Really? I didn't think it warm at all." Her voice was crisp. "If there was anything intolerable in the room, it was your attitude."

He dropped his head in his hands and exhaled slowly, trying to subdue the pounding in his chest. "You didn't tell me they would be having a goddamn party, Amelia."

"I didn't know."

"Didn't you?" He hated the accusation in his voice.

"No. I didn't." She crossed her arms. "But what if they are? I know it's not precisely the cream of London society in there, but they are earnest, well-intentioned people. What have they done, to earn your disdain?"

"Nothing. Nothing."

She didn't understand. And even if he wished to explain it to her, he was in no condition to do so. His head was spinning. He didn't even think he could stand. So many people, such a small space . . . and he hadn't been prepared. When he attended balls in Town, he spent hours preparing himself beforehand—physically, mentally. And he brought brandy. God, what he wouldn't give for a brandy right now.

"Just go on," he said. "I'll be there in a minute."

A bit of solitude was all he needed to get put to rights. Although a minute of it might not be quite enough. Hours worked better.

She dropped onto the bench next to him. "You're truly ill, aren't you?"

"No," he said, far too quickly to sound credible.

Damn, damn, damn.

"You're trembling. And so pale."

"I'm fine."

"Spencer . . ."

The quality of her voice had changed, from scolding to concerned. He would far rather have the scolding. He quite liked the Amelia who scolded him. He'd missed her, in the past few weeks.

"You look as you did that night," she said, "on the Bunscombes' terrace. What is it? What's wrong?"

Bloody wonderful. Why did he have to marry a clever, inquisitive woman? He had two choices now. Let her drag it out of him slowly, or just have out with it on his own terms.

"Nothing's wrong," he said, burying his face in his hands. "It's just . . . something that happens sometimes, when there are too many people about. I don't like crowds."

She placed a hand on his shoulder. "You don't like crowds."

"I can't abide them, actually. Never have been able to. They make me ill. Physically ill." There, he'd said it. He'd never said that aloud to anyone in his life. He wasn't even sure he'd fully admitted it to himself. Oddly, a sense of relief accompanied the admission. His thumping pulse began to slow, and he lifted his head. He'd never been able to comprehend his reaction in these situations. He was a strong, competent, intelligent person in every other respect, and his whole life, this one weakness had maddened him. Perhaps Amelia could help him understand it.

"If I'm prepared in advance," he said, "I'm fine for a time. A half hour or so, at most. If I stay any longer, or I'm taken by surprise . . . something happens to me. I don't know how to describe it. I get warm. My head spins; my heart pounds. The air is suddenly too thick to breathe. It's as if my whole body insists that I must leave, immediately."

"So you do."

"Yes."

"Even if you have to sweep an impertinent spinster off her feet and take her with you."

Smiling a little, he arched a brow at her. "You asked for that." Clearing his throat, he went on, "So long as I'm prepared, I can attend these things. I just make sure to leave before the scene goes bad."

"Yes," she said. "I think you told me that. The key is all in knowing when to walk away. So this is why you only stayed for one set of dances? That whole 'Duke of Midnight' routine . . ."

"Was not my idea. I just wanted to keep my appearances brief, and it's easiest to leave after the supper set. But the whole thing mushroomed, and . . ."

She laughed softly, shaking her head. "All that gossip and rumor. All that speculation. For nothing."

"Not for nothing." He scratched his neck, and her hand slid from his shoulder. "I don't mind the gossip. I've never given a damn what people think of me. It's amusing—and sometimes useful—to be feared."

Or at least it had been, until talk of murder was added

to the mix, and he'd lost the trust of his wife before he'd any real opportunity to earn it.

"Spencer?" She took one of his hands in hers. "As we are baring our secrets, I feel I should confess something. I may have been responsible for starting a most pernicious rumor about you. Worse than any other."

"Oh, really?" he asked, intrigued.

"Yes." Biting her lip, she gave him a doleful look. "I may have told a group of impressionable young ladies that by the light of the full moon, you transform into a ravening hedgehog."

He struggled to maintain a reproachful silence.

She continued, "Well, if it helps, I do regret it now."

"Do you?"

"Oh, yes. It was an insult to hedgehogs everywhere."

A throaty laugh shook free from his chest, and it felt damned good. He squeezed her hand in silent thanks.

"So . . ." she said, "this has been the case all your life?"

He nodded. "For as long as I recall."

"And it's not just ballrooms?"

"No." He only wished it were so simple. "Anywhere with too many people and not enough space. Arenas. The theater." He gave her a meaningful look. "Weddings. Musicales."

"Oh." Her face softened. "And schoolrooms? Those, too?"

He gave a tense shrug. Damn, but it galled him to realize how much he'd sacrificed over the years. It hurt worse that she'd realized it, too. "I know, I know. Everyone else seems to manage those settings with ease. That only makes it more irritating. I don't know what the devil is wrong with me. I've spent my whole life feeling like . . . like a fish with no talent for swimming."

Her fingers went to his temple, feathering through his hair. "Oh, Spencer . . ."

"No." He batted her hand away. "Amelia, don't. For God's sake, don't pity me. I can bear anything but that. It's an annoyance, I'll grant you, but not a deprivation. In the absence of attending frivolous parties, I've mastered some very useful talents. Cards. Horsemanship."

"You've read a great many books."

"Yes. That, too. I'm happy with my life as it is."

"Are you?" She looked doubtful.

"Yes," he told her honestly. Because at this particular moment of his life, he was. Things had been strained between them, to put it mildly, since Jack's visit. He'd almost forgotten how much he enjoyed simply talking with her. He'd forgotten how good it felt to laugh. She had a way of dragging his demons out of the shadows and . . . not ignoring them, or making them over into gleeful cherubs . . . but simply tweaking their ears. Looking them in the eye with that oh-so-Amelia combination of good sense and dry humor.

"Yes, I'm happy," he repeated. "I'm happy with my life as it is. Right now."

Footsteps crunched on gravel nearby.

"I think someone's coming," she whispered. "Perhaps we should—"

He kissed her. Firmly at first—until the shock wore off and she realized that she was being kissed. And then sweetly, tenderly—because she deserved his care. Holding her chin between the pads of his thumb and second finger, he urged her close. He explored her mouth with his lips and tongue, patiently coaxing her to open for him. Wooing her into full participation. Because she was worth that effort, too. This was a woman who ought to have been courted by a legion of suitors. How was it she'd remained unmarried all those years, standing on the fringes of ballrooms? How was it he'd never picked her out from the crowd himself and asked her to dance?

God damn, he was a fool. But a very lucky one.

All too soon, she pulled back. "I think they're gone." She flashed a look over her shoulder, and her cheeks turned a pretty shade of pink. "Quick thinking, that. You really are brilliant at disguising this problem. Honeymooners are forgiven all manner of rude behavior."

"Well, then there's the solution. We'll spend the rest of our lives on permanent honeymoon."

She laughed, as though it were a ridiculous notion. He wished it weren't.

"Honestly, Spencer. I can't help but wonder . . . Surely something can be done. Have you tried—?"

"Yes."

"But I didn't finish my . . ."

"It doesn't matter. If there's something you can think of to try, I've tried it. Nothing has worked. This is just part of who I am, Amelia. I reconciled myself to it long ago."

"Oh." Her chin ducked in disappointment. "I see."

Frustrated, Spencer rubbed his face with his palm. Of course, this was now—not some long-ago time. He was married. He had a ward. And as much as he might have reconciled himself to a life without social events, was it fair of him to ask Amelia to reconcile herself to it, too? Hospitality and friendship . . . those things were part of who *she* was. Not to mention the obligations they would have for Claudia's season. A bitter taste filled his mouth, making him grimace.

"Is there nothing I can do for you?" she asked.

"No, no. Just leave me be."

"I could send for—"

"Leave me be," he said, with too much force. They both cringed. He knew he was only alienating her further, because she lived to be helpful. But in this case, there was nothing she could do. He took a breath and calmed his voice. "When this happens, all I need is to be let alone."

"Very well." She rose to her feet. "I'll go. Stay here as long as you wish, and I'll make excuses with our hosts."

With that, she hurried back toward the entrance of the house. Spencer sighed, feeling a weight of guilt settle about his shoulders. In the past few minutes, he'd felt closer to Amelia than he had in weeks, but this damned condition of his was the brick wall he'd spent a lifetime banging his head against. And no matter what he said, or what she did, they would always remain on opposite sides of it. She needed society to make her life complete; he only felt whole in relative solitude.

Had he really tried *everything*? Not truthfully. In his youth, he'd attempted to overcome the damned problem through any number of strategies—most of which involved drinking and plain force of will—but he'd always been motivated by his own selfish needs and desires. The wish to attend school. The desire to chase girls. Sheer frustration with his ineptitude.

But there was one thing he hadn't yet tried. He hadn't tried conquering it for Amelia.

At the very least, he owed it to her to try.

"Are you quite certain?" Amelia studied her husband's expression for any trace of reluctance.

He leaned against the wall, crossing one ankle over the other. "For the fifth time, Amelia. I'm quite certain."

"You truly don't mind?"

"I don't mind."

She tugged on her gloves. "You know we don't have to go down at all."

"I know it."

"I would suggest we wait until after the dancing's started, but I suspect they'll be waiting on us to begin it. We'll only stay for a dance or two. The moment you want to leave, just tell me. You don't even have to say a word. We'll have some sort of signal. Touch the top button of your waistcoat, perhaps."

"A signal?" He arched a brow. "What are we, spies for the Crown? Can't I just bodily remove you from the hall? It worked well enough last time."

She threw him a disapproving look. Which was difficult, because there was simply nothing about his appearance to inspire her disapproval. Even swathed in silk and pearls, Amelia felt unequal to his simple, black-and-white-attired elegance. He looked splendid.

"Don't give me that look. I think you rather enjoyed it." His eyes darkened. "I know I did."

She blushed. Well, she *had* rather enjoyed it, truth be told. "A discreet signal will do for tonight. Save the bodily lifting for later, in private."

They exchanged smiles, and a giddy flutter rose in her belly.

Something had changed, since the garden that afternoon. He'd opened himself to her, revealing his vulnerabilities as he hadn't done since that conversation in the stables. He was a man who'd spent his life actively wishing to be misunderstood, but he'd bared a piece of his true self to her. And now, each time their eyes met, it was as though a silent message passed between them—sometimes a joke, sometimes an observation, other times a carnal suggestion. They were behaving like a couple, instead of two individuals who happened to be married.

His sudden openness made Amelia imprudently hopeful. Her foolish optimism was only increased by the fact that she knew he was making a great sacrifice, attending this party with her. She worried her heart was in serious peril, but she couldn't bring herself to erect the barriers again. She could only hope for a change in his views. Once they arrived at Briarbank, he would see what her home and family meant to her—how they'd molded her into the person she was, much as his own past had formed him. Perhaps then he would understand how it hurt her to be separated from Jack.

As Spencer looked her up and down, his appreciative expression turned to a frown.

Self-conscious, she put a hand to her throat. "Is there something wrong?"

"No, nothing." But as he stared at her, the little furrow of concentration between his eyebrows deepened. The expression was one of bemusement, as though he'd expected a different image from the one his eyes beheld.

"Does the gown look well?" She twisted a little, hoping he'd praise the dress at least and send her downstairs with a smidge more confidence.

"Quite," he said thoughtfully. "But then, blue always looks well on you."

Well, that seemed to be all the reassurance she would receive.

She took one last fretful glance at her reflection in the mirror and then met Spencer at the door. Before they left the room, Amelia paused a moment to smooth his lapels and waistcoat with her gloved hands.

Their gazes met. She kept her hands flat against his chest. It would have been the perfect moment for a kiss . . . if he wanted to kiss her. In the garden earlier, he'd embraced her so sweetly. But perhaps that had just been one more tactical move in a lifelong campaign of evasion and disguise.

After staring into her eyes a long moment, he reached to open the door. "Shall we?"

As balls went, this was a much more forgiving assembly than a London rout. The country setting not only afforded more spacious rooms, but also kept the guests to a reasonable number.

Still, as they entered the Granthams' modest hall, Amelia felt her husband's arm tense against hers. She had the urge to murmur something encouraging, or give him a soothing touch—but she checked the impulse, knowing it would only add to his annoyance. The last thing he would want was to be fussed over. He just wanted to be let alone.

And of course, they were instantly beset. Fortunately, she'd become acquainted with several of the guests earlier that day. She made quick introductions, and once Spencer had made his typically gruff acknowledgments, she took over the burden of making conversation. They made their circuit of the entire room this way, moving from small group to small group. Spencer made his terse, barely civil greetings, and Amelia gladly did the rest. She inquired after distant relatives' health, exchanged sympathies with those who'd known Leo, deflected impertinent questions about their hasty marriage, and accepted well-intentioned wishes of joy with equal grace. By pushing herself to the forefront, she was able to spare Spencer an undue burden of curiosity.

And as the evening wore on, she found herself enjoying the attention. This was their first public appearance together, and it was really something, to be the lady on the Duke of Morland's arm. Despite his faint, persistent frown, Spencer hadn't touched his top waistcoat button yet, nor tossed her over his shoulder to cart her from the room. The evening was going quite surprisingly well, and Amelia reveled in the freedom to laugh, converse, and joke as boldly as she wished.

In fact, she was having the time of her life.

When she looked up from a conversation to find her father's old friend Mr. Twither had cornered Spencer to question him mercilessly on farriers, Amelia even resorted to a new tactic: shameless flirtation. She sidled up to the old man, complimented the turn of his legs, remarked upon his youthful vigor, praised the delightful shape of his spectacles, and then discreetly pulled Spencer away, leaving a flushed, stammering, and quite-pleased-with-himself Mr. Twither in their wake.

And then, before anyone else could approach them, she loudly decried the heat and closeness of the room, gathered two glasses of cordial from a passing servant's tray, and beckoned Spencer aside.

"There's an alcove just there," she whispered, pretending to sip from her glass as she indicated a paneled screen.

He took the other glass from her hand. "After you."

The musicians picked a fortuitous moment to strike up the first chords of the quadrille, and amidst the excitement of partnering and queuing up, Amelia and Spencer slipped behind the screen. The triangular space was small and mostly occupied by a forlorn-looking potted palm.

Spencer drained his cordial in one draught, then grimaced and wiped his mouth.

"Well . . . ?" she asked cautiously, scanning his appearance for any signs of unease.

"This cordial is abominable." He glowered at the glass before setting it on a ledge behind them. His eyes slanted toward the screen. "And the musicians aren't much better."

"Yes, but how are *you*? I'm so sorry about Mr. Twither. He's harmless, you know, but he holds his end of a conversation like a dog holds a bone. Oh, and those dreadful Wexler twins." She shook her head. "They're shameless. Did Flora truly pinch your bottom, or did it just look that way?"

He didn't answer. Just smiled a little, in that devastatingly handsome and seductive way he smiled on rare occasions. Between that smile and the cordial, a very pleasant tingle warmed her insides.

"You're enjoying yourself," he said.

"I am." She sipped her drink. "I know you hate this sort of thing, and this must be the most trying evening imaginable—"

"Oh, I wouldn't say that."

Something thumped against the screen from the other side, startling her. Spencer's arm slid about her waist, drawing her back. She pivoted to face him, and his hand slid over her waist as she turned, until his palm settled at the base of her spine. A palm frond tickled against her neck. Suddenly stricken with a girlish flutter of nerves, she stared hard at his cravat.

"Are you truly enjoying tonight?" she asked.

"I'm enjoying right now."

"You've—" *Quiet, you ninny. He's here for you. This night is going so much better than you have any right to expect. Don't ruin it.*

"What?" he prompted, absently stroking his thumb over the small of her back.

She forced her gaze up to his and swallowed hard. The cordial must have made her bold. Or stupid. Likely both. "You've been staring at me so strangely all evening. I'm afraid you're disappointed, somehow. With me."

That mild frown he'd been wearing now etched itself into a stern mask of censure.

Words spilled from her mouth. Silly, irrational, painfully truthful words. "You're so handsome, you see. Just ridiculously so. I think you're the finest-looking man I've ever known, and I know I just don't look like your duchess. I know feigned affection wasn't part of our bargain, and I know you don't give a damn what anyone else thinks. But I do give a damn what they think. Just a little one; I can't help it. And I seem to care a great deal . . . far too much, I fear . . . about what *you* think, so—"

"Shhh." He laid a finger against her lips.

And then said nothing.

Did he not know what to say? What a fool she was.

Lie. Oh, please. Just lie to me. Just tell me I'm lovely, and I'll pretend to believe you, and we can forget this ever happened.

He tilted his head toward the screen and mouthed, *Listen.*

"Yes, yes." A matronly laugh resonated through the screen. "Rather a coup for Lady Grantham. Their first public appearance since the wedding, I understand."

"Thank the Lord," the unseen lady's companion replied in a gruff voice. "Now you can cease nattering on about the 'true' reason behind the marriage."

"Oh, yes. Obviously a love match. I never doubted it."

A loud harrumph.

"Well, I didn't!" came the protest. "Amelia always was a delightful girl, but marriage has been very kind to her. And anyone can see His Grace is completely besotted. He won't be torn from her side."

Behind the screen, Amelia nearly burst out laughing. Spencer covered her mouth with his palm.

The man snorted. "Yes, and any man with two eyes can see exactly which of her charms he's drunk on. They're on rather public display."

Amelia felt her eyes go wide. Spencer just flicked a devilish glance at her breasts and kept his hand pressed to her lips.

The man lowered his voice, and she held her breath to make out his words. "I'd keep her close, too, were I the duke. If she flirts that shamelessly right in front of him, imagine what she'll get up to when he's not looking."

"Oh, pish," the lady said. "Amelia's not like that. And what if they are in one another's pockets? Nothing wrong with newlywed bliss."

By this time Amelia was laughing so hard, her shoulders were shaking. Spencer gave her a quelling look, and she struggled to regain her composure. She failed. She giggled helplessly into his hand for a solid minute, tears rolling down her cheeks, until the musicians struck up a livelier tune and the gossiping couple drifted back into the crowd.

She still couldn't stop laughing. If she stopped laughing—ceased acting like everything they'd just heard was patently ridiculous—she'd have to admit how desperately she wished it all were true. If she stopped shedding helpless tears of laughter, she would just be . . . crying.

Is it safe to release you? his expression asked, after a long moment.

She nodded.

"Oh, heavens," she whispered, wiping her cheeks. "I'm sorry, but that was so . . ." Another inane giggle choked on a sob. "Imagine, if they only knew—"

"Knew what?" His hand shot out again. But this time he didn't press a finger to her lips. He cupped her cheek instead, and tilted her face to his intense, searching gaze. "The truth?"

Suddenly, she wasn't laughing anymore. She was barely breathing anymore.

"Amelia," he whispered, "at this moment, I don't think you'd recognize the truth if it pinched you on the bottom."

He dropped a firm kiss on her forehead. She couldn't decide what that kiss meant, or even whether she liked it or not.

"Here is what we're going to do," he said. "When this dance ends, we're going to sneak back out of this alcove the way we came in, and we're going to crawl out of one another's pockets. I'm going to make my passing nod at etiquette by inviting one of those grabby Wexler twins to dance. Hopefully Flora." She bit back a laugh, and he brushed a fingertip over her cheek. "And after that, I'm off to find a bit of brandy and quiet, and no one will notice. I'll come back for you in an hour, and in the meantime, you're to dance and enjoy every minute."

"But—"

"Don't argue. Just enjoy."

The music ended, and he was gone before she could object. Not two seconds had passed, and she missed him already.

She remembered her half-drunk glass of cordial. After downing the remnants in one swallow, she patted her cheeks dry and slipped out from behind the screen. Without her most striking accessory—a duke on her arm—she prepared to spend the next hour resuming her life as Just Plain Amelia. Having a pleasant, if unspectacular time. Chatting with the ladies on the fringes of the ballroom.

Blending into the wallpaper.

Chapter Seventeen

His wife was the center of the party.

From his shadowed gallery overlooking the hall, Spencer nursed his brandy and watched Amelia dance with her fourth partner in as many sets. She tripped gaily down the reel, smiling as she went. Once returned to her place, she exchanged a furtive remark with an adjacent lady, and several people in her circumference laughed. All ears were tuned to her remarks. All eyes were on her—on the shimmering cobalt silk that hugged her curves tight, and the yet more brilliant blue of her eyes.

To be sure, she was a duchess now, and doubtless some measure of the assembly's collective fascination could be attributed to her new title. But a mere title wouldn't hold them all enthralled. It was simply Amelia. Outgoing. Vivacious. Alluring as hell. Gone was the plain, retiring spinster. Tonight, her essence was uncorked and bubbling like fine champagne. Everyone wanted to be near her. To laugh with her. To get just a taste of her intoxicating charm.

And Spencer wanted it more dearly than anyone. A quality brandy enjoyed in solitude was one of life's saving graces, no question, and he did have a hard-earned misanthropic reputation to keep up. But he hadn't *needed* to leave. He hadn't experienced any head-spinning or blood-pounding to speak of tonight. In fact, he'd scarcely noticed the crowd this evening.

Like everyone else, he'd been captivated by his wife.

"What are you doing here?" The voice came from behind him.

He turned. "I ought to ask you that."

"I'm watching the party, of course. Just like you." Claudia stepped forward to join him at the gallery rail, and together they stared down at the dancers. "I'm weary of Bea Grantham. She's a very silly girl."

"I thought she's the same age as you."

"Not in any way that counts." Leaning on the balustrade, she propped her chin in one hand. "Amelia looks rather pretty tonight." There was surprise in her voice.

"Yes, she does."

Hm. Now he had the answer to his question.

The night they first met, if someone had asked him to describe Amelia d'Orsay, he would have called her plain. Unremarkable, at best. By the morning, he'd come to think of her as passable, even lovely in the most flattering light. He'd always found her alluring, in a voluptuous, sensual way.

But when she'd emerged in their suite earlier, dressed in that gown . . . Good Lord. He'd felt as though he'd been kicked in the gut. His heart had stuttered, and then there'd been an ache that settled in his chest. He'd realized, quite suddenly, that he now must count her among the most beautiful women he'd ever known. When had that happened? He'd spent the evening puzzling—was the change in her, or in him?

He had his answer now. It was her, all her. Perhaps she hadn't changed, but she'd been revealed.

"She's very popular with the gentlemen, isn't she?" Claudia's voice took on a cheeky tone. "Perhaps I'll apply to her for advice."

An uneasy feeling welled in his gut. Ever since Amelia had suggested Claudia might be envious of Spencer's marriage, he'd felt uneasy around his ward. He doubted Amelia's supposition was true, but he was afraid to ask and find out. In general, he just didn't know how to talk to Claudia anymore. Not that he'd ever been especially proficient at it, but lately she was so prickly and difficult. He hated that she was growing up, and growing further away from him.

"It's past your bedtime," Spencer told her.

She sighed dramatically. "Do you plan to treat me like a little girl forever?"

"Yes. That's what guardians do." To her sulky pout, he replied pointedly, "Good night."

Once Claudia had gone, he turned to find Amelia in the crowd again. It wasn't difficult. All he had to do was look for the knot of slavering men.

He wasn't alone in his admiration of her, and he couldn't pretend to be pleased. Humbling as it was to admit, he'd rather liked believing she had no better alternatives than marriage to him. That even if he bungled everything—which he was obviously wont to do—he needn't worry about losing her to another man.

He tossed back another swallow of brandy. Tonight, he was worried. Very worried. Behind that screen she'd looked up at him with such heartrending doubt in her eyes. Didn't she have any idea what she meant to him? For God's sake, he was here. At a party. In Oxfordshire. For her. That ought to tell her something.

Evidently it didn't tell her enough. There was no way around it. He was going to have to explain a few things to her. Very slowly, and in some detail. And for a man who'd long ago vowed never to explain himself to anyone . . .

Spencer was rather looking forward to it.

He descended the stairs and entered the hall just as

the first strains of a waltz began. Amelia was already partnered with another man—some local gentleman farmer whose name he'd forgotten already—but Spencer didn't give a damn.

"I believe this is my dance," he said, extending his hand right in front of the waiting man's.

Amelia gave him a reproving look, but the farmer was already gone. Taking her in his arms, Spencer swept his wife onto the dance floor.

"Is it midnight already?" she teased.

"Near enough." He took her through a brisk series of turns. "I owe you an answer, from earlier."

"Oh, no," she stammered. "No, please. I was so silly to even—"

"I've been staring at you all night, you said."

"Just . . . just a little."

"Oh, I have been. So has every man here. Don't tell me you haven't noticed."

"They're only drawn by the novelty."

"Is that what you're calling them tonight?" He cast a glance at her cleavage.

She blushed. "I suppose a well-cut gown does do wonders for a girl's confidence."

"Hm." He tightened his arm around her waist. "No, Amelia, I don't believe it has much to do with the gown, or the novelty. It's just you. They're drawn to you. You've been courting notice tonight. Flirting and dancing and laughing with every man to pass your way. And you've been enjoying their attention. Don't deny it."

"Very well, I won't." Her expression turned wary. "Are you displeased?"

An excellent question. He'd been asking himself the same thing. But he couldn't begin to give an answer here.

"We need to leave," he said. "Immediately."

Her eyes widened with concern. "Oh. Oh, of course.

You're ill." She lowered her voice. "Can you last to the end of the waltz? It will be less noticeable if—"

"Immediately." He brought them to a swift halt.

"Very well, then. You go ahead, and I'll just make our excuses to Lady Grantham."

"You're coming with me."

"But I must—"

Damn it, when would she learn to stop arguing with him? With an impatient sigh, Spencer tightened one arm behind her back, bent to slide the other behind her knees, and straightened, lifting her into his arms. Her breathy gasp of surprise heated his blood.

Around them, all dancing ground to a halt.

It was a struggle to keep from grinning as he said, "We're leaving. Together. Now."

The man was a barbarian.

Amelia could see it in the eyes of the party guests. Because, of course, every eye in the room was on her and Spencer. The guests' expressions mingled shock and glee. A display like this was exactly what they'd come hoping to see, and she pitied poor Lady Grantham, because this excitement would herald a swift end to the evening. The guests would empty the hall immediately, desperate to go home and discuss it amongst themselves, write letters, regale their servants with the tale. Rumors of Spencer's uncivilized nature would double within hours of their exit from this ballroom.

He truly was a genius.

As he carried her past a slack-jawed Lady Grantham, Amelia attempted to take their leave. "Thank you so much for a lovely evening. We'll see you at breakfast, then."

Spencer tightened his grip on her body and said, loud enough for all to hear, "Don't make any promises."

Amelia couldn't help it. She burst out laughing.

And with that, he carried her from the room.

As they headed for the stairs, she expected him to put her down. Obviously, if he'd needed to leave the room so quickly, he must be feeling ill. How brilliant of him, though, to let everyone believe he simply couldn't exist another moment without carting his wife up to bed. It was true, newlyweds were forgiven all manner of rude behavior. And she counted it as a small victory, that Spencer would let a roomful of gawking dancers believe *she* was his weakness, rather than appear simply haughty and rude. The whole scene was immensely satisfying.

"Really," she whispered as they mounted the stairs, "I can walk from here."

He gave a dismissive snort and continued carrying her, taking the risers two at a time. Amelia ceased arguing. This was enjoyable, too.

He did put her back on her feet at the entrance to their suite, and after they reached the bedchamber and closed the door, he stalked off across the room, tugging at his cravat.

Wanting to give him some space to recover, Amelia went to the dressing table and removed her gloves. She undid the clasp of her bracelet and laid it on a gilt tray. "Thank you for tonight," she said quietly, watching Spencer's reflection as he tore off his coat and cast the garment aside. "I know what a trial it must have been."

"Do you?" Stripped down to his waistcoat and shirt, he came to stand behind her.

Their gazes locked in the mirror. His eyes were dark and intense.

Swallowing self-consciously, Amelia reached for the clasp of her earring.

"Leave them on," he said.

Frozen in place by the brusque command, she stared at her husband's reflection. He didn't look pale or ill in the least. To the contrary, he radiated strength and virility. The only one perspiring or trembling was Amelia.

"Leave the pearls," he repeated, settling his hands on her hips. "I want you looking just as you looked down there, in the hall."

She dropped her hands, pressing them flat atop the dressing table. The posture pitched her forward on her toes.

"Yes." The word was a husky groan. "More. Give me a nice, full view of what you've been showing the other men all evening." He yanked her hips back, so that her weight canted onto her arms. The posture thrust her bosom forward, and in the mirror, the twin swells of her breasts puffed for attention. Even she couldn't look away.

His hands roamed possessively over the curves of her backside and hips. "Do you really know what a trial it was, Amelia? To look on from a distance while my wife danced and flirted and captivated every man in the room? Can you truly understand how that feels?"

Yes, she thought. *Yes, you ridiculous man. Of course I know what it feels like, to stand by unnoticed while you hold every woman in the room in thrall.* She hadn't considered it until this moment, but was it possible she'd enjoyed tonight partly out of revenge?

The devil in her said, "Tell me. Tell me how it feels."

His reflected gaze trapped hers. Meanwhile, his hands were doing unseen, wicked things. "Perhaps I should say it made me immensely proud. That wouldn't be a lie. But neither would it be the whole truth."

She felt her skirts lifting in back, tangling about her ankles and teasing the sensitive hollows of her knees. Air rushed over her exposed legs, both cooling and inflaming her.

"The truth is"—his thigh nudged her legs apart—"it also made me angry."

His fingers brushed the sensitive slope of her inner thigh, traveling up to stroke her sex. She was ready for him, her intimate flesh already swollen and damp with excitement, and the discovery dragged a low moan from them both. The hard ridge of his arousal branded her hip.

"It made me want to teach you a lesson."

He roughly prodded her legs apart and moved to stand between them. Excitement rushed through her. In the mirror, the reflection of her breasts rose and fell at a suggestive pace, as though he were already moving inside her. His own breath came faster as he leaned against her, propping her skirts at her waist with his abdomen while his hands worked the buttons of his fall.

Within seconds, she felt him poised at her entrance. Her body ached for him. Wept for him.

"Yes?" he breathed.

"Yes," she answered.

Yes. He entered her in one hard, quick thrust that rocked the dressing table on its legs. Her body cringed at the sudden assault, but he gave her no quarter. He slowly withdrew, pulling out almost to the tip before driving home again, all the way to the hilt.

"This is mine," he said, clutching her hips. He nudged deeper still. "Mine."

He was so deep inside her, so hard and strong. He was all she could feel. Toes, fingers, lips, ears, skin . . . all the fringes of her body melted to insignificance.

Lifting her at the waist, he began to thrust, setting a brisk, unforgiving rhythm. Atop the dressing table, her bracelet rattled on the gilt tray. The reflection of her breasts bobbed in time with his movements, bouncing erotically and threatening to overflow her bodice. As the force of his thrusts increased, the dark border of one areola eased free. Now the neckline chafed her hardened nipple . . . back and forth, back and forth as he moved, hemmed silk rubbing against the exquisitely sensitive nub.

And inside her . . . oh, God, inside her he was reaching places she hadn't known existed. Pleasure coiled in her womb, volatile and intense. A devastating explosion seemed inevitable, and she worried that afterward, she would never be the same again. The strength left her arms. She leaned forward over the table, resting her weight on her elbows. The change in position earned his grunt of approval, and he began to thrust faster still. The folds of her skirt and petticoat wadded between her pelvis and the table edge, and as he moved, the bunched fabric stroked her just where she needed it.

"Spencer," she gasped. She let her head roll forward, resting her feverish brow on one forearm.

"No." His fingers tangled in her hair, pulling her head back up. The sharp yank on a thousand nerve endings sent pain and pleasure rushing from her scalp to her toes.

"Watch yourself," he commanded her. "Watch yourself as you come. Every other man can see you as you were downstairs. Witty. Desirable. Charming. Elegant." Each word drove home with another thrust. "But this is when you're goddamned beautiful, and this beauty is mine. It's for me, and me alone. Now and forever. Do you understand?"

She wouldn't have thought it possible, but he doubled the force of his motions again. A bottle of eau de cologne rolled to the floor, crashing open in a flood of rich scent. Her senses were overwhelmed.

"Mine," he said, on a hard, spanking thrust.

"Yes." She watched, mesmerized, as her reflection flushed pink. Her swollen lips fell apart, exposing the tip of her tongue. She stared into the jewel-like blue of her own eyes, soaring closer to release with each delicious thrust. He was right; there was true beauty there.

"Yes. Oh, Spencer. *Yes.*" Her eyes squeezed shut as she came. She couldn't have stopped them, any more than she could keep her eyes open for a sneeze. The force of her climax was too powerful, too sudden. It went on and on, as he drove into her relentlessly.

As the tremors in her core ebbed, she sensed the shift in him—that slight hitch in his motions that signaled he'd gone past the point of return.

And now she forced herself to look. She watched in the mirror as his jaw went tight, and his lip curled back to reveal gritted teeth. His face was contorted with pleasure, as if it felt so good it hurt. His eyes closed, and his neck arched.

That mask of primal, raw lust—it was for her. She'd done that.

"Yes," she urged him. "Come for me now."

He gave a harsh cry and froze as he spent inside her, digging his fingernails into her hips. She would have bruises there tomorrow. She would cherish them.

They remained there, joined, gasping and shuddering against the much-abused dressing table. He laid his brow on her bare shoulder. Perspiration misted them both.

He withdrew from her body, and she trembled helplessly in his arms. Her knees refused to solidify. She wondered if she'd even be able to stand.

"Oh, Amelia," he finally said, sounding drugged and weak. "Come here."

He helped her to the bed. She lay boneless atop the coverlet while he played lady's maid, removing her gown, stockings, and undergarments. He dampened a cloth at the washstand and swabbed her brow and neck with cool water before dragging the cloth lower, to soothe the tender flesh between her legs.

He stretched out beside her on the bed. "Are you well?"

She managed a nod.

He smoothed the stray hairs from her face and kissed her cheek. Then he kissed her neck. And then that delicate pulse just beneath her ear. He kissed her everywhere. No eager nips or seductive swipes of his tongue. Just tender, reverent brushes of his lips against her skin, from crown to toe. Her exhaustion was so complete, she wasn't even ticklish. He kissed the insides of her elbows, her belly, her knees, and even the broad, fleshy mound of her hip. She didn't so much as flinch. Then he settled between her legs, spreading her thighs to accommodate the breadth of his shoulders. His fingers parted her gently, and he dropped a soft kiss against her sex.

Her hips bucked, just a little.

"I've been waiting forever to do this." He stroked her with his tongue. "You taste so good."

And with that, any fight in her was gone. She lay there, letting the beautiful pleasure sparkle and swirl through her veins. She brought one hand to his hair, sifting through the dark curls as he kissed her languidly. Within her, the need mounted again, and she knew he would soon bring her to another blissful crest—but she didn't want to hurry. In some ways, she couldn't imagine a greater pleasure than this. Knowing that there was a party downstairs and a bottle of brandy next door, but what her husband most wanted to do at this moment was just this: to lie between her legs and worship her body with his lips and tongue. She fought the rising climax as long as she could, wanting to prolong this time they were sharing together.

But she couldn't make it last forever. He pursed his lips around her bud and did something indescribable with his tongue, and her peak was upon her before she even had time to breathe. First piercing, then soft and buoyant as a wave.

Oh. Oh.

Oh.

He rested his head on her belly. "I've missed this."

She smiled, stroking his hair. They'd shared a bed every night for weeks now, and they'd never done exactly "this" before. But she knew what he meant. He meant he'd missed her. Emotion thickened her throat.

"Spencer?"

He lifted his head, a silent question in his eyes.

"Please speak," she begged him. "It's a lovely moment, and this is where you ruin it. This is where you say something arrogant and insensitive. You know, to save me just in time, before I lose my heart to you completely."

He gave her only a smile.

"Oh, dear." She let her head fall back to the pillow. "There it went. I've fallen in love with you now."

"Just now?" Chuckling, he rolled off her and came to a sitting position, resting his forearm on one bent knee. "Well, thank God for belated blessings." He ran a hand through his hair. "It's been coming on rather longer than that for me."

"What?" She sat bolt upright. "What can you mean? Since when?"

"From the first, Amelia. From the very first."

"No. I don't believe it."

"Don't you?" He cast a meaningful look at his waistcoat pocket, where a corner of white peeked out.

"Why on earth are you still clothed?" she teased as her fingertips closed over the bit of linen. Her hands went utterly useless, however, once she plucked the cloth from his pocket and stared at it. It was *her* handkerchief. The one she'd pressed on him that first night on the Bunscombes' terrace. Embroidered with her initials in purple script, twined round with ivy and decorated with a single buzzing honeybee. Had he truly been carrying it ever since? Carrying a *tendre* for her, as well? She could never have believed it, had she not been holding the evidence in her hand.

She looked up at him, astonished. "Spencer . . ."

Color rose on his cheekbones, and he shifted defensively. "Go on, do your worst. You have already accused me of being a romantic and a sentimental fool. I don't know what more you can say to discredit me."

"You are a sweet man."

"God, there it is." He flopped back on the bed, as if shot through the heart. "Repeat that to anyone, and I will have you brought up on charges of slander."

"I wouldn't dream of telling a soul," she said, smiling as she nestled close. "I like it being our secret."

His arm encircled her naked shoulders as he heaved a contented sigh. "Might I be allowed an endearment now? Or will you accuse me of treating you like a horse?"

"That would depend on the endearment, I suppose. What did you have in mind?"

"My dear? My darling? My sweet?" Skepticism tainted his voice as he tested each phrase.

"No, none of those. Too overused to have any meaning."

He rolled to face her. "What about my pearl? My blossom? My treasure?"

She laughed. "Now you're just making fun."

He cupped her face in his palm, and what she saw in those entrancing hazel eyes made her breath catch. A capacity for emotion so fierce and loyal, it flashed with the enduring fire of diamonds. Deeply buried, but worth any effort to reach.

All teasing fled his voice. "My wife. My heart." He tilted his head, considering. "My dearest friend."

"Oh." Emotion pinched sweetly in her chest. "I think I rather like that last."

"So do I, Amelia." He pulled her close for a kiss. "So do I."

Chapter Eighteen

"There's Briarbank."

Amelia's mount pranced sideways as she pointed. Spencer nudged Juno forward and let his gaze follow the indicated direction, scaling down a craggy bluff and winding into a bend of the river. There, tucked against a wooded bank, sat an ancient stone cottage. Smoke puffed in welcome from its chimney, rising above the trees and hovering above the river like a miniature cloud.

"It's a lovely prospect, isn't it?" Her eyes swept the verdant countryside and winding valley.

It was indeed, he thought, surveying the view. Lovely didn't begin to describe it.

The green plateau they currently occupied was home to the ruins of Beauvale Castle. The castle's crumbling turrets had been well positioned for defense. They overlooked the valley of the River Wye, and from this high bluff, one could see for miles in any direction. Miles of forests and farmland, displaying every shade of green in Nature's palette. Dark, mossy glens that swallowed the sunlight; fields of summer alfalfa that sparkled as a mild breeze teased the grass.

"'Once again I see these hedgerows, hardly hedgerows, little lines of sportive wood run wild,'" she recited quietly. "'These pastoral farms, green to the very door.'" She gave him a smile that arrowed straight for his heart.

How could he not love her? He'd married a woman who quoted Wordsworth. And not merely to impress or sound well versed in modern poetry, but because the verse meant something to her, and she kept it in her heart.

She looked at him through her lashes. "You're very quiet. What are you thinking?"

At the anxious note in her voice, her mount moved beneath her. For her first lesson, she was doing quite well, but she still lacked the confidence to fully control a horse. It would be some weeks yet before he could allow her to ride alone.

Spencer calmed Amelia's gelding with a few clucks of his tongue and dismounted from Juno to give her a rest. Likely he shouldn't have pressed a mare Juno's age on such a long journey, but he'd seen with his own eyes the destruction she wrought on her stall and herself when left behind. He needed to secure ownership of Osiris, and soon. But all these were thoughts better kept to himself.

"It's beautiful," he said simply, looking out on the valley. Really, that was God's truth. Caught between the wild, uneven landscape spread below, the primeval forest at his back, and the brilliant blue sky overhead . . . he found his breath squeezed from his lungs. The sight made his heart ache for his own boyhood home. Canada's untamed landscape offered many such vistas, and in his youth he'd often slipped away, paddled hard, ridden far to find them. Now an adult, he rarely let himself feel how much he missed that inspiring beauty.

Nature never did betray the heart that loved her.

Here was a dark alcove of his spirit he'd never examined too closely, but Amelia had forged straight in and drawn back the curtains, illuminating everything. He wasn't especially sentimental, but he *was* a true Romantic, in the vein of Wordsworth and his like. Spencer had never been able to sit in a crowded church pew and feel anything but hopeless and tormented. But Nature was his cathedral. In places and moments like these, he truly felt the presence of the divine. Both humbling and comforting, at once.

It was a good thing, at times, for a duke to feel humbled. The same could be said—or at least tacitly admitted in rare moments of self-examination—that it was sometimes a welcome thing, to be comforted. And he didn't need to go chasing, swimming, or scaling wild landscapes in pursuit of those feelings now. Fortunate soul that he was, he'd married a woman with the wit and generosity to dispense both comfort and humility, and the spirit to keep him guessing which he'd receive on any given day.

And he loved her for it. Such a new endeavor for him: loving. And an intimidating one to undertake. He was a man who tended to excel at a few select pursuits and fail catastrophically at the rest. He hated to ponder the consequences if this one fell into the latter category.

"How long has the castle been like this?" he asked, nodding toward the ranging pile of stone.

"Not so very long," she said. "From what my father told me, it was standing until a few generations ago. It was weakened by fire and then fell into disrepair. Most of the walls are still standing, but there are no roofs or floors to speak of." She turned shining blue eyes toward the castle's entrance, where a stone arch bridged a pair of rounded towers. "Well, except in the gatehouse. That's where my brothers got up to all their mischief."

"And you? Where did you get up to your mischief?"

"I was a good girl," she said, raising her eyebrows. "I didn't get up to any mischief."

He gave her a subtle wink. "Never too late to begin."

To give his mare a bit of rest, he led her in a slow walk about the ruined castle's perimeter. Pity the heap was entailed to her brother. He found himself wishing he could rebuild it for Amelia, make it into the home she deserved. Wake up to this sparkling green landscape and those brilliant blue eyes every morning.

After rounding the castle, he returned to Amelia, observing her delicate profile as she looked down at the river. He could imagine her ancestors standing here, in centuries past. Generation after generation of strong, noble women who partnered the strong, protected the weak, and made the keep worth defending.

"It's well situated," he said, following her gaze to Briarbank. In lieu of their own private castle, he supposed they'd have to make do with the cottage. "But it's dreadfully small."

"Yes. And it will soon be full of people. I'll understand, if sometimes you feel the need to slip away." She smiled. "Anyhow, the neighborhood begs to be explored. There's the river, the forest, all sorts of ruins. Someday we'll ride down to Tintern. That would be an excellent excursion for Claudia."

Spencer frowned at the mention of his ward, shooting a glance back toward the coach. Certainly, the ruined medieval abbey would be an excellent excursion for her—if they could coax the girl to go. Claudia hadn't been riding since her return from York. He didn't know whether her boycott stemmed from resentment toward Amelia, or toward him.

"Come along," Amelia chided, evidently mistaking his frown for reluctance. "You know you want to see the view of Tintern Abbey. 'When the fretful stir unprofitable,'" she quoted, teasing him with another line from Wordsworth's poem, "'and the fever of the world have hung upon the beatings of my heart . . .'"

She arched an eyebrow, extending him a dare.

"'How oft, in spirit, have I turned to thee,'" he finished in a murmur, looking over his shoulder as though there might be someone to hear.

"I knew it." She smiled. "Romantic."

"Our secret, remember." He made his voice deep with mock threat. "You're not to tell a soul."

Four days later, Spencer sat in Briarbank's small library, shaking blotting powder over the letter he'd just finished. A knock sounded at the door. "Come in."

"It's only me." Amelia entered the library, closing the door behind her and approaching the desk with a delicious sway in her hips. A quite promising sway, if he read the signals right.

This place was good for her. He'd noticed the change in her the moment they'd arrived at Briarbank. She was in her element, brimming with confidence and cheer, and for his part, Spencer had been reaping bountiful rewards in their bedchamber. And in their dressing room, and in the bath, and even once in the drawing room. But not yet in this library, and he dearly hoped this afternoon's interruption was intended to remedy that oversight.

He sealed his letter and set it aside. "Well?"

"A rider just arrived from Harcliffe Manor. Lily and the gentlemen are under way. They should arrive within an hour or two."

Spencer received the news with surprising ambivalence. This was the original reason he'd journeyed here—to get Bellamy and Ashworth in one place and put an end to this Stud Club business. But now he'd been enjoying his time alone with Amelia. He hated for the honeymoon to end.

Evidently, she felt the same. Skirting the desk, she sauntered around to his chair and made herself at home in his lap. "Soon the house will be full of people," she said.

"I'll be busy making everyone feel at home. This may be our last time alone for a while."

She wasted no time with coyness. Her hand went straight to his groin.

"Already?" she teased, stroking his erection through the fabric of his trousers.

"From the moment you entered the room." He hauled her further into his lap, taking her mouth in a kiss that was equal parts playfulness and passion. God, he loved her mouth. So sweet and lush, just like the rest of her.

She reached between them, unbuttoning his fall and smallclothes with practiced skill. He cupped her breasts, teasing her nipples to peaks through the thin muslin as she freed him from his trousers. Her cool, delicate fingers wrapped around his thick length, stroking him boldly. He reclined in the chair, reveling in the sensation. She was a quick study, his Amelia. She'd already learned just how he liked to be touched.

Another rap at the door had him jolting in the chair.

"Stay here," she said, scooting off his lap. "One of the servants, no doubt. I'll be back in a trice."

He obeyed her. Because really, he had no desire to stand and greet whoever it was with a rampant erection. He didn't even bother to tuck himself back in, just moved closer to the desk. Amelia conferred with the intruder in hushed tones, and then shut the door and locked it. If his arousal had flagged the slightest bit during the interruption, the sound of that tumbler in the lock had him throbbing again, instantly.

As she hurried back across the room, he pushed back in his chair and surveyed the desk. Would he lay her atop it? Or bend her over it? Decisions, decisions.

Amelia had ideas of her own, however. She walked over to where he sat in the chair, took his eager length in her hand, and sank to her knees.

Oh, hell.

That sweet, lush mouth closed over the swollen head of his cock, and Spencer thought he would erupt. "Amelia, wait."

She backed off and looked up at him.

Damn it. Why the deuce had he done that?

"What is it?" she asked.

"Are you sure . . . ?" He hadn't wanted to push her into this too soon.

Her eyes twinkled. "You told me that if I enjoy something you do to me, there's an excellent chance you'll enjoy the same."

"In this case, it's not an excellent chance. It's a certainty."

"Well, then. Stop interrupting."

She took him in her mouth again, this time smiling while she did it. And it was the damnedest thing, but it felt different when she smiled. Even better than before, if such a thing were possible. Her tongue curled around the sensitive ridge beneath, and her soft palate rubbed against the crown, and a helpless burst of profanity tore from his throat.

Which made her laugh, and then it got even better.

She was a little tentative, but that was good, because if she'd been any more free with her lips and tongue and hands, he would have come in an embarrassingly brief ten seconds.

He fell back into the chair, surrendering to the mounting pleasure. With one hand, he swept a stray lock of her hair aside, to better watch as she sucked him between those plump, coral-pink lips. She looked up and caught him watching, and she gave an erotic sigh that had him clawing the upholstery.

Sweet heaven. Embarrassing or not, he was already close. So close. Perhaps he ought to warn her. She'd never done this before. She might not realize she had a choice, but . . . bloody hell. Why would he want to give her one? Really, of all the times for a man's nobility to be put to the test.

"Amelia," he groaned. There. That was all the warning she'd get. He knew she'd recognize the desperation in his voice.

Bless her, she only increased her efforts. Her very effective efforts. Her brilliant, amazing, soul-shattering, credibility-defying, best-ever-in-his-life efforts.

"Oh, *God*." He arched off the chair, his whole body racked by bliss.

In the aftermath, he stared unfocused at the cracked plaster and roughhewn ceiling beams. Amelia had been right. This drafty little cottage was paradise on earth.

She rose from the floor and sat on the desk facing him, wiggling her bottom backward and letting her legs dangle between his sprawled boots. Her kittenish expression was one of extreme self-satisfaction.

Minx. He would teach her something about satisfaction. Just as soon as he recovered his breath. Reaching out with a leaden arm, he encircled her ankle with his fingers. "Now you."

She shook her head. "Thank you, no. I don't want to get mussed. They'll be here any time now. The beds are prepared, but I'd hoped to gather fresh flowers for each room." Her brow wrinkled. "And I'm still missing a vegetable dish for dinner. How do you feel about parsnips?"

"I'm completely indifferent to parsnips," he said, sliding his hand up her calf. "But I very much want to taste you."

Laughing, she slid back on the desk, out of his reach. "Not now. I've so much yet to do."

"And if you don't finish, what does it matter? Amelia, you are too quick to put others ahead of yourself."

She shrugged and flicked a glance at his lap. "Are you saying you wish I hadn't . . ."

"Of course not. Are you mad?" He grinned. Tucking himself back in, he straightened in his chair and took a more serious tone. "But I've been wondering something. At the Granthams' the other night, you were radiant. Bewitching. The center of attention. If you'd behaved like that in Town, I could not have attended a single ball without noticing you, let alone dozens. How is it I never saw that Amelia in London?"

She bit her lip. "I've been pondering that question myself. Obviously, you're a great boost for my confidence. I defy any woman to be a wallflower with a handsome duke at her side." She tickled his knee with her toes. "But before I met you . . . I think I once mentioned Mr. Poste to you. The squire I was engaged to marry?"

He nodded.

"My father owed him a great deal of money, you see, and he made certain I understood he would forgive the debts in exchange for . . . well, for me." Her voice grew soft. "He had his eye on me, from the time I was very young. Too young. I developed earlier than most girls, and even when I was twelve, I would catch him leering at me. It made me feel so unclean, and I was only a child."

Spencer wanted to hit something. Hard. "Did he touch you?"

"A few pinches, here and there. Nothing more. But I didn't know how to cope with that sort of attention, and I never spoke of it to my parents. I was afraid they wouldn't let me marry him, and I wanted so much to help. In the end, I just couldn't go through with it. My motives were entirely selfish. I dreamed of having my turn at courtship and romance. But even after I broke the engagement, it took years before I could feel a man's eyes on my body and not simply . . . wither where I stood."

Damn it all. There was nothing to make a man feel more useless than the revelation of a wound suffered years in the past, healed over in the present, that he couldn't do a blasted thing to remedy now.

"So if no one saw me, I suspect it was because I didn't want to be seen. Perhaps I didn't feel worthy of attention." She gave him a bittersweet smile. "You see, Poste died soon after our betrothal ended. If I'd endured just a year of marriage to him, my family would have been saved so much trouble. And I'd be a wealthy widow now."

"Surely you don't feel guilty for that."

One of her shoulders lifted in a shrug. A clear admission that she did.

Dear, addled girl. To have carried that misplaced guilt—and the weight of her family's financial distress—all these years. Simply because she'd balked at marrying a lecherous old stick? At least it made some sense now, why she would so eagerly deny herself in the name of helping her brothers.

He caught her hand and squeezed it. "I'm very glad you didn't marry him."

She slanted her gaze away.

He waited, hoping she'd return the sentiment and say she was happy with the way life had turned out, too. That being a wealthy widow was nothing compared to being the Duchess of Morland, and she would not give up Spencer for anything—not even to redeem her father's debts.

But she didn't say any of that.

"I love you," she said.

His heart cinched with disappointment. He knew the words were sincere. The only trouble was, there were a great many people Amelia sincerely loved. And he'd never felt comfortable in a crowd.

Needing a diversion, he dropped his gaze to the

papers scattered on his desk. "Who was that earlier, at the door?"

"Oh, it was Claudia. I told her you'd be along in a minute. A shockingly accurate estimate, in the end."

He gave her backside an affectionate swat as she hopped down from the desk.

"One other thing," she said, turning at the door. "When the men arrive, you're to take them angling. I'm counting on fresh salmon for dinner tonight."

"Here's another." With a quick jerk of his wrist, Ashworth snagged a wriggling fish from the Wye.

Spencer congratulated him and recast his own line, once again marveling at his wife's cleverness. He'd planned this holiday with the intent of disbanding the Stud Club once and for all. But in order to execute his plan, he needed an opportunity to speak with Ashworth without Bellamy present. Amelia had handed him the perfect excuse. Course fishing was a gentleman's sport, a pastoral occupation. As a child of privilege raised in the country, Rhys would have grown up angling on summer afternoons, as had Spencer.

But Julian Bellamy . . . ha. This cottage was likely the closest he'd ever come to a river other than the Thames. The more Spencer learned of the man, the more he was convinced Bellamy's provenance was a direct line back to the gutters of London. His jokes and fashionable attire were enough to grease his way in Town, but not out here in Gloucestershire. Here, he stood out like the impostor he was. He'd balked at the mere mention of angling, making some pitiful excuse about tuning the pianoforte.

Spencer wondered how much Leo had known about the man's true history. By all accounts, they'd been close friends.

"I need funds," Ashworth said, saving Spencer the

trouble of easing into the topic. "That's the reason I'm here. Once we're done, I've decided to go straight to Devonshire, see what's left of my torched estate. I'll need money."

"I happen to have money," Spencer said with nonchalance.

"And I happen to have a token. I'd suggest we make a simple exchange, but . . ."

"But Bellamy won't hear of it, I know." Derision pitched his voice to a drawl. "Heaven forfend we neglect the Stud Club Code of Good Breeding."

They both laughed a little. Just a little, because the joke was Leo's, and Leo was dead.

"We'll play for it," Spencer said. A nibble on his line stole his attention, but as he began reeling in the line, the catch slipped away. "One of these nights, we'll convince Bellamy to sit down to cards. There's not much else to do out here. It shouldn't take long. Just let me take the lead. I know how to play these situations slowly. When I lose ten thousand pounds to you on one hand, you'll lose the token to me on the next."

"I want twenty thousand."

"Fifteen. That's as high as I'll go."

"You offered twenty to Lily."

"She's grieving and pretty. You're ugly and unlikable."

Ashworth shrugged. "Fair enough."

They fell silent again for a time.

"While we're here, the two of us . . . I suppose we're years overdue for a conversation." Spencer took extra care rebaiting his hook. "About Eton . . . I wasn't really fighting you that day." That was as close to an apology as he could get. After all, he hadn't started the fight.

A dragonfly buzzed past. Spencer recast his line.

Finally Ashworth said, "I wasn't really fighting you, either."

"We needn't speak of it further." God forbid they

accidentally wade into heartfelt conversation. Spencer cocked his head, wondering if that was the true reason Amelia had sent them out angling. The little minx.

"So if you weren't fighting me," Ashworth said, "what were you fighting?"

Spencer sighed. Of course it couldn't have been that easy. This would have been an opportune time for a fish to bite and remove all possibility of further discussion.

None did.

"I don't know," he said finally. "Fate."

He'd been miserable at Eton. He was seventeen, and one of the oldest students there, but his Latin lagged behind that of the second-form boys. Then there was his little problem to contend with: breaking into a cold sweat in crowded classrooms. The only boy who'd rivaled him for surliness was Rhys St. Maur—one year younger than Spencer, but already two stone heavier. The two of them had waged a silent competition for the title of Worst Boy in School. Spencer had no idea why Rhys made so much trouble, but on his side, the rabble-rousing was intentional. If he misbehaved enough, his uncle might send him back to Canada. Or so he'd hoped.

Then the letter came that day. It was February and sunny, yet still cold as a bitch. He'd been happy, initially, to be summoned from a Greek lesson to receive the missive. Inside, he found the news that his father had died in Canada, a month before. He'd been an orphan for a month, and he hadn't even known. And now it didn't matter how much he misbehaved. There was no going back home. There was no home to go back to.

He'd been devastated. Angry with himself, his father, his uncle, God.

And Rhys St. Maur had picked that day to start a brawl.

"Fighting fate?" Rhys asked. "You never struck me as that stupid. A man can't win against fate."

"Perhaps not," Spencer said. "In the end I can't say I'm sorry I lost."

Whatever regrets or guilt Amelia might harbor about her past, he had none. Here he was, a duke with every material advantage and a thriving business concern to boot, married to a clever, desirable woman who also happened to be his best friend. He wouldn't change a damn thing. He only wished his wife felt the same.

God, he was a greedy bastard. A few weeks ago, he would have thought nothing could make him happier than to hear Amelia say she loved him in the same selfless, devoted way she loved her brothers. Now he'd heard it. And it wasn't enough. He wanted to be first in her life. First, last, and everything in between.

Rhys pulled in another salmon. "There's three."

"Excellent," Spencer replied, reeling in his line. "Now we can go up to the house, and Amelia will be satisfied."

"Are you going to tell her I caught them all?"

"Of course not. And neither are you, if you want your fifteen thousand." Spencer opened the tackle box. "It's a fair bit of money, fifteen thousand. Enough to take a wife."

"A wife?" Rhys scowled as he helped Spencer untangle the lines. "You should confine your strategy to the card table. That's the worst idea I've ever heard."

"Why? Because you might start smiling?" He persuaded the box's stubborn latch to close. "Bellamy may be an ass, but he may have been right about one thing. Perhaps Lily could benefit from a husband's protection."

In retrospect, that was Spencer's one regret: the rudeness with which he'd rebuffed the idea of marrying Leo's sister. At the time, he'd simply rejected the idea on instinct, without questioning why it felt so unthinkable.

No one could have seen it then—least of all him—but he'd already been half in love with Amelia.

Rhys snorted. "Oh, Lily has a protector. Good Lord, that was a miserable ride today, with the two of them in the coach. Never saw a man working so hard at looking disinterested and failing so completely."

So Spencer had been right. There was something between Bellamy and Lily Chatwick.

Rhys gave him a devilish look. "Perhaps I'll threaten to marry her anyway, just to watch Bellamy's reaction."

Oh, now *that* would be amusing.

"Do me a favor," Spencer said, picking up the rods in one hand and the tackle box in the other. "Make sure I'm in the room when you do."

Chapter Nineteen

"Is it my imagination?" Amelia said, kneading a taut lump of bread dough. "Or are matters tense between you and Mr. Bellamy?"

Lily laughed, propping her elbows on the kitchen table. "Tense does not begin to describe matters between us. Julian won't stop pressuring me to marry."

With a floury hand, Amelia brushed back a wisp of stray hair. "But it's barely been a month since . . ." She bit her tongue.

"Since Leo died," Lily finished. "I know. And his heir has yet to arrive from Egypt. He probably hasn't even been notified yet. The town house and estate are mine to live in for months, but Julian insists I need a protector." She tilted her head at the lump of floured dough. "You make your own bread?"

"Only on special occasions." Or in this case, when a fit of nerves had caused her to accidentally consume, in its entirety, one of the loaves Cook had prepared that morning. She had an old habit of eating when she was anxious.

On the other side of the wall, Julian Bellamy attacked the drawing room pianoforte with vigor. Dark, furious chords shook the plates on their shelves. She wished he had gone angling with the other men, but he seemed unwilling to leave the house. Interesting, that he would choose to occupy himself at the pianoforte. It kept him close to Lily, without her knowing it.

"I can hear him," Lily said, as though reading Amelia's thoughts. She cast a glance at the wall separating the kitchen from the drawing room. "Or rather, I can feel him. He always plays with a great deal of passion, but he used to play happier tunes."

"How can you—"

"Tell the difference?" She glanced up at the shelves. "Happy tunes don't rattle the plates."

Amelia gave the bread dough a thoughtful pat. "Lily, have you considered that Mr. Bellamy might be in love with you?"

"Oh, yes. I believe he thinks he is."

"What do you mean?"

"We've had a friendship for years, but it's never been anything more. Then when Leo died . . ." Lily's shoulders hunched. "I think Julian's grief and guilt are exaggerating the depth of his attachment to me. He couldn't save Leo, so he feels obligated to protect me."

"You don't think he'll act on his feelings? Or imagined feelings?"

Lily shook her head. "No."

"Just as well, then," Amelia said, hoping that her friend did not return the man's affections. Nothing good could come of such a match. Lily was a refined, delicate lady from one of England's most noble families. Julian Bellamy was a hellraiser of indiscriminate origins. That alone wouldn't lower him in Amelia's estimation, but she didn't quite trust the man. Mr. Bellamy couldn't be too terribly in love with Lily, if he'd been bedding another woman—a married woman—the night Leo died.

"You know you'll never lack for a place to live,"

Amelia continued. "You're always welcome to stay with me and Spencer."

"That's very kind of you. And Spencer." Lily gave her a sly look. "Did I not say he would make you a fine husband?"

Amelia blushed, turning the dough and slapping it to the table. "Yes, you did. And it took some time, but he eventually proved you right."

"I'm so happy for you."

Amelia was happy, too. But it seemed uncouth to gush on about it, when Lily was still mourning her brother.

At the thought of brothers, her own heart gave a twinge. More than ever, she hoped this holiday could lay the foundations of reconciliation between Spencer and Jack. Though Spencer remained his usual reserved self, Amelia noticed the signs of her husband warming to Briarbank's beautiful scenery and homely atmosphere. She understood now that he'd been raised on a series of British forts in Canada, then transferred straight to the grandeur of Braxton Hall. He'd never known the comforts of a cozy home and affectionate family. After their time here, surely he would understand why Amelia couldn't turn her back on a member of her own.

She asked, "Are you certain you don't mind sharing with Claudia? It's such a small cottage, only four bedchambers. But if you do mind, we can put someone in the—"

"It's fine," Lily interrupted. "I'm grateful for the company. Even the taciturn variety."

Amelia sighed. "She never talks, does she? I don't know how to reach out to her." She felt a pinch guilty for turning Claudia away from the library that afternoon. She wondered if Spencer had ever caught up with her, to find out what she'd wanted. The coaches had arrived so soon thereafter; he might not have had the chance. "I have to admit, that's why I put the two of you together. Perhaps you can succeed where I've failed. I've tried and tried making friends with her, but she only becomes more withdrawn."

She punched down the dough. Her failure to win over Claudia had her frustrated and, yes, a bit resentful. Strolls along the river, pianoforte duets, even trips to the shops—the girl rejected her every suggestion. She didn't know what more to do.

After setting the bread aside to rise a final time, she clapped the flour from her hands and turned to wash them in the basin.

While her back was turned, she heard Lily say, "What a surprise! I didn't know you'd be joining us."

Had the men returned from the river so soon? It couldn't be Mr. Bellamy—she still heard a haunting melody emanating from the pianoforte. Shaking her hands to dry them, Amelia turned around.

What she saw made her knees go weak.

"Hullo, Amelia."

"*Jack?*" For a moment, she thought she was seeing a ghost. The phantom of Jack's fourteenth summer, when he'd shot up four inches in six weeks and devoured every scrap of food in the house before picking the nearest trees clean of green apples, too. But of course she wasn't seeing a boy, nor a ghost. This was truly her brother standing awkwardly in the middle of the kitchen, like a stranger in his own house. He looked haggard, gaunt. His clothes hung loose on his frame, giving him that boyish, bony appearance. Dark shadows haunted his eyes, and his last shave had been at least three days ago.

Her eyes welled. The tears streaked down her cheeks before she could get them back.

"Oh, come now. Is that any way to greet your favorite brother?"

"Jack." She threw her arms around him, hugging him

close. *What's happened to you?* she wanted to ask. How had he sunk to this low? She was failing him, so miserably. Failing her mother's memory. Failing Hugh's. "It's good to see you." She clutched him tighter still. No matter what Spencer did or said, this time she would not let Jack go. Not until he told her everything, and together they made some plan to get his life put to rights. She'd lost one brother already, and she couldn't bear the pain of losing another.

"We've a full house," she said, wiping her tears and striving for a cheery tone. "Can you make do with the attic while you're here?"

"Of course. Assuming Morland doesn't—"

A deep voice interrupted. "Assuming Morland doesn't what?"

Spencer tromped into the kitchen, holding a set of sleek fish. "Three salmon, as ordered." He flung the fish on the table and turned to Jack.

Amelia's stomach knotted. She didn't know how Spencer would react to Jack showing up again uninvited. Even though he shouldn't need an invitation—not to his own family's house.

Lord Ashworth followed Spencer into the room. At the sight of the giant, Jack held up his hands in a gesture of truce. "I'm not here to make trouble. I've brought the papers from Laurent."

"Papers?" Amelia asked. "What papers?"

No one heeded her question. Amelia held her breath as Spencer dragged a wary gaze over her brother's disheveled clothes and sharply angled form. Would he curse Jack? Dismiss him? Welcome him? It seemed too much to hope for the last, but she couldn't help but dream.

In the end, he didn't speak a word to Jack. "Ashworth, this is Amelia's brother. Jack d'Orsay." He caught Amelia's gaze. "He'll be staying with us for a while."

Tears of relief pricked at the corners of her eyes. Oh, how she loved him. She loved *both* these men, more than she loved her own life. And she adored Spencer for not forcing her to choose between them. *Thank you,* she mouthed to her husband.

"Jack, Lord Ashworth is Lieutenant Colonel St. Maur," she said, clearing the emotion from her throat. "He served with Hugh in the army."

"Then I'm doubly glad to make your acquaintance, my lord. Your courage was legend, from my brother's letters." Jack bowed, then drew a sheaf of papers from the bag slung over his arm. "Your Grace, shall we discuss these in the library?"

"Whatever are you talking about?" Amelia said, inwardly pleased with her brother's sudden formality. She gave Spencer a merry look, as if to say, *See? He's already reforming.* "Dinner will be ready soon. Whatever you need to discuss, it can wait until after we've eaten."

And by then, she would have pulled Spencer aside to learn just what these papers were all about.

"Besides," she continued, "you're all of you men in desperate need of a bath. Go on, get out of my kitchen. Go bathe and dress for dinner, and let me finish here." She briskly shooed them through the door.

Lily rose, too. "If you don't mind, I'll rest for a bit. I'm fatigued from traveling."

"But of course you are. Shall I show you upstairs?"

"No, thank you. I know the way."

Once she was left alone, Amelia braced her hands on the tabletop. She drew a deep, slow breath. And then she began to weep uncontrollably. Great, racking sobs left her cheeks wet and her throat aching. What was wrong with her? She just couldn't stop crying, and she had no idea why. Jack was here, Spencer hadn't thrown him out, and this was her chance to set everything right between them. She ought to be rejoicing, not crying.

From the basin, a salmon accused her with one round, glassy eye. Actually, what she ought to be doing was preparing fillets for dinner. But as she reached for the fish, her stomach gave a wild lurch. Tears forgotten, she grabbed the nearest empty bowl and retched into it.

Oh, dear. Though her head spun, she performed a hasty calculation on her fingertips. Suddenly it all made sense. Her helpless tears, her sudden nausea, her cravings over the past few days—for baked goods and Spencer. All thoughts of her house guests, her husband, even bedraggled Jack and his mysterious papers fled her mind.

She was with child.

When dinner came, Spencer found himself seated across the table from Claudia. He didn't appreciate the childish manner in which she picked at her food. But he truly hated the way in which she shifted her fascinated gaze from one egregiously inappropriate man to the next: Ashworth, Bellamy, Jack d'Orsay. The last passed Claudia a debonair grin along with the bowl of parsnips, and Spencer began to question the wisdom of placing his ward in close society with three men who could be called his enemies.

He tried to catch Amelia's eye, but she'd taken quite an interest in her water goblet. It wasn't like her to be so distracted.

"God's truth, this room is quiet," Jack said. "Tell us a joke, Bellamy. Or one of those amusing stories. You're always the life of the party in Town."

"We're not in Town," Bellamy said. "And I don't feel so amusing, of late."

That was an understatement. From the looks of them, Jack and Bellamy were having a competition to see who could closest resemble a wraith. First man to waste to vapor wins.

Amelia took the nudge, rousing herself to make conversation. "Lord Ashworth," she said, "how do you find the scenery?"

Thick eyebrows knitted in a frown. "I'm not a man inclined to flowery description, but if pressed . . . I think I might use the word 'charming.'"

"I understand you have an estate in Devonshire," she said.

"Yes, in the heart of Dartmoor. The countryside cannot be called charming. Forbidding is probably the word."

"Oh, yes. I've passed that way, when visiting cousins in Plymouth. What a study in contrasts the area is. Such beauty and such desolation." Amelia turned to Bellamy. "And you, Mr. Bellamy? Where were you raised?"

Bellamy took a slow draught of wine. When he put down the glass, he looked dismayed to see Amelia patiently awaiting a response, fork poised in midair.

"Farthest reaches of Northumberland," he said. "Middle of nowhere. Don't suppose you've any cousins there."

Spencer put in, "Actually, I've land in Northumberland."

"Really." Bellamy's tone was bored.

"Yes, really. Mines. Did your people work in mining?"

Bellamy said, "What else is there to do, in Northumberland?"

"Coal, I suppose?"

Bellamy gave him a cold, slashing look, and Spencer leaned forward in anticipation. He'd been waiting to catch this fraud in the act.

"No. Copper."

"Bollocks. There's not a vein of copper in all Northumberland." Spencer's knife clanged the edge of his plate. "And if yours is a Northumberland accent, then I speak like an Ottoman King. Where do you get off, accusing me of crimes? You're nothing but a petty swindler and a fraud."

Bellamy's eyes went to Lily.

Spencer repeated his words, making sure the dark-haired woman could read his lips clearly. "You are a lying bastard, Bellamy."

"Now look here—"

"Just how have you been spending my money?" Spencer asked. "That massive investigation I'm funding has yielded precious little in the way of results."

"Perhaps that's because the killer isn't in Town," Bellamy said, his voice tight. "Perhaps that's because the culprit's been hiding out in Cambridgeshire."

Ashworth groaned. "For God's sake, can we move on from this? Morland isn't a killer. It's not in him."

"How would you know?" Bellamy said.

"Because if he were, I wouldn't be sitting here. I'd have died fourteen years ago."

The room went silent.

Spencer stared at the scarred, hulking warrior. "Are you talking about Eton?"

He remembered the way their fight had dragged on, blow after blow, while boys ringed them and cheered and the schoolmasters stood passively by—helpless to stop it, since both he and Rhys were larger and stronger than any adult there. They were both big youths, but Spencer'd had the advantage of age and the force of grief and anger behind his blows. But no matter how many times he smashed Rhys to the dirt, the mad bastard wouldn't stay down. He'd kept dragging his bleeding carcass off the ground and coming back for more. Until he hadn't even been throwing punches of his own, just lumbering forward on shaky legs to receive Spencer's next punishing blow. At the time, he had interpreted Rhys's persistence as foolish pride, and as he'd been in the mood to keep dealing blows . . . foolish pride seemed as worthy an offense as any.

But when Rhys staggered to his feet yet again, with one eye swollen shut and his chest hunched over broken ribs—on his last blow, Spencer had heard them cracking under his fist—he just couldn't stomach the idea of hitting the idiot one more time. It had become a matter of his own pride, to walk away.

Rhys's expression told Spencer they were recalling the exact same scene. "I wanted you to kill me," he said.

Around the table, eyes widened. Wineglasses tipped.

"Pardon the bluntness." Rhys addressed the group in a diffident tone, forking another bite into his mouth. "I never did master the art of genteel dinner conversation."

"You wanted me to kill you," Spencer repeated.

"That's why I kept getting up. I wanted to die, and I knew if I kept putting my face in front of your fist, you had the strength and fury to do me in." He looked to Bellamy. "But he didn't."

"That's disgusting," Spencer said. "You would have left me with that guilt all my life, believing I'd murdered you in cold blood? What the devil is wrong with you?"

Rhys shrugged. "Too many things to list tonight. You were the first I tried that with, but not the last. Took me a long time to give up on the strategy of picking fights in hopes of getting pummeled into my grave."

"How long?"

"I don't know." Rhys cocked his head. "Until a month or so ago? In the infantry, they kept decorating me for it. Finally realized only the good die young. At any rate, Bellamy, I can assure you His Grace isn't capable of murder."

"That was years ago," Bellamy said. "It doesn't prove a damn thing."

"Perhaps not. But this does." Spencer drew Leo's

token from his waistcoat pocket and tossed it onto the table. "It's his," he said, answering the silent question. "I've seven more upstairs, if you want to count."

"I knew it," Bellamy said, his face going red. "I knew you—"

"It was me," Jack said. "I mean, it wasn't me who killed Leo. But I found that token. It was in the possession of a wh—"

Spencer threw his fist down on the table. "Not now," he growled, casting a look at Claudia. For God's sake, he suddenly realized they'd been discussing violence and murder right in front of her. They weren't going to discuss whores, too. "We're not having this conversation in front of the child."

"I'm not a child!" Claudia protested, banging a fork against her plate. Her eyes swam with tears. "When are you going to realize that?"

"Eat your salmon," he told her.

"I'm not going to eat the dratted salmon." She stabbed it with her fork and muttered, "I hate you."

Spencer sighed. He didn't suppose that comment was directed at the fish. He looked to Amelia, hoping she would intervene and use her hostess's charm to rescue this wreck of a dinner. But his wife wouldn't meet his gaze. She was staring down at her own salmon, wearing a puzzled frown. All evening, she'd been strangely preoccupied.

Bellamy said, "Send the girl to bed if you must. But I've been slaving day and night for the past month to find the men who killed Leo, and if anyone at this table has information, I want to hear it now."

"I found the token," Jack said. "It was in the possession of the wh—" He absorbed Spencer's cutting glare. "Of the *witness* to Leo's attack. The one who called for the hack and delivered him to your house."

"When did you recover it?"

"Just the day after his death."

"And you told no one?"

Jack shrugged. "At the time, I didn't know you were looking for it, or even that it was Leo's. I met with her in Covent Garden, but I suppose she'd made a special excursion to Whitechapel that night for the boxing match. Anyhow, when I tried to find her again, she'd disappeared. I'd given her a guinea in exchange for the token. Seems she'd decided to take a holiday with her windfall and gone to visit her mother in Dover."

Spencer caught Bellamy's gaze. "That's why neither of us had any luck finding her ourselves."

"What do you mean, 'neither of us'?"

"Later." He most definitely was not discussing his day of searching Whitechapel taverns and brothels in front of Claudia. "But at least we know this. Whoever killed Leo, they weren't after his token. Otherwise, it wouldn't have ended in the hands of a passerby." He turned to Jack. "But you did find her?"

"Eventually, yes." He gave Spencer a look. "Thought it might help."

Interesting. So now Jack wanted to help him? Spencer had no doubt what sort of help Jack would ask in return.

"And then you just left her again?" Bellamy speared both hands through his unkempt hair in exasperation. "Where is she now?"

"Relaxing in finer accommodations than she's ever enjoyed in her life," Jack answered. "Don't worry, she's not going anywhere. Someone's watching her."

"Did she have any further information? Did she see his attackers?"

"Only glimpses, in retreat. Her descriptions of them are vague at best. Tall, broad-shouldered, dressed in coarse attire. She couldn't describe them with any helpful detail. What was interesting"—he raised an eyebrow in a theatrical pause—"was her description of Leo's companion."

Silence.

"What?" Bellamy finally managed. "But . . . but he was alone that night."

"No, he wasn't. There was another man with Leo when he was attacked. The harlot remembered his features quite well—hair, height, clothes, looks." He turned a steely gaze on Bellamy. "From her description, the man looked a great deal like you."

Chapter Twenty

Julian Bellamy's face went pale with shock. "He looked like *me*?"

Oh, Spencer was going to enjoy this. Not only was he cleared of all suspicion, but now he could repay Bellamy the favor. "Well, well. This is an interesting development."

"I was not with Leo that night," Bellamy said. "I wish to hell I had been, but I wasn't."

"Then it's curious, isn't it, that Leo was seen with a man who matched your description?"

"I set the trends for fashion. Men *try* to match my description. Every brainless toff in London wants to resemble me." He gestured toward Jack. "He's one of them, for the love of God. Why would you take his word, anyway?"

Spencer picked up the token from the table. "Perhaps because the brainless toff was able to locate in a matter of days the person you've been seeking for nearly a month? The fact that he found Leo's token proves he's not fabricating the tale. And it would certainly explain a great deal, if you were involved. Like why Leo's body was delivered to *your* house that night. Why your vast investigation has gone nowhere. And why you've been so eager to pin the blame on me."

"I wasn't with Leo," Bellamy said edgily. "I have an alibi."

"Ah, yes." Spencer narrowed his eyes. "What was her name again? Lady Carnelia? I don't suppose she'd rush to confirm your story. What makes you think a married noblewoman would invite public scandal just to save your miserable hide?"

Bellamy shot a look at Lily, as though hoping she hadn't understood Spencer's remark.

Lily bowed her dark head quickly and pushed back from the table. "Lady Claudia," she said, extending a hand, "would you kindly show me the way to our chamber? Silly me, I've forgotten."

Reluctance was plain on Claudia's face, but Lily clutched the girl by the wrist and fairly dragged her from the room. In unison, the men rose from their chairs. Because, naturally, that was the polite thing to do when driving two innocent ladies from the dining room with talk of murder and whores.

Amelia remained seated, looking stunned and pale.

"Well?" Spencer said. He didn't truly believe the man had killed Leo. He'd witnessed Bellamy's shock that night, and he could see plainly the toll recent weeks had taken on him. Even Julian Bellamy wasn't a gifted enough performer to pull off the role of grief-stricken friend so convincingly. Whether Leo had been alone or with a friend, the simplest explanation for his death was still the most likely—he'd been the unlucky victim of random thievery. But let Bellamy know, for a moment, just how it felt to live under unfounded suspicions of murder. Let him watch the woman he cared for scurry from the room.

"We're going to discuss this alone, Morland," Bellamy said. "In your library."

"Ashworth comes, too," Spencer said. "And we're going to do more than discuss the matter." He tossed the disc of brass in his hand. He hadn't planned to do this so soon, but this was the perfect opportunity—when emotions and enmity were running high. "We're going to sit down to cards. It's time to disband the Stud Club once and for all."

"Fine by me," Ashworth said.

Spencer turned to Bellamy and stared him down, filling his gaze with unspoken challenge. This was the moment. Unless the lying bastard balked, victory would be his, tonight.

"All right." Hatred was keen in Bellamy's eyes. "Let's end it. And then you'll tell me where this bit of skirt's being put up, and I head back to London in the morning. I need to question this woman as soon as possible."

"In the library, then." Spencer moved aside as Ashworth and Bellamy stalked from the room and crossed the narrow corridor to enter the library.

He shot out an arm to prevent Jack from following. "Not you."

"Come on, Morland," Jack muttered. "Let me play."

"Where's the harlot?"

"The Blue Turtle Inn in Hounslow."

"The papers?"

"Here." Jack withdrew them from inside his coat and slung them on the table. He lowered his voice. "Now let me play. I found that token. I found her. You owe me a seat at that table."

"Absolutely not." That was all Amelia needed, for Jack to run up a fresh debt of thousands just when he was on the verge of getting clear. "You've done what you came to do. You'll leave tonight."

"Tonight?" Amelia finally jolted from her reverie. "He's just arrived. And this is our family's house. You can't boot him out."

"*Our* family's house?" Jack turned an accusatory gaze on Spencer. "You didn't even tell her, did you?"

"Tell me what?" Amelia asked, rising from her chair.

Spencer sighed. He hoped she'd take this well, in the spirit it was intended. "I'd planned to tell you tonight. I'm buying the cottage."

"Buying the cottage?" She looked to the rafters. "*This* cottage? Briarbank?"

"Yes, to all three."

"You can't possibly buy this cottage. It's entailed."

"No, it's not. The land surrounding the castle, yes. But not this property."

"So those papers . . ." Her eyes fell to the table.

"Will make the house mine." *Damn it.* "Ours."

"But . . ." She blinked furiously. "But this house has belonged to the d'Orsay family for centuries."

Bollocks. She was not taking it well. Not well at all.

"You really should have told her," Jack said.

"Get out," Spencer snapped. He needed to discuss this with Amelia in private.

"No, don't." Amelia grabbed her brother's arm. "Stay. Don't you let him chase you from this house."

"Damn, but the two of you are exhausting in your demands," Jack said. "I'll just go to bed. If I'm allowed."

After his brother-in-law left the room, Spencer placed his hands on Amelia's shoulders. In a belated attempt at tenderness, he stroked his thumb back and forth along her collarbone. "Amelia, I've made inquiries in recent weeks. Your brother owes a vast sum of money. Thousands. To a man far less forgiving than I." He didn't give the man's name; she wouldn't recognize it anyhow. But Jack's creditor was the proprietor of several of London's most infamous gaming halls, and he was a man known for his ruthlessness. It wasn't a business a man rose to the top of without excelling at ruthlessness.

The tears began to spill from her eyes. "He looks so terrible, so haunted."

"I don't doubt it. He's probably living in streets and taverns, unable to go to his own home for fear of endangering his safety. If he doesn't make good on the debts soon . . ." He let the fear in her eyes complete the sentence for him. "I can't countenance simply giving him the funds, but I will purchase this house. For you."

"Why on earth would I want it for myself?"

A small spark of hope warmed him inside, to know that she'd so completely forgotten the terms of their original agreement. "I intended to buy it in case you were unhappy living with me. After a child is born." He reached to wipe a tear from her cheek. "Of course, now I'm hoping it can be a summer retreat for us both."

"Spencer, this place is a piece of d'Orsay history. Our house in Town is long gone, and you've seen the ruins of Beauvale Castle. This cottage is all we have left. Our family pride is the very mortar holding these stones together. I can't believe you would so callously strip it from us."

"Callously? Perhaps this place belongs to Beauvale in name, but you are the one who cares for it so deeply. And what of *our* family? Why can't we begin a new chapter of this house's history, together?"

"What sort of chapter begins with tossing my brother to the wolves?"

By the devil, he was tired of hearing about her brother. When he managed to speak, his voice vibrated with anger. "How long are you going to keep defending him? You heard Jack. He's on the verge of clearing his debt, once this transaction is completed. And all he wants is to get right back at the gaming table and drown himself again. He's on course to meet with true disaster, and he has no compunction about dragging you along with him. If he stays in this house, he will work on you, make you all manner of promises . . . and then just devastate you all the more when you wake up one morning to find he's made off with your pearls."

"He wouldn't do that." Her hand went to her throat as she shrugged away. "And if you truly thought I'd be so happy for you to purchase Briarbank, why didn't you tell me? Instead you've gone behind my back, manipulating everyone to your own purpose. Even the first week of our marriage . . . you held my brother's debt over my head, just to get me to the card table and get your hands on my—"

With a gasp, she pulled up short. She gestured toward the library and lowered her voice to an accusatory whisper. "That's the entire reason for this house party, isn't it? That little card game you're about to play. You've arranged this whole holiday just to win those tokens and that dratted horse."

He shrugged, unable to refute it.

Closing in on him, she jabbed a finger in his chest. "And you would lecture me on misplaced priorities. You led me to believe we were welcoming these people as friends and guests. I thought you wanted to be open and honest with them, gain their trust and cooperation. But no. Forget sincerity, we're back to gamesmanship. All I ask is for you to give Jack a chance. Talk with him, help him see his errors, let him learn from your example. But you won't hear of it—and no surprise, given the manner in which you treat your own kin. You never did speak with Claudia today, did you?"

"No." He heaved a guilty sigh. No, he hadn't. He could have offered some excuse, but it would have been a lie.

"I didn't think so. My brother may have his problems, but you're delusional if you present yourself as an exemplar of behavior. You're so closed off and insular, it's a wonder you can see beyond your own nose. The wealthy, intelligent duke who welcomes all manner of insidious gossip rather than admit to feeling uneasy in crowds? Who'd stand accused of murder rather than fall under suspicion of possessing a heart?"

He blinked, wounded. How could she say that? Perhaps he *was* reserved with everyone else, but he was different with her. She'd pulled him out of that insular, smug, goddamned lonely existence and made him yearn to be a part of this—this family, this home. Why couldn't she see that he wanted it not just for her, but for them?

"Amelia . . ." As he began, his voice broke. He cleared his throat and started again, clearly and calmly. It shouldn't be so hard to say this. "You are everything to me. The world is welcome to know it."

"How would they? Because you've carried me out of a few ballrooms and tend to throw punches when I'm around? You're wrenching this house away from my family. Uprooting it from centuries of d'Orsay history." A sob caught in her throat. "Meanwhile you've been *using* me and my love for this place, just to gain custody of a horse. And now you'd cast my brother out, again."

He caught her by the shoulders. "Damn it, you are the one who is letting Jack come between us. You're so invested in this selfless martyr role. Somewhere inside you is that sixteen-year-old girl who believed she deserved her own happiness. The woman who has captivated me from the first time I held her and found I couldn't let go. I've done my best to be understanding, but—"

"Your *best*? Oh, Spencer. I know you too well to believe that. If you would accuse me of denying myself, then please queue up for your share of the blame. I've never known a man so remarkable, so complex and caring . . . and so determined to hide it from the world. If I were ever so lucky as to glimpse your true, shining best, I'd probably expire where I stood from the brilliance."

If she'd intended those words as a compliment, they damn well didn't feel like one. They felt like brilliant shards of glass.

He sighed. "Say what you will, Amelia, you can't deny that I'm making an effort. And I'm tired of coming in second to Jack for my pains. At least I'm trying to secure your happiness."

"My happiness? How can I possibly be happy, when I know my brother is living on the London streets, brushing sleeves with danger every moment of the day?"

"I don't know, but you'll have to learn. Because Jack isn't going to change." He tipped her chin and lowered his voice. "Sooner or later, you'll have to decide where your loyalties are. With him, or with me?"

She stared at him as though he were some sort of monster. Damn it, he wasn't a monster. He was human. He wanted to know his wife loved *him* above any other man. Wouldn't any husband want the same?

"If you knew me at all," she said in a shaky voice, "you would understand how dearly I love my family. And if you ask me to deny them . . . you've made the choice yourself." She grabbed the sheaf of legal papers from the table and clutched them to her chest. "These aren't signed yet. So long as this house belongs to the d'Orsays, my brother is welcome in it. Jack stays."

"Nothing good will come of it," he warned. "He'll only hurt you again."

"Not half as much as you're hurting me now."

"Amelia . . ." He slowly stretched a hand toward her, but she flinched away before he'd halved the gap.

"Go," she said, jerking her chin toward the library. "Go win your damn horse. We both know where your loyalties are."

She was so prickly and emotional and filled with

wrongheaded notions . . . he couldn't even conceive of how to argue with her.

So he did what she'd asked. He went.

The library was small, and they huddled around the desk to play. Their game was brag. Piquet was Spencer's forte, but it was only a two-player game.

It took time to lay a trap, and no small amount of patience. The first and most difficult task was to create the illusion that chance had a seat at the table. For the first hour or so of play, Spencer won a few hands and purposely lost several others. On a few occasions, his opponents' superior play truly caught him off guard. He knew he ought to be using this time to observe Bellamy carefully. Every man, even the best of players, gave unconscious physical clues to what sort of cards he held. But Spencer just couldn't focus on the arch of Bellamy's eyebrow or the tapping of his finger. Memories of Amelia kept distracting him. He kept seeing her lovely blue eyes marred by redness. He heard her bitter words rattling in his ears. And other parts of him recalled the way she'd lavished her passion on him earlier that day, as he'd sat in this very chair. She had him more than distracted. He was damned confused.

She was right, to some extent. He *had* manipulated her with this holiday, along with everyone else. Purchasing the cottage in secret, conspiring with Rhys to get Bellamy to the card table. But did Amelia truly think her own imagining of this house party would have culminated in success? In her fantasy, she would open her house, her arms, and her heart to everyone, and Spencer would reveal a few long-held, mildly embarrassing secrets. Add in a week of angling and parlor games . . . conflict resolved. The three men would emerge as friends.

A naïve, impossible notion. Wasn't it?

As Bellamy shuffled the cards and prepared to deal,

Spencer cleared his throat and looked to Rhys. "Say, Ashworth . . . we're not friends, are we?"

A healed gash scored the soldier's face, and his eyebrow split as he looked up in surprise. "I don't know. We're not enemies."

"Any further traumatic childhood incidents you feel moved to discuss?"

"Not particularly. You?"

Spencer shook his head. "None."

Bellamy rapped the deck to square it, then began to deal. "While we're having this little chat, I'll take the opportunity to say I despise you both. And as far as you two are concerned, I was born to nomadic goatherds in Albania."

That settled it. So much for friendship. Spencer gathered his cards. No pair, few prospects. Time to make good on his deal with Rhys. "Let's stop mincing around, then. Ten thousand." He scratched the sum on a piece of paper and shoved it to the center of the table.

Play turned to Rhys. "I don't have ten thousand."

"I'll accept your token as an even wager against mine."

"Ten?" His eyes said, *I thought we agreed on fifteen.* "Twenty, and we'll call it an even exchange."

Sly bastard. Spencer didn't even feel like arguing. He just wanted this over. With a stub of charcoal, he altered the notation on the paper. "Done."

Ashworth shook the brass token loose from his purse and laid it on the table before him, giving Spencer an enigmatic look. "It's up to fate now."

"I make my own fate, thank you." Bellamy lifted the corner of his cards where they lay on the table. His face remained impassive. Spencer expected the man to get out of the way, wait to see how things shook out between him and Ashworth before risking anything of his own.

But Bellamy wasn't that clever. He reached into his breast pocket and withdrew a brass coin. "Let's do this. I'm tired of pushing pennies back and forth. I need to talk to that whore before her memories fade any further and find out who was with Leo that night. Perhaps his companion could lead me to the killers."

"Perhaps his companion died too," Ashworth said.

"We would have known by now, if another gentleman of the *ton* went missing or turned up dead the same night. That wouldn't make sense." After a pause, Bellamy added thoughtfully, "Unless he had something to do with the attack . . ."

Spencer groaned. "For God's sake, stop looking for vast conspiracies in a random crime. No, it doesn't make sense. By definition, a senseless tragedy never will. Maybe the prostitute was lying, or simply confused."

"Maybe." Bellamy tapped his coin on the table testily. "But the sooner I talk to her, the sooner I'll know, won't I?" He flung the token to the center of the table. "One hand. All ten tokens. Winner takes all."

"I've already put in twenty thousand," Spencer protested. "You expect me to put in all my tokens, too?"

"Do you want the horse, or don't you?" Bellamy's eyes were hard. "This is your only chance. Win or lose—after this hand, I get up from the table and walk away."

Spencer stared hard at the man's expression, scanning in vain for some tic in his jaw or telltale dilation of his pupils. Damn it, he ought to have forced himself to concentrate earlier. If he had, he might have known whether Bellamy truly had the cards to back up his bet, or just wanted to scare Spencer off, so he could leave the table with his token and dignity.

Regardless of what cards Bellamy held, Spencer knew his own were worthless. True, there were more cards to be dealt and he might catch a stroke of luck, but if

Spencer called this bet, the odds were he would lose everything.

Well, not *everything*. The excessive drama of the thought struck even him as overwrought. What was truly at stake here? A few lumps of brass and an aging stallion? Suddenly, none of it seemed worth a damn. His wife, on the other hand—now, Amelia was irreplaceable.

He'd been pursuing this goal with such focus, for so long . . . giving it up simply hadn't been an option. After all this time, he'd practically lost sight of why he wanted the stallion in the first place. If he gave up on Osiris, he'd reasoned at the outset, he would be giving up on Juno. And to give up on Juno would have felt uncomfortably close to giving up on himself. *Would have,* in the past. But this was the present. More to the point, this was the beginning of his future. The only reason they were gathered was because Leo Chatwick, his peer and contemporary, had died far too young. Was this truly what Spencer wanted inscribed on his own grave marker? "Brilliant cardsharp, good with horses?"

For a moment, he imagined what would happen if he lost. He would leave all ten tokens and any stake in Osiris on this table, and then go upstairs to make amends to his wife. Pledge to make her his priority, and hope and pray that she could one day find it in her heart to return the sentiment. Cover her body with kisses; whisper words of love against her skin. Make love to her until neither of them had the strength to stand.

How would losing feel? It would feel damn good. It would feel remarkably like a victory.

This was the moment to walk away.

Apparently, Bellamy had decided the same. He picked up the token and replaced it in his pocket as he rose. "Well, then. If you haven't the stones—"

"Sit down," Spencer told him, flipping Leo's token

into the center of the desk. "We're going to finish this tonight. The other tokens are upstairs. Let me send a servant for the lockbox."

He rose from his chair, but before he could even reach the door, Amelia burst through it. Behind her came Lily, dressed in nightclothes and wrapper, her unbound hair hanging to her waist. Both women wore expressions of fear.

"Good God, what is it?" Spencer moved to take Amelia in his arms. To the devil with horses and cards . . . At that moment, embracing her was the only thing in the world he wanted to do. It seemed the thing he'd been made to do. She needed him, and she'd come to him. He wouldn't let anything hurt her now.

But as he reached for her, her arms stiffened. She held him off.

"We've no time," she said, swallowing hard. "Claudia is missing."

Chapter Twenty-one

"Missing?" Spencer's face turned the color of ash. He gripped her elbow. "Are you certain? Perhaps she's only—"

"No. She's gone, and she's not alone." Amelia swallowed hard, wondering how she could possibly tell him this next. But she had to do it. If there was any hope, it depended on swift action. "She's gone with Jack. They left a note."

Raising her fist in the gap between them, she bade her fingers to relax. In her palm lay the crumpled scrap of paper she'd found tacked to the kitchen doorjamb, in that pockmarked patch just below the lintel where countless coats of enamel had worn through to the grain. Her brothers had always left their messages there. The d'Orsay Post, they called it. And true to form, Jack's message was succinct:

We're for Gretna.

The paper was signed by them both.

Spencer stared at the words so fiercely, Amelia would not have been surprised to see the scrawled letters roust themselves from the paper and rearrange to spell different words, just to escape his displeasure. She too wished there were some way she could alter the facts.

"How long?" he asked brusquely.

"We . . . we don't know. Obviously sometime since dinner, so a few hours at most. The horses are all still here, so they must be on foot." Surrendering the note, she knitted her fingers in a tight clasp. "I can only imagine he's after her dowry."

"I'm so sorry," Lily said from behind her. "I retired early, and of course I didn't hear her go out."

"Don't apologize," Spencer said. "My ward isn't your responsibility."

He gave Amelia a sharp look, stabbing at her conscience. Of course, Claudia was partly her responsibility. And Jack . . . Jack wouldn't even have been here, if she hadn't insisted he stay. "I'm so sorry," she said feebly. "That he would run off with her like this, in the middle of the night . . . I simply can't believe it of him."

"Of course you can't. You haven't believed anything I've told you of him. No matter what he does, you defend the rogue. Why should you stop now?"

"Perhaps there's some misunderstanding, some other explanation," she said feebly. Feebly, because even she knew the words were foolishness.

Steeling his jaw, he headed for the desk. "I told you nothing good would come of letting him stay."

"Yes, you did." But she'd been willing to take that risk, assuming stupidly that hers were the only feelings at stake. That if Jack wrought more mischief, he would be hurting only *her*. She'd never dreamed his actions could affect Spencer and Claudia, too. Oh, Lord.

By this time, Bellamy and Ashworth were on their feet.

"What's going on?" Bellamy asked.

"My brother has eloped with Claudia," Amelia told him. When Spencer shot her a look, she added, "It's not as though we can hide it from them. For God's sake, let them help."

"Which way would they have gone, Morland?" Ashworth asked.

"Well?" Spencer looked to Amelia. "You know the area best."

She shrugged helplessly, catching one fingertip between her opposite thumb and forefinger and pinching it hard. "Any number of ways. Most likely toward Gloucester, to catch a mail coach headed north. But to get there they might have gone north through Colford, or east, toward Lydney. Then there's the river. They might have headed south toward the Severn, intending to ferry over to Aust and continue to London. The fastest coaches to Scotland leave from there. Or they could have hoped to board a ship . . ." Her voice dwindled, along with her hopes. The possibilities seemed endless; the likelihood of catching them, slim. "In any direction, they're not much more than a half-dozen miles from transport."

"Well," Ashworth said, "there are three of us."

"I'll order my fastest horses saddled," Spencer said, pulling open a low drawer of the desk. "We'll each take a different route."

"Precisely when did I offer my assistance?" Bellamy asked.

"Just now." Spencer withdrew a pistol from the desk drawer. With a bit of show, presumably for Bellamy's benefit, he jammed the gun into the waistband of his trousers.

At the sight of the weapon, Amelia's joints went weak.

"All right, all right." Bellamy acquiesced with an impatient tug at his hair. "I'll go south, toward the Severn and Town. If I find them, you'll hear of it. But I'll continue on to London if I don't."

"Fair enough. You'll find her at the Blue Turtle, in Hounslow. You'll probably need to pay her account."

Amelia had no idea what that last bit meant, but Bellamy seemed to understand.

"I'll go north," Ashworth said. "If they've taken a coaching route, someone ought to have seen them on the way to Gloucester."

Spencer said, "I'll take east, then, through the forest."

Bellamy drew a deep breath and riffled his hair. "I'll be needing proper boots."

He left the room, and Lily slipped out the door after him.

Ashworth went next, tossing a parting comment over his shoulder: "We'll meet you at the stable."

Spencer's reply was a curt nod.

Amelia stood alone with her husband, hugging her arms across her chest. She watched as he shook open a pouch and counted shot into his palm, then replaced the round balls of lead and cinched the bag tight.

"I'm so sorry," she said.

"Save the apologies." He exhaled roughly, plucking his coat from the back of the chair and shrugging into it. Bracing his hands on the desk, he fixed her with a look of sharp concentration. "Give me the route. Road names, landmarks. Any description you can offer."

She did her best, though it had been years since she'd traveled straight through the Forest of Dean. And what details she remembered—the primroses and violets, the carpets of ferns dotted with mushrooms, the remarkable sight of ducks nesting in a chestnut tree—weren't likely to help him tonight. She forced herself to focus and gave him what information she could: stream crossings, steep grades.

Until she was interrupted by a pattering sound.

"Bloody hell," Spencer muttered, stooping to peer through the window glass. "Now it's raining."

Could this get any worse? Amelia hoped it would only be a brief summer shower. The thought of Jack and

Claudia on foot in the rain . . . not to mention, the three gentlemen in pursuit on horseback, riding over slippery, unfamiliar terrain . . . And all of this in the dark of night, with no moon.

Bloody hell, indeed.

He brushed past her on his way to the door. She caught his arm, swiveling him to face her. "Spencer, wait. Do you blame me for this?"

"I don't have time to stand here and discuss blame, Amelia. I have to find them and bring Claudia back before she's lost her reputation. Or worse."

She cringed, understanding his meaning all too well. Jack might be desperate, but surely her brother wouldn't defile a fifteen-year-old innocent? She wished she could reject the idea with greater certainty. At this point, she hardly knew what to think. "Is there nothing I can do?"

"Stay here." Cupping her chin roughly, he tilted her face to his. "Do you hear me? Stay here, in case they come home."

She swallowed hard and released his sleeve. "What will you do, if you find them?"

"I'll do whatever is necessary to protect Claudia."

Fear drummed in her chest. He meant he would deal harshly, even violently, with Jack if he felt it necessary. And given the circumstances, she would not have asked him to show mercy . . . if Claudia's abductor were any other man.

"Please," she choked out. "Please don't kill him. I just couldn't bear it if—"

"If you lost your brother," he finished bitterly. With one last wounded glance, he turned to leave. "I know what he means to you, Amelia. Believe me, I know it all too well."

After two hours of pacing the drawing room, Amelia thought she would go mad with worry. For her brother, for Claudia, for Spencer . . . even for Lord Ashworth and Mr. Bellamy. The more time that passed, the harder it became to imagine any happy outcome. If Claudia and Jack spent the night together away from home—the girl would be ruined. Whether or not they were found before reaching Scotland, whether or not Jack had actually touched her. Spencer might be forced to let them marry with his blessing, simply to preserve some shred of her reputation. He would *not* consider that a happy outcome, and neither would Amelia. Jack and Claudia would no doubt live to regret it, too.

Assuming Spencer let Jack live.

Her skin prickled with dread. She'd been desolated by the mere idea of choosing between them. Now the events of this night threatened to make the decision for her. And Spencer might never forgive her if Claudia came to harm.

Lily dozed fitfully in an armchair nearby, but Amelia knew she'd never find sleep. Her mind buzzed, her thoughts flitting from one possibility to the next. None of it made any sense to her, and that was what kept her circling the carpet, trailing her fingers along the mantel, skipping to the windowsill, then tracing the back of the divan. She understood why Jack would wish to elope with Claudia—obviously a duke's ward would come with a significant dowry. But why on earth would Claudia agree to go with him? Jack was handsome enough, and he could be charming when he wished to be . . . but he certainly didn't look his fittest at the moment, and the girl had scarcely spent any time in his company. Claudia obviously resented Amelia and Spencer's marriage, but was she so thoroughly steeped in adolescent rebellion that she would go so far as to elope out of spite?

And . . . Scotland? He would have to forgive her for saying it, but Jack just didn't seem industrious enough to stage an elopement to Gretna Green. It was a long, hard journey, and an expensive one. He obviously had no funds, and Claudia's pin money wouldn't go far. Perhaps they had some goods they hoped to sell.

Had they taken things from the house?

Driven by a sense of dread, and the desire to be anywhere but the drawing room, she grabbed a candlestick and charged up the stairs to her and Spencer's bedchamber. She yanked open the small corner closet and pried up the panel at the bottom, holding the candle over the hidden cache . . . straining her eyes into the darkness, searching . . .

There. It was still there, the cloth-wrapped bundle of Mama's jewelry. None of it was worth a great deal—not in coin, anyway. But the strands of seed pearls and topaz earrings were priceless to Amelia.

After replacing the secret panel, she stood.

And immediately crumpled back to the floor. She had to pull herself together. Her heart pounded in her chest, and she felt so lightheaded.

Oh, God. Suddenly it all made sense.

Stay here.

Those were his words to her, his only request. *Stay here, in case she comes home.*

"Forgive me, Spencer," Amelia muttered as she stepped over the cottage threshold. She wrapped her foul-weather cloak around her shoulders and closed the door behind her. The rain was lighter now, but cold. The moon shone through a gap in the clouds, but Amelia didn't trust it to last. She reached for the carriage lamp hanging beside the door. Splashing through shallow puddles, she made a hasty sprint for the stable.

She simply couldn't stay put in the cottage and wait. If her suppositions were right—and the small voice in her gut told her they were—Claudia was in even greater danger than Spencer realized. But the girl might not be so very far away.

Ducking into the humble stables that temporarily housed beasts bred for kings, Amelia saw that her mature, steady gelding had been left behind. Of course, the men would have taken the fastest mounts.

"Now there, Captain. Would you like to go for a ride?" She extended her hand and let the horse sniff it before cautiously giving him a pat. Stretching up on her toes, she unlooped his halter from the ring. The gelding shuffled forward, and Amelia realized that—logically—her saddle had been removed. As had the bit and bridle. She swung the carriage lamp and her gaze toward the tack hanging on the wall. Could she even remember how it all went together?

"Oh!" Startled by a sudden nudge at her waist, she nearly dropped the carriage lamp. It was only Captain nosing her pocket, looking for a treat. But it made her realize she was completely out of her depth. It would be stupid of her to try to saddle him herself, and perilous to her unborn child if she took a kick or a fall. She would have to go on foot.

The decision made, she left the stable. Eschewing the smooth but circuitous carriage lane, she hurried toward the narrow, winding footpath that climbed the bluff. Few trees grew here, and the way was paved with exposed limestone and moss—rain didn't improve the traction of either surface. She slipped and stumbled as she went, at one point clawing her fingernails into a bit of turf to keep from tumbling headlong into the river. Somehow she managed to reach the bluff's plateau with body and carriage lamp intact.

She allowed herself a few moments' rest and thanksgiving. And then she dashed for the ruins of Beauvale Castle. That was where the d'Orsay boys had always got up to their mischief. As she covered the half-mile's distance to the walls of crumbling stone, she said a prayer that old habits would have endured.

By the time she reached the gatehouse, she was gasping for breath. Her heart lightened as she saw the door was already ajar. She pushed the slab of oak open and thrust the carriage lamp inside.

Jack stood in the center of the darkened tower. His hair was matted to his forehead in thick, pale locks. He scarcely looked surprised to see her.

"I didn't know, Amelia." He cast a glance over his shoulder. Behind him, Claudia shivered in the corner, hugging her knees to her chest. "I swear to you, I had no idea."

"You're a fool," she said, hanging the lamp on a candle sconce blackened with centuries of soot. She brushed past him to go to the girl. "Do you think she'd agree to run off with you on the basis of a dashing smile? You're not so very handsome as that."

Hurrying to the corner, Amelia knelt before Claudia. The girl's lips were blue and quivering; her eyes, unfocused. Tears and rain streaked her face.

Amelia untied her cloak and quickly arranged it around the girl's trembling shoulders. "It's all right, dear. Everything will be fine. *Claudia.*" She waited until the girl met her gaze. "It's all right. I know. I know everything."

And then the girl fell into Amelia's arms, sobbing helplessly against her shoulder. Amelia held her tight, murmuring words of reassurance. The poor dear. She'd been needing this embrace for so long, and Amelia had been too absorbed in her own problems to realize all Claudia's rudeness had been aimed at pushing her away—not because she resented Amelia, but because she was afraid of anyone learning her secret.

Even Amelia couldn't have possibly guessed the truth until today, after that tearful epiphany in the kitchen.

The girl's aloof demeanor, her strange moods, her wild fluctuations in appetite and illness in the coach . . .

Claudia was with child.

"You poor thing." She stroked the girl's wet hair. "I'm so sorry." What a terrible burden for a fifteen-year-old girl to struggle under on her own. "Did it happen in York?"

Claudia nodded against her. "My music master. I was so lonely there, and he was so kind to me, at first. He promised I wouldn't . . ." The girl's voice broke, and Amelia held her tighter still. "Oh, Amelia. I was such a fool. And how will I ever tell him?"

Amelia knew she wasn't referring to the music master.

"I can't bear it," the girl sobbed. "He'll be so furious with me."

"Shh," Amelia said, shifting to cradle the girl in her arms. She rocked them both, gently. "I will tell him. And if he reacts with anger, it won't be anger at you. He cares for you so much."

"I thought . . . if I ran away, married—"

"Everyone would believe the child was Jack's," Amelia finished for her. "And you would never have to tell the truth." She rubbed Claudia's back briskly, feeling the girl warm in her arms. Wet muslin clung to her body, clearly delineating a rounded belly—the telltale sign her high-waisted gowns had heretofore concealed.

"It was all her idea." From the other side of the small room, Jack spoke up. "I didn't know she was with child until the rain soaked us through. You must believe me. She just came to me, and I was so desperate . . ." His back met the stone wall, and he slid down it until he sat on the floor. "I haven't touched her, I swear it."

"Yes, but why, Jack? How can you do this to me? Don't you know how I've defended you? Again and again, I've helped you, believed in you. And this is your thanks, absconding with my husband's ward?"

"I'm in a bad way, Amelia."

"Yes, Spencer told me."

"It's worse than even he knows. Exile or death, those are my options." He buried his face in his stacked arms. "Not sure I'd mind the second."

His words caught Amelia sharply in the chest, driving a wedge between her ribs and slowly levering them apart. She thought of going to her brother, but then Claudia whimpered. Instead, she tightened her arms about the girl to offer more comfort and warmth.

And then she began to shiver with fear. Between Claudia and Jack, the two of them needed so much. Not only comfort and warmth, but reassurance, assistance, absolution. Amelia wasn't sure she had enough within her to give them, and even if she did . . . there might be nothing left. Perhaps she would simply disappear.

"You mustn't blame him," Claudia whispered. "He's right. It was all my idea."

"Yes, but he should have known better. You're fifteen years old."

"Nearly sixteen," she sniffed.

"Sixteen." Jack raised his head and stared unfocused toward the ceiling. "Don't you remember the summer you were sixteen, Amelia? You were engaged to Poste. Hugh and I, we spent the whole summer up here at the gatehouse, plotting to stop the wedding. We may have been only thirteen and twelve, but we were blood sworn to never surrender you to that decrepit troll. We made black-powder grenades to create a diversion, a catapult . . ." He gave a hollow chuckle. "There was some strategy involving riled-up chickens, as I recall."

Tears welled in Amelia's eyes, even as she laughed to imagine the confluence of chickens, black powder, and a catapult interrupting her wedding. Old Mr. Poste would have likely expired on the spot. "What valiant plans. You must have been gravely disappointed when I cried off."

"No." His gaze met hers—utterly devoid of cynicism or deceit. "We were relieved, Amelia. Not just me and Hugh, but everyone. You deserved so much better. That's why . . ." He cleared his throat. "It's damned miserable, knowing I've driven you to marry Morland now."

"Jack, that's completely different. Spencer is nothing like Mr. Poste. I love him."

"You love everyone, no matter how undeserving. He's still not good enough for you. No one is." He shook his head. "If Hugh were alive, we'd have found a way to interrupt that wedding, too. Chickens, black powder, whatever it took."

Had they laid siege to all Bryanston Square, she doubted Spencer could have been dissuaded. If he wouldn't stop the wedding to answer murder allegations, a homemade catapult wouldn't have stood a chance.

"Of course," Jack said, "if Hugh were alive, everything would be different, wouldn't it?" Her brother tipped his head back against the wall and stared up at the leaking ceiling. "We spent our boyhoods in this crumbling heap. Couldn't bear to come back here, after. Thought I'd be relieved to see it sold, but . . ."

Her heart squeezed. So that's why she hadn't been able to get Jack out here last year. The same memories that comforted her were simply too much for him.

"I should have gone with him. I hated Laurent for buying Hugh a commission, and not me. I always followed him everywhere."

"I know," she said. "But you can't follow him now, Jack. Not to the grave."

"Can't I?"

"No," she said forcefully.

Water dripped slowly from the rafters. Plink, plink, plink. And then a realization exploded inside her.

"My God. That's why you're just sitting here, isn't it?

You *want* to be found. You want Spencer to call you out."

Again, he said nothing.

Her brother wished to die. It was an admission that should have wrung her heart till it hurt—and it did. But it also angered her beyond belief.

"Have you considered anyone but yourself, with this plan of yours? I know you loved Hugh. We all loved Hugh. His death devastated the entire family. So now you would inflict that devastation on us again, by goading my husband into a duel?" Her voice shook. "I tell you now, that will not happen. Spencer is not a murderer, and I won't allow you to make him one."

She smoothed Claudia's hair. "And this girl is fifteen years old, Jack. I don't care whose idea it was, or what assumptions you were laboring under when you took her from the house. Nothing excuses this."

"I know, I know." Jack hugged his own knees and rocked himself. She thought she heard him weeping.

The sound only frustrated her further. Her brother wasn't the frightened, ill-used, powerless child in this room. That role was Claudia's, and in his self-centered myopia he'd done nothing to help the girl. For God's sake, she was pregnant, terrified, chilled through with rain, and Jack was keeping her huddled in this drafty tower. He hadn't even offered her his coat.

Strangely enough, Amelia was glad of it. That small example of thoughtlessness might be inconsequential compared to his other misdeeds—but it was this final ounce of selfishness that tipped the scales. For many months, she'd believed she could save her brother if only she loved him hard enough. But she saw her error clearly now. She'd accused Spencer of being insular, but Jack was the one incapable of seeing beyond his own grief. Other men lost brothers, friends, even children and wives—and still avoided abject dissolution. Why Jack had stumbled into the chasm when others managed to skirt it, she would never know. But she finally understood it was beyond her power to pull him out.

She murmured to Claudia, “Do you feel well enough to stand?” At the girl’s nod, Amelia hooked a hand under her elbow. “Come, then. I’ll take you home.”

“What about me, Amelia?” Jack asked weakly. “What becomes of me now? You’re so fond of telling me what to do.”

She shook her head as she helped the girl to her feet. “I don’t know, Jack. I truly don’t know.”

Chapter Twenty-two

In the final black hour of night, Spencer crested the ridge of forest and began his descent toward Briarbank. The moon shone brightly now, though a mist still hung over the earth, blanketing the ground with moisture.

The scent of powder clung to his clothing. His boots were spattered with blood. His limbs were boneless with fatigue, and the early morning air was so humid, he felt as though he were swimming through it. Struggling, flailing. Drowning.

He could only pray Ashworth or Bellamy had succeeded where he'd failed.

He passed the stables on his way to the house. He was almost afraid to turn his head as he walked past the small, humble horse barn—but he made himself do so, wondering if he would see either of the other men's horses returned. He didn't. But what he did see chilled his blood.

Captain was missing. Amelia's steady gelding, gone. He'd been tied near the barn entrance, and with the moon so bright, Spencer ought to have been able to glimpse his gray coat from here. Nothing.

His legs—or rather, the numb, wooden stumps currently occupying his boots—quickly pumped to life, propelling him toward the barn. He rushed inside, looking frantically from stall to stall. No Captain to be found. Oh, Christ. She barely knew how to hold the reins. Surely she hadn't dared to take the horse out herself. With her inexperience and these conditions, to do so would have been an invitation to disaster.

His breath came quick and panicked now, and with every inhalation pain stabbed his side. He pressed an arm to his ribs, wondering if he'd broken just one, as he'd initially thought, or several. Wincing in pain, he half ran, half stumbled out of the barn and toward the cottage. The windows were dark, save a faint light from the library window. He moved toward it, drawn by that warm glow that seemed the embodiment of hope itself. Leaving the paved walk, he headed straight for the window and peered inside.

There she was. Seated in a chair by the wall of bookshelves, a sheaf of papers in her hand. Alone.

Gratitude swept the last bit of strength from his knees. He propped a hand on the wall for support, sucking in a lungful of air and relief. If he'd lost her, he couldn't have borne it.

Well, she might be lost to him yet, after tonight. And God only knew where Claudia was right now. But he stood there for a moment, gazing through the window glass at her pale, lovely profile and trying to imagine he wouldn't emerge from this night a complete failure at protecting everyone and everything he'd ever loved.

He went to the door and found it unlatched. Within seconds he stood in the entry of the library. His jaw worked a few times, sliding his thirst-thickened tongue over a tooth that had jarred loose. He couldn't think of a word to say.

"She's here." With shaking fingers, Amelia swept the papers aside. "Sleeping upstairs. She is safe."

Relief flooded his lungs, until his chest ached with it.

Still, he couldn't find words. So he crossed the room, knelt before his wife, laid his head in her lap, and wept.

"Oh, Spencer." Her fingers smoothed the hair from his brow. "Lord, you smell of death. And you're all scratched and bruised. What's happened to you?"

"It's nothing," he said, curling one arm around her legs. "Captain is gone from the barn. When I saw it, I thought perhaps you'd . . ." He clutched her tighter, feeling that moment of black terror more keenly than before. "God, Amelia. You must promise to never leave me."

Her fingers stilled in his hair. His heartbeat scudded to a stop, as well.

"I have news," she said at length. "It will be difficult for you to hear."

He wanted to keep his face buried in her skirts out of sheer cowardice, but he forced himself to sit back on his heels, rub his bleary eyes clear with one hand, and face this "news" like a man.

She pressed her lips together, hesitating. "There is no easy way to say this."

"Then say it straight out." He propped his arms on either side of her skirt, bracing himself for the worst.

"Claudia is with child."

"*Claudia.* Claudia, with child?" Emotion struck him in the chest. Several emotions, as a matter of fact, hitting him one after the other in quick succession, like a series of punishing blows: shock, disbelief, sorrow, guilt. Fury. A dozen questions tumbled in his mind, but only one really mattered. "Whose?"

"Not Jack's," she said hastily. "It couldn't have been. It was her music master in York."

"I'll kill him," Spencer bit out.

"What good would that serve? The man doesn't even know. And from Claudia's own account, it seems the tutor seduced her, but she was not . . . unwilling."

The mere idea of a man touching his ward sent nausea rolling through his gut. "She's fifteen years old. A child."

"Not any longer." Amelia grasped one of his hands and folded it in both of hers. "She's so frightened, Spencer. She's known for some time, but she's terrified of how you'll react. Just the same, I think she meant to speak with you. Earlier."

Earlier. When he and Amelia had been . . . otherwise engaged in this very room and they'd sent her away. And afterward, Spencer never had spoken with her as promised. Truth be told, he'd been avoiding speaking with Claudia for weeks.

"The elopement was her suggestion," Amelia continued quietly. "But Jack seized the idea eagerly. He's desperate for funds; she was desperate to conceal her pregnancy. It was a ridiculous plan, and I think they both knew it. They didn't make it any farther than the castle gatehouse, in the end. That's where I found them, wet and chilled through."

"You climbed up there? In the middle of the night?"

"Well, the idea did cross my mind to take Captain, but I realized quickly what a stupid notion that was."

"Thank God." He bent his head to her lap again. "I should have known you were too clever to attempt a stunt like that."

She laughed a little. "If it had been just my safety at stake, I might have been tempted to try, but . . ." He felt her sigh. "I know you must blame me for this. If only I hadn't insisted Jack stay, he—"

"Don't," he said, lifting his head to capture her gaze. "Don't blame yourself. Nothing excuses Jack's actions."

"I know," she said in a rush, squeezing his hand. "I know."

"It's my right to deal with him, Amelia. He all but kidnapped and ruined an innocent girl, and he must be made to face consequences for it. You can't keep protecting him any longer."

"I . . . I've already sent him away."

He rocked back on his heels, stunned.

"For both his good and yours. This can't end in violence." Averting her eyes, she swallowed hard. "I've promised to meet with him soon. I let him borrow Captain, but I swear you'll have the horse returned to you."

"Blast the horse." As if he gave a damn about the horse. He'd give every last stallion, mare, and gelding in his stables this instant to undo this night's events. "Where's Jack gone?"

She wouldn't look him in the eye. "Spencer, you know I can't tell y—"

"You can. And you will, because I'm asking it." He grabbed her chin and forced her to face him. Devil take it, he couldn't abide this any longer. "You have to choose, Amelia. I'm damned tired of always coming in second to that brigand, watching you squander all your sympathy and tenderness on him. This time, you cannot be loyal to us both. He abducted my ward. Either you tell me where Jack's gone and let me deal with him, or . . ."

"Or?" Red rimmed her eyes.

"Or you leave. You go to him, and you leave me. I can't keep doing this."

All throughout his brain, alarms trumpeted, trilled, blared. *Recant, you idiot. Take it all back, before she realizes what you've said.* He knew, rationally, that he'd just made the most impulsive, ill-calculated, goddamned foolish wager of his life, forcing the issue now. Asking her to make such a choice on a morning when lives and futures hung in the balance. But his brain wasn't making the decisions at the moment. His heart was speaking for him, and his heart was in shreds. He needed her—*all* of her. And if she couldn't give him everything, he'd best face it now and start learning to live with the pain.

Her eyes told him her answer, long before her lips could form the words.

"I'm sorry. I must go to him this morning."

The alarms in his brain muted, one by one, leaving only a low, mournful bugled dirge: *It's what you deserve, you witless fool. Now she's leaving you. This morning.*

It was nearly morning, wasn't it? Faint light seeped into the room, illuminating the sweet, familiar features of her face. God, she'd always been so lovely at daybreak. Even that very first morning, in the carriage. He'd decided then and there to marry her, claim her, make her his own. And somewhere between that dawn and this one, he'd grown to love her best when she clearly belonged to herself. It just wasn't in him to force her to stay. He wanted her willing, or not at all.

Dawn might be breaking over the river bluff, but a dark, endless night loomed inside Spencer's soul. He stared down at the crescents of blood and grit beneath his fingernails, the milky white quarter-moons of hers.

She said, "You should take Claudia home to Braxton Hall. She ought to be seen by her physician, for one thing. But more than that, she needs comfort and guidance. The girl needs *you*, Spencer."

"But . . ." Oh, hell. He should just say it. "But I need *you*. I've no idea what to do with her, or even how to talk to her about such a thing."

She gave him a wry smile. "You're a man of frightening intelligence. I have faith in you to figure it out." She reached for the papers on the desk and furled them into a scroll, but not before he recognized them as the still-unsigned purchase agreement for Briarbank. "I'll be taking these with me."

He blinked furiously. "I see."

Yes. In the light of morning, it all was too painfully clear. When her feelings for him clashed against her obligations to family . . . the d'Orsay pride would win out every time. She would tend to her brother's needs before his. She wouldn't allow *her* family cottage to become *theirs*. And by refusing to share her, Spencer had driven her away. He'd forced her to choose between her husband and her family, and now he must abide by her choice. No matter how much it hurt.

And damn, did it hurt. As he shifted his weight from one knee to the other, his ribs gave a sharp twinge.

Her gaze fell to their hands as she continued, "There is one thing more I must tell you. I suspect I, too, am with child."

"Oh, God. Oh, Amelia." Never had words filled him with such bright joy and such utter misery at the same time. The image of her body swelled with his child, the thought of cradling their infant in his arms . . . it was like a small star had burned through the atmosphere and blazed a trail straight for his heart. He wanted a family with her as he'd never wanted anything in his life, and nothing should have made him happier than this news. But at the same time, his own arrogant words came back to haunt him. *I give you security; you give me an heir*. She was leaving him this morning, and she carried within her the perfect excuse to never come back.

Spencer said a fervent prayer to God for a girl.

"Are you well?" he asked, swallowing hard. "Is there anything you—"

"I'm fine," she assured him, smiling a little at her belly. "Very fit indeed. D'Orsay women are built for breeding, you know. Sturdy."

Before he could grasp a few of the thousand adjectives that described her with far greater justice than "sturdy," her gaze slanted away.

"You never finished your game," she said.

He followed her gaze to the desktop. Atop the blotter, their cards and wagers lay untouched, frozen in time. In the center were his note for twenty thousand pounds and two of the Stud Club tokens: Rhys's and Leo's. Bellamy had never laid his token down, and Spencer never had the opportunity to fetch the remaining seven from upstairs.

Not that it mattered anymore.

He rose to his feet slowly, feeling aches in muscles he hadn't known he'd strained. He suspected his injuries would take turns announcing their presence over the course of the next few days. As he took a step, pain shot through his ribs, and he grimaced, leaning one hand on the desk for support.

"God's mercy, Spencer." She was at his side. "What's happened to you?"

With morning light filtering into the room, she was no doubt noting the abrasions on his skin, the gore spattering his boots, the shredded cuff of his sleeve.

"Took a fall," he said, drawing a painful breath. "I've broken a rib or two, I think."

"I'll send for the doctor immediately. Are you cut somewhere? There's so much blood . . ."

"It's not mine."

She didn't ask for an explanation. Unfortunately. He could have deflected a question, but this damn endearing patient silence thing she always did . . . he had no defense to that.

"I was on Juno," he said quickly, wanting to have it out and over with. "On the way back from Lydney she stepped in a hole and fell. Threw me clear of her, fortunately. I could have been banged up far worse. But her leg was broken, in more than one place. She was in a great deal of pain. No way to get her back here for treatment, and even if there was, she'd have been completely lamed, so . . ."

"Oh, no." Her voice broke. "You had to shoot her."

His eyes burned as he confirmed her suspicions with a nod.

"Spencer." Wiping her eyes with her hand, she surveyed his torso. "Will I hurt you terribly if I give you a hug?"

"Probably," he said. "But I'll take it anyway."

She moved toward him gingerly and slid her arms beneath his coat, around his waist. And then, with agonizing slowness, she brought her body flush with his and buried her face in his shoulder. It still wasn't enough. He wrapped one arm around her shoulders and crushed her tight to his chest. And yes, it hurt like the devil—but not nearly as much as it was going to hurt when he inevitably had to let her go.

"I'm so sorry," she said, weeping against his soiled coat. "I'm so terribly sorry, for Jack, Claudia, Juno, everything. I wish things were different."

"So do I."

Sniffing and dabbing at her eyes with her wrist, she pulled away. "I'd best go dress and pack my things."

"Wait." He pulled a handkerchief from his breast pocket and held it out to her, knowing she'd recognize it even without opening it to view the stitching. If she was truly leaving him, he ought to give it back. Somehow he mustered the ghost of an irreverent grin. "Can't a duchess afford handkerchiefs?"

Wordlessly, she took it. Stared at it a moment. And then she left.

He stood there for a while, exhausted and in too much pain to move. It might have been a short while or a long while—he really didn't know. He likely would have still been standing there at midday, had Ashworth not rapped on the door.

"I hope they're here," he said, "because they're nowhere between Colford and Gloucester."

"She's here," Spencer replied. "He's gone."

Ashworth grunted. "As it should be, then." His eyes narrowed as he took in Spencer's gory boots. "Now, when you say 'gone,' do you mean . . ."

"No."

"Not that I'd blame you."

"It's not his," he said, indicating the blood spattering his boots. "My mare took a bad fall. Had to . . ." He swore, glancing at the waxing trapezoid of sunlight shining through the window. "I have to get out there and bury her."

"I'll go with you," Ashworth said. "I've dug a grave or two in my time."

"No, no." He pinched the bridge of his nose. "You've been out all night already. I can't ask you to—"

"You didn't ask. I offered. And I've worked through a night or two in my time, as well." He kicked his boot against the doorjamb. "It's no more than any friend would do."

"Are we friends?"

"We're not enemies."

"In that case . . ." Spencer sighed, dragging a hand through his hair. "I'd be grateful for the help." He gestured toward the desktop and the aborted card game. "Don't neglect to take your winnings."

The soldier's brow furrowed. "We were interrupted. I don't recall anyone winning."

"I left the game first. Anything on the table is my forfeit. Technically, Bellamy never placed a bet. Besides, my cards were rubbish. I would have lost anyway." He shook his head. "I wanted to end this joke of a club once and for all, but it seems Harcliffe isn't through poking fun at us yet."

"You think Bellamy will find the man responsible for his death?"

"I think he finds him every time he looks in a mirror. That's the damn problem." Spencer took the note and two tokens and held them out. "Just take them, Rhys. Aren't you the great believer in fate? Perhaps it was meant to be."

They took their time returning to Braxton Hall, traveling at a slow pace out of consideration for Claudia's stomach and Spencer's healing ribs. He rode with her in the coach. It seemed right to keep her company, and he needn't worry about giving Juno exercise anymore.

God. There'd been so much lost in the past week, he didn't know where to begin grieving. Juno, his marriage, Claudia's innocence—all were casualties. The fault was shared among many, but he blamed only himself. Amelia had been right. If he'd only been more open with those around him, all of it might have been avoided.

Still, he didn't know how to begin fresh. He and Claudia traveled the entire journey in silence, save for the most banal of discussions. Which inn to choose for their stopover; whether the weather would hold fair. He didn't want to press his ward to talk until she was ready. They had months yet. Ample time to discuss.

They reached home on the fourth day, rather late. But the days were still long in summer, and an extended gray-gold twilight stubbornly held the night at bay. While the servants brought in the trunks and prepared their rooms, Spencer ordered a light supper brought to his library and invited Claudia to join him.

To his surprise, she agreed.

They shared a tray of sandwiches, and then he watched her eat tarts and sip chocolate. When the hour grew late enough that their rooms ought to have been readied for bed, she addressed him.

"Would you read to me? Like you used to do when I was a girl?" She gave her cooling chocolate a deep, searching look. "I . . . I rather miss it."

He cleared his throat. "Of course. Have you any particular book in mind?"

"No. You choose."

He chose Shakespeare—the comedies, naturally. God knew they'd seen enough tragedy of late.

Leafing through the volume, he located Act I of *The Tempest* and began to read. Claudia curled her legs under her skirt and rested her head on the arm of the divan, closing her eyes. He couldn't tell whether she was still listening or had fallen asleep, so he just kept reading, for himself. It had been too long since he'd read through Shakespeare. The plays only made sense to him when read aloud, and it felt deuced awkward to sit around by oneself, reading to the candlewick.

He read clear through to the end that night, then drew a blanket over Claudia's sleeping form and left her to rest undisturbed. The next evening after dinner, he read through three acts of *A Midsummer Night's Dream* before her light snoring intervened. They finished the play the next night, and then she asked for an old favorite: Johnson's *Rasselas*. He remembered how, as a girl, Claudia had enjoyed the story of the fabled Abyssinian prince traveling the world in search of contentment. It was the adventure that held her attention then—the princesses and pyramids. Spencer wondered if she remembered that in the end, the prince never found the happiness he sought.

As he paused to sip his brandy and turn a page, Claudia suddenly sat up on the divan. "What will become of me?"

At last, here they came to it. Feeling both grateful and apprehensive, he laid aside the book. "There are a few alternatives."

"What are they?"

"As I see them, they are three. If you wish to be married, I could find a man to marry you. A good man of limited means, who will benefit from the connection. He must agree to raise the child as his own and delay any further"—he shifted in his chair—"childbearing until you are ready."

She studied her palm. "I don't particularly like that alternative."

Thank God. Neither did he.

"If you wish to preserve your reputation," he continued, "you can give birth in secret. The child would be fostered with a local family, and you would be free to have your debut season, be courted by suitors, and marry where you liked. Perhaps you might see the child on occasion, but you would never be able to acknowledge him as your own."

"Her. I think it's a girl." Placing a hand on her belly, she said, "Go on. You said there was a third."

"The third option," he said quietly, "would be to give birth and keep the child. You would be disgraced, and your chances of making a good marriage would be slim. You most certainly would never know the excitement of a London season."

"But I would have my baby."

"Yes."

He allowed her a moment's contemplation.

Leaning forward and bracing his elbows on his knees, he said, "They are none of them easy choices. Your life will be drastically altered, no matter which you take. But you should also know this. Whichever course you choose, you may be assured of having my support, both material and otherwise."

"And Amelia's as well?"

"I . . . I can't speak for Amelia." God, saying her name aloud after so many days apart . . . He missed her, terribly. What he would not give to have her here. She would know what to say to Claudia, how to comfort her. How to cross the room and fold the girl into a warm hug, in a way that didn't feel awkward and forced. But she wasn't here, and he had no one to blame for her absence but himself. What the hell had he been thinking, forcing her to choose between him and her family? Her love for her family was in her blood; it was who she was. It was the reason they'd even met. He should have known he could never offer her anything to compete.

Claudia took the words from his lips when she said, "I've made a muddle of everything, haven't I?"

"You've made a mistake. I've made my share, as well." Such as believing she'd outgrown these evenings spent reading aloud, and that he had nothing more to offer her. "But now you must decide how you can live with that mistake."

"What do you think I should do?"

"I think you should make your own choice, in your own time." He hesitated. He didn't want to make the decisions for her, but if she asked for guidance, wasn't it his duty to give it? "I will say this much. We both know what it's like to grow up without a mother. It isn't easy. I don't believe the avoidance of gossip is a good way to choose the direction of one's life. And as for marriage . . . How much do you remember of your father?"

"I remember you were always fighting with him."

He chuckled. "We had our disagreements. A great many of them, as a matter of fact. Most of that was my fault. It was devilish hard laboring under his expectations. Easier sometimes to purposely misbehave, rather than make the effort and come up lacking."

"Yes," she said softly. "I understand."

He winced, hating himself for ever making her feel that way. "No matter our arguments," he said, "I had tremendous respect for your father, and for my own father, as well. They were good, honorable men, and exceedingly loyal. When your mother died, your father could have married again, with hopes of getting a son of his own to assume the title. But he couldn't bear the idea of remarrying, that's how much he loved your mother. So he sent for me from Canada instead, and I gave him so much hell in those first few years, it's a wonder he didn't reconsider. But he never did remarry. And neither did my father, after my own mother died. That's why I wouldn't like to see you trapped in an unhappy union, Claudia. Love, for a Dumarque, is not a passing fancy. We remain devoted to the grave."

"You feel that way about Amelia?"

"Yes," he said simply. No matter how many differences he'd had with his father and his uncle, here was one thing they shared in common. He was a Dumarque man at his core. He would love one woman until he died, and there could never be another. God help him if she didn't feel the same.

Claudia looked askance at him. "If you truly feel that way, you could do a better job of showing it."

"You're right," he agreed. "I could do a better job of it with you, too. I plan to improve."

Her eyes shimmered. "Do you plan to start soon?"

When he was seventeen years old, Spencer had spent five miserable weeks aboard a two-masted brig to cross the Atlantic Ocean. That trip had been a pleasant afternoon jaunt compared to the arduous journey he made now. He rose from his chair, crossed the vast expanse of the library carpet, and sat down beside his ward.

He placed a hand on her shoulder. "Whatever you decide, Claudia, you will always have a home here. And you will always be loved."

She started to weep. He hoped they were a good sort of tears. Regardless, he slid his arm around her shoulders and gathered her into a hug.

He felt rather proud of himself for it, but evidently he still needed practice to perfect the art. After a moment, Claudia sniffed and said, "I miss Amelia."

He gathered her even closer then, because he needed to be hugged back. "I miss her, too."

"When is she coming home?"

"I don't know. She may not come back to Braxton Hall."

Claudia straightened, pulling back to stare at him. "Whatever do you mean? Go fetch her!"

"But . . . I'm not certain exactly where she is at the moment."

"You're the Duke of Morland. Find her!"

"I'm not sure she wants to be found." He could scarcely believe he was discussing this with Claudia . . . but then again, who else did he have to ask? "I bullied her quite a bit at the outset, and I don't want to make the same mistake again. I miss her, yes. But I want her to be happy most of all. If she comes back, I want her to come freely. Willingly."

Her eyes went wide. "Then *convince* her. Fall at her feet and grovel. Make some grand gesture of apology. Tell her that sweet little story you just told me and profess your undying love. Really, Spencer, don't you know anything about romance?"

Chapter Twenty-three

It was a fine summer morning on the Bristol docks, and for once a ray of fortune was shining on the d'Orsays. A merchant brigantine called the *Angelica* sailed with the tide, bound for Boston.

Jack would be on it.

Amelia's nose wrinkled as she squinted at her brother through the blaring midday sun. She wished she'd thought to purchase him a hat with a wider brim. With his fair skin, he'd be crisped to currant red after one day at sea.

"Well?" he said.

In a last sisterly gesture, she smoothed the lint from Jack's coat sleeves with her gloved hands. "What a grand adventure you're going to have. I believe Hugh would be very envious."

"I like to think he's coming with me."

"Perhaps he is." She threw her arms around her brother and hugged him tight. "I love you," she whispered fiercely. "Don't ever dream otherwise. But I just can't take care of you any longer. It's time you learned to take care of yourself."

"I know," he said. "I know."

She pulled back and withdrew a small bundle from her reticule. The knotted handkerchief contained a heavy clutch of coins. "Your passage is already paid. This is all I have to give you for expenses."

"Thank you," he said, reaching for the makeshift purse of gold and silver. "I'll do my best not to lose it the first night out from land."

She tried to laugh, but she knew the danger of him doing just that was great. She kept her hand on the handkerchief, refusing to let him take it yet.

"If you do lose it, don't write me for more. If you wander home a few months from now, having landed yourself in trouble again and looking for my help . . . I won't give it." Much as it pained her to speak those words, she knew she had to say them. *Cut the leading strings*. Perhaps if Jack understood she wouldn't be there to catch him, he might take greater precautions not to fall. "This is the very last time I save you, do you understand? I will pray for you and always love you. But after this, not a penny more."

With that, she let go of the handkerchief. It was much easier to release her grip on that bit of linen than it was to let go of her responsibility for him. But she had to do both. She deserved to be happy, too, and she couldn't imagine happiness without Spencer. She simply couldn't risk letting Jack come between them again.

Spencer was right; she did have to make a choice. But this wasn't a matter of deciding between her brother and her husband. It was a matter of deciding to seize happiness and let go of guilt.

Amelia was choosing herself.

"I'd best be going, then." He glanced over his shoulder at the *Angelica*'s gangplank. "I hate to leave you alone here. Is Morland coming for you?"

She shook her head. "He's taken Claudia home to Cambridgeshire. I've sent an express to Laurent. He'll help me close up the cottage, and then we'll travel back to London together."

"Amelia?" He chucked her under the chin. "When I said no one's good enough for you, I meant it. And I include myself. I know I haven't deserved half the help you've given me, but . . ." His lips twitched at the corner, tugging on Amelia's heart. All the d'Orsay men made that face when they were struggling not to cry. "I'm grateful for it. Thank you for loving me, even when I've done my devil's best to be unlovable."

The look in his eyes, the catch in his voice . . . her heart squeezed. She was a breath away from flinging her arms around his shoulders and vowing to take him back home, solve all his problems for him.

Taking a step backward instead was quite possibly the bravest thing she'd ever done. But she knew in her heart, it was best for them both.

"Goodbye, Jack," she said. "We'll miss you. Please take care."

Then she turned on her heel. Took one step. Then two. Every pace she took away from him felt like a step taken on wobbly foal legs, but as her boots clopped hollowly on the planked dock, she slowly gained in coordination and confidence. It had taken a little time and much sorrow, but she'd finally mastered the lesson Spencer had given her the night they first met:

Turn those hapless d'Orsay fortunes around. Learn when to walk away.

"Where shall I take you?" As they neared Charing Cross, Laurent turned to her on the carriage seat. "Home?"

Home.

Amelia mused on the word. She wondered which house her brother referred to: the Duke of Morland's, or his own? Which one was "home"? That was the question for her to decide, she supposed.

"I'll come with you, if you don't mind." No house felt

like home without Spencer in it. And though he would still be at Braxton Hall, she couldn't abide the thought of rattling around that cavernous town house alone.

"Of course you're welcome. Winifred's planned some sort of party tonight. Lucky for me we're returning in time for it. She'd have my head if I left her alone to host."

"Is it a large party?" Now this might change Amelia's mind. After two days of carriage travel and a week's worth of melancholy, a busy social gathering wasn't really how she wished to spend her evening.

"No, no. A few couples over to dinner. Perhaps a bit of cards and dancing after, you know."

Well, that didn't sound too dreadful. As a matter of fact, dinner itself sounded most welcome. And as for the amusements afterward—she could easily plead a headache and slip upstairs. It wouldn't even be a falsehood. She'd done so much ruminating and pondering and reconsidering in the past two days, her brain ached.

"Did I do the right thing?" she asked her brother, for likely the tenth time since Jack had sailed with the *Angelica*. "Will he be all right?"

"I don't know how he'll fare," Laurent answered, reaching for her hand and giving it a reassuring squeeze. "But you did absolutely the right thing."

"I just still feel guilty, letting him believe his debts will remain unpaid."

"You know he never would have left otherwise."

"I know." She bit her lip. "Will you have a difficult time finding another buyer?"

"I don't expect so. It's a choice piece of land, even if the cottage is modest. The Earl of Vinterre expressed some interest in it. Wants to tear down the place and build an Italianate palace overlooking the river."

"Oh, dear. I may vomit."

Laurent passed her the basin. It wouldn't have been

the first time she'd been ill on this journey. Nor even the second, or fifth. Apparently her unborn child didn't enjoy coach travel any more than she did.

Afterward, he soothed her back. "Don't be upset. I'll find another buyer."

"No, don't." She pressed her sleeve to her mouth. "I think it would be easier to see Briarbank razed than inhabited by another family. Sell it to Vinterre, and do it quickly."

The sooner all the dealings were completed, the sooner Jack's debts could be paid. And the sooner that happened, the sooner Amelia could return to Braxton Hall, pockets empty but heart undivided. She would set about convincing her husband that she was devoted to him, above all.

The coach made its creaking turn into Bryanston Square and soon lurched to a halt before the house. Laurent helped her alight from the carriage.

At the door, they were met by a wild-eyed Winifred. After sparing Amelia a brief nod, she latched on to Laurent's arm. "Oh, thank goodness you're finally home. I'm beside myself, utterly. We need to order more wine—whole casks of it, likely. And spirits for the gentlemen." She pulled her husband into the house, and Amelia followed them over the threshold.

"The fish course is a horrid dilemma. Naturally this would happen on a Monday, when there's no decent fish to be had for gold or silver. Naught but common oysters in the market." Her voice pitched a half-octave closer to hysteria. "I can't serve oysters to a duchess!"

Amelia laughed. "I shall do just fine with oysters, thank you. You've served them to me many a time before."

Her sister-in-law turned to her, wearing a puzzled expression. "Forgive me, Amelia. But of course I didn't mean *you*."

Of course not. Amelia sighed.

Winifred's voice lowered to a whisper. "Her Grace, the Duchess of Hampstead will be joining us for dinner. I've just received the note from one of my dinner guests, Mrs. Nodwell. Her cousin is married to Her Grace's nephew's adopted brother, you see?"

Amelia didn't, but she nodded politely anyway.

Winifred turned back to Laurent, pulling him into the Rose Salon, where servants were removing porcelain cherubs from the shelves and pushing the furniture to the sides of the room. "Obviously," she said, "I couldn't decline. And then Mrs. Petersham sent a note round, asking if she might bring her cousins visiting from Bath. I couldn't say no to them, either. And now these cards keep coming . . ." She gestured toward the row of calling cards propped on the mantel. "I do believe tonight we're going to be overrun with Quality."

"But . . ." Amelia shook her head to dispel her confusion. "At this time of summer? Why?"

"For you, of course! They all assume you and Morland will be in attendance. Everyone is desperate to see your first public appearance in London since the marriage." She lifted an eyebrow. "There are some very interesting"—she pronounced each syllable distinctly, *EEN-ter-est-ting*—"rumors coming out of Oxfordshire, you know."

A bittersweet smile curved Amelia's lips. She'd known there would be gossip, after that display at the Granthams'. The memory of that night—the dancing, the lovemaking, the conversation and sweet embraces lasting into morning—it wrung her heart with surprising ferocity. The pain made her think of Spencer's broken ribs. She hoped they were healing well.

Lord, she missed him, with everything she had.

Moving to the side of the room, she took a seat on a recently relocated footstool. "Well, I fear your guests will be disappointed," she told Winifred. "I'm not feeling well enough for socializing this evening, and the duke is not even in Town."

"But he is!"

Amelia's jaw dropped. "He is?"

"Yes, he arrived this very morning in Mayfair, and the news has already appeared in the afternoon papers." Winifred snapped her fingers at a footman. "Not there. By the window."

Amelia quietly reeled, trying not to betray the magnitude of her shock. Spencer was here in Town? Could he have any idea of her own arrival? And what about Claudia? Where was she?

As Winifred went into another flurry of instructions for the servants, Laurent crouched at Amelia's side. "Shall I have the carriage take you to Morland House?"

"No, no." She couldn't see him like this, not yet. She wasn't prepared. She wasn't even certain he'd *want* to see her. "I will send him a note."

With a few more snaps of Winifred's fingers, a lap desk and quill materialized before Amelia. The paper was a terrifying expanse of white. She was afraid to lay her pen to it at all, fearful of marring that blank perfection with the wrong word and mucking up everything again. In the end, she simply wrote:

I am here in Town, at my brother's house. You are invited to dinner this evening.
—A.

There. If he wished to see her, he would know where to find her. Laurent dispatched a runner with the note, and Amelia passed two fretful hours unpacking in her old, modest bedchamber whilst Winifred renovated the downstairs. Finally, just as light was fading, she glimpsed the runner through her open window as he made for the house's back entrance. She rushed down the service stairs to find the boy.

"Well?" she asked him breathlessly, once she'd collared the youth. He held a folded paper in his hand. "Is that my reply?"

He shook his head no. "The duke weren't at home, ma'am. Footman told me he'd gone out for a game of cards."

A game of *cards*? He'd come back to London just for a game of cards?

"Go back there," she told the boy. "Find out where he's gone, and find His Grace to give him that note. Don't bother coming back until you do."

"Yes, ma'am."

She released the lad, and he darted off the way he'd come.

Circling one palm over her belly—a habit she'd already developed, even though her abdomen didn't protrude yet—she took deep breaths and tried to remain calm.

Hours later, she was panicking.

Laurent's house was crushed, wall to wall, with guests. They'd begun arriving shortly after sundown and continued to stream in even now. The entirety of Bryanston Square was congested with coaches and teams. Most of the recent arrivals didn't even seem to understand they were lacking an invitation. Amelia wasn't certain they knew whose house they were at; they were just following the crowd. Winifred's food had run out hours ago, much to her despair, but her reinforcements of wine and spirits were holding strong for the moment. No one showed the slightest inclination to leave.

In the hall, the hired quartet gamely played over and through the din of rumor and laughter. A few couples carved out enough space to dance a cramped quadrille.

Amelia couldn't imagine why they all hadn't given up and gone home hours ago. The duke's absence was obvious, and tonight she lacked the spirit to compensate with flirtation and witty remarks. Even with every window thrown open to the night air and the barest minimum of candles burning, the air in the rooms was exceedingly close, and Amelia had done her best to seek out the few pockets of relative seclusion. Whenever someone asked after Spencer, she murmured a few words of excuse. Recently arrived in town, delayed by business . . . et cetera.

She was on the verge of slipping out entirely and hiring a hack to Morland House, where she could perhaps find some restful quiet and wait for Spencer in peace. Then the musicians struck up the first few bars of a waltz, and a raucous male voice called out, "Not yet! Not yet!"

Bemused, she watched as every head in the room swiveled toward the ancient clock, where the short hand wavered just on the brink of twelve. A collective hush amplified the tick, tick, tick . . . as then the long hand swept past the ten. Amelia suddenly understood why the guests wouldn't give up on the duke and simply go home.

They were waiting for the hour of twelve, of course. Breathless with anticipation to see if the Duke of Midnight would remain true to his name.

And that realization began the longest ten minutes of Amelia's life.

She passed the first five minutes asking after and then slowly imbibing a glass of tepid lemonade.

By straightening every seam of her gloves, she managed to while away another two.

Then there came a dark, endless minute in which guilt and regret swamped her, and doubt followed close behind. Perhaps he wouldn't come because he was still angry and didn't want to see her. Perhaps he had no use for her now, since she was already with child.

Another minute ticked past, and she scolded herself. If he didn't appear tonight, it meant nothing. Except that he was off somewhere else, and she would see him the next day. Or the next.

And then the entire assembly passed the final minute simply waiting, watching, listening to the clock's inexorable ticks. When the slender minute hand finally clicked into unison with the squat hour hand, the room went dead silent. And then the clock's cuckoo bird popped out from its window and cheerfully mocked them all.

Cuckoo! Cuckoo! Twelve. Dratted. Times. The wretched little wooden creature had probably never enjoyed such a rapt audience.

It was midnight. And no duke had arrived.

Well, that was that.

Now the party was truly over. The musicians struck up a waltz, as they'd no doubt been bribed to do, but no one cared. The guests murmured amongst themselves on mundane, uninteresting topics, in the way people do when they're thinking of leaving a party.

A week's worth of fatigue settled on Amelia's shoulders. For heaven's sake, she needed to rest. She pressed forward through the packed drawing room, heading for the little pocket door behind the pianoforte. It led to a service corridor, and she could use it to make her escape upstairs.

"Amelia, wait."

The deep voice rang out over the crowd. Over the musicians. Over even the violent pounding of her heart.

"Wait right there. Please."

Well, that couldn't be Spencer. She'd just heard the word "please." She wheeled around anyway and felt positively biblical when the crowd thronging the hall parted like the Red Sea. And there, standing at the other end of that freshly carved valley of humanity, was her husband. The tardy Duke of Midnight.

"It's ten past," she couldn't help but say. "You're late."

"I'm sorry," he said earnestly, starting toward her. "I came as soon as I could."

She shook her head, astonished. Not only "please," but "sorry" now? In public, no less? Was this man truly her husband?

But of course he was. There was no other man on earth so handsome.

"Stay there," he said again. "I'm coming to you."

He took an awkward, hobbled step in her direction, and then another. A grimace pulled at his mouth. His injuries were clearly still paining him. As gratifying as it was to watch him at long last moving across a dance floor toward *her,* and not some preening debutante, she realized this was going to take far too long.

"For heaven's sake, stay put," she said. Her heel caught on the carpet fringe as she hurried toward him, and she would have fallen to the floor without the well-timed assistance of a smartly dressed gentleman in green velvet. It made her conscious, as she met her husband halfway and he pulled her into a tight embrace, that they were being observed by one and all. And "all," in this case, referred to hundreds.

Of course she didn't mind the attention herself. But she knew how Spencer hated crowds. She pulled him as far to the side as possible, putting his back toward the horde of onlookers.

"There now," she said, keeping her arms laced around his neck. "Just pretend we're dancing."

He winced. "The ride from Braxton Hall nearly killed me. With these ribs, pretense is all I can manage."

"Why are you in town at all? I heard you were playing cards."

"Well, I meant to. That's the reason I came to London. I'd no idea you'd be here. My intention was to win back Jack's debt from the gaming lord himself. I'd arranged the game, prepared my stakes and sharpened my strategy—do you know that man's one of the best piquet players in England?"

"I suspect you're better."

His mouth tipped with an arrogant grin. "I suspect I'd have proved you right, in the end. It might have taken me hours, though, and we were just sitting down to the table when your boy found me, and I read your note. And after that . . ." He blew out a breath. "After that, I just said to hell with it. I wrote him a bank draft instead."

She gasped. "You didn't!"

"I did. Because whatever amount your brother owed, it wasn't worth a single hour's delay in seeing you." He swallowed hard. "All Jack's debts are paid, Amelia. You needn't worry about his safety anymore."

"Oh, Spencer. You're very good to have done that. But I wish I'd had the opportunity to speak with you first. Jack's gone. He sailed from Bristol on a brigantine bound for America. You were right. I was doing him more harm than good. He's my brother, and I'll always love him. But I'll have to love him from afar just now. Our marriage is more important to me than anything." She lowered her voice and gripped him tight. "*You* are more important to me than anything. I'll never let anything come between us again."

"I . . . I can't believe it." He blinked away a glimmer of emotion. "What of the debt?"

"Laurent has another buyer for the cottage." When he began to form a question, she added, "The debts are ours to dispatch, not yours. We'll repay you every penny. Jack is our problem, our family's responsibility."

"Your problems *are* mine. Your family too, if you'll have me. I was a complete bastard to ask you to choose. And you can't give up that cottage. It's your home."

"It's a house. Just a pile of stones and mortar, and a

crumbling one at that. It's meaningless without love to fill it. My home is wherever you are." She felt a smile warming her face. "Here we are right back where we started, aren't we? You owning my brother's debt, me with only a drafty cottage in Gloucestershire as collateral."

"Is it wrong of me to demand Briarbank in payment anyhow? The property needn't change hands. A very long lease will suffice. I love it there, and I love being there with you. And I love you. God, I haven't said that to you nearly enough, but I'm going to make up for it now by telling you five times a day. I love you, Amelia. Since the very first night, I knew you were the only woman for me. Until the day I die, I will love you. I love—"

"Hush." She put a finger to his lips. Had he gone mad, or had he forgotten the crowd of onlookers at his back? Leaning in close, she teased, "It's a quarter past midnight. Don't exhaust all five so early in the day. I'd like something to look forward to, once we get home."

He grasped her hand and kissed her fingers warmly. "You needn't worry on that score." He brought her close and whispered in her ear. "God, how I've missed you. Not only in bed, but especially in bed. It's a very big bed, and it's damned empty without you. Life is empty without you."

Feeling it prudent to change the subject before she went to custard, she cleared her throat and asked, "How's Claudia?"

"At Braxton Hall. I've promised to return quickly. She's still considering her options, but I've told her she'll have my support, no matter what her choice."

"She will have *our* support."

He released a deep sigh. "Thank you." He raised a hand to her face, cradling her cheek in his palm. "And you? You are well?" He flicked a glance downward, toward her belly.

"Yes." She smiled. "Both of us."

As his thumb stroked sweetly over her cheek, his eyes warmed to rich shades of gold and green. He gave her one of those rare, devastating smiles. "What a beautiful mother you'll be."

He bent his head, clearly seeking a kiss.

She put a hand to his chest, holding him off.

"Spencer," she whispered, darting a glance to either side. "There are hundreds of people about."

"Are there? I hadn't noticed."

"Your heart's pounding."

"That's for you."

And now her own heart skipped a beat. She'd spent her whole life loving those around her, and still she'd never dreamed she could love someone this much—so much it stretched the very seams of her soul. Better yet was the knowledge that the love would only grow, and she would have to grow with it.

"You realize, you do have a certain reputation," she murmured. "Everyone here is expecting to watch you cart me from the room in a scandalous, barbaric display."

"Then they'll be disappointed. I'm scarcely fit to lift a kitten at the moment, and even if I were . . ." He cupped her face in both hands, and his gaze reached so far into hers she felt it warming her toes. "It's never been my desire to conquer you, Amelia. If you leave this room with me, it must be at my side. As my wife, my lover, my partner . . ." His thumb brushed her lip. "My dearest friend. Would you do that?"

She managed a tearful nod.

"Then may I kiss you now, in front of all these people?"

She nodded again, this time smiling through the tears. "On the lips, if you please. And do it properly."

Read on for an excerpt from

Twice Tempted by a Rogue

by Tessa Dare

Published by Ballantine Books

Rhys St. Maur, newly Lord Ashworth, was a broken man.

Literally.

By the age of twenty, he'd fractured his left arm twice—once in a schoolboy brawl at Eton, and then again during an army training drill. Cracked ribs . . . he'd lost count of those. Fists driving through barroom haze to connect with his face had snapped the cartilage in his nose a few times, leaving him with a craggy profile—one that was not improved by his myriad scars. Since sometime around his thirtieth birthday, the little finger on his right hand just plain refused to bend. And in damp weather like this, his left knee throbbed with memories of marching through the Pyrenees and surviving the Battle of Nivelle unscathed, only to catch a Basque farmer's hoe to the knee the next morning, when he left camp for a predawn piss.

That left knee was on fire tonight, sizzling with pain as Rhys trudged through the granite heart of Devonshire, leading his horse down the darkened road. The moisture in the air kept dithering between fog and rain, and the night was thick with its indecision. He couldn't see but a few feet in front of him, which was why he'd decided to dismount and lead his horse on foot. Between the poor visibility and the surrounding terrain littered with chunks of stone and boot-sucking bogs, the risk of fatal injury was too great.

For the horse, that was. Rhys wasn't in the least concerned for himself. In fact, if he thought this godforsaken moor had any chance of claiming his own life, he'd cheerfully saddle his gelding and charge off into the gloom.

But it wouldn't work. It never had. He'd just end up with a lamed or dead horse, another broken rib perhaps, and the same curse that had haunted him since boyhood: unwanted, undeserved, and wholly wasted good luck.

No matter what misfortune befell him, this or any night, Rhys St. Maur was doomed to survive it.

The wind's low moan played his spine like a fiddle string. Behind him, the gelding balked. With a reassuring shush for the beast's benefit, Rhys marched on, turning up the collar of his coat to keep out the mist.

Yea, though I walk though the valley of the shadow of death, I will fear no evil . . .

He'd been walking through this valley for a long, long time. Trod so far into death's shadow he'd felt his feet turning to dust in his boots, the breath in his lungs burning acrid as sulfur. A living ghost, that's what he was. He'd returned from war to a newly-inherited barony, and his sole duty now was to haunt the English aristocracy. Hulk awkwardly in the corners of their parties, terrify their delicate young ladies, and cause the gentlemen to rub their temples self-consciously as they tried not to stare at the gnarled scar marring his own.

As Rhys rounded a sharp curve in the road, a vaguely familiar sight emerged from the gloom. If he'd read his landmarks right, this had to be it. The tiny village of Buckleigh-in-the-Moor. At this distance, just a meager constellation of amber pinpricks against the black night.

The horse, scenting straw and safety, picked up his pace. Soon the cluster of stone and cob buildings came into focus. It must not be as late as it felt. A fair number of the cottages still showed light through their windows—yellow eyes peering out from beneath thatched-roof hats.

He halted in the center of the road. Wiping the moisture from his eyes, he squinted in the direction of the old inn. Fourteen years he'd been gone, but the same sign still creaked on its chains above the door. It read, in retouched gilt letters, The Three Hounds. Below the words, the pictured trio of dogs remained at perpetual attention. A burst of coarse laughter rattled one of the inn's unshuttered windows. Old Maddox was still doing a brisk trade, then.

Though his mount stamped with impatience, Rhys stood motionless facing the inn. Finally, he tilted his face to the sky above it. Fog covered the village like cotton wool, obscuring the craggy tors that loomed high on the steep slope beyond. Without their ominous shadow, the village of Buckleigh-in-the-Moor—this hated place he'd been running from since before he could remember—almost appeared . . . quaint. Charming. Welcoming.

And at that fool notion, Rhys almost laughed aloud.

This place would not welcome him.

No sooner had he formed the thought, than the inn's front door swung out on its hinges, tossing a shaft of light and warmth into the courtyard. The dull wave of laughter he'd heard earlier now swelled to a roar of excitement—one punctuated with a crash of breaking glass.

"You bastard son of a bitch!"

Ah, now that was the sort of reception he'd been

expecting. But unless the old superstitions were true and some witch had foretold his arrival, Rhys knew the words couldn't have been meant for him. No one was likely to recognize him at all—he'd been just seventeen years old when he'd been here last.

Pulled forward by curiosity and the smells of ale and peat smoke, he approached the open door, stopping just outside.

The tavern was cramped, and much as Rhys remembered it. Just big enough to hold a small bar, a half-dozen tables, a mismatched assortment of chairs and stools, and—on this particular occasion—complete pandemonium.

"That's it! Pound 'im good!"

Two neckless apes faced off in the center of the room, spitting and circling one another as the onlookers pushed aside tables and chairs. The taller of the two brutes took a clumsy swing that caught nothing but air. The momentum carried him into a startled onlooker's arms. That man took exception and shoved back. Within seconds, the room was a blur of fists and teeth.

Standing unnoticed in the shadowed doorway, Rhys shifted his weight. An echo of bloodlust whispered in his ear. As a younger man, he would have hurled himself into the thickest knot of violence, eager to claw and punch his way back out. Just to feel the surge of his racing pulse, the slice of broken glass scoring his flesh, the tang of blood in his mouth. The strange, fleeting sensation of being alive.

But he wasn't that young man anymore. Thanks to the war, he'd had his fill of both fighting and pain. And he'd long given up on feeling alive.

After a minute or two, the peripheral scrabbling defused. Once again the two louts faced off, huffing for breath and clearly hungry for more. They chuckled as they circled one another, as though this were their typical Saturday night fun. It probably was. Wasn't as though life on the moor offered a wealth of amusements other than drinking and brawling.

Now that he studied their faces, Rhys wondered if the two might be brothers. Or cousins, perhaps. The taller one had mashed features, while the shorter sported a beaky nose. But their eyes reflected the same empty shade of blue, and they wore identical expressions of willful stupidity.

The shorter one picked up a low stool and taunted his opponent with it, as if baiting a bull. The "bull" charged. He threw a wild punch over the stool, but his reach fell short by inches. To close the gap, Bull grabbed a brass candlestick from the mantel and whipped it through the air, sucking all sound from the room.

Whoosh.

Beak threw aside his stool, and it smashed to splinters against the hearth. With Bull's attention momentarily diverted, Beak dove for a table still set for a meal. Half-empty dishes and bread crusts were strewn over white linen.

Rhys frowned. When had old Maddox started bothering with tablecloths?

He stopped wondering about it when Beak came up wielding a knife.

"I'll teach you to raise a club to me, you whoreson," he snarled.

Everyone in the room froze. Rhys ceased leaning against the doorjamb and stood erect, reconsidering his decision not to intervene. With a brass club and a knife involved, someone was likely to get seriously injured, or worse. As tired as he might be of fighting, he was even more weary of watching men die.

But before he could act, a series of sounds arrested him where he stood.

Crash. A bottle breaking.

Plink, plink, plink. Glass bits trickling to the floor.

Thud. Beak collapsing to the table unconscious, rivulets of wine streaming down around his ears.

"Harold Symmonds, you'll pay for that wine." A slender, dark-haired woman stood over Beak's senseless form, clutching what remained of a green-glass bottle "And the tablecloth too, you great lout." She shook her head and tsked. "Blood and claret will never come out of white linen.

"And as for you, Laurence—" She wheeled on the second man, threatening him with the broken bottle's sharp glass teeth. Though he was twice as big as the barmaid and a man besides, Laurence held up his hands in surrender.

In fact, every man in the room had gone still. As though they all feared the harsh discipline this tiny barmaid might dole out. Interesting. To a man like Rhys, who'd spent several years commanding soldiers, that snap to attention spoke volumes.

Jabbing the bottle at Laurence, the barmaid backed him up against the wall. "'Twas your own master who brought that, you know."

"This?" He stared at the candlestick in his fist. "It's Gideon's?"

"No, it's the inn's." She wrenched the brass club away from the stunned brute and curled her arm, lifting it to eye level. "But Gideon delivered it. Hauled it and its mate all the way up from Plymouth just last week. The set came very dear, and I'll thank to you keep your grimy mitts off the bric-a-brac."

The thing must have weighed a stone, but it cost her no effort to heft the candlestick up on the mantel with one hand and nudge it back into place.

"There," she said to herself, apparently satisfied with the symmetry. Standing back, she threw the jagged remnants of the bottle into the fire, and a wine-fueled blaze surged in the hearth.

The reddish flare illuminated the woman's face, and Rhys got his first good look at her.

Holy God. She was beautiful.

And young.

And . . . and beautiful.

Rhys had never been especially good with words. He couldn't have described exactly what it was about this woman that made her appearance so striking. He just knew he'd been struck.

She had pale skin and dark hair coming loose from a thick plait. Her figure was slight, yet feminine. Her eyes were large and wide, but to discern their color he would've had to stand much closer to her.

He wanted to stand much closer to her.

Especially now that she was no longer armed.

Fury radiated from her slender form as she propped her hands on her hips and scolded the assembly. "It's the same damned scene, again and again." Her tone was sharp, but the voice beneath it was husky, warm. "In case you haven't noticed, this inn is all we've got in Buckleigh-in-the-Moor. I'm trying to build a name for this place, make it a respectable establishment for travelers. Now tell me, how am I to make this inn fit for the Quality, what with you overgrown clods destroying my dining room once a fortnight?"

She swept an angry glare around the room, silently confronting each offender in turn. When her gaze collided with Rhys's, he noted the first crack in her veneer of poise. Her eyelashes fluttered. That was the extent of her visible surprise. The rest of her remained granite-still as she said, "And all this in front of a guest."

Rhys sensed every head in the room swiveling to face him. But he couldn't have torn his gaze from the barmaid's if he'd tried. Jesus, what a woman.

Between the travel and the damp, his body had been grousing at him all night. He wouldn't have believed one more part of him could stiffen . . . but evidently it could. His riding breeches pulled snug across his groin. He'd gone hard enough to rival that brass candlestick. He hadn't reacted so intensely to a woman since he'd been a randy youth. Perhaps not even then. His heart pounded. Blood surged through his veins, carrying orders to his every limb. He felt his whole body tightening, mustering strength, readying for a purpose. A very specific, very pleasurable purpose.

Damn. He felt *alive.*

Still holding his gaze, she said steadily, "Now put this place to rights."

Rhys blinked. He didn't recall this woman—he couldn't possibly have forgotten her—but had she somehow recognized him? Was she calling him out for his gross negligence as lord? It would be a fair enough accusation. If there was anything that needed putting to rights in Buckleigh-in-the-Moor, the responsibility should be his.

But as the men before him lurched into motion, scraping chairs and tables against the slate floor as they dragged the furniture back into place, Rhys realized her words hadn't been meant for him. He was almost disappointed. He would have liked to put things to rights for her. Starting with that mussed dark hair.

With an impatient sweep of her fingers, she tucked a lock behind her ear. "Welcome to the Three Hounds," she said. "Are you coming in, or aren't you?"

Oh, he was coming in. He was most definitely coming in.